Fade Up From Black

The Return Of Harry James Denton

ALSO BY STEVEN WOMACK

The Harry James Denton Novels:

DEAD FOLKS' BLUES

TORCH TOWN BOOGIE

WAY PAST DEAD

NOBODY'S CHAIN LAYS STRAIGHT

A MANUAL OF MURDER

DIRTY MONEY

The Jack Lynch Novels:

MURPHY'S FAULT

SMASH CUT:

THE SOFTWARE BOMB

Standalone Suspense Thrillers:

RESURRECTION BAY (with Wayne McDaniel)

BY BLOOD WRITTEN

FADE UP FROM BLACK

The Return of Harry James Denton

STEVEN WOMACK

Nashville

Fade Up From Black

The Return of Harry James Denton

ISBN: 978-1-7321899-7-3 (Hardcover)

ISBN: 978-1-7321899-8-0 (Trade Paperback)

Published by Spearhead Press

Nashville, Tennessee

Dedication

This book is affectionately dedicated to all the readers who've reached out to me over the years, asking if we were ever going to hear from Harry again…

Well, my friends, he's back.

Chapter One

Damn it, I thought I was ready.

The day the call finally came, it's not like I was surprised. We'd all been waiting for weeks. I was determined not to let it throw me.

The last few days, though, I'd been more restless than ever, on some kind of raw edge that wouldn't let me sit still for longer than a minute. Not sleeping much, no appetite. I mean, I knew it was coming, but somehow you're never really…

Ready?

How do you get ready for something like this?

I was in my new office that afternoon, the one we'd moved the company into just a few months earlier. The word *company* may be a stretch. There were only five of us.

On the other hand, these days it doesn't take many people to run a company. In 2012, Facebook bought Instagram for a billion bucks; at the time, it had fifteen employees.

Thirty years earlier, 60,000 people worked at the Rochester headquarters of a company called Kodak. The same year that little prick Zuckerberg bought Instagram, Kodak went tits up with just a couple thousand employees still on the books.

Obviously, I'm distracted right now. Can't focus… Thoughts rocketing through my head like a bunch of middle-schoolers playing Laser Tag in my brain.

These new offices of ours are on the twelfth floor of a

brand-new building in a downtown Nashville no one recognizes anymore. A couple of decades or so ago, I used to bitch about Nashville traffic. Now, to paraphrase Woody Allen, I'd sell my grandmother to the Arabs to get 1990s traffic back again.

The last decade, especially, had seen a building boom that dwarfed anything any of us had ever seen before. No one who was born and raised in Nashville—the few of us who are left—can get their heads around any of this. The state bird's the crane—the construction kind—and the skyline is speckled with siege after siege of them, their angled necks snaking into the sky like hungry baby birds waiting for momma to regurgitate breakfast down their throats.

Being the boss, I had the corner office, with a phenomenal view that overlooked the Cumberland River just as it curved around Nissan Stadium where the Titans play, past the pedestrian bridge named after one of the heroes of my life, John Siegenthaler. Two weeks earlier, we'd thrown an Independence Day party and all gone up on the roof to watch one of the greatest fireworks displays in the country, surrounded by towering skyscrapers that reflected the fireworks bursts in a funhouse mirror maze, like a reboot of Orson Welles' *The Lady from Shanghai*.

This ain't no hick little hillbilly music town anymore…

So now it's the middle of July and we're well into three figures of heat index, although you couldn't tell it behind the polarized darkened-glass exterior walls of my office and the silence of the HVAC units.

I stared out, across the river. Below, the General Jackson was paddle-wheeling by on its way back to Opryland, its decks packed with sun-broiled tourists. My cell phone chirped. I pulled it out of my shirt pocket, held it a beat, touched the screen.

"Hello, sweetheart," I said.

"Daddy," she said. She sounded more exhausted than ever before. Way too tired for someone who had yet to see a sixteenth birthday…

She was silent for a moment. "Daddy," she sniffed.

"Yes, baby."

"It's…" She hesitated, took a shallow breath and held it for a moment. I knew her, knew exactly what she was doing, could see her doing it in my mind's eye. She was steeling herself, trying to keep it together one five-second block at a time.

"It's over."

I looked down at my desk, my uncluttered, organized, suddenly infuriating desk.

"When?"

"Twenty minutes ago," she said softly.

I closed my eyes for just a second, then opened them again. The General Jackson had moved about four inches across my window glass from right to left.

"The Genworths are there, right?" I asked. "Like we planned…"

"Yes."

"You're not alone?"

"No. But why can't I just stay here with Estella?"

"Alex, we talked about this. You don't need to be there right now. It's just one night."

There was silence for a long moment.

"Okay."

"Good," I said, relieved. "I'll call Uncle Lonnie and Aunt Sheba. We'll leave first thing in the morning, be there early afternoon."

"Can we pick you up at the airport?" she said, her voice almost pleading.

"Honey, you know how it is. Schedules are tough to keep in a private plane. I'll call you twenty minutes out. We'll just take an Uber."

I heard what sounded a little like a laugh. "Daddy, you know I hate Uber."

"Okay, Lyft, taxi, whatever. Straight to the Genworth's after we land."

There was a long silence, almost as if neither of us knew what to say next.

"I…" She stopped.

"What, sweetheart?"

"I don't think it was too bad."

"We can be grateful for that," I said. "That's good to know."

"I love you, Daddy."

"I love you, Alexis." The only time I ever used her full name was when I was telling her I loved her, as if calling her by her full name gave it more weight. "Can I call in an hour or two? Just check in? Or you want to call me when you get settled?"

"I'll call when we get to the Genworths'."

"Okay. If you don't, you know I'll be speed-dialing you," I said. Alex had a way of forgetting to return calls and texts. It's a teen thing, I think. Hormone-induced memory loss…

Or maybe it was stress-induced. She's had a lot on her these last few months.

"All right. I'll talk to you soon."

A moment later, we disconnected. I set the phone down on my desk and turned, staring out the darkened, glazed windows into the searing blue Nashville July sky. The colors all seemed distorted now, as if the world was somehow different…

It was.

Marsha Helms, the mother of my daughter and the great broken love of my life, was dead.

⁂

I stood there a long time, staring out the window, as the General Jackson disappeared and the constipated interstate highway over the river started clogging up and slowing down. I don't think I was really thinking much of anything; every thought that could be thought had pretty much been thought.

Marsha and I had *processed* about as much as we could process in the months leading up to the end. I'd flown out to Reno just last week, staying in the guest room on the top floor of the mansion on Mount Rose Marsha had inherited from her Aunt Marty almost a decade earlier.

Aunt Marty didn't much like me when I showed up at her door some sixteen years ago. After all, I'd knocked up her niece and, in her view, caused Marsha to lose her career and to have to retreat to Reno with her tail between her legs. After a while, though, she learned the truth and came around. Marty and I were side-by-side when Alex came into the world.

For the last years of her life, Marty and I were the closest of friends, long after Marsha and I gave up all hope of ever making it. The five or six times a year I came to Reno to see Alex, Marty had welcomed me into her house and treated me like the son she never had.

She was a grand old lady and I was proud to be one of her pallbearers.

And she left everything to her only living relative: Dr. Marsha Helms. Now, nearly ten years later, that would be passed down to our daughter. I only know this because, in the conflicted and twisted pattern of emotions that defined our relationship, I was now the executor of Marsha's estate and the trustee for my daughter until she came of age.

That, combined with the rest of it, made my daughter, Alexis Martha Helms Denton, a very, very rich young woman…

❧

I stood there so long my legs started to stiffen and go numb. Finally, there was no way to get around the next part. I dreaded this, mostly because I knew the anguish it was going to cause. But like everyone else, she knew it was coming.

I picked up my cell and hit the button. "Hey, Siri…" I said.

Alex was always giving me grief for using Siri. No self-respecting adolescent would use something that so obviously impressed the late middle-aged. I gave it right back to her, said Siri was the only woman I'd ever known who always did what I asked without question. The only problem was, I'd let Lonnie have my phone one night to do what he called an "update." Ever since, Siri wasn't always so cooperative.

In fact, she'd developed kind of an attitude.

"*S'up, Harry?*" Siri answered back.

"Call Sheba, mobile…"

"*Okay, if you insist. Calling Sheba, mobile…*"

A couple ringtones later: "Harry." I'd always loved the sound of Sheba's voice. Some people just have that kind of voice. Lonnie was a lucky guy.

"Hi, Sweetie," I said. "How are you? Where are you?"

"Fine and at the condo. You?"

"I'm okay," I said, then after a long beat, "I got the call."

Like I said, she knew it was coming. But there was something about having it finally arrive. She let out a gasp, then a sound like a kitten mewing.

"Oh, god, I'm so sorry."

"I know. Me, too."

She tried to hold back a sob, with only a little success, then: "Alex? Is she okay?"

"Better than I would've thought. She's with Hal and Marie."

"I'm glad. I've been so worried about her. She's an amazing young girl."

"Fortunately," I said, "she's got her mother's toughness."

"And equally fortunate," Sheba added, "her father's disposition."

Sheba and Marsha had never really warmed up to each other, mainly because Sheba always considered me one of the good guys and, sometimes, Marsha didn't. They'd reached an uneasy peace over the years, and when Marsha came down with the cancer Sheba took it as hard as we all did.

"Let's not rush to judgment on how fortunate that is," I said. "Where's he at? The farm?"

"He's with Captain Jimmy at the hangar," Sheba answered. "They had a couple maintenance issues to take care of. I think he knew the call was coming."

"Will you let him know?" I asked. "I hate making these kinds of calls."

"Typical guy," she said. "You're still coming to dinner, right?"

"You don't have to do that. I know you probably got a lot to do before we leave."

"No, no way. You're coming for dinner tonight and that's all there is to it. I'll ring up that new pizza place around the corner from Yazoo and have something delivered."

"Well, don't go to too much trouble."

"No trouble at all," she said. "Besides, I don't want you to be alone tonight."

"Thanks, love. I appreciate it. Seven-ish, right?"

"Lonnie should be back by then, but if he's not, you and I'll open a bottle of champagne, rip our clothes off, and make mad passionate love on the living room floor."

I laughed.

"I mean it," she said. "We'll fuck like crazed bunnies..."

I laughed again. "That'll teach him to be on time."

⁂

Outside my office, at her L-shaped desk in the lobby, my assistant Ashley Meadows sat in front of her bank of computer monitors. We didn't actually get a lot of walk-in traffic here at Denton & Associates, but Ashley's was the first face the rare visitor saw.

She'd been with the company a little over a year, having joined us after finishing her MBA at Vanderbilt's Owen Graduate School of Management. In that year, I'd never been able to quite figure her out. She was twenty-eight, looked about ten years younger, rail thin, high cheekbones, thick strawberry blonde hair, intense brown eyes that could bore straight through you.

Row of studs down her left ear, a couple in her right, and a tiny gold stud through a left pierced nostril... I'd try to describe how attractive she is, but I learned a long time ago that it's a bit awkward to try and describe how attractive a woman is when you're old enough to be her grandfather.

Not to mention that I knew ten minutes into the interview that she was among the half-dozen or so smartest people I'd ever met. If she had an IQ of less than 150, I'd be shocked. She'd been a Dean's Scholar at Vanderbilt, full ride, graduated with a 4.0.

"So why do you want to work here?" I asked after about an hour. "With your credentials, your degree, you could go anywhere. Any of the majors would snatch you up in a heartbeat. New York, London, Paris…"

She stared at me across the conference room table. "Okay," she said after a moment. "My last module at Owen, I did an independent study on a local entrepreneur and his start-up. Wrote a thirty page paper on him. I'd like to get it published someday, but I think it would really piss him off."

I cocked my head. "And that local entrepreneur was…"

She hesitated just a moment, then with her right hand, she rolled up her left sleeve and turned the inner part of her forearm toward me. In deep blue ink, a series of Greek letters were tattooed in a straight line.

I don't read Greek, but I recognized this one word. "Really?" I said.

"Asfáleia," she said.

"Tattooed on your arm?" I shook my head. "Man, that's intense. You a stalker or what?"

"I'm fascinated by how a man with no college degree, no formal computer training, a failed country music singer before he became a repo man and a bounty hunter, could start a computer security company in a trailer home in East Nashville and turn it into a billion dollar company."

I smiled. "Two-and-a-half billion, actually. Made the cover of Inc. Magazine."

"Oops. My bad," she said softly.

"I still don't get it," I admitted. "Yeah, Lonnie started Asfáleia

Technologies in a run-down trailer in a junkyard and sold it a dozen years later for a fortune. He's the fifth richest man in the state of Tennessee and somewhere in the lowest quadrant of the Forbes 400. But he's out of the business now. He's got a couple of people who work for him, mostly attorneys and development people who help him give the money away. He dabbles in some venture capital projects, monitors investments. But he's not hiring."

"I don't want a job from him. I want to learn from him and everyone around him. And you're the closest one to him, right by his side from the get-go."

I leaned back in my chair and studied her a moment. "Lonnie and I go back a lot farther than Asfáleia Technologies... The stuff I could tell you."

She leaned in, her elbows on the table. "Look, you're right. I could go to work for a hedge fund, Goldman Sachs, one of the S&P 500s and make a lot of money, start climbing that ladder. But I don't want that. I want to build something of my own. My own Asfáleia Technologies."

Asfáleia... The Greek word for *security*.

"Harry, my daddy's a third-generation tobacco farmer outside Baxter, Tennessee. I grew up in the hollow. I'm the first person in my family to go to college. The last thing in the world I want to do is become some faceless part of a corporate machine."

I looked away. "I get it. The last couple of years at Asfáleia, that's what I felt like. We got so big, so successful, the machine ran itself. Truth is, I was bored to hell. And I think Lonnie was too."

She grinned. "I'll bet."

I cleared my throat and scooted in toward her. "You know

what we do here at Denton & Associates. We're primarily contract workers for the Austrian/German conglomerate that bought Asfáleia. That was part of the buyout deal. We generate documentation, monitor networks, perform analyses, advise and consult. We get paid a lot of money for it, don't work very hard, and half the time I don't know what the hell the guys here are talking about."

"Okay…"

"I'm not even sure what you'll be doing, but we'll find something."

"I'll keep myself busy," she said.

I found myself staring at her for what seemed like a long time. Hell, it *was* a long time, long enough for a little discomfort.

"What?" she asked softly, her forehead furrowing.

"I'm going to give you your first test," I said after a few more moments of silence. "Are you trustworthy?"

She stared back at me for a couple of seconds. "I think so," she answered. "I always have been."

"Then I'm going to tell you the secret of how a failed aspiring country music singer, repo man, and bounty hunter started a company that eventually made him a billionaire. I expect you to keep that secret."

Her eyes lit up; she scooted forward and rested her forearms on the edge of my desk. She nodded her head.

"Lonnie Smith is not a dumb ignorant redneck hillbilly. He's from Brooklyn, where he graduated first in his class, valedictorian, from Brooklyn Technical High School. If you don't know what that is, Google it some time. But trust me, it's damn impressive."

She nodded again.

"He got a full ride to MIT. Some kind of computer

engineering… He was on a *summa cum laude* track. The summer between his sophomore and junior years, he married his high school sweetheart. He had everything. Then late one night, deep in the winter of his junior year, some crazed son of a bitch junkie broke into their apartment in Cambridge while he was doing an overnight in the computer labs. The guy raped and murdered his wife…"

Ashley sat up straight, sucked in a deep breath. "God," she muttered.

"Lonnie found her when he came in at five in the morning. In the decades that I've known him, he's only talked about it once to me. He said he didn't remember much for months after that. They caught the guy; he went away for a long time. Lonnie kind of cracked up, crashed and burned. Took a long road trip, wound up in Nashville, never left."

"Wow," she whispered.

"You can't ever let him know I told you that."

"I understand."

"Deal," I said. We stood and shook hands across the table.

"Thanks, Harry. You won't be sorry," she said, letting go of my hand.

❧

And I hadn't been, especially in the last few months when I'd been flying out to Reno on a moment's notice and leaving everything in her lap. She'd become essential to the operation, so much so that I'd begun to worry that we wouldn't be able to keep her, although I kept that part to myself.

I walked out of my office to find her leaning in to a monitor, intently watching some kind of moving graph on the screen. Lately, she'd been working on a project with Hugh Caulfield, our head IT guy, and Donnie Hazzard, the guy who keeps the servers running around here. They were kind of closed-mouthed about it, but since we were in the cybersecurity business, I assumed it was something in that arena.

"Ash," I said, clearing my throat. She turned.

"I'll be leaving for Reno tomorrow."

Ashley shot up out of her chair and crossed to me in a few steps. She threw her arms around me and gave the biggest hug she could with her 115-pound frame.

"Harry, I'm so sorry," she said. "I am so terribly sorry."

I patted her back, returned the hug, then we stepped apart. "I appreciate that," I said. "Thanks."

"Are you all right? How's Alex?"

I'd introduced Alex to Ashley almost a year ago on one of Alex's visits to Nashville and they'd become instant buds. "You tell me," I said. "You're the one on Snapchat with her. You see her more than I do."

"Don't take it so hard. Everybody ghosts their parents on Snapchat," she said. "Try her on Facebook."

"She bounced outta Facebook a year ago. Says that's where grandparents post pictures of their grandkids. Look, I'm gonna take off. I've got a lot to do before we leave tomorrow."

Ashley's face seemed to lose a little color. "Oh, God," she said. "This has happened at the worst possible time."

"What? What's happened?"

"Your door was shut and I didn't want to bother you. I tried to get rid of him. Honestly, I did."

"Get rid of who?" I asked. I could feel the tension rising in the back of my neck.

Ashley crossed her arms, almost defensively, and shook her

head. "I tried to get rid of him, but he insisted. Said he had to talk to you. I told him to make an appointment, but he kept saying this couldn't wait. A matter of life and death..."

"What in God's name are you talking about?" I demanded.

"This man, he dropped in about fifteen minutes ago. Said he had to talk to you. He was insistent, even relentless. I parked him in the conference room, told him he'd have to sit there until you were available, *if* you were available."

I cocked my hands on my hips, completely exasperated now. "He's *here*?"

She nodded toward the conference room. "He's in there now. I'm sorry, Harry."

"Oh, damn it, this is too much. Let me go—" I turned and took a few steps toward the conference room. I stopped, turned back to her.

"What's this guy's name?"

"Leo," she said. "Leo Walsh."

"Well, let me just go give Mr. Leo Walsh the old heave ho."

Chapter Two

The Denton & Associates conference room was down the hall past Ashley's desk, through a door on the left. The room was long and narrow, with an expensive wooden conference table down the center. Eight leather chairs, one on each end and three down each side, filled the center of the room. At the far end, a small cabinet hung over a wet bar. A sixty-inch flat screen filled the wall at the other end nearest the door.

I stopped at the door, knocked twice, and stepped in.

On the far side of the room, in the middle chair, a thin older guy with thick salt-and-pepper curly hair sat in a blue wool blazer that was far too heavy for the summer heat. He scooted back in the chair and stood up in his brown khakis with the frayed leather belt. He was maybe six-feet tall, weighed barely 150, and had this overwhelming air of exhaustion and weariness about him. His face was heavily wrinkled, his nose spider-webbed with thin red lines and broken vessels, and his eyes were encircled by blue and green bags that seemed to make the wrinkles sag even more. The smudged pair of Ray-Ban Clubmaster bifocals he wore did a lousy job of hiding the damage.

"Mr. Denton," he said. He extended his hand and I stepped forward, cautiously took it. His handshake was firm, but not like that of somebody trying to prove something. "I appreciate you taking the time to see me."

I motioned for him to sit down, then took the seat across from him. "This is all a little unusual, Mr. Walsh. We don't get a lot of walk-in traffic here and this is a really bad time. I'm leaving town tomorrow morning."

"I'll try not to take much of your time," he said.

"Okay," I answered. "How can I help you?"

He looked down at the table for a moment, then back up. He seemed uncomfortable.

"You're a private investigator," he said.

I squinted a little and tried to focus on his eyes through the bifocals. Something about him seemed suddenly familiar.

"I'm sorry, Mr. Walsh," I said. "You've been misinformed. Denton & Associates is a computer security consulting firm. We work exclusively with large corporations."

"I know that. But *you're* a private investigator," he said.

I looked away from him for a beat, trying to put my finger on something that just wasn't there yet. Then I turned back to him.

"I used to be," I said. "A long time ago. That was a couple of careers back."

"Yeah," Leo Walsh said. "But you've kept your license current. I checked."

"Mr. Walsh, keeping a private investigator's license current in the state of Tennessee means paying an annual fee and taking a few hours of continuing education units. I did it more as an exercise than anything else. I haven't done any private investigating in almost fifteen years."

"You used to be a newspaper reporter," he said. "I read your stuff all the time. You covered politics, mostly, and you did a good job. I was a real fan."

Okay, so now I was beginning to worry that I had a stalker or something in my office. This guy seemed to know more about me than I was comfortable with.

"Yes, and I got in trouble at the newspaper and was fired. I left the field after that."

Leo Walsh grinned, revealing a row of yellowed teeth. Age? Smoking?

"I know," he said. "I appreciate a man who gets in trouble now and then. I've had quite a bit of trouble myself. Got some right now, in fact."

I stared at him for a moment. "I have no doubt of that, Mr. Walsh. But truth is, I don't do that kind of work anymore."

I put my hands on the conference table to push myself back, then stood up. "And in fact, I'm very busy right now. So if you'll excuse me…"

He sat there, looking up at me, unmoving.

"Mr. Walsh, I really need to…"

"I want you to investigate a murder," he interrupted.

"A murder? You mean, like a homicide?"

He nodded.

"Mr. Walsh, yes, I have a legal, valid private investigator's license, but I am not a law enforcement officer of any type. If you have knowledge of a crime, you need to go to the police. If a murder has been committed, you need to go the police. If you are involved in a murder, then you need to retain the best counsel money can buy. That's my advice for you."

He sat there, still unmoving, looking up at me. His eyes seemed even heavier, almost mournful. Then I suddenly saw the resemblance. Curly mound of thick salt-and-pepper hair, deeply lined face, heavy bags under his eyes…

Guy freaking looks like those photographs Jill Krementz took of her husband Vonnegut in the last decade of his life, after a lifetime of smoking, hard-drinking, surviving wars and divorces, battling endless blank pages, little things like that.

I shifted uncomfortably.

"Mr. Walsh," I said softly. "Whose murder do you want me to investigate?"

"Mine," he whispered.

Then it hit me. It all came abruptly back, from over twenty years ago. I sat back down in my chair, stunned.

"You're Leo Walsh," I said. "*The* Leo Walsh…"

He nodded again.

"So," I said after a moment. "How do you take your coffee?"

Twenty-five years ago, Leo Walsh came out of nowhere with a first novel that blew everybody's socks off. Called *The Sphinx Confessions*, it was a sprawling historical epic set in the Middle East during the late twenties, at the dawn of the Great Depression, just as the seeds of World War II were germinating. It had elements of romance and adventure, politics and intrigue, but it was also highly literary and garnered great respect from the Ivory Tower. *The New York Review of Books* and *The Atlantic* frickin' loved it.

It performed amazingly well for a first novel. It made both the *Times* and the *USA Today* best-seller lists and stayed there for a long time. This was during the mid-nineties when it was going up against books like *Angela's Ashes* and *All The Pretty Horses*, *Midnight in the Garden of Good and Evil* and *Bridget Jones's Diary*. We're talking some pretty stiff competition here.

I vaguely remembered talk of a movie.

Nashville was a much smaller town then, and frankly a much better book town than it is now. At one time, there were three locally owned bookstores, but they've long since gone under. There's only one independent bookstore left in Nashville that didn't make its bones on the used-book trade and selling used DVDs and video games. The biggest bookstore in Nashville now is off an I-40 exit ramp and has the feel of a literary pawn shop.

Leo Walsh's success was a big deal. I went to one of his book signings at Davis-Kidd back in the nineties and had to wait in line almost an hour for an autograph. He was on the cover of magazines, interviewed on TV, the featured keynote speaker at conference after conference. *Nashville Magazine* named him to its list of Nashville's Most Influential People.

For a few moments, he seemed to be everywhere.

He was short-listed for a Pulitzer Prize and, I think, the National Book Award. I woke up early one morning and turned on the television and there he was, being interviewed by Joan Lunden on *Good Morning America*.

Then he just…

Well, he just *disappeared*.

I think there was a second book, maybe a third. I can't even remember the names of them. If I'd ever given him or his books any thought, I would have considered this a great mystery. He slid out of sight so fast, though, that I never noticed.

And now here he was, sitting in my conference room, nursing a cup of coffee and staring across the table at me with a questioning look on his face. Then he reached into the side pocket of his wool jacket and half-extracted a rumpled pack of Pall Malls. He raised an eyebrow.

"I'm sorry, Mr. Walsh," I said to his unasked question, "but this is a no-smoking building."

He shrugged, stuffed the pack away. "Just, you know," he said. "A cup of coffee and a smoke… Kinda go together."

I raised my cup and took a sip. I didn't ask her to very often, but when Ashley made coffee, it was amazing. I don't know how she did it and she wasn't telling anybody.

"So what happened after the second book?" I asked.

He leaned back. "Well, it's the mid-nineties. I'm in my forties, with seven unpublished novels and a drawer full of rejection slips. Been writing books over twenty years and can't give one away. At least not one with my name on it."

I smiled. "And then one takes off."

He nodded. "Like something nobody's ever seen before. Best-seller lists, award nominations. Didn't win any, but hey, *it's an honor to be nominated...*"

"So what—?"

He held up a hand. "I'm getting to that. The first book's published by some small press in Georgia, outside Atlanta. They gave me a twenty-five-hundred dollar advance, which was the most they'd ever given anybody. Then the book takes off and my agent starts negotiating the next book."

He picked up the coffee cup, took another long sip.

"Obviously, the small press hasn't got a chance. They're the first ones to drop out. I got five houses in New York City that want the book. So I tell my agent I want a million bucks..."

"A million dollars?" I asked. "For a second book?"

He half-shrugged again. "Started to believe my own press. Plus I'd been doing this shit for twenty years. Figured I was due some back pay. The book goes out to auction, top bid's five-hundred grand. I turn it down. My agent tells me I'm crazy. She goes back to the publisher, comes back with another offer. Three-quarters of a million, with performance bonuses tied to the book that will boost it over a mil if it performs. I turn it down. The agent goes bat-shit, starts yelling at me over the phone."

I set my cup down, leaned on the table with my elbows planted, my jaw half-open.

"Yeah," Walsh said. "Crazy. So I say to my agent *You're not listening…* I want one-million American dollars on the table as an upfront advance. And every time they come back with an offer for less than a million, my price goes up a hundred-fifty-thousand, which is your fucking commission."

He stopped for a moment, as if staring off at something way far away in the distance.

"The next offer was for one-million dollars," he said quietly.

"Wow," I muttered.

"So I sign the deal," he continued, "and the next day, fire my agent for not believing we could pull this off. And I've got a year to turn the manuscript in. Meantime, my agent in L.A. gets an offer from a studio. I tell him part of the deal is I get to write the script. He tells me that's impossible, no first-time novelist without a track record ever gets that deal. I tell him I just sold a book for seven-figures, so I don't exactly need the money. But I've always wanted to be in the Writers Guild. So if they want the book, those are the terms…"

He went silent for another moment.

"So they agree," he said, his voice dropping in volume. "Everything's roses. I've got a million-dollar book deal. Just been signed to adapt my own novel for the movies, which means another six figures."

Then he stopped for a moment and, I swear, he started humming the first few bars of *Young at Heart…* Something about fairy tales coming true and how it can happen to you.

I let him go on for a few beats, then: "So what happened? I'm assuming this did not have a good outcome."

He looked up. "So I'm working like crazy, writing a novel and working on a screenplay. The pressure's getting to me, I'm starting to drink a little more than I used to. Not sleeping much, pretty cranky most of the time. My first wife, despite all the money and fame and bullshit, starts to—well, let's just say I wasn't a very good husband during this period.

"So I get the script turned in and the director fucking *hates* it. I don't mean he thinks it's got problems, needs some rewriting, *blah blah blah*. He *fucking hates* it. I'm in his office in L.A. and he throws the script across the room at me. *This is shit, Mr. Walsh!* He fires me and this makes the trades like crazy. Suddenly, I'm like the most untalented hack anybody's ever seen. But my agent got me a pay-or-play contract, so no matter what, I get the money. But I'm off the project. They bring on another writer, do a page-one rewrite. A year later, the project goes into the black hole of development hell and never comes out."

He suddenly pushed away from the table and stood up, too agitated to sit still. He paced back and forth behind the conference table, his hands in his pockets.

"The worst thing is, I get what in Hollywood is the kiss of death. *I'm difficult to work with.* So I go 'eff it,' I'll take the money and run. Meanwhile, I'm cranking out the next book, the one that sold for a million. I finish it in four months and I turn the draft in and my editor loves it. She sends me back the copyedited manuscript with some very complimentary notes and her best wishes on my future endeavors…"

"What?" I asked.

"Nine months before pub date, she takes another job," he said, his face tightening up. "I get assigned another editor, but she comes on late in the game. It's not her book; I'm not her author.

She's got no investment in the project. She's not the one who talked them into writing a million-dollar check, so why should she stick her neck out? When the book comes out, nobody's got its back. It's completely orphaned. No real promotion, no real support…"

"And?"

He looked away for a moment. "The book tanked. Went nowhere. Came and went as fast as a Harlequin romance. Magazines have a longer shelf life. I'd made a huge chunk of change in a short amount of time, but the New York agent took fifteen percent, the L.A. agent got ten. Uncle Sam gets a huge slice of the pie. The wife and I bought a nice place in Green Hills and that sucked up a truckload of cash."

He leaned against the wall, his hands still in his pockets, one ankle crossed over the other. "I figured I could come back from this. Life's full of second acts, you know. I got a year-long appointment as a visiting writer with the Vanderbilt English department. That was at least a little respectability and some badly needed cash. I figured I'd just write another book."

"Did you?" I asked.

He nodded. "Took another year-and-a-half. I couldn't even get an agent to take it on. Meantime, my visiting writer contract is up, I'm depressed as hell, drinking too much, making life miserable for my wife. So she decides she's had enough. Files for divorce. Tennessee's a community property state, so she got half and the house, plus we'd been married over ten years, so she got spousal support."

I shook my head slowly. "Holy crap."

"So one evening I'm in black tie at Columbia University being honored as a Pulitzer Prize nominee and four years later I'm packing my shit into a U-Haul and moving into a two-bedroom apartment in Antioch."

I leaned back in my chair and studied him. His clothes were worn, his eyes puffy and red, and he needed a haircut.

"I am so sorry, Mr. Walsh, that's a terrible ending. But you asked me to investigate a murder and you tell me you're the victim. Obviously, you're still on the right side of the dirt. Why do you think someone's going to kill you?"

"First of all, that's not the ending. Hard to believe, but it gets a lot worse. I started writing screenplays and wrote two more novels. I went through a couple of agents in L.A., but they both turned out to be not only crooks, but complete incompetents. I actually sold one of the novels, to a third-tier publisher in Minnesota. They printed 1250 copies in paperback and didn't bother to proofread the cover…"

"And it went?"

"Nowhere. Meanwhile, I'm adjusting to life in an apartment complex and gradually getting back on my feet. Money's tight, so I get a job teaching in a local community college. Creative writing, a screenwriting class, three sections of freshman English comp. Like working in a factory, the Walmart of academia, but it pays the bills. Sort of. As long as I don't count my alimony as a real bill. And then lightning strikes…"

I gave him the classic *what???* look.

"I fell in love," he said wearily. "Again. A colleague in the English department, a woman a dozen years younger than me. She'd written a novel, wanted me to read it. It was pretty good, although I should have paid more attention to the fact that the protagonist was a depressed, troubled young woman who hated all men."

"Yeah," I agreed. "That's often a dead giveaway."

"You know how it goes," he continued. "Late-night editing sessions, intense conversations. Lots of eye contact, fingers brushing against arms. Then it's late and we're tired. *Hey, let's have a glass of wine.* Next thing you know, we're necking like a couple of teenagers. Then the clothes come off and we're doing the deed on the couch in my faculty office after hours."

He smiled. "I gotta tell you, I was proud of the fact that at my advanced age I was still getting laid on a couch like a high school linebacker."

"You're a hopeless romantic," I said.

"Actually, that's part of my problem. I am. Anyway, we got married and a year later, she's written two more novels, sold one for a pretty fair advance, and gotten herself a tenure-track position at an actual college. Meanwhile, I'm still trying to teach third-grade English to 19-year-olds who made 13s on their ACTs and wishing cocktail hour would get here."

"And so she..."

He nodded. "...Files for divorce and gets half of the little that's left."

"So is she the one who's planning to kill you?"

He shook his head. "Oh, no. I mean, yeah, she hates my guts, but death would be too easy an out in her eyes. She wants to see me suffer. So she sabotages what little career I got left. I didn't have tenure at the community college, so she starts trash-talking me and calling in favors and the next thing you know, my contract doesn't get renewed."

I rolled my eyes. "Jeez," I muttered. "This is amazing."

He nodded. "Yeah, so now I don't even have my crappy job anymore. The money's running out and the pucker factor is climbing. So I get approached to teach in, of all places, a film school."

"In Nashville?" I asked.

"Not many people know it, but Music City's got a slew of film schools. The first film school in the state of Tennessee was started in Nashville in the mid-nineties. It caught on and now there are like five of 'em. Can't swing a dead cat..."

"So you started teaching film?"

"Well, scriptwriting. Lotta people think you don't need a script to make a movie, but you really do, right? I tried to get on with the legitimate ones, but to teach in most film schools you gotta have, like, credits and shit. A Master of Frickin' Arts or some such. But then this for-profit starts up. The Nashville Academy of Cinema Arts. NACA, for short..."

"Yeah," I confessed. "I've seen their commercials. Late at night. The French lady..."

He grinned. "That's Ursula," he said. "Ursula Gilbert, only she pronounces it *Jeel-bear*. She's a piece of work. She was doing this startup, needed somebody with a little name recognition on her faculty."

He looked away for a second. "At least I still had that..."

"Did something finally work out for you?" The question came off more brutal than I intended.

"Are you kidding? This is an unaccredited, for-profit clown college that's somehow managed to qualify for federal financial aid. She brings in seven figures a year scamming returning vets out of their G.I. benefits and talking kids into racking up a fortune in student loan debt."

"How long you been there?"

"Three years," he answered. "She's under investigation by

the Feds. *How do I know that*, he asks? Because the Feds have talked to me."

"So you think she might be the one who—?"

"Maybe. Either her or the third one."

"*Third* one? You mean, third wife?"

"Yeah," he said. "Some people never learn. We lived in the same building at the apartment complex. We ran into each other in the laundry room, the parking lot. She was cute, kind of frisky in a flirty, harmless way. And she had this boyfriend and they had a bad breakup. So we started hanging out together. Next thing I know, she's spending the night at my place and then we get absolutely shit-faced one night and wind up in a small town just across the Alabama state line. A good, old-fashioned elopement…"

I looked up at the clock above his head on the wall. We'd been talking over an hour now. As fascinating a tale as this was, I needed to wrap it up. I gotta get ready to go help my daughter bury her mother.

"So why do you think she's going to kill you?" I asked bluntly.

He studied me for a few seconds, then stepped back over and sat back down at the table. He clasped his hands together in front of him and looked down at them.

"Right at the end of my first marriage, when the money was still coming in, I bought a million-dollar term life policy and prepaid the entire term. I thought it would display my concern and love for my then-wife. I was wrong. She didn't want to wait for me to check out and make it finally worthwhile for her. She wanted to be rid of me and get her share now. I never told my second wife about it. My third wife's a high school graduate who works in retail. She thought since I was a famous published *arthur* that I had a lot of money. When she found out I didn't, she was…"

"Disillusioned," I offered.

"And really, really pissed. One night, in an attempt to placate her, I showed her the paperwork on the insurance policy where I'd changed the beneficiary. That calmed her down for a while."

"Look, if you think she's going to kill you for the insurance, then you and she both need to remember that the chances of getting away with that are about zip and none. And if you're really worried about it, there's one simple solution, Mr. Walsh."

"Yeah?" he asked.

"Cancel the policy."

"I thought of that," he said. "But truth is, I actually care about her and if I do kick off, there's not much else there for her."

"So why now?" I asked, confused. "How long have you two been married?"

"Just over a year."

"You get along okay most of the time?"

He shrugged. "Can get a little rocky," he said. "Thank God for boxed wine and make-up sex."

I smiled. "If nothing else, I admire your honesty. Can't say much for your judgment, but at least you seem to own it."

"I do. I've made a lot of mistakes. I've owned up to them and paid a hell of a price."

"So why now?" I asked. "What's the urgency?"

He took a deep breath and exhaled it slowly. "Because," he said, "the insurance policy expires in two weeks. If she's going to do it, she's got to move now."

I stood up. "Look, Mr. Walsh, I've enjoyed talking with you, but the truth is your wife has to know that no one ever gets away with something like this. But in any case, even when I was a private investigator, this was not the kind of thing I could take on. My advice to you is to get a good lawyer and take his advice. Maybe he'd suggest letting the insurance expire."

"Oh, it's going to expire. I can't afford the premium to keep it going."

"Then it'll be a moot point," I said. "In any case, I've got to be going."

I extended my hand. "It's been a pleasure, Mr. Walsh. I've enjoyed talking to you."

He shook my hand and I let him out into the reception area. He looked kind of downcast as I held the door open for him. "Good luck to you, sir. I hope things get better for you."

Leo Walsh nodded to me, turned and shuffled out, like the old, weary man he was.

I shut the door and turned to Ashley, who sat at her desk with her mouth open.

"What the hell?" she said. "You were in there over an hour. I was beginning to wonder if he'd taken you hostage."

"Ashley, I have had the weirdest frickin' day I've had in years. Only problem is, I don't have time to tell you about it."

She stood up as I went into my office for my backpack. As I headed for the door, she gave me a quick hug. "You're on my mind," she said. "I'll be thinking about you guys a lot. Give Alex a hug for me and call if you need anything. The guys and I'll send some flowers."

I stared at her for a moment and thought of Leo Walsh and his decades-long struggle to find a love that worked. I didn't know which was worse: go through life alone but unbattered, or keep going back to the rodeo over and over even though you know you're going to get your ass thrown into the dirt every time.

"Thanks," I said. "I'll be in touch."

Then I walked out into the world, a world that suddenly felt like it had a great big hole in it.

Chapter Three

Shit's changed.

Almost twenty-five years ago, broke, alone, divorced, and fired from my job as a newspaper reporter, I found a nice little old lady in East Nashville who had an apartment above the house she and her husband had bought for about eight grand in the late Fifties. She was a widow, hard of hearing, wore frumpy house dresses, and loved gardening. She made me a sweetheart deal on the rent if I'd cut the grass during the summer months.

Both of us being pretty much alone, Esther Hawkins and I soon became friends. Even after Marsha and I got together, I still spent a fair amount of time drinking tea with her and chatting at her Formica and chrome kitchen table that looked like something out of a Fifties soda shop. We'd sit in her linoleum-floored kitchen with the painted wooden kitchen cabinets and the thirty-year-old Kenmore stove and the same Kelvinator refrigerator she and Mr. Hawkins had bought new in 1958 and she'd tell me stories about growing up in Nashville during the Depression. The house she lived in had been one of those brick faux-Tudors that had been put up in the early-Thirties after a tornado cut a huge swath through this part of the city, flattening everything in its path.

East Nashville was a lot different back then. Until about the mid-nineties, this was where you lived if you couldn't afford anywhere else. It was mostly blue-collar working-class, with interspersed pockets of hard-core poverty and crime. Muggings, rapes, car thefts, even murders were pretty common and if you walked down a few blocks past the old Bailey School to the other side of Porter Road you had to be careful not to step on the used, discarded syringes left by the junkies over by the railroad tracks.

Then the artists and the musicians discovered it, the gays and lesbians, the gentrifiers, and the young entrepreneurs. That was then, as they say, and this is now.

Anyway, a little over four years after I moved into that tiny, one-bedroom attic apartment, I went downstairs to borrow Mrs. Hawkins's phone because mine had been disconnected. That's what happened back then when you didn't pay the bill. Guess it still does, but it's been a while for me since that happened.

I knocked on the door, then I beat on the door and yelled. No answer. Weird. She almost never left the house. Worried, I went upstairs, dug around in a drawer until I found the key she'd given me. I let myself in, did a room-to-room, then found her curled up on the bathroom floor.

Heart attack… Marsha said she probably never knew what hit her. That's something, I guess.

A week or so later, I sat in her attorney's office in a state of complete gobsmackery. Esther Hawkins left me the house and about 75-grand in cash and CDs. Her legacy turned my life around just about the time East Nashville's fortunes started changing as well. In the last twenty years, bungalow after bungalow, cottage after cottage, house after house—not one of which ever sold new for more than ten grand—was refurbished and renovated, or bulldozed over to raise the notorious "tall and skinnies" that dotted the neighborhoods like alien spaceships descended from the heavens.

I'd had plenty of offers for Esther's house over the years, but I turned them all down. Then when things finally turned around for me financially, I started putting money into the place. A while back, I spent the better part of a year having the house gutted, wall-to-wall and floor-to-ceiling. Everything went out but the load-bearing walls.

I had the attic apartment repurposed as a second floor and a staircase put in, which was where Alex's bedroom, a guest bedroom, another bathroom, a small media room and a ton of storage are now. I put up a three-car garage at the back of the lot and fenced the yard with custom-designed wrought-iron fencing. I had an aggregate driveway put in. A company pressure-washes it twice a year. A crew of landscapers turned my yard into a magazine cover and maintained it immaculately year-round.

Inside, the Formica countertops were now granite, with top-of-the-line stainless steel appliances picked out by my sexy blonde interior designer with the lower back tattoo, including a six-burner Garland stove and a Sub Zero Pro 48 with the glass door. Custom cabinets line the walls. The fixtures are all Waterworks brushed nickel.

I had the hardwood floors redone by the Verchotas, the house totally wired with internet, smart sensors, everything controlled by a network and apps I could pull up on my smartphone.

I have absolutely no idea why I put all that work and money into the place. I still lived there alone, except when Alex came to stay, and I didn't have many guests. Lonnie and Sheba came over for dinner a couple times a month, but that was about it.

I don't really know why I did it, except that it was my home now and I could. Last month, I turned down a blind offer of 2.5 million.

Yeah, shit's changed.

Down in the office parking garage, I unplugged the Tesla and stowed the charging cable, then backed out and headed into the Nashville traffic. I slogged through the pack a few feet at a time, catching up on the news off the satellite radio and trying not to feel too morose. Finally, the traffic eased up a bit and I made it across the Shelby Street Bridge and into East Nashville.

I pulled into the driveway, then hit a button on the touchscreen and the gate slowly rolled open. Another touch on the screen and the garage door on the far left opened and I pulled the T into the first bay. Next to it, the restored 1965 candy apple red Mustang convertible, just like the one my father bought when I was a toddler, sat collecting dust. I hadn't driven it in months. On the other side of the Mustang sat the year-old Ural Gear Up, which was an overpriced Russian sidecar motorcycle I'd bought to cruise around on weekends.

Toys… Yeah, I could afford me some toys.

I plugged the Tesla into the charger, then buttoned everything up and went inside, where I loosened my tie, laid down on the bed, stared at the ceiling, and tried to relax.

That didn't last long. My brain was in overdrive. I couldn't turn it off. I'd met Marsha right in the middle of what was probably the lowest point of my life. I'd had a marriage go south, then the newspaper business kicked me to the curb, which, as it turned out, was probably a favor because these days the newspaper business is just about out of *bidness*.

Back then in the state of Tennessee, a private investigator's license went for $75.00 if you could pass a background check, which in those days meant no verifiable felonies and no record of having been habitually drunk or crazy.

I qualified, barely.

The hardest part was finding the extra $75.00. Eventually, I raised the cash, found a cheap office, and hung out my shingle as a P.I. Over the next couple of months I nearly starved to death, until finally an old girlfriend hired me to help out with a problem her husband was having. Unfortunately, her husband's problems were worse than she knew, because somebody killed him the day after she hired me.

In the middle of this mess, I met Marsha. Dr. Marsha Helms was the assistant medical examiner for Metropolitan Nashville and we were almost immediately drawn to each other. She was a couple inches taller than me, really smart and almost kind of nerdy, and had a mouth on her that could out-smartass me any time she wanted to. I found this aspect particularly appealing.

There was also a dark, moody side to her and since I've always had a thing for women who sleep hanging upside down, that made the whole dynamic even more powerful.

We had our conflicts. She was driven, intense, a real Type A, and very successful. She made a lot of money, drove a Porsche 911, and had what even in the mid-Nineties was considered an expensive condo in Green Hills. I, on the other hand, rarely had more than twenty bucks in my pocket, lived in an attic apartment, and drove cars that were largely duct-taped together by Lonnie Smith, my future billionaire buddy who at the time was a repo man living out of a trailer in Inglewood.

The chemistry was intense, the passion electric, but the problems underneath probably doomed us. We were together almost three years before the conflicts made their way to the surface, like bubble rust on an old car that came through no matter how many coats of paint you sprayed on.

You can't Bondo the human heart.

Truth is, we were about to call it quits when I got involved in a case that turned really ugly. In the end, I had to kill a guy, the first and only time that ever happened. It was a him-or-me situation and there were other people at risk. I did what I had to do, but sunk into the worst funk I'd ever been in after it was over.

Then, at the absolute lowest point ever, Marsha turned up pregnant.

We tried to make a go of it, but reality kept butting in. There was a scandal at the Medical Examiner's Office and Marsha wound up as collateral damage. She got fired, then decided to move to Reno and hide out with her Aunt Marty until the airborne fecal matter settled and the baby was born.

I thought I'd never see her again, and then about a month before Alex was born, she called and asked me to come to Reno. In the end, I was there for Alex's birth, which was the single most incredible moment I've ever experienced. I stood behind the doctor as she brought Alex into the world, and to this day I swear we made eye contact, even though Marsha told me for years afterward that just wasn't possible.

But it was too late for me and Marsha. We couldn't let go, though, because of this being we'd made together. It took some doing, but we finally made peace with each other and over the years I became a regular visitor to Aunt Marty's Mount Rose mansion. I watched Alex grow up. Once she was old enough, she spent a month every summer with me and I saw her most holidays. The three of us settled into a rhythm that was predictable and worked for us. Alex and I talked every couple of days, and when technology evolved we FaceTimed and kept in touch on social media. She sent school essays to me for proofreading and copy-editing and I tried hard not to just take it over and do the work for her. When she had parent/teacher conferences at school, I either flew out there or video conferenced.

Other than living half-a-continent apart, it was almost like being in a normal family. Life went on.

Becoming a parent, especially a late-life one, I suddenly found myself focusing more than ever on career and money. Before Alex, I'd always been a little loosey-goosey about money and work, just taking things as they came along. The newspaper reporter in me never quite went away and after my biggest cases, I found myself recording certain aspects of the work I'd done in a series of books that never really went anywhere. I mostly did it for myself, but after Alex I was too busy.

A couple years after Alex was born, Lonnie—who'd always been a backyard, garage tinkerer—turned his attention back to computers and information technology. He took what he'd learned in almost three years at MIT and started to build on it. In one of my cases, he'd actually hacked a couple of websites, including a credit bureau, to get some information I needed. These early attempts at hacking on the down-low led to a growing interest in cybersecurity. Lonnie polished up his coding skills and I soon found myself completely lost when he started talking.

He developed a software package that made it exponentially harder to hack a website or an account. Then he developed a piece of software that could track hackers back to the source no matter how many ghost ISPs they tried to hide behind. A couple of years later, he developed an app that would penetrate any Virtual Private Network, grab the virus or malware the bad guy was intending to launch, and turn it back on the hacker.

Being a fan of *Hamlet*, he called it *Cyber Petard*, as in hoisted with…

Lonnie's never been one for publicity. He'd rather be the guy behind the curtain pulling the strings that no one ever sees or even knows is there. So when he started his company— Asfáleia Technologies—he brought me in as a kind of public information officer, communications specialist, and tech writer. I wrote copy, manuals, marketing materials (although Lonnie almost never advertised in a conventional sense), and even did some presentations and selling.

Lonnie did one thing that marked him as different from other tech entrepreneurs. In the early days of computers and software, legendary guys like Jobs and Gates sold equipment, computers, software. They recruited new customers by developing new products and kept a revenue stream going through constant updates and revisions. They obviously reaped fortunes beyond anything we've seen since the Gilded Age, and thousands of other entrepreneurs and innovators copied them and revolutionized the world.

Lonnie, on the other hand, never *sold* anything. He never created an actual physical product, never had a retail store in a mall, never went out with an IPO. Lonnie simply developed the most effective cybersecurity software package in the world and then *leased* it only to A-list customers. S&P 500 companies, international conglomerates, credit bureaus, and other massive institutions were his clients, and the software he created was so powerful that it quickly became essential. It was expensive as hell, but worth every cent to a huge corporation. He took care of the clients and never tried to make a quick killing. He wasn't interested in short, big money. He was in it for the long run.

He brought in ten of us in the early days, and since he didn't have any money, he gave us stock in the company. We quickly outgrew that trailer in the middle of Lonnie's junkyard in

Inglewood. When the money started coming in, he paid us.

Well.

A dozen years after starting the company, Lonnie confessed he was getting bored with it all. When a consortium of German and Austrian IT companies approached him with a buyout, he decided it was time to move on.

The ten of us who'd gone in early with him were, in deference to the company name, the O.G.s—*Original Greeks*. Only the past couple of years the newer kids in the company started calling us *Old Guys*. The other nine O.G.s called it quits, took the money and ran, but for some reason or other, that just didn't appeal to me. So I took a few of the guys with me to form Denton & Associates, and as part of the acquisition deal we got a five-year contract to provide consulting and support.

Truth is, it's mostly make-work. I just wasn't ready to bail. What was I going to do, work on my handicap? The one time in my life I tried to play golf, it made me talk ugly.

When the contract expires, the Krauts'll shitcan us for sure. By then, I'll figure out what's next. I'm just trying to take care of my guys so that when the end comes, they'll have a soft landing.

There are lots of truths, though, and another big one is that I can retire any time I want to. When Lonnie sold the company just over a year ago, I owned the biggest share of the ten O.G.s—7 ½ percent.

Do the math.

When Lonnie sold Asfáleia Technologies for 2.5 billion dollars, the guy who twenty-something years ago had to scrape together seventy-five bucks to get a private detective's license walked away with $187,500,000.

Like I said, shit's changed.

Chapter Four

An hour later, I'd showered, changed into a pair of jeans and a cotton shirt, and headed over to Lonnie and Sheba's. I crossed the river, maneuvered my way to Charlotte Avenue, then headed west. It was after six, but the traffic was still moving like automotive sludge. No wonder people had set up Twitter accounts to bitch about Nashville traffic. Half of them were probably tweeting in the middle of it.

I turned left off Charlotte onto 11th, then slowed as the traffic thickened between the new Manhattan-style apartment houses and the massive, ancient Nashville Electric Service facility. Almost thirty years ago, when I started as a rookie reporter at the afternoon daily in Nashville—which has long since gone under—the newspaper building entrance fronted on West End, but the printing operation and the freight and delivery docks were a level below the street and opened up into an area known as The Gulch.

Back then, The Gulch was pretty much a wasteland, with empty warehouses, run-down factories, a railyard, a couple of seedy bars and street lights that turned the place into a film noir soundstage at night. The advantage, though, was that the land was so cheap some brave gentrifying pioneers opened up businesses and the area started trending hipster.

Then the city decided it was time to get serious about revitalization and created the Gulch Business Improvement District. Over the next ten or twelve years, the most amazing transformation in the history of American cities took place.

The warehouses and empty factories were razed and in their places blossomed high-rise apartment buildings and condos, microbreweries galore, trendy expensive restaurants, hipster retail outlets like Urban Outfitters and Lucchese, faux English pubs, organic juice bars, and exotic pizzerias that were to Pizza Hut and Dominos as a Ford Fiesta was to a Maserati. It was a city within a city; the hippest, trendiest, coolest place to be in Nashville.

In short, a real pain in the ass…

A couple of years ago, right about the time Lonnie sold the company, a new condo complex went up near the intersection of 12th and Division. I don't know squat about architecture, but this massive twenty-story tower was some kind of commercial-residential fusion of Art Deco and ultra-modern steel and glass that had absolutely nothing to do with any historical or artistic context I'd ever seen in Nashville.

Called *The Travertine*, I have no idea why anyone who had any connection to this city or its history would have wanted to live there. And it goes without saying that the entire development was pre-sold before the first steel girder was set in place.

Lonnie and Sheba bought the two-story penthouse. Not quite four-thousand square feet, four bedrooms and three bathrooms, surrounded on two sides by a terrace that looked out over The Gulch, toward downtown, Bridgestone Arena, and the state capitol, I think he picked it up for somewhere between three and four million.

I'm just guessing, though. What the hell do I know? I live in a renovated bungalow in East Nashville.

I saw about a five-heartbeat gap between the oncoming cars on Division Street and jetted into the entrance of The Travertine's underground parking garage. I tapped the card with the magnetic stripe against a sensor and a gate went up. Two floors underground, Lonnie's parking spots were a short walk to the glass-enclosed area that held a pair of elevators.

Lonnie's black Ford pickup took up one of the slots, with Sheba's Mercedes SUV parked next to it. I took the slot on the other side, then walked over to the bank of elevators. The security here was amazing; I had to tap my card on a sensor to get into the parking garage, then tap it again to get into the elevator lobby, all the while under constant video surveillance.

I guess when you're this rich, you're safe…

The elevator opened and I had to tap the card on a sensor again to make the "P" button light up. When you hit the button for the penthouse, the elevator became an express straight to the top unless Sheba or Lonnie had turned a key upstairs and disabled it.

A quick ride later, the elevator opened into an anteroom off the entrance foyer. "Hey guys," I called.

"In the kitchen," Sheba answered from off to the left. I walked into the living room, all chrome and glass and modern, with the draperies pulled to let in the July late afternoon natural light. The sky was a palette of beautiful blues and shimmering golds. Air pollution on the Nashville skyline made great eye candy from this vantage point.

Sheba came out of the kitchen wearing a pair of white jeans and white button-down Oxford cloth shirt. Her mane of blonde hair—hence the nickname *Sheba*—fell down over her shoulders and, as always, she wore almost no make-up.

"Harry," she said, coming toward me and wrapping me in a hug. "How are you?"

I hugged her back. "Hanging in there."

"C'mon, let me get you a beer. Lon's in the shower. He got back about twenty minutes ago and you know what happens when he gets around a set of tools."

She grabbed my hand and pulled me into the kitchen, then opened one side of a massive, steel side-by-side. She peeked around the door at me.

"Yazoo summer seasonal?"

I smiled. "Sure. Sounds great."

She reached for a bottle opener, closing the refrigerator door with a right knee nudge.

She handed me the brown bottle, condensation already forming on the side. I downed a third of the bottle in one swallow.

"Great," I said. "I've been waiting all day for that."

She leaned against the counter, her arms folded across her chest. "And what a hell of a day it's been," she said. "How're you holding up, Harry? Really?"

I shrugged. "I don't know," I answered. "Something tells me the hard part's not here yet."

She picked up her glass of chardonnay off the counter, took a sip, and studied me over the top of the glass. "I'm worried about you."

"I'll be okay."

"Harry, you're staring straight into sixty, you've been through about a decade-and-a-half of roller coaster agony, and now you've got a teen-aged girl coming to live with you."

"Now, wait a—"

She cut me off with a raised palm. "Yes, granted, she's the

greatest teen-aged girl in the universe. We all agree. But c'mon, Harry, you gotta figure this is going to be an adjustment."

I was quiet for a second, looked down at the floor and back up at her, then let out a long, deep breath. "Sweetie, I don't even know where to begin."

Behind us, footsteps padded down the hallway. "Don't know where to begin what?" Lonnie said as he walked barefoot into the kitchen. He wore jeans and a T-shirt and was rubbing his wet hair with a bath towel.

I'd known Lonnie over twenty-five years and he wore the same size jeans now that he'd worn then. He once grew his jet-black hair long and pulled it into a ponytail, but had cut it back in the last ten years to where it was just fashionably long and moving toward salt-and-pepper.

Sheba opened the refrigerator door and pulled out a beer. She tossed it to him; he twisted the cap off in one motion.

"Don't know where to begin getting my head around how you can drink so much beer and never put on a pound."

He smiled, took a long chug off the bottle. "It's not the calories you take in," he said, and then he winked at me *sotto voce*. "It's how you burn 'em off."

Sheba laughed. "Yeah, and you burn about a thousand a day running that mouth."

Lonnie raised an eyebrow. "Yeah, baby, but it's *where* I run it…"

"Okay, you two," I said. "I can come back later."

Lonnie laughed loudly enough that it approached guffawery. "C'mon, I know it's July out there, but let's go sit on the balcony. My hair's never gonna dry in all this AC."

"When I first met you," I said, following as he and Sheba led the way, "you didn't have any AC."

"That's right," he said, sliding open the 12-foot-high tinted glass doors. "That old window unit in the trailer'd gone out and I needed about three more repos to replace it."

We settled in at the black wrought-iron patio table with the glass top. It was the height of July, but there was a nice breeze blowing and we were far enough up that it was about as pleasant as July ever got around here.

Lonnie leaned back in his chair and put his feet up on the table supports and stretched. "So how's Alex?" he asked.

"She sounds okay, I guess. I'm glad she's with Marie and Hal. I was going to call her in another couple of hours if I don't hear from her."

"Listen, we've had a little snag on the plane," Lonnie said. "Nothing major. Little wet spot on a hydraulic line. Captain Jimmy wants to have the A&P look at it. They'll send a guy over first thing in the morning. We should be outta here by lunchtime."

I grinned at him. "You flying left seat by yourself?" Lonnie'd been signed off on the Citation about three months earlier, but still hadn't built up a ton of time. Reno would be the longest cross-country he'd ever taken.

"Well, if it was just our two old scroungy asses, I'd say let it go." He motioned in Sheba's direction. "But with this one and Alex coming along, better safe than sorry. Captain Jimmy'll take right seat. We'll get him a rental, put him in a room at the Hyatt in Lake Tahoe. He can play a little blackjack, lose some of my hard-earned money while we take care of business."

"Cool. I'm mostly packed."

"Harry," Lonnie said, suddenly almost serious, "we been through some shit before, buddy. We'll get through this. I want you to know that. Sheba and I'll have your back."

Sheba nodded. "You're family, Harry."

"I appreciate that, guys. More than you know."

Lonnie raised his beer, polished off the last of it, and slid the bottle onto the table. "You know, we both had some problems with the way…"

He hesitated for a moment. "Well, the way she treated you sometimes."

Sheba gave him the look. "We said we weren't going to go there."

Lonnie turned to her, batted his eyes. "We're just talking here, sweetheart. That's all."

"It's ancient history. Nothing can change the past. And I'm going to go refill my glass and grab you two another beer."

She got up, crossed over to the door and slid it open.

Lonnie sat up, put both feet on the floor. "Is there anything we can do?"

"What do you mean, anything you can do? You're flying me out to frickin' Nevada in your private jet to bury my daughter's mother and bring my kid back home with me. Don't you think that's enough?"

"That's not even what I mean," he answered. "Hell, in the end that's just money. I mean, is there anything we can do to make this easier?"

I thought for a moment. "Alex is going to need a lot of propping up. And I can't be everything for her. She's awfully close to Sheba."

"Well, you know Sheba's gonna be there for her. But what about you?"

I shook my head. "No, nothing for me. I grieved over losing

Marsha a long time ago. It's not like I was pining for her or anything. I kept going out there for Alex's sake."

The door behind us slid open again and Sheba came out with her right hand wrapped around the necks of two beer bottles and a fresh chardonnay in her left.

"I wonder sometimes," Lonnie said.

"Wonder what?" she asked, setting the bottles down.

Lonnie looked up at her. "This guy tells us he was over it years ago and that the only reason he kept going out there was for his daughter."

"Can't you buy that?" Sheba asked again. "Sometimes, you just gotta take people at their word."

"And yet in fifteen years, this guy's barely gone on a date."

"Wait a minute," I interrupted. "I said I was over her. I didn't say she wasn't a tough act to follow."

Lonnie rolled his eyes, leaned over and grabbed his beer off the table.

"Besides, I have been on dates, lots of 'em. Just nothing permanent, long term…"

Lonnie chugged about a third of the beer, then sneered. "C'mon, when's the last time you got laid?"

"Lonnie!" Sheba snapped.

"C'mon," he said. "You said it yourself. We're family…"

"And families have the right to know the last time each member got laid?" I asked.

He smiled. "Interesting that you should deploy the word *member*. Besides, you're just dodging the question."

I grabbed my fresh beer off the table, took a pull, then leaned back in the chair and stared out over the horizon. "Okay, so it's been awhile. Long dry spell."

"Define long dry spell," he said.

"Five years?" I answered, unsure of that exact number myself. Never thought I'd get to a point where I literally couldn't remember the last time I had sex.

Sheba put her head down in her hand, covering her eyes and slowly shaking her head side-to-side.

"*Five years!*" Lonnie yelped. "Jesus, as long as we're in Reno, let's get you out to the Mustang Ranch."

"Been there, done that," I said. "Besides, the dang *gummint* tore it down."

Lonnie cocked his head toward me. "How—? I mean, how have you not... *exploded*?"

"Look," I said, on the defensive, "I just haven't found the right person. Plus, if you recollect, I've been a little preoccupied the last year or so with helping my daughter get through her mother's cancer."

"This is depressing," Sheba said. "Let's change the subject. Harry, have you got Alex's school situation straightened out?"

"I think so. I met with the admissions person at Bealesworth last week when I got back from Nevada. Everything looks good. Put down a deposit..."

"Bealesworth?" Lonnie asked.

"Private school out on Highway 100, other side of Warner Park just before you get to the Loveless Cafe, near Vaughn's Gap Road. Good school. Great college prep. She can play field hockey and lacrosse."

"Yeah, out by the entrance to the Natchez Trace." Lonnie leaned forward. "Just got one question. They gotta wear those little plaid skirts and the knee-high white socks?"

"You're disgusting," Sheba said, trying not to encourage him by laughing.

"No," I answered. "It's not a Catholic school."

"Sounds expensive," he said, leaning back. "Plus a helluva long way from East Nashville."

"It is," I said. "But I hope driving her to school will just be daughter/daddy alone time. I'd put her in Metro, but the public schools here are…"

"Problematic?" Sheba offered.

I nodded. "Yeah."

Lonnie stretched out, laced his fingers behind his head. "Face it, Harry," he said. "You're just an old, rich, privileged white guy."

I turned and leered at him. "Takes one to know one," I said. "Pass the caviar."

❧

We each had another cold one and I told Lonnie and Sheba about the strange little man who came to my office today, and his bizarre story of wanting his own murder investigated.

"I never heard of the guy," Lonnie said. "Leo Walsh?"

"I vaguely remember him," Sheba said. "He was famous for a while, kinda' like that Dan Brown guy. You know, guy who wrote that Rembrandt Code-thing."

"I think it was Da Vinci. They made a movie out of it," I said, shaking my head. "God, as if the day wasn't strange enough," I said.

"What are you gonna do?" Lonnie asked.

I shrugged. "Nothing to do. I mean, the guy's got problems, but they're way beyond my pay grade."

Sometime between the third and fourth beers, we ordered a couple of pizzas from this trendy new hipster place down

Division, near 8th. Sheba pulled up the menu online and I found myself still struggling to get my head around the new world order. Pizza to me was tomato sauce, cheese, and either pepperoni or Italian sausage. If you were trying to be healthy, then you threw on some green peppers or a handful of spinach.

As Belushi used to say: *But noooooo…*

Sheba insisted we try the caramelized onions, apples and goat cheese pizza. In case that didn't work, we ordered a strawberry balsamic pizza with chicken, sweet onion and Applewood bacon as backup.

Lonnie and I got into an eye-rolling contest, which drew, shall we say, a sharp rebuke.

Then Sheba and Lonnie explained to me that the only pizza delivery you could get anymore was from the cheap franchise chains. Now any restaurant worth its salt outsourced deliveries to one of the gig economy operations designed to screw their employees out of decent pay, steady schedules, and benefits like health insurance, vacation or sick pay, and pretty much any other basic human right. When Sheba submitted the online order and came to the buy page, those two pizzas, delivered, cost more than my first private investigator's license.

Mmm, I'm sure that'll be some tasty pizza.

Actually, it was. An hour later, in the middle of it, Alex called and I put her on speaker and we all got to catch up. Alex still sounded exhausted, but she perked up when I told her Sheba and Lonnie were in the house. She and Sheba chattered away like old girlfriends and it made me feel better that she and Lonnie would be in my daughter's life when she started her new life here.

I didn't know if I could do this alone.

Chapter Five

Sleepless night. One of many… This one was worse, though. A day so long that it was now officially the next day.

You lie there staring up at the ceiling, only it's dark and you can't really see the ceiling. But what you can see is the dim amber glow of the digital alarm clock numbers as the seconds and minutes seem to click on endlessly. Around 4 A.M., I got up, poured myself a glass of white wine and turned on the flat-screen television mounted on the wall on the opposite side of my bedroom. Flipped around—news, shopping channels, the endless digital media streaming downriver to nowhere…

Finally, on Turner Classic Movies, an oldie but a goodie: *Crime School* with Humphrey Bogart and Gail Page from 1938, just a couple of years before Bogey broke out forever onto the A-List with *High Sierra* and *Maltese Falcon*. It was one of those Warner Bros. social justice movies that really starred the Dead End Kids, who grew up and became the Bowery Boys.

I drifted off, and when I came to, Mickey Rooney and Judy Garland were singing something, but I flipped off the TV and staggered into the shower. It was going to be a long day and I'd be halfway across the country before it was over…

The lunch rush hour was in full-on mode by the time I snaked over to the freeway entrance ramp on Broadway. As I turned right onto the highway, I glanced to my left. The drive-through line at the White Castle wound around the building into a good twenty, thirty minute wait.

A semi laid on its air horn like the Titanic leaving Southampton as I slid into the lane just in front of it and jammed the pedal. When you do that on the Tesla, it feels like it's pulling a couple of g's. If this yutz in the Peterbilt thought I couldn't get out of his way, I showed him how wrong he was, just like a true asshole Nashville driver.

I jinked my way across the next three lanes until I was all the way over to the left and sailing around the steeply-banked bridge that melded into I-40 West. The traffic thinned out a bit the further away from downtown I got and next thing I knew I was hitting the ramp onto the northbound lane of Briley Parkway, headed toward Ashland City. Fortunately, I wasn't going that far.

I always get a little nostalgic taking this route. You go around a curve and up a slight incline and, way off to your right, like a distant castle or a decaying Disneyland, sits "The Walls," the old Tennessee State Prison. Now over a hundred years old, it resembles the ghost of an abandoned medieval castle, complete with turrets and battlements, shattered windows, eroding flow coat exposing crude brick, and weeds sprouting everywhere. From the mid-eighties until it closed in 1992, I was out there eight or ten times a year to interview inmates or cover stories. I even covered the 1985 riots, although there wasn't a whole lot to see because no reporters were allowed inside until the rumble was over. When they went back on lockdown, we essentially got a tour of a garbage dump.

After The Walls closed in 1992, the Department of Corrections turned it into a movie set. That worked for awhile, with movies as far apart as *The Green Mile* and *Ernest Goes to Jail* being shot there. Somewhere along the line, though, it occurred to somebody that maybe all that stuff flaking off the walls onto the actors and crew should be tested. That's when they discovered the toxic soup—everything from lead paint to mold to asbestos and a carcinogenic smorgasbord of eroding insulation—that inmates had been sucking in for nearly a century.

Now it's totally off-limits: abandoned, crumbling and creepy as hell, not to mention dangerous. It's one of those parts of my life that I remember fondly. But I don't want a do-over.

Anyway, I wasn't there to reminisce.

❧

The exit ramp loops back under Briley Parkway onto Centennial Boulevard. A few miles ahead, in an area that's mostly industrialized, the Cumberland River makes a big hairpin turn called Cockrill Bend. Hidden away in Cockrill Bend is John Tune airport, a single-runway field that is the only way to fly into Nashville without hassling with the crowded and complicated Nashville International Airport.

It's a commuter airport, with hangars and tie-downs for people well-off enough to have their own planes, and a couple of flight schools for people who hope to be that affluent someday. I turned right off Centennial Boulevard and drove up the narrow road toward the terminal. Twenty years ago, you could just turn off the road onto the tarmac and drive on the asphalt up to your hangar, but 9/11 had put an end to all that. Now this airport, like all others, was surrounded by chain link fence and razor wire, with entry to the actual tarmac card-access only.

I parked in front of Compact Aviation, one of the FBOs—Fixed Base Operators—that serviced, maintained, fueled and provided hangar space for the rich guys who parked their expensive toys there. I pulled my backpack, suitcase, and hanger bag out of the back of the car and rolled my way into the office.

A young blonde in jeans and a polo shirt with the Compact Aviation logo looked up from her desk and smiled.

"Can I help you?"

"I'm Lonnie Smith's passenger," I answered. "I'm supposed to meet him here at noon."

She pointed toward a hallway. "Mr. Smith and Captain Jimmy are out preflighting the plane. I believe Mrs. Smith's in the pilots' lounge."

I had to smile. Somehow, I never thought of Sheba as *Mrs. Smith*, even though that's precisely who she'd been for over a decade. I was surprised that she took Lonnie's name when they got married, but the longer we all lived with it, the more natural it seemed. Still, she was always just Sheba to me.

I hitched my hanger bag higher on my shoulder and towed the rolling bag down the hallway and into the lounge, which was nicer than a lot of the apartments I'd lived in. Leather sofas, HDTV mounted on the wall, four computer stations, a cooking area with microwave and a refrigerator and a large picture window that looked out over the airport. Sheba stood at the window facing away from me, wearing a pair of white jeans, sandals, and a silk blouse. Her hair was pulled behind her but untied, draping over her shoulders. Her arms were crossed as she stared quietly out over the airport, the heat shimmering off the asphalt in the July sun.

"Hey," I said.

She turned, faced me with a blank look. "Hi."

I laid my hanger bag and backpack down on the nearest sofa. "Everything okay?"

She nodded toward the window. "They're out there doing a once-over."

I crossed, stood next to her. Lonnie's latest toy, a Cessna Citation CJ4 twin-engine jet, sat parked on the tarmac. Lonnie'd had it about three months, had been signed off in it pretty quickly, but still hadn't built up enough time to be comfortable flying cross-country.

Lonnie'd taken up flying almost five years ago, just as he started to get bored with running the company and simultaneously had made so much money he could do just about anything he wanted. He started out, as all pilots do, in a two-seater, single-engine trainer and he'd taken to it like he was born with a set of wings glued to his ass. Within a couple of months, he'd gotten his pilot's license, then an instrument rating, multi-engine, commercial, and now type ratings in the Citation, a twin-engine jet. Along the way, he'd become best buds with his flight instructor, Jimmy Wilbert. I almost found myself a little jealous from time to time. I wondered if Sheba didn't get a little of that herself.

"How's it going, Harry?"

I shook my head. "Weird morning. Sometimes it feels like the world has shifted off its axis."

Sheba turned back toward the window, away from me. "It has," she said.

The Citation was parked with its nose to the right. It gleamed white in the sun, except for the interlaced blue and red trim stripes that ran down the side of the fuselage. The airplane's rudder was a T-tailed configuration and seemed big for the size of the plane, but what did I know? I'm just the passenger.

Emblazoned across the tail was the aircraft's N number: N999AT.

On the port side of the jet, Lonnie climbed down the drop-down entry door, followed by Captain Jimmy. The two walked around to the nose of the aircraft, then squatted to examine something on the nose wheel. Lonnie stood up, turned toward us and waved, then motioned for us to come on out.

"Where's your bag?" I asked. "Need any help?"

"Already on the plane," Sheba answered. "Besides, you look like you're loaded down enough."

I hooked my backpack strap over my right shoulder, then draped the hanger bag over it, grabbed the rolling bag with my left hand, and followed Sheba out of the lounge. Outside, on the asphalt, the heat was building up fast. I could feel it through my shoes and see it shimmering off the pavement ahead of me.

"Hey," Lonnie called, "let's get rolling!"

As we approached the plane, Lonnie stepped forward and grabbed the suitcase out of my hand. He turned to Captain Jimmy.

"Which one?"

Jimmy turned and eyeballed the suitcase. I'd only met him a few times, but he was the kind of guy who stuck in your mind. He was in his mid-sixties, his face weathered and creased like he'd been a heavy smoker in his earlier years. He wore a pair of blue slacks and one of those short-sleeved pilot's shirts with the epaulets and the gold braid. His hair was cut short and he had a perpetual half-smile on his face.

"We're traveling light today," he said. "Shouldn't be any weight-and-balance issues. Just stow it in the aft compartment with the others. There's a bar in the cabin for the hanger bag."

I walked up to Jimmy and extended my hand. "Can I keep the backpack with me?"

"Sure," he said.

"I really appreciate you doing this, Captain. Means a lot to me."

He grinned as he shook my hand. "Glad to do it," he said. "You call, we haul… That's all, ya'll."

Sheba went up the stairs into the cabin, with me a step or two behind. The engines were shut down and there was no AC, but the blackout shades had been lowered on every window so it was bearable inside.

When Lonnie told me he was buying the plane, I clandestinely looked up what one of these things costs. Base model, reasonably equipped, ran almost nine million. But Lonnie'd had this one tricked out with every mod available, including custom leather seats, an upgraded lavatory at the rear of the plane and God knows how much on the avionics. I'd never actually asked him, but I'd be surprised if he spent less than ten on it.

And to top it all off, it still had that new car smell. Sometimes I'm staggered by all this…

As I hit the last stair step and entered the cabin, I looked to my left onto the flight deck. This was my third ride on the Citation, so I'd seen it all before. Still, I couldn't help being blown away by the high-tech, total glass cockpit. Lonnie'd explained to me that the old-school, analog steam gauges and instruments were long gone. Everything was digital and glass, computer controlled and automated. He told me the Citation was actually an easier plane to fly than the old 152 he'd learned on.

I turned right and followed Sheba down the aisle between the single line of seats on either side. The interior was all blues and browns, rich and calming. Leather seats, a flat screen mounted on the wall at the front of the cabin…

"Which side you want?" she said.

"Makes no difference," I answered. "You choose and I'll take the other."

Sheba slid into a seat on the left side and I sat across from her. Up front, Lonnie was already settling into the pilot's seat on the left side of the aircraft as Captain Jimmy was hauling up the entrance door and securing it.

"You actually gonna let him fly left seat in this thing?" I called out.

Captain Jimmy howled. Lonnie turned around, leaned into the cabin. "Hey, buddy," he said, raising his right bird finger to me. "Got ya joystick right here. Fly this!"

"Hey, I don't care one way or the other. Long as I know where the parachutes are stowed."

Jimmy laughed again as he was strapping himself into the right seat. "You guys just kill me," he said.

"Let's hope not," I offered. "Say, how long's this little joyride gonna take?"

"Reno Tahoe International Airport is precisely 1809 miles away as the crow flies," Jimmy answered. "Our enroute flight time, depending on the winds, should be under four hours."

I turned to Sheba. "That seems quick."

She leaned in toward me. "Lonnie told me this little puppy poots along about 500 miles an hour…"

"That's *pooting*?"

The lights in the cabin flickered and I saw Lonnie and Captain Jimmy flipping digital switches and calling off stuff to each other. Then, from behind us rose the slow whine of two engines spooling up. In just a few moments, the engines hit idle speed, the lights flickered again, the blackout shades lifted on the windows, and I felt a steady stream of cold air coming down on me from a vent above. We sat there for a couple of minutes, then the Citation began slowly moving. Lonnie taxied the jet forward, then turned to the left, past the hangars and onto a taxiway. The taxiway seemed bumpy, the airplane almost lumbering down the asphalt, the swept-back wings seeming to dip and rise with each bump. Then we stopped for a few moments as Lonnie and Captain Jimmy did whatever pilots do just before taking off.

Next thing I knew, we turned hard left onto the runway and Lonnie gunned it. The engines roared up to full throttle, although it seemed quieter than what I remembered. I felt myself being pushed back into the seat, then Lonnie pulled back on the yoke and the nose lifted.

Everything smoothed out as we went wheels-up. Then there was the gentle thunk of the landing gear tucking itself up and we were on our way.

In about five hours, I'd have Alex back in my arms again.

The flat-screen monitor mounted on the front wall of the cabin displayed a map of the U.S., with our little airplane meme just over west Tennessee and moving to the left. We'd only been airborne about fifteen or twenty minutes and it looked like we were almost to the Mississippi River. Lonnie hit the cabin intercom, just like a real pilot on a grown-up jet, and announced that we'd arrived at our cruising altitude of 28,000 feet. We'd picked up a good tailwind, he said, and were right on track to hit Reno by midafternoon local time.

I looked over at Sheba and she was leaning against the bulkhead, her eyes closed. I settled as deep into the cushioned leather as I could and leaned down to look out the window. Just over five miles below me, the west Tennessee countryside passed like a patchwork quilt of browns and greens, shades of earthy color with a brilliant coating of blue on top. Wispy cotton balls splayed across the sky in random puffs.

It was beautiful. And I couldn't fathom how I got here. So much of this still seemed unreal...

At some point, I actually drifted off. The flight was so smooth, so quiet, and unlike flying commercial these days, so damned comfortable that I couldn't help it. I woke up only because I had this sense we were losing altitude. I came to and looked out the window and saw we were descending through a thin layer of cloud and suddenly the stark, frightening but beautifully barren high desert was skimming by below us. Off to one side, a range of reddish brown and gray mountains with barely a hint of green stood against the haze. There was a highway below us, and increasingly, housing developments pushing farther and farther out into the arid, dry rock.

I looked across the aisle. Sheba gave me a soft, sweet smile. "How long have I been out?"

She shrugged. "Couple hours, maybe. I took a little snooze myself."

I grinned back at her and motioned to the cockpit. "Hope they're awake up there."

"Doesn't matter," Lonnie called from the left seat. "Autopilot works just fine."

"How much longer we got?"

"Reno Approach has got us," he said. "We'll be on the ground in fifteen minutes tops."

"Jeez," I said, reaching for my phone. "I gotta text Alex..."

I pulled up her number and typed: On the ground in 15 minutes. We'll grab a cab to Marie & Hal's. Can't wait to see you. Love--Daddy

A minute later: GREAT! CAN'T WAIT. WE'RE ALL HERE! XXXOOO

In a few more minutes, we were on final descent to Reno Tahoe International. Lonnie settled the Citation back into a slow easy approach and raised barely a squeak when the tires greased the runway.

I turned to Sheba. "Damn, he's good…"

She nodded.

The plane slowed, then turned right off the runway, jogged to the left on some taxiway, and the next thing I know we're pulling to a stop in front of Atlantic Aviation, the main FBO at Reno. I unbuckled myself and stood up in the aisle, stretching to relieve the stiffness after almost four hours sitting. You stiffen up after awhile, even in luxury.

Sheba headed forward while I got my hanger bag and backpack strapped on, then turned and made for the exit. Lonnie and Captain Jimmy were standing on the tarmac while a couple of ramp attendants retrieved our bags and loaded them onto a cart. I took a deep lungful of the thin, high desert air of Reno, air that was so different from the thick, heavy air of the South. I'd grown to love this air, to love the brilliant sky a color of deep blue I'd never seen anywhere else. I'd grown to love this country in a way that I never thought possible.

I'd been here less than three weeks ago, just as Marsha was moving into hospice care. Now Aunt Marty's property belonged to our daughter, to be held in trust until she was old enough to decide what to do with it. If she wanted it for herself, it was hers to keep. I'd made that promise to Marsha when she asked me to be the executor of her will and the trustee of the estate.

I intended to keep that promise.

There was twenty minutes' worth of paperwork to be

completed before we could head into Reno. Atlantic Aviation would service Lonnie's toy, clean it, make sure everything was taken care of, then have it fueled and ready for us when we headed back to Nashville in five days. Sheba and I walked through the plush private terminal. Outside we hailed a taxi van and loaded the gear into the back. I gave the driver Hal and Marie's address and he typed it into his GPS.

A couple of minutes later, Lonnie and Jimmy exited the building and climbed into the van. It was almost four local time and there was a growing knot in my stomach. All this stuff started flooding over me as the van driver maneuvered his way out of the airport and headed west on Plumb Lane. A couple minutes later, off to our left, the Peppermill rose up out of the ground like an explosion of light.

We kept on Plumb, then turned northbound on South McCarran Boulevard. I'd been to Marie and Hal's house a couple of times over the years, but I couldn't seem to bring up much of a memory. Just snapshots in my head. I remembered they lived in a really plush house in a gated community just off the Caughlin Parkway, near some country club that I have a vague memory of steak and cocktails with Marsha and the two of them years ago. We'd been their guests that evening and it had set them back a pretty penny.

They could afford it, though. Hal Genworth was one of Reno's most successful realtors and his wife, Marie, was the Chief Medical Examiner and Coroner for the Washoe County Regional Medical Examiner's Office.

Which was how Marie and Marsha got to be such good pals. After Alex was born and it was clear Marsha wasn't moving back to Nashville, she needed something besides motherhood to occupy her time and keep her brain busy. So she signed on as a contract medical examiner with Marie's office. She could pick her own hours, make some extra money, and most importantly, occupy that high-powered brain of hers.

The van driver turned onto Caughlin Parkway, with its high six-figure, low seven-figure homes all in a similar 18th century Spanish hacienda style. A half-mile or so down, he turned through an open gate into a circular driveway that led up to the Genworths' house. The lawn was manicured and as green as an Irish golf course. The driveway was gray flagstones, the house itself a contemporary modern showcase.

"Holy cow," Sheba muttered.

"Yeah, it's kind of breathtaking," I answered. "I don't think the Genworths have any kids."

The house was hard to describe. The bottom floor was like a contemporary ranch house, only with several wings spreading out from a center core. Over that main part of the house there was a second story with a line of rectangular windows on all four sides. The house itself was sided in wood. Cedar maybe? Something more exotic?

Hell if I knew. I was just waiting for the driver to pull up front and stop. As he braked, I hit the Send button on my phone to text Alex: We're here…

I stepped out of the van just as the front door to the house flew open. Alex came running down the walk and I managed to take two steps toward her before she flew into my arms and nearly took me down.

I wrapped my arms around her and lifted her an inch or two off the ground. I wouldn't be able to do that much longer; she'd be taller than me in another year.

She buried her face in my shoulder and began to sob. I put my cheek down on the top of her head. Her thick, straight black hair, just like her mother's, smelled clean.

"Daddy," she whispered.

"Hello, baby," I said. "I'm here. I'm here."

Everything was all right now, even if nothing was ever going to be the same.

Chapter Six

The hugging and the sobbing went on awhile, as it tends to do at times like this. Sheba was next, with the two of them clamped together almost desperately. Even Lonnie seemed to be fighting something back.

Marie and Hal Genworth stood behind us, at a distance. I turned, walked over to them. Hal was early 50s, tanned, close-cropped hair. He wore khaki trousers, sandals and a Polo shirt. He looked like what he was, a realtor and a golfer, but somehow I never held that against him.

Marie was a couple of years younger, maybe twenty pounds heavier. As long as I'd known her, which was coming up on ten years, she'd struggled to keep the weight off. She was attractive though, and as sweet as she could be for somebody who cut up dead bodies for a living.

I'd once thought the same thing about Marsha.

I took Hal's outstretched hand with my right hand and grabbed his shoulder with my left. "Guys, I'm so grateful. I don't know what we would have done without you. Thank you so much."

Hal shook my hand. "Harry, it's our pleasure. I'm just so sorry we had to."

Marie opened her arms and I stepped into them. She gave me a tight hug. "Harry, I'm sorry," she whispered. "We're all going to miss her so much."

I pulled back. Her eyes were wet, glistening. I struggled for a moment to keep it together myself. "I just appreciate you so much being there for her and Alex."

"Wouldn't have had it any other way," she answered.

I turned, my arm still around her shoulder. "C'mon," I said to Hal and Marie. "Meet the southern branch of the tribe."

❧

Death is more about contrast than anything else. The stillness of the dead contrasted with the frenzy of the living left behind. The end of pain for the dead and the ongoing agony and grief of the living.

So damn much to do when all you really want is to curl into a ball and shut the world out…

We carried all our stuff into the Genworths' house and parked it in the foyer. Marie had set out a buffet full of snacks for us, which was especially welcome because it never occurred to me to actually eat that day. Alex scooted her chair close to me and I ate with my left hand while my right arm was around her shoulder. It seemed to me she'd grown in just the short time since I'd last seen her.

Maybe she just seemed older.

The plan was for the Genworths to give us a ride up Mount Rose to the three-story Alpine mini-mansion Aunt Marty'd left Marsha. Lonnie, Sheba, and I would stay there with Alex. Once we got settled in, Lonnie would drive Captain Jimmy the rest of the way up the mountain to the Hyatt in Incline Village. There were three cars at the house—all of which, I suppose, now belonged to my daughter—so there wouldn't be any problem with getting everybody where they needed to be.

Today was Tuesday. Alex and I would head back into Reno tomorrow and settle the last details at the funeral home. There would be a brief visitation Thursday morning, with the funeral to follow. Marsha had decided, to my surprise, that she wanted a conventional, traditional ceremony. After that, she'd be laid to rest in the mausoleum next to Aunt Marty. Over the years, we'd often talked about how we wanted to say goodbye to this world. I personally always liked Hunter Thompson's idea of having my ashes shot out of a cannon, but that was just my innate flair for the over-the-top.

Marsha had talked about being cremated and having her ashes scattered over the desert, or the ocean, or off the top of the Eiffel Tower or someplace equally glamorous. I think that all changed when she had Alex. Suddenly, the idea of catching the bus when your kids are still around becomes a lot weightier. I think she thought if there was a place where Alex could visit her that maybe it wouldn't be so much like they'd never see each other again.

In many ways, the hard part would come after that. Alex would have to say goodbye to the house she'd lived in all her life and the high desert she loved so much. The three of us had talked about Alex staying here to finish high school, but she had two more years left and she didn't really like the private school her mother put her in all that much anyway. Living up on the mountain meant a lot of time alone. After Marty passed, it was just Marsha, Alex, and Estella, who'd now been the housekeeper there for something like a quarter-century. After Alex moved back to Nashville to live with me until she went off to college, Estella would continue to live there as the caretaker, presumably for as long as she wanted or could.

The last time I'd been to Reno, almost three weeks ago, Marsha was fading in and out most of the time. The hospice nurse went from twice a week to every two days to every day. Alex, I, and Estella started packing up Alex's things. She'd carry a few suitcases with us on the way back to Nashville, but movers would bring the rest in a week or so.

In the middle of all this, with Marsha slipping away a few doors down the hallway, I kept having the oddest sensation as we were packing Alex's things. There would be some book, or something like a yearbook full of autographs, or a piece of clothing, or some decoration on her desk. An expensive digital camera I didn't know she had. A ticket stub from a concert she'd never told me she'd been to. And I'd look at whatever it was and, for a moment, I'd have this sensation of *I've never seen that.*

That's when it began to hit me. I loved my daughter very much, from the moment she was born. Never any question, any doubt. We'd traveled together. Talked or FaceTimed together nearly every day for years. I'd visited her here; she's visited me there.

But we'd never actually lived together.

And I began to see that I didn't really know her.

⁂

Estella Avillar must have heard us coming up the driveway. She was standing on the long front porch waiting as we pulled to a stop. She wore a flowered print dress and flat sensible shoes, her silver-streaked black hair pulled up in a tight bun. Like Marty, Estella had been most suspicious of me in the beginning. The first night I'd met her, after finally making it to Reno from Nashville, she made me shave and shower, then change out of jeans and into a pair of khakis before letting me into Marsha's room.

Even then, she was reluctant to leave us alone. Like we were two teenaged kids who were going to misbehave.

Marie parked the Suburban in a space across from the veranda as Hal pulled his Lexus SUV into the slot next to us. Back in the day, Marty used to do a lot of entertaining, so when she had the house built back in the late seventies, she made sure there was plenty of parking.

"Alex!" Estella called out. "Querida!"

Alex smiled and waved as she climbed down from the car. I opened the back door and slid out onto the aggregate, the heat instantly radiating through to my feet. Even at this higher altitude, the fierce July sun was relentless. I unloaded the bags from the back of the Suburban, while Captain Jimmy and Lonnie unloaded the other car. Sheba went up the steps and introduced herself to Estella, then followed Alex into the house.

I hefted my backpack onto my shoulder, then lifted the suitcase and threw the hanger bag over my other shoulder. At the top of the stairs, I set all the stuff down and hugged Estella.

"Señor Harry," she said, her English a lot less-accented than it was when I met her almost sixteen years ago. "It is good to see you again, but I am so sorry."

"Thank you, Estella," I said. "I am sorry for you, too, my friend."

Estella was nearly seventy, but had only just begun to put on a little weight in the last few years. She had become what most people would characterize as *matronly*, but clearly had been an attractive, even striking woman in her younger days. I don't know why she never married, or even if she had ever married. There are some boundaries you just don't cross.

We finished unloading the cars and lugging the baggage into the house. Sheba and Lonnie had never been here before and Sheba just stood in the foyer kind of staring. The house was designed like a Swiss chalet, all polished wood and beams. The house towered three stories above the ground, but the bottom floor was partially underground, set into the side of the mountain. There was a media room, laundry, wine cellar, home office and Estella's apartment on that floor, which opened up into a three-car garage.

Marty made a lot of money in the hedge fund business.

"This is amazing," Sheba whispered. A large living room with an adjoining library was off to the right of the entranceway, with the dining room, kitchen, and access to the master suite off to the left. A grand staircase led to the top floor, where there were four other bedrooms. Alex had the largest one, and over the years the next largest kind of evolved into mine. There were two other guest rooms.

"Yeah," Lonnie agreed as Estella swept past us into the kitchen. Alex stepped over next to me and wrapped her left arm around my waist, my right arm across her shoulder. She was very quiet. Suddenly, everything seemed very quiet.

I leaned down. "You okay?"

She nodded. "It's not the same," she whispered.

"I know. And it won't ever be. But it can become something else if you want it to be. Or you can let it go. It's up to you."

She turned her head up and looked directly into my eyes, surprised, as if I'd said something that caught her completely off guard.

"That's right," I said. "This is yours now."

❧

We made small talk and killed time for a while, then Lonnie and Captain Jimmy loaded up Marsha's Jeep Cherokee in the garage and took off up the mountain to Incline Village, where

Captain Jimmy would have a few days paid R&R at the Lake Tahoe Hyatt Regency. I don't think anyone actually came outright and said it, but we all understood that Lonnie and Jimmy would grab a steak and a couple of drinks, then hang out in the casino for a while. After they left, Sheba huddled in a corner of the living room, with its sprawling picture window looking down over the Mount Rose forest. She seemed tired and completely happy to have Lonnie and Jimmy out of her hair.

Estella made the best arroz con pollo I've ever had in my life and I took it as a sign of great affection that she always made it my first night here. Sheba and I went down to the wine cellar and came back up with a couple of bottles of Albariño, a crisp, dry white wine that was kind of the Spanish equivalent of a Pinot Grigio. It was perfect for a chicken and rice dish on a hot July day. Estella and Alex went about wordlessly preparing dinner like they'd been doing this a long time, which I supposed they had. Sheba and I wandered out onto the porch with our glasses of wine and gazed down over the mountain as the sun started its slow fade to black behind us.

Sheba leaned on the rail, staring silently. Then she stood up and turned to me. "You're being too quiet," she announced.

I took a long sip of the wine and thought about that. "Am I? What should I be saying?"

"You could talk about what you're feeling," she offered.

"That'd be a lot easier if I knew what that was. Marsha used to try to get me to do that. *Talk about my feelings*, as if somehow becoming emotionally more accessible would miraculously fix everything. Sometimes it just feels like vomiting."

She smiled. "Stiff upper lip, right? You know, sometimes purging is good for you. Get it out of your system."

I sat down in one of the redwood Adirondack chairs and tried to relax my shoulders. "How do you just get something like that out of your system? It's not like you caught a bug and need to let it pass or you ate a chunk of stinky French cheese that didn't agree with you."

I sat there a moment. Sheba turned and faced me.

"I don't know where to put this," I said. "I'd had relationships before, had even been married before. But then this thing with Marsha started… And then it went bad in ways and for reasons I'm not sure I understand even to this day. Jesus. And if we had just let it go, maybe things would have been different, but then Alex came along and we were basically stuck in something, and neither of us could ever really define what it was."

I looked up at Sheba and suddenly felt tense all over. "I wasn't the only one who never had another serious relationship after that. Marsha never moved on either. How do you unpack all that stuff?"

Sheba walked across the deck and laid her hand gently on my shoulder. "I wish I had an easy answer for that," she said. "Maybe you just give yourself time."

The next morning, Alex and I pulled up in front of the Higgins & O'Brien Funeral Home a few minutes before our 11 A.M. appointment. Neither of us had slept well or much and nobody had any appetite for breakfast. Truth is, I'd had the better part of a bottle of wine by the end of the evening and all I really wanted the next morning was a shower, a couple of aspirin, and coffee.

Alex was quiet the whole way down the mountain. We waded into the flow of Reno traffic and Alex pulled up directions to the funeral home on her phone. The parking lot was nearly empty as we pulled to a space in front.

I wondered as we walked in if there was some universal funeral home architectural firm that cranked out cookie-cutter funeral homes like fast-food franchises. Like so many other funeral homes I'd been in, this was a one-story, sprawling brick ranch building with two wings off a central area and an arched entrance that led into a marbled foyer. After that, thick red carpet everywhere, overstuffed ottomans and sofas. Ornate wainscoting and formal trim in every room and hallway…

A middle-aged woman with sprayed hair wearing a stiff dress and glasses from the seventies sat behind a polished reception desk. She looked up as we entered.

"We're the family of Dr. Helms," I said. "We had an eleven o'clock."

"Of course," she said, standing up. "Please have a seat. I'll go get Mr. Higgins. Would you like some coffee or some water?"

I looked at Alex. She looked pale, drawn, and shook her head slightly.

"We're good."

The receptionist turned and silently padded down the hallway. There was no one else around. I stood there nervously.

"I don't feel like sitting down," I whispered.

"Me, either."

I put my arm around Alex's shoulder, but she seemed tense and uncomfortable, so I didn't leave it there long.

"Hey," I said. "You don't have to do this. I can take care of it."

"No, Daddy," she said. "I want to be here."

A large man in a brown suit and shoes polished to a sparkle came down the hall, followed by the receptionist. His short hair was brushed back over his skull and he had a thick walrus moustache and brown, horn-rimmed glasses.

"Mr. Denton, it's good to meet you finally," he said brightly. I took his hand, shook it, and instantly wished I had a paper towel with me.

"Thank you, Mr. Higgins," I said. He turned to Alex.

"And you must be Miss Alexis," he said. Alex nodded shyly and shook his hand.

"I just wish it were under better circumstances. We are all so sorry for your loss. Dr. Helms was a valued member of the Reno community. She'll be missed."

He led us back to his office, past a row of funeral parlors, each with an inspirational or religious name to it. He stopped at one, *The Chapel of Eternal Hope*.

"This is where the service will be tomorrow," he explained. We looked inside. It was one of the larger parlors, with an alcove off to the side, fixed rows of church pews and an overflow room for folding chairs if needed, and a large flat-screen TV mounted on the wall behind the podium. Part of the funeral package was a multimedia presentation that would screen during the visitation.

"We hope it will be satisfactory," he said.

Alex reached over, took my hand, and squeezed.

"It'll be fine," I said.

We sat down in the visitors' chairs in his small office and he pulled out a stack of papers. We began reviewing the details of the funeral package, the billing, all the ancillary charges, which went on for three printed pages. I'd already paid the bill through an EFT from my bank in Nashville, but there was still the final review.

Then there were multiple copies of the death certificate and all the legal paperwork. I had this thought flash through my head: that after all the bodies Marsha had autopsied over the decades, the law didn't require one for her. She died of natural causes, at home, no suspicious circumstances.

For a moment, I almost wanted to laugh. *Define irony…*

After going over the mountain of paperwork that rivalled a mortgage closing, he shuffled and jogged it all into a neat pile, sealed it up in a custom-made magenta portfolio case emblazoned with the Higgins & O'Brien seal in gold, and handed it to me.

Twenty-seven grand…

Life may be cheap these days, but death sure as hell isn't.

Mr. Higgins sat back in his chair and cleared his throat. "Now that that's taken care of," he said solemnly, "would you like to see Dr. Helms? We have her in a private viewing room for now. Sometimes it's helpful for the immediate family to see her for the first time without the crowd at the service."

Alex drew in a sharp breath. I turned to her, laid my hand on top of hers. "We don't have to," I said. "It's up to you."

She turned, her eyes glistening in the fluorescent light embedded in Mr. Higgins' office ceiling.

"No, I want to…" She hesitated. "Yes, let's do."

We stood up as Mr. Higgins held the door open for us. I let Alex go through first, then followed her. Higgins led us down the hallway, then right into a shorter hallway with a series of closed doors on either side. He stopped at one, opened the door, then reached in and flicked a light switch.

"I can stay with you," he said, "or I can give you some private time. Whichever will be most helpful to you."

I held Alex's hand tightly as we stood there. "I think we'd like to be alone with her," I said.

Higgins nodded and opened the door for us. It was a small room, with an open casket at the far end with a recessed ceiling light shining down on it. There was a sofa and a wing chair, with an end table on one side that held a vase of fresh flowers and a couple of boxes of tissue. The lights were down low, the room cool and dry.

Alex stepped in. I followed and Higgins pulled the door closed behind us.

I took Alex's hand and together we approached what seemed like a huge bronze casket. As we got closer, Marsha came into view.

She wore a royal blue dress with a white lace collar and lace cuffs, her hair fixed, eyes closed. Funeral makeup gave her a reddish glow on her cheeks. She wore a strand of pearls and her hands were folded on her torso. This time it was my turn to take in a sharp breath.

"I don't remember that dress," I said. "I've never seen that dress."

"Estella and Marie picked it out," Alex whispered. "I… I couldn't."

I held her close to me as we stared down at Marsha. I'd been to plenty of funerals in my life and not once had I ever agreed with that idiotic funeral comment that the person in the casket looks so good. The dead don't look real. It's hard to imagine that the object lying in the casket was someone you once ate with, argued with, lived with.

Made love to… Woke up next to.

I tried to remember if this was Alex's first. She was six when Marty died and we'd taken her to the funeral, but I doubt she had much memory of it beyond snapshots.

I felt Alex start to tremble and instinctively pulled her closer. Then she sobbed. "Momma…"

My eyes filled when Alex started to go over the edge. "I'm so sorry, baby," I whispered, pulling her as close into me as possible. That's when it all gave way. We stood there for what seemed like a long time, her lanky frame shaking and heaving, me trying to be as solid as I could for her.

Finally, the worst of it passed. She sniffed loudly, then stiffened and pulled away from me. She grabbed a couple of tissues off the table and handed one to me. We wiped our eyes and noses and cleaned ourselves up a bit, then stood there gazing at her for a couple more minutes.

"You know," I said. "The dress really doesn't work for me. She should be wearing scrubs."

Alex laughed. "The last few years," she said. "It was jeans, a denim shirt and cowboy boots."

Alex took a step closer to the casket, then leaned down and kissed her mother's forehead. "Goodbye, Momma…" she whispered.

I felt something in my own chest jump. As Alex turned and stepped away, I leaned down and kissed Marsha's forehead as well. She was cold and waxy.

"Goodbye, love."

Chapter Seven

It wound up being a great day for a funeral.

After the service. the pallbearers—including Lonnie, Hal, and Captain Jimmy in his full-dress pilot's uniform—carried Marsha to the hearse and we began the short, long drive to Mountain View Cemetery.

On its best days, there is no sky anywhere near as blue as the high desert sky over Reno. Maybe the gods decided to give us a break, but the July heat even let up a bit and a slow but steady wind from the west over the Sierra Nevada pushed every cloud out of sight. The sky was clear, a brilliant, radiant blue that somehow matched the strange and unfamiliar dress she wore in the casket. The bare mountains were especially orange and brown and brightly-colored rust.

Mountain View Cemetery fills a 160-acre tract wedged in between I-80 on the north and West 4th Street on the south. The Reno traffic dutifully and respectfully sidelined itself as the long procession wove its way on. It only took about twenty minutes and soon we were lined up outside the three-story Mountain View Mausoleum, which has the distinction of being the largest mausoleum in Northern Nevada.

Marty had bought four crypts in a row on the top floor. She was entombed in the one farthest to the left, with her name MARTHA BISHOP and her dates—1932-2006—on a bronze plaque. Next to hers, a bronze plaque read JACQUES BARRONE, with the dates 1929-2004. Jacque and Marty had spent twenty years together before he passed away, but never bothered to go through with that whole marriage thing.

Alex seemed stiff and wooden next to me, alternately taking my hand and edging in closer, our shoulders just meeting in the middle, and then pulling away as if she were kind of disembodied from it all.

I get it…

Alex, Estella and I sat in the front row of folding chairs as the hired preacher said a few last words, and then the workers lifted her casket and slid it in. Alex started sobbing, her shoulders hunched and shaking, wet phlegmy gurgling sounds bubbling up from somewhere deep inside her. I held her close and Sheba patted her back. Estella stood off to the side, silently bearing up and bearing witness.

The workers sealed her in, and it was over.

❧

Marie and Estella put together a reception at the Mount Rose house after the service. The forty-minute or so drive seemed a bit much to me, but this is The Wild West, where people drive two hours for a carton of milk, a loaf of bread, and a pack of Marlboro Lights.

Estella had offered to cook, but I put my arm around her shoulder and told her that she was more than an honored guest; she was part of the family. If she wanted, she could go back to being the person who ran and took care of the house tomorrow. In fact, we'd all go back to doing our jobs.

Tomorrow.

Today, she was going to let other people serve her.

So she reluctantly let the caterers do their job and about three-quarters of the sixty or so people who showed up for the funeral made the trek up the Mount Rose Highway. Aunt Marty's well-planned parking area was soon put to good use, with cars overflowing onto the street.

I half-expected the reception to be morose and somber, but I was wrong. It was still an exquisitely beautiful day with hours of bright sunshine left before the slow slide into dusk. There were washtubs full of iced-down local craft beers and bottles of wine out on the veranda. Tons of food was spread over several tables. In recognition of Marsha's separate-but-equal roots in the American West and the American South, there was a lot of barbecue and baked beans and fried okra and the truest of all healthy Southern vegetable dishes, macaroni and cheese.

People tend to separate by gender at these sorts of affairs. I noticed that most of the women stayed inside, chatting around the kitchen and the dining room, while the men tended to move toward the shaded veranda, which is where most of the washtubs were. The caterer had unloaded a truckload of folding chairs, which were soon occupied by male middle-aged backsides holding sweaty brown bottles.

Over the past few years, as Nashville's beer-snobbery factor grew exponentially, I found myself moving toward the craft beers myself. Can't remember the last time I had something like a Pabst Blue Ribbon, even though the Pabst Brewing Company was going gangbusters since they were brought back to life in 2014 and rebranded as the most hipsterish of all hipster beers.

So I reached into the washtub and pulled out the first bottle my hand touched. I looked at the label and guessed it was designed by some—no doubt—gifted young unpaid graphic design intern.

Mustang Ranch Irish Red Ale the label read, with a stylized drawing of the Mustang Ranch logo. I almost burst out laughing;

a craft beer named after the now-defunct Mustang Ranch, the world's most famous legal brothel. My last major case as a private investigator had been when I came out here for Alex's birth. I was hired to go undercover at the Mustang and got a job as a maintenance man. In the end, I helped nail the guy who was running a money-laundering operation out of the Mustang and who murdered one of the girls, who also turned out to be an undercover C.I.

Yeah, the big private dick in a whorehouse had cracked the case and nearly gotten himself killed in the process.

Maybe that was why I decided to go the corporate sell-out route and just make money. Same reason Marsha had herself entombed less than an hour away from the family home, rather than have her ashes shot into space or sprinkled over Mount Everest.

Enough of this, I thought, as I opened the beer and took a long swallow. It was perfect; ice cold and hoppy enough to clear your sinuses, the way beer should be, and like a breath of clear desert air.

I looked around the long porch. Hal and Lonnie were standing there with a beer in hand, with Captain Lonnie back in civvies so he could drink without reservation as well.

There were a few women on the porch, but it was mostly guys with their jackets off and folded over the rails and the backs of chairs, their ties pulled down or off, their sleeves rolled up.

"Ladies and gentlemen!" I yelled, tapping my beer on the side of a washtub. The murmur and chatter died down as all turned in my direction.

"I want to thank you all for being here!" I yelled brightly. "It means a lot to all of us who loved and admired Marsha. We're all going to miss her, but we're not here right now to mourn her. We started that at the funeral and we can all continue that in the silence of our own hearts and heads. What I want us to do today is to celebrate her!"

A few cheers erupted.

"And to remember her for what she truly was: the most intelligent, driven, passionate woman I've ever met. She was totally committed to her work, her family—"

I turned and noticed Alex had stepped out onto the porch and was standing at the back of the crowd watching me.

"—and especially to our daughter, Alex. She was an incredible mother and as a result, we have an incredible daughter!" I raised my beer bottle in Alex's direction and saluted her.

More applause…

"But she was more than that. She was the funniest, quirkiest, and in many ways, the oddest and most interesting woman I've ever met in my life. She cut up dead bodies for a living and was so proud of it she had a vanity plate on her Porsche that read *Dead Folks*. She was stubborn as hell and had a mouth on her that was sharper and faster than a Stryker saw. She's the only woman I've ever known that I could be madly in love with and want to strangle at the same time."

This time, genuine laughter erupted. These people, I thought, knew Marsha.

"She could autopsy a murder victim and then two minutes later make the most God-awful black humor joke you've ever heard. The first real conversation I ever had with her took place when I was a private detective investigating my first case for the widow of a murder victim. Marsha—or as she often reminded me back then, *Doctor* Helms—told me the victim had just had sex before he was killed.

"Amazed, I asked her how she knew this. She winked at me and said *Remember, Harry, rigor mortis is just an all-over hard-on.*"

The place exploded. Guys—a fair number of them either in the Medical Examiner's Office or the funeral home business—doubled over, spit beer out of their noses they were laughing so hard. I should have pursued a career in standup.

Over in the corner, Alex displayed a tight-lipped, if genuine, grin, her arms crossed. She was also blushing.

"At the same time," I continued, a little more seriously, "I've seen her with the families who'd just lost someone. And there was no one kinder, more sensitive, more loving and compassionate than anyone I'd ever met toward people she didn't even know."

I raised my bottle again. "Ladies and gentlemen, when they made her they broke the mold. To Dr. Marsha."

A sea of beer bottles and glasses rose in tribute, accompanied by a fair amount of cheering. There was a lot of hugging and back-slapping, like guys do when there's a big emotional release accompanied by beer. Lonnie and Jimmy made their way over to me, cornered me against the rail.

"Damn, Harry," Lonnie said. "Tha'z beautiful. How long'd it take you to write that?"

I stared at him a beat, then look a long pull off the Mustang Ranch Irish Red. "Totally off the top of my head."

Then I turned and made my way toward Alex.

It was almost ten o'clock by the time the last of the guests pulled out of the driveway and headed down Mount Rose Highway toward the city. Alex and I stood on the porch, waving goodbye, and then we stood there a while longer, arm-in-arm, staring up at the night sky. It was a beautiful, coal-black sky peppered with glittering sparkles and just off the northwest horizon, a sliver of moon.

Alex put her head on my shoulder. "She's up there now," she whispered.

I nodded. "Yes, I believe she is."

We turned and slowly walked inside. The caterers had cleaned up most of the mess, but Estella was still futzing around, straightening things, adjusting furniture, collecting the last few glasses and picking up coasters, making sure no watermarks were left on furniture.

I locked the door and armed the burglar alarm. Estella walked over to Alex, wrapped her in a hug. "Querida," she asked, "can I get you anything? Is there anything I can do for you?"

Alex smiled and hugged her back. "No, thank you. I'm just beat. I think I'll take a shower and then head to bed."

"It has been a long day," she said. "Your Tía Estella is very tired, too. But you have to promise me that if you need anything, you will let me know."

"I promise," she said. Then Estella walked away and we were alone in the kitchen. Against my better judgment, I opened the refrigerator and grabbed one last beer. Alex smiled.

"I've never seen you drink so much beer," she said. "You okay?"

"Well, it's been a special day." I cocked the bottle toward her and saluted. "I've been pacing myself. I'm okay."

She looked at me for a beat. "Can I have a sip?"

I cocked an eyebrow. "You're not old enough."

She shrugged. "I know. I won't tell anybody if you don't."

I eyed her over the top of the bottle. "You ever tried beer before?"

"C'mon, Daddy," she said. "I'm in high school. I've been to a few parties."

For some reason or other, it felt good that she could be that honest with me. I opened the refrigerator and pulled out another beer, twisted the top off, and handed it to her.

"We're not going to make a habit out of this," I said. "But we'll toast your mother."

She took the cold bottle and eyed the label. "Mustang Ranch," she read. "I've heard of that."

"Someday," I said, "I'll tell you a story about *that.*"

I raised the bottle and tipped it toward her. "To Momma," I said.

"To Momma," she repeated. We took a sip. Alex's mouth screwed up like she'd just taken a swallow of vinegar. "Ugh, that's terrible. It doesn't taste like Bud Light."

I laughed. "No, it doesn't. It's real beer."

"Oh, I get it," she grinned. "It's a *manly man's* beer."

"Something like that. You don't have to finish it."

She set the bottle down on the counter. "I won't."

"Why don't you sleep in tomorrow?" I asked. "You've had a hell of a few days."

"I thought we were leaving tomorrow."

"We've got some wiggle room," I said. "We can leave tomorrow or over the weekend. I think Lonnie needs to be back by Sunday night and I probably do as well. But we can take our time. That's the beauty of not flying commercial."

She stared down at the floor, lost in thought for a moment. Then she looked up at me. "Daddy, if we can pull it together, I think I'd like to go tomorrow."

I was padding down the stairs in my sock feet early the next morning when I heard the sobbing. At first, it was a soft, indistinct sound that was almost unrecognizable. Then, as I crossed the dining room and neared the kitchen, it became clearer.

I stopped, listened.

Alex was sobbing, and Estella was talking low to her. I peeked around the corner and saw the two of them, their backs to me, huddled together in front of the kitchen island. Alex had her head in her hands, her shoulders hunched over and shaking. Estella was holding her tight, trying to prop her up.

And then they started talking, rapid fire, staccato…

In what sounded to me like perfect Spanish.

⁂

Captain Jimmy had the Hyatt Regency shuttle stop off and pick us up on its way down the mountain. Alex had managed to shoehorn enough clothes and the rest of her belongings into four suitcases, a duffle bag, and an overstuffed backpack that was mandatory issue for students these days. The movers would have the rest to us in a week or so.

Estella put together one last grand meal for us all, including a very grateful, rather thin young van driver. There was a lot of laughing and hugging as we loaded up. Alex made Estella promise to come see us before school started. I promised her the grand tour, which for anyone coming to Nashville, of course, means the Grand Ole Opry. She also said she'd never been to an NFL game before, so Lonnie piped up and offered that he knew somebody—meaning his private banking firm—who owned one of the 177 luxury suites at Nissan Stadium. Depending on the timing, he'd get us all pre-season or the real deal…

Then the hard part came. I thought Alex was going to lose

it again when we finally said goodbye, but apparently she and Estella had worked all that out earlier this morning. There were smiles and waves all around as we pulled out onto Mount Rose Highway and Casa Marty faded into the rearview mirror.

Alex and I sat on the last row of the shuttle. She got really quiet and pulled out her phone and started texting, Snapchatting, Instagramming. Hell, I don't know. Whatever it was, it seemed to occupy her until we pulled into the terminal and parked in front of Atlantic Aviation. I kept wanting to ask her if she was okay. That's what guys do in cases like this. They ask if you're okay and then hold their breath and hope they get the right answer. Like they can fix anything if you're not…

Lonnie and Jimmy had phoned ahead and the ramp guys at the FBO had towed the Citation around in front of the terminal. It was washed and polished to a sheen, fueled and prepped and ready to go. Lonnie and Jimmy did the walkarounds anyway as the guys got the baggage and started stowing it away, with Captain Jimmy keeping a close eye on them.

The July heat had returned, payback-style, and it was as hot and dry today as it hadn't been yesterday. We were all in jeans and light clothes, but even then, it wasn't good to stay out in it too long. The FBO had brought out an auxiliary power unit, so the Citation was already cool and dry inside. I gave the driver a folded pair of bills and he went away with a smile on his face.

Alex and I walked around the jet a couple times, oohing and making other appropriately impressed noises.

"Daddy, I've never seen anything like this," she whispered to me, gazing up at the tail from the aft end. "Can Uncle Lonnie actually fly this thing?"

I nodded. "Yeah, and he's pretty good at it. I think he brings

Captain Jimmy along because he likes to have somebody to talk to about flying. And, *hey, it ain't me, babe*."

As we climbed up the short stairs to the cabin, she actually stopped in the entryway. She turned around, eyes wide, mouth open.

"Is this for real?"

I nodded.

"This is what Momma used to call high cotton."

I grinned. "Get in. Grab a seat."

Twenty minutes later, we were all strapped down, clearances and flight plans filed, the engines spooling up. We went wheels-up at 2:35 local time. We'd be back in Music City in time for a late dinner, and then Alex and I would drive into East Nashville and begin our new lives together as single daddy and high-school daughter.

Lonnie levelled out at 24,000 feet. Sheba and Alex sat across from each other in the first aisle and I settled into the starboard seat behind them. They were alternately leaning into each other, chatting away, and then gazing out the windows as the Rockies drifted by below us.

I found myself strangely tired, but unable to sleep. I pulled out my mobile and tapped the app for the ABC affiliate in Nashville. I'd been out of the loop on the local news, so thought I'd catch up on the carjackings and home invasions.

Instead what I got was a lead story that made me glad I was strapped in my seat. I stared at the tiny screen, stunned:

LEO WALSH, PULITZER NOMINATED AUTHOR,
FILM SCHOOL PROFESSOR FOUND BRUTALLY MURDERED

Chapter Eight

I was in a fog for the rest of the flight. Lonnie and Captain Jimmy landed the Citation at John Tune Airport, taxied up to the Compact Aviation ramp, and let the engines spool down into silence.

Then Lonnie opened the hatch and a literal fog rolled in.

We'd gone from the dry, crisp desert air of Reno to the oppressive literal fog of a July night in Nashville. It was 7:30 when we landed, and the faint orange glow in the west signaled the sun was almost completely down. The temperature was still in the low 90s, though, with the dew point not far behind.

A blast of heat rolled into the cabin as soon as the door was down. A row in front of me, Sheba let out a loud groan.

"Welcome home," she said.

"It's like a steam bath," Alex said, unbuckling herself and standing up. "I'm gonna need another shower." She pulled at the sleeves of her shirt as if they were already glued to her skin.

We pulled backpacks and all the other junk together, then climbed out onto the hot concrete. The heat waves rising off the asphalt and concrete shimmered in the dusky orange light that was a surreal mix of sunset and runway lights. In the distance, layered on top of the tree line that was on the far side of the runway, a thick cloud of steamy fog sat heavy and still.

Captain Jimmy and Lonnie emptied the baggage lockers and lined the suitcases up on the tarmac. Lonnie stepped over and leaned in to me.

"I know you guys are tired. We don't have to do anything here. The night ramp guys'll button up the plane and tow it into the hangar. Jimmy and I can head out here tomorrow to check it over."

I pulled out my mobile and motioned for him to follow me a few steps away.

"What's up?" he asked as I pulled up the app for the local news station.

"You remember me telling you about the guy that came to my office? The strange guy who wanted to hire me as a P.I.?"

Lonnie looked confused for a moment. "The day before we left?"

"Yeah."

"I was a little preoccupied, Harry," Lonnie said. "We were getting ready to fly across country for a funeral."

"I know that," I snapped. "But that crazy guy who wanted me to investigate a murder, and when I asked him who's murder, he says *mine*."

"Yeah, okay. I remember."

I held the mobile up. "Well, somebody did him."

Lonnie's eyes widened and he took the cell out of my hand. He squinted in the dim light and used his index finger to rake the screen up as he scanned the article.

Three screens later, he handed me back the cell. "Holy shit, Harry," he muttered. "That's freakin' freaky."

I tucked the phone into my shirt pocket. "I guess the guy wasn't as crazy as I thought."

"Yeah," Lonnie said, staring off at the tree line. "Now he's not anything."

After a moment, he turned back to me. "What are you gonna do?"

Behind us, we heard footsteps. "So what's going on, boys?" Sheba called. "Why the man-huddle?"

I turned. "Oh, nothing," I said. "We're just trying to figure out what to do next."

"Yeah," Lonnie added. "You guys want to follow us to the Gulch? We can have a beer, order some more outrageously expensive pizza."

I turned to Alex. "I don't know. What do you think, sweetie? What are you hungry for?"

Alex shrugged, her hair already frizzing at the edges in the humidity, her forehead glistening. "I'm not really hungry," she said. "More tired than anything else. A shower would be nice."

"Maybe we should just load up the car and go get settled in," I offered. "We've got a lot to do over the next few days. I think there's enough stuff at home to rustle up a snack."

Alex turned to Sheba. "Would that be okay?" Sheba smiled, extended her arms and wrapped Alex in a hug.

"Of course, sweetheart. You must be exhausted. Let's get you home."

"And out of this heat," Lonnie added.

We rolled the luggage across the tarmac and into the Compact Aviation offices, then back out the other side onto the parking lot. Sheba's black Mercedes SUV was two slots down from the Tesla, with Captain Jimmy's pickup at the end of the lot.

"So this is the Tesla," Alex commented. It was then I realized how long it had been since Alex had come to Nashville. She generally flew out at least four times a year, but right after her trip over fall break last year was when Marsha'd gotten her cancer diagnosis.

I flew out there for Christmas, and after that Alex wouldn't leave her mother.

"When did you get it?" Alex asked, walking around the car.

"End of March," I said.

"Hmm," she said. "Should still have that new car smell."

We managed to shoehorn five suitcases, a couple of backpacks, and a purse into the car, then it was hugs in the heat all around. Captain Jimmy smiled and waved as he pulled out of the parking lot.

"You guys gonna be okay?" Sheba asked.

I looked down at Alex. "I think so. We've got some adjusting to do."

Alex nodded. "It'll be all right."

Lonnie and Sheba turned to her car and started to walk away. A few steps later, Lonnie looked back. "Hey, Harry! Call me tomorrow, okay? Give me a news update."

I nodded. "You got it."

Alex and I climbed into the Tesla and I booted it up. As we pulled out of the parking lot, Alex fished her iPhone out of her purse.

"You mind if I Bluetooth my Spotify playlist into the car?" she asked. She leaned over and turned on the car radio.

I tried to pretend that I actually understood the question.

"I haven't done that yet, so I don't really know how."

Alex grinned and pressed the Menu button on the touchscreen. "Don't worry, Daddy," she said. "I'll take care of it."

~

From that moment on, there was something subtly different. On every other trip to see me in Nashville, Alex had either just listened to whatever was on satellite radio in the car or plugged her own earbuds in. It never occurred to me that she thought of herself as a visitor to my home. I always wanted her to think of it as *her* home. Clearly, until now she'd never felt comfortable enough to play her own music. It was a little thing, I guess, and I don't want to make too much of it.

But this was *different*...

She wasn't a visitor now; she lived here. She could Bluetooth her own playlist into *our* car.

And, man, what a playlist. As we made our way from Cockrill Bend to East Nashville, I listened, silently gobsmacked, as my not-quite-16-year-old, clean-cut, well-scrubbed, suburban, private school white girl daughter blared the nastiest rap music I'd ever heard in my life. I could only catch snatches of the lyrics, but it was something about being a dangerous man with money in my pocket and *bad bitches and ya' ugly-ass friends*, mixed in with *Spend ya' money like money ain't shit*...

I pulled onto the entrance ramp to Briley Parkway, headed home to East Nasty. I turned to Alex: "Who is that?"

She reached over, turned the volume down to just below ear-splitting. "I'm sorry, Daddy," she said. "It's Bruno Mars. Is it okay?"

I smiled at her and shook my head. "Sure. Kind of a catchy tune, actually."

She cranked the sound back up and the car shook. It was a whole new world.

❧

Alex opened the door to her bedroom and flicked on the light. She carried her backpack and one suitcase, with me behind her lugging two more. Her room had once been the single bedroom in the apartment Mrs. Hawkins rented me. When I did the renovations a few years ago, the apartment was swallowed up into the house. The living room and kitchen in the old apartment had been done away with, so the bedroom was now a lot larger.

Alex and I had done a few things to the room during the years she visited. I thought it was actually pretty nice; certainly better furnished than when it was my apartment twenty years ago.

Back then, the windows were dry-rotted wood, single pane, and they continuously leaked cold air in the wintertime. In the hot Nashville summers, the whole apartment was cooled by a single ancient window unit in the combination kitchen and living room. The whole apartment had basically been two rooms and a bathroom. For the first three years, the only entertainment had been a sixteen-inch black-and-white television. Then I splurged and bought color.

Now, Alex had a 48-inch plasma-screen mounted on the wall across from her canopied double bed, with home theater surround sound, her own control for the central heating and air, and super-high-speed broadband WiFi. There was a double chest of drawers against one wall, nightstands on either side of the bed, and a desk with shelves above it against the other wall. It wasn't bad for a teenager's room, but I figured Alex had a lot of work to do to actually mark the territory as hers.

"Once we get settled," I said, as she lifted her suitcase onto the bed and unzipped it, "we can do whatever you need to. You want your own furniture in here, we can get this stuff out. Decorations, stuff you want on the wall… Whatever will make this home for you."

Alex turned, a tired smile on her face. "It's already home, Daddy. Thank you very much."

She stepped into my arms and gave me a long hug. "You hungry?" I asked. "I've got barbecue in the freezer. Only take a few minutes to thaw it out. Cole slaw and baked beans. Sort of welcome you back to Nashville."

"That sounds great," she said. "Have I got time to grab a shower and change?"

"Of course," I said. "Just come on down when you get ready. I'll grab the other suitcase and leave it on the landing."

I walked downstairs and out to the car, retrieved my suitcase and Alex's last one, and got them squared away. Then I went into the kitchen, popped a pound of frozen barbecue I'd picked up take-out from Jack Cawthon's on Charlotte Avenue into the microwave, and set it to defrost. I turned on the oven and pulled out some leftover cornbread and baked beans from the fridge.

Dinner started and the shower running upstairs, I went into the living room and turned on the television. It was a couple of minutes before nine and the Fox affiliate ran their local news an hour before the other stations. Most of the time, I tried to avoid local television news. I hate cheerful banter. Tonight, I was going to make an exception.

The screen came alive just as the local news teaser came on.

"Coming up on Fox 17," a voiceover said as the credits from some incredibly popular show I'd never seen began rolling, "the local film community reacts to the brutal murder of one of its own."

I walked back into the kitchen and grabbed a beer. By the time I got back, the blow-dried, white-haired guy in the tailored suit and the attractive young woman in the skin-tight wrap dress were hard at work at the anchor desk.

"Thanks for joining us here on Fox 17! I'm Billy Brawner with tonight's headlines," the guy said.

"And I'm Melissa Matthews," the bright young woman said.

"Tonight, the local film community is in shock at the brutal murder of one of Nashville's most famous writers and teachers."

"Yes, Melissa," answered the guy, who managed to muster an awful lot of gravitas for a guy named *Billy*. "Sixty-six-year old Leo Walsh had been a fixture in the Nashville writing and film community for nearly three decades. The discovery of his body last night in a dumpster behind an all-night diner on Murfreesboro Road has left the community reeling, as Fox 17's Cameron Alvarez reports…"

Cut to a live newsfeed in the parking lot of the Pancake Palooza just off Murfreesboro Road near Spence Lane. A dark-haired young woman in a tight pair of slacks and a white blouse stood under a harsh, sulfurous parking lot light holding a microphone and waiting for the uplink to connect.

"Yes, Billy," she said after that awkward pause that always seems to accompany live remotes, "two local homeless men apparently out for a night of dumpster diving found the body of Leo Walsh in the far corner of the parking lot right behind me."

The camera shifted slightly to reveal a couple of dumpsters that were still surrounded by the standard yellow crime scene tape, with a blue-and-white Metro squad car parked nearby. Wonder what the Pancake Palooza was doing with all their trash…

"A police spokesman said Walsh appeared to have been robbed and beaten, although the official cause of death is pending the results of an autopsy."

The scene reset to a daytime interview in the parking lot, with an unnamed reporter holding a microphone off-screen. A caption below read: Deputy Chief Vince Moss, MNPD Spokesperson.

"It appears that Mr. Walsh was the victim of an assault and robbery, although we are still interviewing witnesses to determine if anyone saw this heinous crime. We ask that if anyone has any information related to the murder of Mr. Walsh, that they please call our anonymous Crime Stoppers line or any Metro police precinct."

Cut back to the live remote with the bright young woman standing in the gritty, Nashville nighttime parking lot. "Billy, that's the latest from the crime scene at the Pancake Palooza on Murfreesboro Road. I'm Cameron Alvarez with Fox 17."

Back in the studio, Melissa Matthews spoke directly to us through the camera. "Fox 17 reporter Mary Ellen Caldwell looks back at the life and career of one of Nashville's most iconic literary figures."

Iconic literary figures I whispered. Do these folks know Leo Walsh lived in an apartment complex in Antioch?

The screen switched to thirty-year-old newsreel footage of a crowd in the long-gone Mills Bookstore in Hillsboro Village, with a much younger and better-groomed Leo Walsh standing at a podium in front of the throng.

"Leo Walsh exploded on the local literary scene almost three decades ago with the publication of his *New York Times* best-seller, *The Sphinx Confessions*. The novel went on to become both a Pulitzer Prize nominee and a nominee for the National Book Award. For a few years, Leo Walsh became a national celebrity along the lines of Stephen King, Dan Brown, and a host of literary luminaries—"

The screen cut to the set of *Good Morning America*, where Leo was being interviewed by Joan Lunden, then switched to a copy of *People* Magazine with Leo on the cover.

The voiceover continued: "The film rights to Walsh's novel were acquired for a near record-breaking sum, but the movie was never made. A few years later, Leo Walsh turned to teaching, where he became one of Nashville's most distinguished film professors."

My jaw dropped. What planet were these people on? Or was the guy in my office five days ago an imposter?

The screen cut to a close up of a late-middle-aged woman with a huge mound of salt-and-pepper hair swept up and pinned above a fur collar.

"Ursula Gilbert," the voice-over continued, "is the president and founder of the Nashville Academy of Cinema Arts. In an exclusive interview with Fox 17 just this afternoon, she describes what a loss this will mean to the local film community."

"We are broken-hearted at the loss of Professor Walsh," the woman said in the thickest French accent I'd ever heard outside of France. "Leo was a great writer and teacher and a founding faculty member of the Nashville Academy of Cinema Arts. He anchored our screenwriting program and mentored hundreds of students. He was an invaluable and beloved member of our film community. I don't know what we will do without him..."

Ursula Gilbert's voice trailed off and she looked, for a moment, like she was fighting back tears.

"A sad ending for one of Nashville's great literary treasures. This is Mary Ellen Caldwell for Fox 17," the voiceover intoned.

Behind me, the microwave dinged as the TV anchors moved on to the next story. I stared at the screen wordlessly, trying to process the disconnect between the Leo Walsh I'd met in my office Monday morning and the Leo Walsh being eulogized on the television in front of me.

The impatient microwave dinged again. I turned just as Alex came down the stairs. She was barefoot, wore a T-shirt, a pair of sweats, with a towel wrapped around her head. She'd scrubbed her makeup off, which in some strange way made her look more like the little girl I still thought of her as.

She must have caught the look on my face. "You okay?" she asked.

I held out my hand, pointed the remote at the screen.

"I suddenly drew a blank," I said. "Do you like the vinegar-based sauce or the Carolina sweet?"

Chapter Nine

Sometimes you just can't turn the human brain off.

I don't know how long I'd been lying there but I knew the covers were in a twist and I was splayed out in what felt like six different directions. The two pillows I slept on felt like bags full of gravel, and the air conditioning seemed to be cycling on and off just often enough to drive me crazy. Every time I thought I was about to drift off, there'd be another blast of cold air wafting down strong enough to pull me out of whatever fog I'd hoped to be in.

I leaned over and fumbled on the nightstand for the alarm clock, then pushed the little plastic bar on top. In the darkness, the red numerals seemed to light up the whole room.

3:17.

I sat up and switched on the lamp, flooding the room in yellow light. A knot rose in my stomach.

Why can't I sleep? I thought. On the surface, I've got nothing to keep me awake all night. I'd gotten through the stresses of the last six months, my daughter was safely home with me. The constant stress and worry over money had long since faded into history. I had more money than I'd ever be able to spend. My daughter would be well taken care of, to the extent that I worried about what real wealth would do to her. I wanted her to have a career, a purpose, a mission in life and not just be one of the one-percent.

Maybe I'd been alone too long. I often felt a bit lonely and hadn't shared a bed with anyone in years, but hell, I was used to that. Over the last decade or so, I'd learned to do quite well on my own, thank you very much.

So why all this unease? Why so many sleepless nights? Why this dull, throbbing, low-level anxiety?

I climbed out of bed and walked across the bedroom to where the built-in bookcase and desk sat piled high with clutter. I opened my MacBook Pro and booted it up. While it was coming to life, I walked through the living room as quietly as I could. I went into the kitchen, extracted a half-empty bottle of Chardonnay and poured a glass of the cold wine.

Crossing back to my bedroom, I stopped and glanced up the stairs. A thin sliver of light shone out from the bottom of Alex's bedroom door. Either she was still up or she'd fallen asleep with the light on. I thought briefly of knocking on her door and making sure she was all right.

No, give her some space. She had a better reason for a sleepless night than I did.

I settled back into bed with the pillows fluffed behind me, the wineglass next to me, and my laptop settled on my… well, *lap*.

I double-clicked the icon to open my home page. Normally, I'm a sucker for clickbait. Give me a celebrity teaser or a catchy lead and I'll boost your click-through rate in a heartbeat.

Not this time, though. I went to a search engine and typed in "Nashville Academy Of Cinema Arts." A beat later. www.nacanashville.com popped up. There was a flashy graphic and a photo of a film set, with a crew of bright young film students in T-shirts and khakis and jeans. They looked eager and filled with promise. There was nothing on the home page about Leo Walsh's death.

I clicked the menu button labeled "A Message From The President." A page appeared with a photo of Ursula Gilbert, standing in front of the grand mahogany desk in her office, her arms folded in front of her, her hips pressed against the desktop. Behind the desk, a massive framed poster of Jean-Luc Goddard's *Breathless* dominated the wall.

She was dressed in a pair of black slacks and a grey turtleneck, her thick, long hair piled on top of her head, wearing a pair of chic European-style red-framed glasses. She looked like a famous European auteur director. All she needed was a lit Gauloises dangling from her lips with a thick cloud of blue smoke drifting up toward the ceiling.

The message was an inspirational one, describing to prospective students how they could pursue their dreams of being great artists and filmmakers, of finding an outlet for their passions in a community of like-minded writers, directors, cinematographers, editors, and producers.

Yeah, I thought. *All with a like-minded shiteload of student loan debt…*

I pointed the cursor back at the menu bar. A couple of clicks later, I was on the faculty page. The Nashville Academy of Cinema Arts had one full-time faculty member for each of five different disciplines. Some guy named Jack McEwen taught directing. He was thin, tall with thick salt-and-pepper hair swept back and tied in a ponytail, intense dark eyes. He was maybe fifty, although it's always hard to tell these things from a website photo and God only knew how old the picture was. In any case, he looked like he could be a little intimidating on a set. There was a short paragraph of his qualifications, which included directing a couple of cable shows back in the late nineties and early two-thousands, along with a couple of independent horror films I've never heard of.

The editing teacher was a middle-aged woman who, like Ursula Gilbert, looked foreign. Raisa Petrov wore thick glasses, a black turtleneck sweater, her hair pulled back in a ponytail behind her. I read her bio and saw that the resemblance was more than a coincidence; she and Ursula Gilbert had worked on a couple of films together in France in the late eighties.

The cinematography teacher, Christopher Weyreuth, had short black hair, pointy ears, with a certain wolf-like look. He had the only film credits I recognized, which were a couple of sequels to action/adventure films from maybe fifteen or twenty years ago. I recognized the names, but had never actually seen the films. I didn't know there'd been a *Spy Kids 7: Return of The Undead Spies*.

Justine Moye was the next-listed faculty member. From her picture, she was a good twenty years younger than anyone else on the page. Her hair was dyed a bright scarlet red. She had a row of piercings down one ear that was visible in the picture and she wore a sleeveless top that revealed an elaborate tattoo of a multi-colored dragon crawling up her left arm. She taught producing and, in many ways, seemed the oddest one of all. Not that I knew anything about the film business, but I always imagined producers would be the most like ordinary business executives. Suits and ties, even, with business cards and calculators...

This young woman, though, looked like she should be slinging drinks in some hipster East Nashville bar.

Then there was Leo. Poor, bedraggled Leo, who even in the staged, posed photo against a dark gray background wall, looked weary and depressed. There were bags under his eyes. He needed a haircut, and if I had been there I would have begged him to sit up straight. He was slumped in one of those canvas director's chairs like he was carrying the weight of the world on his shoulders.

Not any more, though. The dead don't carry.

I double-clicked Leo's photo and it expanded to fill the whole screen. I took a long sip of the wine and stared at the picture a while. Five days ago, he'd come into my office and asked me to investigate his own murder. I'd blown him off. Then somebody beat him to death and threw him behind a dumpster.

The early news reports made it sound like a robbery. Another stupid, senseless crime in a city that was increasingly dangerous, congested, and way too expensive…

I sat there, staring at the screen, and I suddenly realized why my stomach had been in a knot.

Something about this stinks. I don't believe in coincidences, at least not this kind. I can believe it when an earthquake just happens to trigger a tsunami when a family of seven from Salem, Oregon just happens to be spending Christmas vacation on a beach in Thailand. That I can buy.

But this?

No. I don't buy it. And I realized, as I swallowed the last sip of wine, set the laptop aside and switched off the light, that I wasn't ready to let this go.

⁂

I came swimming up out of a fog so deep I couldn't see the top of it. There was a shaking noise somewhere off to my left. When I pried my eyes open, the light burned and it felt like my eyelashes had turned inward and were sandpapering my eyes.

I groaned and rolled over toward the buzzing coming from

the nightstand. I picked up my mobile and stared at the screen for a beat, then pressed the button.

"Hey," I said, more asleep than awake.

"God, Harry," Sheba said. "It's after eleven…"

I tried to focus on the alarm clock. "Barely," I answered. "Three minutes after."

"You okay?"

"Couldn't sleep. Finally passed out sometime after four."

"Is Alex okay?"

I shifted and forced myself to sit up. "Guess so. Haven't been out of my room yet. Certainly quiet enough here."

She laughed. "Didn't mean to wake you, Mr. Slug-A-Bed. But Lonnie's gone off to John Tune and left me all bereft and alone again."

"What?" I mumbled. "So you need me to come over and keep you company?"

"Hah, fat chance," she said. "You'd just find some excuse to abandon me as well. No, I thought maybe your lovely daughter would like to join me for lunch. There's a little place in Green Hills near the mall. We could do a little shopping after, maybe get a massage and our nails done."

"Sheba, my darling," I said. "You are a lifesaver. I was wondering how we were going to fill this day and I've got some things I have to take care of."

"Tell her I'll pick her up in an hour. Afterwards, we'll come back here and you can join us for dinner."

"That is what I call a plan," I said, relieved. "Thanks."

We rang off and I pulled myself out of bed, then stumbled into the bathroom. I did the morning routine, dressed, then headed to the kitchen. All was quiet in the house; Alex's door was still closed with no light peeking out from underneath.

I got the coffee going, then fired up the laptop and started going through my email at the kitchen table, followed by my daily walk through the *New York Times* website, the *Wall Street Journal*, Slate.com, Salon.com, and a few others. There was a time when I would have walked down the driveway and picked up the morning paper, but that seems so long ago as to defy recollection. Nashville was once a two-newspaper town, with a fiercely independent liberal morning newspaper and an equally fiercely independent afternoon paper competing for eyeballs. I was a reporter for the afternoon paper a few decades ago, but it had been bought out by a couple of rich investors, who then sold it to the chain that bought the morning newspaper, who then closed the afternoon daily down.

By then, I was long gone. The once-powerful chain that bought the morning newspaper ran it through the corporate deflavorizer so many times that it quickly became unrecognizable. Only old people who don't know how to open a web browser read it any more, and as for the corporation that bought the newspaper and beat the soul out of it, it now trades as a penny stock.

Hard to wrap your head around that one; the largest newspaper publisher in America opened on the New York Stock Exchange this morning at $1.41. Nowadays, most of the country gets its news off Facebook…

So much for the Fourth Estate.

I heard a shuffling behind me as Alex walked into the kitchen. She wore rumpled plaid sweatpants and a tie-dyed tank top. Her hair was splayed out in fifty directions at once and she clearly hadn't gotten the sleep out of her eyes.

"Morning, sweetheart," I offered. "Coffee?"

She groaned and nodded, then sat down at the table. I poured her a big mug and set it down in front of her. The half-and-half and sugar were already there.

"So how'd you sleep?"

She groaned and shook her head. "I didn't. Not much, anyway."

I grabbed my mug and sat down opposite her. "I had trouble going to sleep myself. In fact, I went to the kitchen sometime around 3:30 and saw your light was still on."

She took a long sip of the coffee and this time the groan was one of pleasure.

"Anything in particular keep you up all night?" I asked. "Or was it just stuff?"

She nodded. "Just stuff. Everything."

"Look, this is all still so new," I said. "It's going to take some time to adjust. There'll probably be quite a few sleepless nights before we settle into this."

She smiled, kind of. "It'll work out."

"On the exciting news front, your Aunt Sheba called. She wants a girls day out. A fancy restaurant in Green Hills, followed by a massage and a trip to the nail salon…"

It just goes to show what I know about women when I didn't get the big grin I was expecting. In fact, Alex's eyes darkened and she gripped the coffee mug so hard her fingers changed shades.

"She'll be here in about a half-hour or so," I said. "I thought it would be okay. I've got a few phone calls to make and some things to take care of. Thought you might appreciate the company."

She set the mug down on the table and stood up. "Well, I guess I'd better hit the showers before the babysitter gets here."

"Alex, I'm sorry. I thought you'd enjoy it more than sitting around an empty house."

She stared at me for a moment. "I guess it just would have been nice to be asked."

Then she turned and walked away.

I sat there for a second, trying to figure out just what the hell had happened. I polished off the last of my coffee, then stood up to carry the mugs to the dishwasher.

Then she shuffled back into the kitchen. "Daddy?"

I turned. "Yeah, sweetie?"

"I'm sorry. Didn't mean to snap at you. I'm tired, I didn't sleep well, and I started my period."

I cleared my throat softly and looked away. I wasn't used to having this sort of discussion with my daughter and though I like to think of myself as a contemporary male with a little bit of woke in me, truth is I'm an aging baby boomer firmly rooted in an era when discussions of menses were couched in terms like *female trouble.*

"Well," I said, "as Uma Thurman said to John Travolta in *Pulp Fiction*, that was a little more information than I needed..."

Chapter Ten

I gave Alex a hug—thankfully, she returned it—as she and Sheba walked out the back door into the steamy Nashville sun. By the time she finished her coffee and got a shower, there was a smile back on her face. She seemed almost eager to get out of the house and back out into the world.

I stared out the window as Sheba pulled her hulking black SUV out of the driveway and the gate slid shut. The heat was so intense you could see waves shimmering off the pavement. The new super-energy-efficient and nearly silent HVAC system I'd had installed during the renovation struggled to keep up.

My head, which had been as cluttered and jammed up as Lower Broadway on a Friday night, suddenly went quiet. Next steps are always hard to figure out. My first instinct was to sit down in front of my laptop and play about ten hands of Microsoft Solitaire, which was the extent of my knowledge of video gaming. But I knew if I went down that rabbit hole in the frame of mind I currently occupied, I might never come out.

It had been a decade-and-a-half since I'd done anything near this kind of investigative work. The muscle had atrophied, gone soft. Part of me wondered why I was even bothering.

But the other part of me was too curious and, truthfully, too enraged to let this go.

I went back to my bedroom, which was large enough to accommodate an L-shaped desk which served as a home office. I opened a drawer on the short side and grabbed an old, dusty, dried-out vinyl folder, one that I hadn't opened in years.

Inside the folder was an album of glassine sheets subdivided into slots just big enough to hold a business card. I don't know if people even use business cards anymore. I think I have some somewhere in my office downtown, but it would take a ten-man search team to find them.

Somewhere in this folder was tucked a business card of someone I used to work with and go to war with regularly. He retired about the same time I got back from Reno on my last case just over fifteen years ago.

"There," I whispered. Spellman Investigations, the card read, with a phone number and an address in Rosemary Beach, Florida.

Lieutenant Howard Spellman had been head of the Metro Nashville Police Department's Murder Squad when I first got my Private Investigator's license all those years ago. Over the better part of the next decade, he and I did an elaborate tap dance with each other. As most cops do, he held P.I.s in very low regard.

I got myself in a couple of jams and there were a few times when Spellman thought he was going to have the supreme pleasure of nailing my hide to the wall. Over time, he gradually realized that while I may not have been the most accomplished of investigators I was one of the good guys, and occasionally my instincts were as good as anyone's. On a couple of cases, I even helped him out.

As a result, we reached an uneasy but workable peace with each other. And now, I needed him again.

I dialed the number on my mobile and got luckier than people usually get making phone calls these days. Nobody seems to answer the phone anymore, but this time, a human voice came on the line.

"Emerald Coast Charters," the voice said. I recognized the voice and grinned.

"Charters?" I asked. "I always suspected you'd rather fish than play cop."

There was a long pause. "Who is this?" the voice asked, wary.

"Howard Spellman, this is a voice from your past. Harry Denton."

Another long pause, then a loud snort. "Harry James Denton. Son of a bitch, I never expected to hear from you again. Damn…"

"How the hell are you?" I asked. "And whatever happened to Spellman Investigations?"

"*Shee-yit*, I got out of that hamster cage years ago. And you're spot on, buddy. I'd rather be on the water."

"So you gave up a P.I. agency and started a fishing boat charter, but kept the same office number."

Spellman laughed. "Office number? Hell, it's just my cell phone."

I had to laugh too. "So you're taking people fishing on the Redneck Riviera."

"Redneck Riviera, my ass. The rednecks can't afford it anymore. They had to move their trailers about thirty miles inland. This is the Emerald Coast now, buddy, and property down here goes for upwards of four-hundred a square foot. That is, if it's within walking distance of the beach. Anything closer goes up from there."

"So whattaya' got?" I asked. "Big-ass rowboat?"

"Big-ass rowboat, my ass," he spat. "Me and the my boy's got a 65-foot Bonner. We can take 12 people out for overnights that can go up to a week. Hell, all the way to Cuba and back if we want."

"That's great, Howard. I'm happy for you."

"Okay, Harry," he said. "You didn't call just to catch up. What are you up to? I heard you got out of the detecting business."

"Yeah," I admitted. "After I became a pappy, I went the corporate sellout route. Decided to go for the steady paycheck and the health insurance. Went into business with Lonnie Smith."

"Lonnie Smith!" he barked. "That raggedy-ass, cowboy country singer repo man?"

"Yep, only that raggedy-ass, cowboy country singer repo man is now the fourth or fifth richest man in the state of Tennessee, just a couple slots back from Martha Ingram and the Frists."

He whistled. "Damn…"

"No kidding. He's done real well for himself, and he's been damn good to me and a bunch of other people as well."

"Good for you. So how's that little girl of yours, Harry? And what's up with you and Dr. Marsha?"

I took in a breath and held it for a beat. "My little girl's about to turn sixteen, Howard. And she's living with me now. Dr. Marsha passed away."

This time, the silence came from his end. "Damn, Harry," he said after a few seconds. "That's tough. I'm really sorry."

"Yeah, the cancer got her. But they took real good care of her, all the way up to the end. I don't think she suffered too much."

"That's something."

"Listen, Howard, I actually do need your help. I'll make this as quick as possible, but the day before I went out to Reno for the funeral, this guy came to my office. Said he wanted me to investigate something for him. I tried to explain I was out of that business, but he was kind of persistent.

"Anyway, he kept pressing me and I finally said, 'Okay, what do you need me to take a look at?' And he said he wanted me to investigate a murder. When I asked him whose murder, he said *mine*."

Howard whistled again. "Okay, that's not something you hear every day."

"It gets weirder. On the way home from Reno, I brought the local news up on my cell and there it was. Somebody really did murder him…"

"Whoa, I'll have to go check that out," Howard said. "How'd it happen?"

"They found him beat to death behind a wannabe Waffle House. Found his body jammed between a couple of Dempster Dumpsters."

"No shit…"

"And it's kind of gotten to me, Howard. I feel real bad. The guy asked me for help and I blew him off. I'd like to help catch whoever did this. That's why I'm calling you, old pal. I need you to hook me up with whoever's running Murder Squad since you retired."

"Well, that's a bit problematic, Harry. You see, there ain't no Murder Squad anymore."

"What do you mean, there ain't no Murder Squad? They give murderers a pass in Nashville now?"

"From what I hear, it seems that way. But no, just over a decade ago, maybe longer, they did a complete reorganization of the department. It's a *hunnert* percent decentralized now. Each precinct covers whatever crimes occur in their area. So where'd the murder take place?"

"Tiny restaurant off Murfreesboro Road, between Spence Lane and Thompson Lane."

"Hmm," he said, thinking for a moment. "Great area.

Mexican mafia on one side, Laotian gangs on the other. That's South Precinct. Hold on for just a second…"

He disappeared for a few moments and I thought I heard faint clicking in the background. Then he was back on the line.

"I went on the website," he said. "Investigative lieutenant's a guy named Akers, Garrett Akers. Don't know him. But of course, I've been outta there nearly fifteen years myself. People come and go."

"Yeah," I said. "They do. So I should just call him directly?"

"You can try," he answered. "From what I hear, this new administrative structure's a mess. Hard to get in touch with anybody. And nobody's a specialist anymore. If a homicide goes a year without being solved, it goes to the Cold Case Unit, which I hear is busier than ever."

"Okay, I'll scrub the website, get his number and give it my best shot."

"A lot's changed, Harry. The department's not what it used to be. You could make connections, get to know people in the old days. Not so much anymore. I'm sure they'll want to talk to you if you know anything, but they might bite back hard if you try to get involved yourself."

"I'm used to it," I said. "The last time I looked in the mirror, I still have your teeth marks on my butt."

He laughed. "The solution to that's simple. Stop looking at your own ass in the mirror. It's good to talk to you, Harry. You take care of yourself. Hey, what's life like in Nashville these days? Haven't been back there in years. Hear the traffic's worse than ever and nobody can afford it anymore."

"Howard, old friend," I said. "You wouldn't recognize it."

I went to the Metro Nashville Police Department website and started noodling around. The South Precinct was on Harding Place just past the Antioch Pike intersection. It had been years since I'd been to that part of town. Nashville's now a big enough city that you can go years without setting foot in huge parts of it.

The website had some YouTube videos encouraging people to join the police department and some other community outreach efforts. One video encouraged people to lock their cars and not leave valuable stuff like cell phones and laptops in plain sight. Guns, especially, seemed to be particularly attractive targets for thieves, although why anyone would leave a loaded pistol lying on a car seat in the first place was beyond me.

Happens all the time, though.

There was a list of the command staff, from the Chief on down, in a flowchart that eventually landed on the individual precinct commanders. I clicked on the South Precinct commander's picture and was hyperlinked to the South Precinct page. There was a picture of the station and a coverage map. I blew up the map to where I could read it and spotted the area where Leo Walsh's body was found.

Howard was right: South Precinct.

There was a list of staff down the right side of the page, with the Day Shift Lieutenant's name at the top. Further down the list was the name of the Investigative Lieutenant Howard Spellman mentioned, Garrett Akers.

Well, I thought, it's a Saturday afternoon but crime never sleeps. May as well take a chance… I plugged in my earbuds and dialed the South Precinct phone number. It rang about twenty times before someone finally answered.

"South Precinct, Harper speaking."

"Hello," I said. "I'm trying to get in touch with Lieutenant Akers."

"Who? Akers?"

"Yes, Lieutenant Akers."

There was a muffled, scrambling kind of noise on the other end, then a low voice in an aside: "We gotta Akers here?"

Then a muffled, indecipherable answer.

The voice turned back to the phone. "Akers?"

"Yes, he's listed on the website as the investigative lieutenant at the South Precinct."

"I don't know. Let me put you on hold while I check."

I rolled my eyes. Was this guy a weekend sub who didn't know anybody? "Okay, I'll wait."

I looked over at the clock. A full minute ticked by before Harper—whoever the hell he is—came back on the line.

"What's this about?" he demanded.

"I wanted to speak to Lieutenant Akers or whoever's in charge of the Leo Walsh homicide. I may have some information that would be useful."

"The what?"

"The Leo Walsh homicide," I said. "You know, it's been on the news."

"Who?"

"Walsh," I said louder, the one nerve I had left starting to fray. "Leo Walsh."

"Awright," he said. "Hold on."

Another two minutes ticked by.

"Okay," Harper said, papers shuffling in the background. "I found him. Hold on."

Then another click and silence again. Intermittent buzzing,

then another voice, deeper and older.

"Akers."

"Lieutenant Akers, my name is Harry Denton. I'd like to speak to the investigator in charge of the Leo Walsh homicide."

"Hmm," he said after a beat of dead air. "Okay, you got him."

"I might have some information about Walsh."

"And you are?" The guy sounded a bit stressed.

"Denton," I repeated. "Harry Denton. I'm a local businessman, and last Monday Leo Walsh showed up at my office. He insisted on seeing me and my assistant parked him in our conference room. I didn't have a lot of time, but he was kind of persistent, so I met with him."

"And why would Leo Walsh want to see you?" Akers asked.

"Well," I said, hesitating. "I used to be a private investigator, although I haven't done any work like that for about fifteen years. But Walsh somehow found out I still had a valid license, so he tracked me down."

"What did he want?"

"Well, it was the strangest thing. He wanted me to investigate his own murder."

There was a long moment of silence before Akers spoke again.

"Would you be willing to come in to the station and make a statement?"

"Of course," I answered. "When?"

"I'll be around here for another couple of hours. Can you come this afternoon, say about 2:30?"

"Absolutely. I'll see you then."

After we hung up, I told Siri to call Ashley. She copped an attitude with me but eventually came around.

"Hey," Ashley said brightly. "How are you?"

I smiled. It was good to hear her voice. "Don't mean to disturb you on a weekend. Hope I haven't caught you at a bad time."

"Not at all," she said. "I'm actually in the office."

"In the office on a beautiful July Saturday afternoon? You should be out at the lake or sunning yourself by the pool."

"What, you want me to develop a melanoma? You know how hot and sticky it is out there right now?"

"And we do have state-of-the-art air conditioners in the office," I offered. "So what are you working on? Didn't know we were that busy."

"Hugh and I are working on a project," she said. "I'm actually proofing and debugging some code for him. Kinda fun, actually."

"Boy, do you guys know how to party…"

She laughed. "So how are you, Harry? When did you guys get back?"

"Late last night," I said. "Well, it was a little after nine. Just felt later. It was an exhausting few days."

"I'll bet. How're you holding up? How's Alex?"

"Neither of us got much sleep last night, but I hope things'll settle down in time. So did you hear about that guy that came by the office?"

I could feel her shudder over the phone, almost as if a cold wind went through her. "God, yes, Harry. How weird was that? And how awful?"

"Yeah, and here's the weird part. I called the cops and told him he was in the office Monday. Now they want me to make a statement. In fact, they may eventually want to talk to you."

"I didn't say ten words to the guy," Ashley said. "But if they want me to corroborate what you tell them, I'm here. Just remember, you took off without even telling me what he wanted."

"That's right," I said. "Tell you what, I'll get you completely up to speed Monday. Right now, I gotta get cleaned up and get going."

"So Harry, where do you have to go?" she asked.

I thought about Antioch and the southeastern part of the city and the little house out there where I'd spent the first three years of my life, when my father was just starting his insurance agency, before he hit it big and we were able to move on.

"The dark side of the moon," I said.

Chapter Eleven

No matter how long I live here, I still maintain the naïve hope that somehow I'll hit that sweet spot in the middle of the day when the Nashville traffic lightens up just a little bit. You'd think I'd have learned over the decades of driving in this town, but as that smart-assed English poet wrote a few centuries ago, *hope springs eternal.*

Unfortunately, 'twas not to be.

I cut over to 16th, passed the Holly Street fire station, then down the hill and back up to Shelby Avenue. I turned right, and it was deceptively smooth sailing for awhile. Shelby clogged up near the interstate, but after a little juking around, I got onto the freeway, over the river, then cut left and merged into I-65 South. Even though it was a sweltering Saturday afternoon in July, the traffic was as thick as any other work day.

At least it was moving, though. I was headed for the Harding Place exit. I'm terrible with directions, but I knew I wanted to head out Harding toward the airport, which meant circling around the concrete ribbon and merging with the eastbound traffic.

That's when it all went, to continue riffing on the Brits, *tits up*.

I stood on the brakes just in time to avoid smashing into the ten-year-old battered Ford F150 with the MAGA sticker in the back window and a silhouette of Donald Trump flipping me off. The dump truck behind me grew larger by the millisecond in the rearview mirror and I braced for impact. The squealing monster brakes on that truck stopped six inches off my bumper.

I white-knuckled the steering wheel, put my head down and sighed a guttural *Jeezus*...

I took a deep breath and looked back up. A herd of stopped cars stretched out in front of me for blocks, with the oncoming lanes empty, blank asphalt. Every few seconds, a brave soul who could get to the far left made an illegal U-turn and went back the other way. Far ahead, bursts of blue light sparkled and flashed above the car roofs.

The clock on the car display read 2:13. May not make a 2:30 appointment, I thought. Hope the lieutenant doesn't put out a warrant on me.

As I sat there another two minutes, the traffic slowly began to move, or rather it did that thing you do in Nashville traffic jams, which is move five feet, slam on the brakes, move five feet, slam on the brakes. Rinse and repeat.

Another five minutes of this and it finally came into view. Sometimes you see stuff that just makes you shake your head in wonder. On rare occasion, you see something so truly, spectacularly awful that you struggle to wrap your head around it.

Ahead of me, at the intersection of Harding Place and Trousdale, just before you get to the Shell station on one side and the Cracker Barrel further down, a tractor pulling a car hauler was on its right side, blocking all but one of the lanes in both directions. The nose of the tractor was turned to the right, as if trying to make the right-hand turn onto Trousdale.

The traffic stopped and I just sat there, staring. Apparently, the poor dumb schlub who was commanding this automotive Titanic tried to make the turn too fast, and the tons of metal behind and above him decided to take on a life of its own. The trailer had gone up on one side like somebody flying the tub on a sidecar motorcycle, and in doing so had pulled the tractor up and over on its side as well.

I imagined this all taking place in slow motion just a few minutes before we got there, with the whole rig balancing on the right side wheels for a split-second before momentum took over and it all crashed down.

Standing next to the wreckage, staring up dumbfounded next to two cops, each with a clipboard, was a skinny guy in a pair of jeans, boots, and a cowboy shirt with the sleeves ripped off. He had his hands on his hips, flashing pencil-thin, blue-inked arms to the whole world, staring at the wreckage of the trailer, his overturned tractor, and very likely, his future.

His mullet flapped in the wind.

The traffic began to pick up, and by the time I funneled into the one lane that was moving past the wreck I was making a good three, four miles an hour. I took one last glimpse at the other side of the crash and saw that the brand new cars on the top shelf of the car hauler had snapped their chains on impact and gone a-flyin'. Now some poor guy had four beautiful Ford Mustangs, wheels to the sky, scattered in his front yard.

There's a certain splendor to it. This was becoming a really special day.

I don't think there's a section of Nashville, with the exception of East Nashville, that has shifted identities more than Antioch. When my father came home from the war, Antioch, Tennessee, was actually a separate municipality, a small unincorporated rural town that was mostly farmland.

Then, as Nashville spread slowly outward like an overfed amoeba, it swallowed Antioch up and kept growing relentlessly. Antioch was still known then as a rural, even redneck part of town. Then there was a rash of gentrification as Nashville got more and more expensive and working class folks who wanted to own their homes had to move further and further out. My father's insurance agency had grown by then and we were able to move out of the four-room cracker box he bought with a VA loan for about eight grand and into a split-level suburban house that he paid the incredible sum of $19,500 for. I was a toddler then, and we had a big back yard and swings and trees to climb and build treehouses in. It was great.

For a while.

In the seventies, the Great Migration began. At first, a growing, prosperous, middle-class African American community, buoyed by more progressive regulations regarding minority mortgage qualifications, began moving to the suburbs, which only motivated the middle-class white folks to put For Sale signs in their front yards.

Property values went down and the prosperous, professional middle-class blacks—doctors, dentists, business owners—who had been housing pioneers started looking for more upscale and safer places as well.

Then the Great Migration continued on through the late seventies and eighties and is still going on today. Cheaper housing attracted first Latinos, then Laotians and Ethiopians, and even later, Kurds. Nashville now has the largest Kurdish population in the world outside of the Middle Eastern Mesopotamian plains.

Nashville, Tennessee—home of the Grand Ole Opry—is today actually one of the world's great melting pots. And as I passed Harding Place and Nolensville Road, it felt like I had crossed over some kind of border into a strange and foreign land, which I guess in a sense, I had.

A supermercado was off to the right, with a crew of stocky Mexicans in the parking lot standing around grilling meat over a smoking oil drum turned on its side. On top of a hill to the left, looming over Nolensville Road, a massive grocery store/warehouse complex advertised and sold Indian food and groceries. The billboards were in Spanish and Arabic and a dozen other languages, and every other one seemed to be a lawyer advertising immigration services. There were crowds of pedestrians everywhere, the usual cast of homeless folks on every street corner hawking copies of *The Contributor*, the local newspaper that made it possible for the homeless to make some kind of a living.

I'd bought copies of *The Contributor* before, from many of the regulars who set up shop on almost every East Nashville street corner. It was one of the last print publications in this area, and not a bad little newspaper.

Flags from all over the world, most of which I couldn't identify, waved from every flagpole, every awning, in every shop window.

The traffic at Harding Place and Nolensville Road choked to a halt as the traffic light let a few cars through at a time. I made it through the intersection, and the flow seemed to speed up. A few minutes later, I crossed over I-24 and realized I could have gone down that freeway instead of I-65 and probably shaved a half-hour off that trip.

But then I would have missed the tractor-trailer and the airborne Mustangs…

This stretch of Harding was one strip mall after another,

interspersed with standalone liquor stores, gun shops, pawn shops, car customization shops, and off to the right just past the Antioch Pike intersection, a gigantic Sam's Club, with hundreds of cars parked in neat rows.

Just past the Nashville Athletic Club, a side street to the right led into a massive complex of buildings, the first of which was the South Precinct. It sat diagonally on the square lot, with rows of parking in front. The building was brick and poured concrete, with a latticework of orange painted beams arching over the entranceway. I parked the car and stepped out into a steambath.

The lobby was mostly empty. The County Court Clerk's row of windows—where the entire population of Southeast Nashville came to renew its car tags every year—was closed. There was a reception desk and area enclosed in what I assumed was bulletproof glass in the center of the lobby.

I walked up to the glass. An older uniformed officer in need of a lifetime membership in Weight Watchers and a few thousand sit-ups looked up at me.

"I have a 2:30 appointment with Lieutenant Akers," I said. "Sorry I'm a little late. There's a wreck up on Trousdale."

"So I heard," he said. "What's your name?" He reached for the handset of his phone.

"Denton," I answered. "Harry Denton."

He spoke into the phone just low enough for me to be unable to hear. After a few exchanges, he hung up.

"Lieutenant Akers will be right out," he said. "I need some I.D."

I pulled out my wallet, extracted my driver's license, and slipped it though the slot at the bottom of the window. He grabbed the license, studied it for a moment, then scribbled my name and the time down on a clipboard. Just as I was stuffing the license back into my wallet, the door to my right opened.

A tall, thin man with short salt-and-pepper hair stood in the doorway, wearing a pair of dark slacks and a police-department-blue Polo shirt. He was clean shaven, totally professional. "Mr. Denton," he said.

I nodded. "Yessir. Sorry I'm a little late. Traffic."

"It's okay. C'mon back."

I walked past him into a brightly lit corridor leading away from the lobby. He let the door close behind us and we walked past a row of closed doors. He stopped at one and pushed it open.

"We can talk in here," he said. I stepped into what was obviously an interview room. A bare, utilitarian table sat in the middle of the small room with a couple of metal chairs on each side. A digital tape recorder sat on the table.

"Please, take a seat." He motioned to the far side of the table. Above me, mounted in the corner, a CCTV camera's blinking red light caught my attention.

Suddenly, I felt more like a suspect than a witness.

I pulled the chair out and sat down as he sat across from me. "I thought we'd do this in an office or something," I said, trying not to sound nervous. "Why do I feel like I need a lawyer?"

He smiled. "You don't. This is just how we do these. I hope you don't mind if I record this. I'm a terrible note taker and this way, I can make sure we get everything right. And if need be, I can have this transcribed and you sign a copy. Just for the record…"

I nodded. "Sure. Not a problem."

He reached over and pressed a button on the recorder. "This

is Lieutenant Garrett Akers, investigative lieutenant, South Precinct and today is Saturday, July…"

He droned on with the formalities, then turned to me.

"State your name, occupation, and address for the record, please."

"My name is Harry Denton. I own a consulting firm that specializes in corporate internet security and I also hold a current private investigator's license in the State of Tennessee…"

I filled in the rest of the blanks. Then Lieutenant Akers turned to me.

"Let's start with how you came in contact with Mr. Leo Walsh. How did you know him?"

"I *didn't* know him. Last Monday afternoon, which I guess would have been the 11th, I was in my office which is located in the 300 block of Fourth Avenue, preparing for a trip I was scheduled to take the next day. Mr. Walsh came in without an appointment and insisted on seeing me. My assistant told me, basically, she couldn't get rid of him. So I went down the hall to the conference room to see what he wanted.

"When I got there, as I told you over the phone, he said he wanted me to investigate a murder. When I asked him whose murder, he answered that it was his."

I spent the next twenty minutes or so retelling the story of Leo Walsh's surprise visit to my office, including the ex-wives and the Nashville Academy of Cinema Arts, and the whole long tale.

As I spoke, I noted the expression on Akers' face. He seemed interested at first, but then he began to look almost confused.

When I finished, he kept the recorder running. "So Mr. Walsh knew someone was going to kill him?"

I nodded. "Yes, that's what I said. He knew."

"But he didn't know who was going to do it?"

"Apparently, there was more than one candidate."

Akers hesitated for a moment, thinking. "Did he know why someone wanted to kill him?"

I thought for a moment, searching my memory. "You know, that's one thing he didn't touch on and I'm sorry to say I didn't ask. He was mostly just telling me this incredible story."

Akers leaned back in his chair and cradled his hands behind his head. He leaned so far back the front legs of the chair came up off the floor.

"You know, Mr. Denton, we're flummoxed by this one. We've got a late middle-aged white guy who lives in a not-great part of town. He drives a fourteen-year old beater and works in what looks like a fly-by-night trade school and winds up dead, wedged between two Dumpsters in the middle of the night in the parking lot of a cheap restaurant in the back of a bodega in a part of town where you usually don't see normal looking old white guys wandering around. Unless they're looking for something they shouldn't be looking for."

I stared at him for a moment. "So you think he was doing something he shouldn't have been doing and that got him killed?"

"I been in this business a long time, Mr. Denton," he said lazily. "Nine times out of ten, a homicide like this is the result of somebody doing something they shouldn't have been doing with somebody they shouldn't have been doing it with, in a place where they shouldn't have been."

"Like what?" I asked.

"The South Precinct is the busiest precinct in Nashville. We got a little bit of everything going on here. That stretch of Murfreesboro Road is notorious for, let's just say, your nocturnally based, freelance niche physical therapists. Of every persuasion imaginable…"

"So Leo Walsh was trying to pick up a girl?"

Akers shrugged. "Girl, boy," he said. "All of the above. Either one can get you in a lot of trouble."

I stared at him a few moments longer, and then it hit me.

"You don't know who he was, do you?"

Akers stared at me a moment, questioning. He unclasped his hands from behind his head, let his arms fall to his side, and settled back down so the chair was on all four legs. Then he sat forward and put his arms on the table.

"I saw the news reports," he admitted. "But why don't you tell me who he is."

I leaned forward, putting my elbows on the table. We were faced off now.

"Twenty years ago, Leo Walsh was famous. He was a Pulitzer Prize nominated writer, rich and in demand. He wrote novels, movies, was a visiting writer at Vanderbilt. He was on the Today Show, Oprah, the whole nine yards. And then it all came crashing down. He lost everything and he made a lot of mistakes and pissed off a lot of people in the process."

Akers brought his left hand up and rubbed his chin. "So you think somebody in the business did this?"

I nodded. "It was a target-rich environment. I don't think this was a random one-off. Was he mugged, robbed?"

Akers thought for a moment, then shook his head. "No. He didn't have a lot of money on him, but his wallet was in his back pocket and there was cash inside."

"There you go," I said. "If it was a trick gone south or some kind of setup, they'd have taken the cash, right?"

"Yeah," he said slowly. "Maybe."

"Can you tell me any specifics about this?" I asked. "Was he actually killed there in that parking lot?"

"I can't really go into specifics," Akers said. "And we're still waiting on the final reports from Forensics Services. But it's starting to look like he was killed somewhere else and dumped in the back of that parking lot, jammed in behind the two Dumpsters."

"Can you tell me the cause of death?" I asked.

Akers hesitated for a moment. "C'mon," I said. "Sooner or later, it'll be public information anyway."

"Blunt force trauma," he answered. "Somebody beat him to death, and brutally. They didn't sneak up behind him and hit him once with a crowbar. It looks like somebody beat him to death with their bare hands."

Something inside me cringed. That was a crappy way to die. "A rage killing," I offered.

Akers nodded. "That's why we thought it might be some kind of sex crime. Maybe he picked somebody up on Murfreesboro Road and when the transaction didn't go as planned, well… Anything can happen."

There was a long moment of silence while we both sat there. My mind was racing. Was there anything he told me that I'd missed, some clue, some indication of who might want to do this to him? He had a couple of ex-wives who hated him, but that was years ago. And besides, as he mentioned, at least one of his exes would have considered killing him, but it would be too quick and easy. She wanted to see him suffer.

"What's your interest in this, Denton?" Akers suddenly asked. "You didn't just come in here to give a statement. You're asking too many questions yourself."

I smiled. "Fifteen years or so ago, when I actually had an office and was working as a P.I., I used to knock heads with the guy who ran the Murder Squad, back when all homicides were investigated out of downtown. Guy named Spellman..."

Akers grinned back at me. "You knew Howard Spellman?"

"Not knew him, know him," I said. "Talked to him this morning. He's the one who explained to me how they've outsourced investigations to individual precincts. He looked up South Precinct on the web. Said he didn't know you."

"I was a rookie, had just graduated from the Academy a year or two before he retired. Saw him work a couple of cases. He wouldn't remember me."

"He used to get really hacked at me when I'd stick my nose into things," I said. "But sometimes it couldn't be helped. We managed to make it work."

"So you're thinking about sticking your nose into this?" Akers asked.

"Lieutenant, the guy came into my office and needed my help and I blew him off because I was too busy and too... preoccupied with my own problems. Turned out he was right, somebody did want him dead. And I feel real bad about that. I'd like to help find who did this if it's okay. Do you guys have a policy about P.I.s?"

"Policy about private investigators?" he asked, his voice rising a bit at the end.

"Yeah, I mean, is it going to cause a problem if I just nose around a bit? On the condition that anything I come up with goes straight to you?"

"Hmm," he said. "You know, I'm coming up on twenty years

on the force and you're the first person who ever asked. Let me think about it."

Chapter Twelve

I stepped back out onto the hot asphalt with Lieutenant Akers' warning still ringing in my ears. He'd made a couple of calls while I sat in the interview room alone and clearly had obtained some official guidance. This was a police matter, he said, and I was to stay out of it. He was pretty clear on this point.

The thought went through my head that I probably should just mind my own business. Leo Walsh had pretty well screwed up his entire life and a once-promising writing career. He'd left a string of angry women, failed books, and dashed dreams behind, and one could make the argument that in the end he probably got precisely what was coming to him.

No, I whispered, *no*... He may have been a screw-up who made some really bad choices in life, but he wasn't a bad guy. Nothing he did justified being beaten to death and chucked out like trash behind a Dempster Dumpster.

A low roar behind me grew louder by the second, then exploded into an ear-splitting scream as a Southwest Airlines jet flew overhead not more than a couple thousand feet up, its wheels dangling beneath it like the claws of a raptor. I knew we were close to Nashville International, but I had no idea we were right under the approach path.

I booted up the car and rolled out of the parking lot, only this time I turned left onto Ezell rather than right. More out of curiosity than anything else, I wondered what was on the other side of the South Precinct. The road dead-ended perhaps fifty yards on at the entrance to a recycling center. Before you got there, however, you had to pass the Davidson County Sheriff's Office facility, which included something called the "Offender Reentry Center."

And next to that, the CoreCivic Detention Facility was safely and securely surrounded by chain-link fence topped by concertina wire. CoreCivic was originally founded as the Corrections Corporation of America, its name modeled after the Hospital Corporation of America. So that's two things besides country music we can all be proud of here: the modern for-profit American health care system and the for-profit prison business model.

I'm so full of pride I could just bust.

It was pressing 3:30 by the time I pulled back out onto Harding Place and headed away from Antioch toward Murfreesboro Road. It was the height of the afternoon and according to the display in the car, it was a gentle 97 degrees outside, with about 90% humidity. I was supposed to meet up with Alex, Sheba, and Lonnie in a couple of hours for dinner. I had a little time to kill, so thought I'd take a drive out Murfreesboro Road and see what I could find.

My mobile was Bluetoothed into the Tesla's audio system. I pressed a button on the steering wheel. "Hey, Siri," I said.

A beep, followed by an annoyed feminine robotic voice. "*What now, Harry?*"

Damn, I thought, I am never letting Lonnie near my iPhone again.

"Directions to the Pancake Palooza restaurant," I said in my best instructional tone, adding in a whisper: "And no more lip."

A few seconds later, a moving map came up on the display.

I curved around Harding Place and made my way to the light at Murfreesboro Road, right next to the abandoned Highway Patrol station where, just over forty years ago, I took my first driving test.

Murfreesboro Road was literally five or six hundred yards away from one of the runways at Nashville International. As I turned left, an American Airlines jet on final approach sirened above me so close it felt like I could've stepped out of the car and spit at it.

In the years before I came along, if you were this far out of town, you were in the country. Murfreesboro Road is also US Highway 41, and before the freeways were built in the early to mid-sixties, this was the way summer vacationers got to Florida. Only it took two days of hard driving back then rather than the seven or eight hours it does now. This was the suburbs when I was a boy, the upscale suburbs full of developments peppered with three-bedroom, bath-and-a-half ranch houses that were the earmark of upward mobility back then.

Now they were rundown, tired, not aging well at all. Kind of like me…

I drove on a few miles in thick traffic, past the smorgasbord of restaurants: Ethiopian, Mexican, Laotian, Indian, even a Polish restaurant. Supermercados and pawn shops, used tire places, cheap cell phone outlets, repurposed fast food restaurants that were now cash advance stores for people needing to borrow against their car titles to make rent. Discount tobacco and vaping supplies…

Homeless people pushing grocery buggies bulging with everything they owned on this earth; Muslim women garbed head to toe pushing baby carriages in the broiling sun, brawny

Mexican construction workers in hard hats and florescent yellow company T-shirts jackhammering a huge hole in the asphalt.

My head swam and I felt isolated, alone, disconnected from the world.

Further down Murfreesboro Road, there was a huge apartment complex on the right, and on the left, a series of cheap motels. One, I noticed, was abandoned and for sale. Wonder how many squatters found their way inside once the sun went down…

Siri's sweet voice instructed me to turn left onto Plus Park Boulevard in another 600 feet. I slowed, the light changed, and for once I got through an intersection without stopping.

Plus Park Boulevard runs through a kind of industrial complex: office buildings, warehouses, almost all of it commercial real estate. Most of it looks pretty upscale and respectable, well-groomed and landscaped.

The road curved uphill and to the left, then back right. I slowed as Siri told me I'd arrived at my location.

To my right, an old, run-down convenience market had been repurposed and was now called the "Kwik Alto—SuperMercado y Carniceria." It was gaily painted, even a bit garish, with Spanish signs and lettering all over the building. A Mexican folk art mural of a young woman tilling a field covered one wall. A locked wire cage full of propane tanks for gas grills sat just to the left of the door near a picnic table so old the wood was slate gray. An overturned pallet sloppily spray-painted a bright blue leaned against a fence that enclosed an outdoor eating area.

I turned in to the parking lot, curious. Siri said I'd arrived at my location, but where was the Pancake Palooza restaurant?

Then I saw it, a tiny sign off to the far side of the parking lot that read PANCAKE PALOOZA, with an arrow that pointed to the left, behind the Kwik Alto Super Mercado.

I slid into a parking spot next to the sign and powered the car down. I stepped out onto the asphalt, which was so hot it felt soft beneath my feet.

How did this place stay in business? I thought. You can't see it from the road, there's practically no signage. And the restaurant itself was tucked in behind another building, almost as an afterthought.

I walked across the parking lot like I was tap dancing across a hot griddle. I turned the corner and there it was, the tiny Pancake Palooza diner. I stopped and stared in shock. The Pancake Palooza resembled about a quarter-sized replica of one of my favorite restaurants in the whole world: The Empire Diner on the west side of Manhattan, in the heart of Chelsea.

It looked like a streetcar, all art deco chrome and glass. Three painted wooden steps in the center led to the entrance door.

Diagonally across from the front door, two grimy Dumpsters sat on the back edge of the parking lot just in front of a thick copse of trees, dense brush, and undergrowth. The rusty, stained green metal was heavily in shadow, with a scattering of garbage where somebody'd missed the Dumpster gate.

I walked slowly over to the two Dumpsters. The yellow crime scene tape was gone. There was no sign that just a couple of short days ago, the body of a man who might have been a successful, even great, writer if he just hadn't screwed it all up, was tossed onto the ground like a discarded mattress.

I pushed into the brush a few feet, then plodded to the right another ten feet or so and peered through the thick leaves. Just beyond the parking lot, the ground descended into a steep gully, at the bottom of which ran a trickle of nasty water. I couldn't tell if it was drainage or a small creek, but it seemed steep enough and slick enough to make it impossible to sneak a body onto the site from the rear of the lot.

I stood there for a moment, thinking. If Leo's body hadn't been brought in from the woods behind the lot, that meant that whoever dumped him drove into the lot, crossed it and stopped next to the Dumpsters.

Which meant, I realized, there could have been witnesses.

Surely, I thought, the police must have realized that too. I disentangled myself from the vines and brush and crossed the lot, then went up the steps and through the front door of the long, narrow restaurant.

A blast of cold air hit me as I entered and I suddenly realized I'd been sweating like crazy. The door dinged as I walked in and a young couple at the far end turned and looked at me. It was a little after four now, too late for lunch and early for dinner.

There was a counter with old-fashioned diner stools that ran down the center, with small tables scattered about in the rest of the room. There were only three tables filled and no one at the counter.

I took a stool as a young woman with purple streaks in her bright red hair, her freckled arms covered in tattoos, came out from the kitchen. She had bright green eyes, pierced nostrils, and wore jeans and a tight T-shirt. She looked like one of the battalions of young hipsters who'd migrated to Music City in the last couple of decades, ever since we'd become the "it" city.

"Hi," she said brightly. "Welcome to the PP."

"Thanks," I said, pulling my damp shirt away from where it had stuck to my chest.

She handed me a menu. "Need a minute or know what you want?"

I opened the menu. Sure enough, the signature meal at the Pancake Palooza centered around some kind of pancake. I suddenly realized that I'd, once again, forgotten to eat lunch.

"I can be quick," I said, scanning the menu. I was having dinner in a couple of hours so I didn't need to pile it on. But a snack sounded good.

"Maybe the buttermilk pancakes, short stack, with a side of bacon. And I'm burning up, so a glass of iced tea with lots of ice."

She smiled and took the menu out of my hand. "Super," she said. "Sweet or unsweet on the tea?"

"Well, I'm from here but even I can't take Southern sweet tea. Half-and-half."

"You got it," she said. She turned and clipped my order to a stainless steel wheel in the opening into the kitchen, then spun it around.

"Order up!" she called. Half-a-minute later, she set a tall glass of tea in front of me. It was so cold that condensation dripped onto the counter.

"This is my first time here," I said. "Nice place. Little hard to find."

"Yeah," she said, wiping the counter around the glass. "We do okay, though. Place is so small you can only get about twenty people at a time in here."

"I imagine that's part of its charm," I offered.

She cocked her head and smiled. Way cute, even flirty…

"So you're a Nashville native," she said.

I nodded. "Yep, aren't many of us left. Where're you from?" I took a long sip of the tea. It was exquisite.

"Moved here from East Tennessee," she answered. "Little

town called Petros."

I leaned back on the stool and did my best Jed Clampett. "*Ooh whee*," I squealed. "Petros, Tennessee. Home of Brushy Mountain State Penitentiary."

She laughed. "Yep, my granddaddy was a guard at Brushy. Thirty years…"

"And the inspiration for my favorite John Hiatt song," I said.

"*Tennessee Plates*!" she said loudly. "I love that one!"

"I saw him do it live once at the Franklin Theater," I said. "It was one of the highlights of my life. So how'd you wind up here?"

"Just decided to move to the big city," she answered. "Ain't much future in a town of less than 600 people."

"I get it, although sometimes I feel like there ain't much future in a town of two million people either."

"Nashville that big now?"

"Will be soon," I said. I held out my hand. "Harry Denton. Glad to meet you."

She took my hand. "Micki Hicks. A pleasure…"

There was a ding behind her as the cook set my order in the window. She turned and in one smooth motion, grabbed a couple of plates and set them down in front of me. She reached under the counter and handed me a knife and fork rolled into a napkin.

"We got about eight kinds of syrup," she offered. "What's your pleasure?"

"I'm a great believer in keeping it simple."

She smiled that incredibly sweet smile again. "Works for me," she said as she reached under the counter and slid a small pitcher of maple syrup over to me.

I dug into the pancakes, the smell of which made me even hungrier. I don't know if you should really deploy the word *perfect* when talking about something as ordinary as pancakes and bacon, but I was sorely tempted.

Micki Hicks crossed from behind the counter and went around the tables, checking on the other customers. Inside of about ten minutes, I'd wolfed down breakfast and was sipping the last of my tea. Micki went behind and down the counter and stood across from me.

"That was quick," she said. "Get you anything else? Coffee?"

"Maybe a refill on the tea. And some answers if you got 'em."

She reached behind her and lifted two pitchers off a tray, one sweet and one regular, then poured both into my glass at the same time without spilling a drop.

"You've done this before," I offered.

She nodded her head. "Every day."

Then, a moment later: "Answers… If I had answers, Harry, I might not be slinging pancakes in a third-rate diner."

"Hey, c'mon now. Second rate at least."

"So what answers are you looking for?" she asked, suspicious now.

I looked at her for a moment and decided to just go for it. "Were you here Thursday night?"

Her brow wrinkled. "Thursday night?"

Then it hit her. "Oh, Thursday night…"

"Yeah. How late is this place open on Thursday night?"

"We're open until ten every night except Friday and Saturday. We're open 'til midnight then."

"So you were gone by ten."

She nodded. "Look, Harry, you don't look like a cop. And

the homicide guys have already interviewed us. None of us saw anything. We were all gone. So who are you?"

I reached into my back pocket and pulled out the thin leather wallet that had been stuffed in the back of my desk for so long I had to dig for it this morning. I opened it up, showing my P.I. license on one side and generic badge on the other.

Micki studied it for a second. "Private investigator?"

I closed the wallet and stuffed it back into my pocket. "Leo Walsh came to my office a few days before he was killed. He thought somebody was gonna murder him and wanted me to dig around and learn what I could. At the time, I couldn't do it. Now I can."

Micki looked down for a second, thinking. "Damn, Harry, this is the creepiest thing I've ever seen in my life. To think that a guy was murdered fifty feet away from where I work. Makes me want to go back to Petros."

"But you didn't see anything?"

She shook her head. "We're outta here by 10:30, 10:45 every night. There's a bunch of homeless folks that swarm the Dumpsters after we leave looking for food. If we've got anything left, we try to set it out in clean boxes so they're not eating food somebody else's had first. Bad enough to have to eat garbage. But to find a dead body on top of that..."

She shook her head again. "Saddest thing I've ever seen."

She looked for a second like she was about to tear up. I reached across the counter and patted her hand. "You're a good soul, Micki Hicks. Sorry to be so damned inquisitive. How much do I owe you?"

She pulled a pad out of her apron and tore off my check. "Nine-eighty-five," she said.

I pulled my other wallet out, extracted a Benjamin, and slid it across the counter.

She stared at it a moment, like it might bite. "I'm not terribly sure we can break that right now. Been a slow day."

I winked at her. "No worries, pal. Keep it. I'll see you around."

"Thanks, Harry," she said softly, folding the bill in half. "I appreciate it. Come back sometime."

I smiled. "You got it."

Chapter Thirteen

So I met a sweet young girl who came to the big city to get away from a dead-end town and wound up, as she said, slinging pancakes in a third-rate diner. She comes to work one afternoon to find the place swarming with cops, forensic services techs, news vans, and gawkers.

I hope they had Leo gone before she got there. Hate to think she actually saw what was left of him.

It was past four by the time I got back out in the Murfreesboro Road traffic. The car display read 98 degrees now with a good hour before things really started to cool off. I'd gotten sweaty and sticky nosing around the parking lot at the Pancake Palooza. If the traffic cooperated and I didn't dawdle I could head home and grab a shower and a change of clothes before dinner.

I turned left off Plus Park Boulevard onto Murfreesboro Road and headed for the interstate exchange just a quarter-mile up. Once I hit the freeway, I could be back home in twenty minutes.

The light changed at Spence Lane and I sat there, heat waves shimmering off the asphalt in front of me. The light turned green and, without thinking or making a conscious decision, I drove straight on, past the entrance to the freeway.

The shower would have to wait.

I drove on down Murfreesboro Road, past what was once a massive bread bakery and was now a car museum, past what had once been a car dealership but had been leveled and was now the main police headquarters complex.

Has everything in this city either been demolished and replaced or repurposed?

I am entirely too insulated these days. I need to get out more.

I saw a billboard advertising the old Drake Motel. At least it hadn't been torn down or converted to an Airbnb. The Drake had been a respectable motel back in the '50s and '60s, but as the area went downhill, let's just say the Drake began to appeal to an entirely different demographic. The area started to turn around in the late 90s and the early 21st century and now the Drake was considered almost iconic, a museum commemorating famous country music stars who'd stayed there before they became rich and famous, then crashed and burned.

I turned right, though, before I got to the Drake, onto Fesslers Lane. This area, too, was almost all commercial, warehouses and small businesses. I got through the heavily clogged intersection at Elm Hill Pike, then over I-40/24.

I was depending on memory to navigate this time. Didn't feel like getting into conflict with Siri.

Boswell's Harley-Davidson was up on my left now and I slowed to make the left-hand turn just past it onto Calhoun Avenue. A quarter-mile or so down, almost to the dead end, a one-story building squatted in the middle of a massive asphalt parking lot, baking in the July sun.

The Nashville Academy of Cinema Arts.

The picture on the website was clearly photoshopped. On the website, the colors popped brightly, the landscaping neat and groomed to the point of perfection. The signage was young and hip, even inspired. It made you just want to come here and hang out with cool, smart young kids and make movies.

But the reality was different. The grounds were in need of

tending, the building clearly another repurposed warehouse constructed of aging concrete and aluminum. The signage was just as hip, but upon close inspection it was cheaply made and basically tacked to the side of the building.

I pulled into the nearly empty parking lot and slid into a slot right in front of the entrance. I could see through glass doors into a dark, empty lobby. I sat there quietly for a few moments, imagining Leo Walsh driving here from his cheap apartment in Antioch in his beat-up, rusting car, having to face his own failures and lack of options each day.

I backed out of the slot and drove slowly through the parking lot around to the left side of the building. This part of the lot was fenced off in high chain-link fence, but the gate was open. I drove through the gate and saw a couple of small trucks with the NACA logo painted on the side. Two freight docks were on the side, their metal doors down.

I was just scoping the place out, not even sure what I was looking for. Leo had said something about the Nashville Academy of Cinema Arts being a for-profit school that was being investigated by the Feds for something, although I don't remember him saying what. I suddenly wished I'd taken notes of our conversation, but I'd been so preoccupied with getting out to Reno, to Alex, that I hadn't paid as close attention as I should have.

Truth is, I never expected to hear from or anything about Leo Walsh ever again.

Now he was soaking up what little bandwidth I actually had left.

I thought about parking the car and seeing if the place was open, but I needed time to pull together some sort of strategy.

Sometimes in this line of work, you can just walk into a situation and wing it. If you're lucky and the timing is right, you can get away with it.

Most of the time, though, it helps to go in with a plan.

I turned the car around and drove away.

***

I stepped off the elevator into the anteroom of Sheba and Lonnie's rooftop condo. "Sorry I'm late," I called.

Alex rounded the corner just as I passed through the living room and came into my arms. "Hi, Daddy," she said brightly.

"Hi, sweetheart. Have you had a good day?"

She leaned in to me. "Great," she said, her voice lowering. "Sheba's a lot of fun."

"That sounds ominous," I said. "Hope you guys didn't get in too much trouble."

We walked into the kitchen, where Sheba stood at the stove, stirring a pot of marinara. A large pot steamed on the burner next to the sauce.

"Sorry I'm late," I repeated. "I had a few errands to run and I got really hot and sticky out there. Ran home and took a shower…"

Sheba turned, smiling. "Well, Harry, on behalf of the women of America, *thanks*. Now grab a beer and join Lonnie on the veranda."

I walked over to the refrigerator and pulled out another Yazoo seasonal. "We're not going to eat out there, are we? It's like a sauna."

Sheba turned. "Are you kidding? Alex's got the table set."

I grinned. "It's my turn to thank you."

"Dinner'll be ready in ten," Sheba said.

"Well," I said, "I'll leave you two to the women's work."

As I walked away, I felt a kitchen towel hit the back of my head.

Lonnie was on the roof in a pair of worn jeans and a T-shirt that depicted a graphic of a plane landing on a runway. His bare feet were stretched out on the chair next to him. A couple of empty beer bottles sat on the table, with a fresh one in a foam koozie.

I sat down next to him. "Fly today?"

Lonnie turned. He looked tired, even a little haggard. "Only hangar flying today. Too damn hot…"

"You look a little pooped," I said.

"Didn't sleep for shit last night. Guess it was jet lag."

I laughed. "Jet lag? We crossed two time zones."

"You know what I mean," he said. "All that emotional stress and exhaustion, being in a strange place. Carrying somebody to their grave. Shit catches up with you after awhile."

"I get it," I said, then took a long swig of the beer. Okay, now I can deploy the word *perfect*. "Neither Alex nor I slept for squat. I think half the time these days I'm running on adrenaline."

He lifted the beer bottle and took a long swallow. "Heard you been out playing private dick today."

"Who said that?"

"Sheba said you were in a hurry to get on with your day. I figured it had something to do with that guy on the news. You're not that hard to figure out, you know."

I leaned back in the chair and rested my head. "Just curious," I said. "It really doesn't make much sense."

Lonnie turned, stared at me for a beat. "Kinda like the good old days, huh?"

I smiled. "There's only one problem with the good old days, Lonnie. They sucked."

"Bullshit," he said. "You didn't have two nickels to rub together to make a dime, but you loved every minute of it."

I thought for a moment. "Maybe. There were certainly moments. But there were also times when I didn't know if I was going to survive it."

He sat up and planted his feet on the floor, then turned to face me with a look on his face that was almost angry. "Yeah, I remember a couple of times when I had my doubts. So what the fuck are you up to, Harry? Trying to recapture your lost youth?"

"Damn, Lonnie, ya' ain't gotta get all up in my grill about it."

He sputtered a laugh, then relaxed and leaned back down in the chair. "You're full of shit, but you do kinda grow on people after awhile."

We sat there staring off toward the horizon, where the sun was just touching down off I-40 westbound.

"Seriously, man," he said, "what are you trying to accomplish here?"

I took another sip of the beer to hold off having to answer that for a moment. "I don't know," I said. "There's something about this poor sonofabitch that got under my skin, I guess. I don't know if I'm gonna dog this one like the old days, but I might do a little digging around. See what I can come up with."

"Well, let me just remind you of one little thing you might want to keep in mind."

"Yeah?"

"You're not in your thirties anymore and so broke you got nothing to lose. Back then, it was okay to take stupid chances. Shit's different now. You're old, you're rich, and there's a lot more at stake."

Then he shrugged his shoulders and motioned with his head in the direction of the kitchen.

I turned in the same direction. "Yeah," I said. "Shit's different. I keep telling myself that."

~

As soon as we dove into dinner, I forgot that I'd eaten breakfast just a couple of hours earlier. Sheba uncorked a couple of fabulous bottles of chianti and the spaghetti was great and the garlic bread was crispy and almost pungent. Being a Southern male, I generally am not a big salad fan. But tonight, even the green stuff was exciting. We laughed and ate and kidded each other, and for a little while the world seemed all right.

"So what about this hoity-toity private school you're starting in August?" Lonnie asked.

Alex—who'd been content enough with her soft drink, but occasionally eyed one of us enjoying the chianti—pursed her upper lip and lifted her nose in the air.

"Oh, *dah-link*, you mean The Bealesworth School?" she said with a pretty spot on fake British accent. "Well, it certainly won't compare with the sophistication and taste of what I'm used to back in the big city of Reno, but *papa* says it will have to do."

Sheba broke out laughing.

"Of course, my *deah*," I chimed in with my fake British accent. "It represents a hardship, but one simply has to make do, doesn't one? We are, after all, in the birthplace of *country music*."

"Yes, *papa*, we will just have to carry on," Alex said brightly. "Stiff upper lip and all that…"

Lonnie was rolling his eyes and Sheba was trying not to spit bread crumbs.

"Seriously," I said, reverting back to a normal voice, "we're taking a tour this week. Alex'll get to see it for the first time."

Alex looked up at me. "I will? When?"

"Uh, it's in my calendar," I said, pulling my cell phone out of my shirt pocket. I swiped across the screen and touched a couple of places. "Yeah, Tuesday at 11 AM. We'll meet with the Admissions Director and get a tour, then we have a 12:15 with the Headmistress, or whatever they call her."

"*Headmistress*," Lonnie said. "I'm seeing whips and chains, leather thigh-high boots…"

"Behave yourself," Sheba warned.

Alex sat still, staring at dead air for a second, and I suddenly felt something unsettling.

"I told you a couple weeks ago, remember?"

"Yeah, I'm sorry," she said. "In the middle of all this, I forgot."

"Are you okay with it?" Sheba asked.

Alex turned to Sheba with something that looked like fear in her eyes. "I guess so. I mean, everybody's gotta go to school somewhere, right?"

Sheba leaned over and took her hand. "It'll be fine," she said. "I did some checking into the school."

I turned to her. "You did?"

"Of course," she said, holding on to Alex's hand. "I wasn't going let our girl here go off to some place without doing our due diligence."

She smiled broadly and that seemed to drain off some of the tension. Alex smiled back at her and squeezed her hand.

"Thanks, Aunt Sheba."

"It seems like a fine place," Sheba offered. "There's lots of extra-curricular stuff, trips over vacations. And you like your field hockey, right?"

Alex smiled. "You know I love field hockey."

"Well, their girls team was ranked number one in the state three years in a row. Last year, they went to Atlanta for the regionals and took third place."

"Oh, wow," Alex said.

I'm not even sure I knew what field hockey was, let alone that they played it in Tennessee.

"And they have a scuba club. Your Uncle Lonnie can tell you how great that is."

"Second only to flying as the most fun you can have with your clothes on," Lonnie, who was on about his fourth glass of wine, said.

"Lonnie!" Sheba snapped.

"I'm just kidding," he said. "You're gonna love it. It's one of the few sports that women are actually naturally better at."

"Yeah?" Alex asked.

"Once you're underwater, everything's weightless. So physical strength is no advantage. Plus, women suck less air than men so they can stay under longer."

Sheba lowered her head and faux-glared at him over the bridge of her nose. "I think it's fair to say that in most things, women suck less than men."

Alex giggled.

"So rest assured," Sheba added. "We checked it all out for you. It's going to be fine."

Alex was smiling big-time now. "Thanks," she said. "I'm excited."

And I sat there, silently, as if I wasn't even there.

Chapter Fourteen

I rolled over and pulled the covers off of me, then trudged into the bathroom for what was getting to be an irritating routine every night. Men facing their sixties rarely get a continuous night's sleep. Afterward, I trudged out to the kitchen for a glass of water, which one would think could be counterproductive. Couldn't help it though; I was scratchy-throat thirsty.

The digital clock on the microwave over the stove read 3:25 in bright blue. I groaned and turned on the spigot, drank half a glass of water, then turned back toward the bedroom. As I crossed the living room, I glanced up the stairs.

Light filtered out through the crack under Alex's bedroom door.

Don't teenagers ever sleep?

Then I remembered. Of course they do, during the day. Adolescents are nocturnal creatures.

Then I headed back to bed. In the end, it was a good night. I only had to get up two more times.

Alex finally rolled out of bed in time for lunch. She sat down at the kitchen table, her eyes puffy, her hair still wet from the shower, and stared at the cubical box on the table next to her coffee cup.

"What?" she said groggily.

I smiled. "Go ahead, open it. I think I got the size right."

She reached up and pulled one of the flaps open. I'd opened

the box when it came in last week to make sure everything was okay, then folded the flaps back down.

Her forehead wrinkled. Then she reached in and pulled out a royal blue, full-face motorcycle helmet.

"It's a helmet," I said.

She grinned at me. "No kidding."

Alex turned it around and saw the graphic on the front of it.

"How do you pronounce it?" she asked.

"It's pronounced *sho-way*," I answered. "It's Japanese. One of the best helmets in the world. Thought we'd go for a ride today."

"On that thing in the garage?" she asked suspiciously. "I've been meaning to ask you about that. What in heaven's name is it?"

"It's my new toy," I explained. "I bought it last year. I'd been wanting one for a long time. Call it middle-aged crazies, but when the merger went through and all that cash came in, I decided to splurge."

"But what is it?"

"It's a Russian bike called a Ural. They're old school, retro. Based on a pre-World War II BMW that the Nazis used in the Wehrmacht. Legend had it that before Hitler and Stalin got into a pissing contest, Hitler gave one to Stalin as a gift. Stalin had it reverse-engineered and started mass producing them by the thousands. They've been making them ever since, and while they're a lot more high-tech and reliable than they used to be, they're still basically the same."

She held the helmet up and rotated it in her hands, studying it. "And that bathtub-looking thingy on the side?"

"It's called a sidecar. During the war, the Russians would mount a machine gun on the sidecar. One guy in the sidecar, one as passenger, one driving. They'll go anywhere."

"And you want to take me for a ride in that thing?"

"There's a great barbecue joint I'd like to show you up in Hendersonville. Thought we'd get dinner or a late lunch, whatever. Unless you're hungry and need to eat now."

She shrugged her shoulders and set the helmet down on the table. "I'm good. Just coffee…"

I lifted my coffee mug and toasted her. "You are definitely your father's daughter."

Thirty minutes later, I was showing Alex how to be a sidecar passenger. The Ural's heavy and cumbersome, all steel and with a low center of gravity. The engine's a 750cc boxer, two cylinders horizontally opposed, across from each other and lying on their sides. For a bike this size, it's a pretty small engine. It's got a lot of torque on the low end, but it tops out at about 65 or 70 miles an hour. Definitely not for high speed freeway driving…

But it's got a sound like a low-pitched sewing machine and it turns heads everywhere it goes.

"How'd you get turned onto these things?" she asked as I was showing her where to hold on and what to do when we went into turns.

"I pulled into a gas station off the interstate one day and there was a guy there filling up," I answered. "It was painted olive drab, the old shade of green the military used to use and it had World War II markings on it. Man, I had to ask what it was. I'd never seen anything like it. We talked for nearly forty minutes standing there at the gas pump."

She grinned and shook her head. "Boys and their toys."

"Yeah, you're right. And the older the boy gets, the more expensive the toys. These things are a niche market. There aren't many of them around, but people that love 'em really love 'em. They cost about three times what an equivalent Japanese bike would cost."

"Oh, well," she said, lifting her left leg and folding herself into the sidecar. "Could've been worse. You could have bought a jet plane like Uncle Lonnie."

A few years ago, they finally got rid of the carbs and fitted the bikes with EFI, so they're a lot easier to start now. The bike kicked over and began purring, that distinctive idle like nothing you'll ever hear from any other kind of engine. The two most unique engine noises in the world are a bike equipped with that BMW boxer-style engine and the Rolls-Royce 12-cylinder Merlin that powered Spitfires and Mustangs.

The Ural only has four gears—not counting the reverse that you engaged by reaching down behind you near the back wheel and jerking up on a lever—and changing gears produces a loud metallic thunk that sounds like something came loose inside.

I dropped into first gear, gave it a little gas, and slowly let out the clutch. The bike rolled forward out of the garage and I hit the key fob to shut the door behind us. A second button on the fob started the front gate swinging forward. I goosed the throttle a little more and we drove onto the street, the gate shutting behind us.

I ran the Ural up to third gear and wound our way through the East Nashville side streets down to Porter Road, then over to Riverside Drive. It was a gorgeous day, just a few stratus clouds here and there. A front had come in overnight and dropped the temperature down to the mid-80s, which was downright pleasant for a July in Nashville. There wasn't much traffic on Riverside so I ran the bike up all the way to about 45, then turned around.

"You okay?" I yelled over the roar of the engine and the wind.

Behind me and to my right, Alex was holding onto the sidecar handgrips with a little bit of white knuckle. There was a great broad grin on her face, though, and I could tell she was all right.

She nodded, the helmet bobbing up and down.

We drove on down Riverside, where there were still a few of the grand old houses that were a century old now or more, the few that had survived the March 1933 tornado that ripped across East Nashville, then on through Donelson and Hermitage. A lot of the houses that were built in the years afterward were now being taken down, one after the other, by developers who were putting up six- and seven-figure tall and skinnies in their place.

I cut right into the side street that went under the railroad tracks and drove slowly through Shelby Park. The speed limit through the park was barely above a fast walk, which meant you could just meander without having your ears blown out by engine noise. It was one of my favorite rides and it was even better having Alex with me. I turned and smiled at her as we drove under an especially thick canopy of old growth trees. She grinned back and gave me a thumbs up.

We pulled out of the park and back onto Riverside Drive. Riverside curves first one way, then the other, for a few miles and then it shrinks from a divided road with a landscaped median down to two lanes next to each other and does what most Nashville streets eventually do: changes names.

So we took Greenfield up to Gallatin Pike and turned right, then headed north toward Hendersonville. Riding a motorcycle on Gallatin Pike, even a heavy slow one like the Ural that won't tip over, is taking your life in your hands. Despite it being a lazy, warm Sunday summer afternoon, the traffic was thick and frustrating. Some guy in a pickup truck that looked like a prop from *Sanford and Son* pulled out in front of us in Madison and would have taken us out, except that I could see he was going to run the essentially meaningless red light he was facing, and I hit the brakes.

When I got the bike last year, Lonnie gave me a piece of advice I've never forgotten: *when you're riding a motorcycle in traffic, just assume that every son of a bitch out there is trying to personally kill you.*

We made it past Rivergate alive, though, and were soon headed out of Nashville.

Just across the Sumner County line, where Gallatin Pike changes its name to Main Street in Hendersonville, sits a little joint called Center Point Barbecue. The place is tiny, with maybe a dozen tables with plastic checkered tablecloths on an elevated stage off to the right and a counter that might sit ten people on a good day.

Alex looked around as we came in, unimpressed.

"So this is the world's best barbecue?" she whispered.

I pulled off my helmet and cradled it under my arm. "I'll tell you how good this place is," I said. "Ten years ago, when Lonnie and I were about to go under, we got an appointment to go pitch our software to an S&P 500 company in Manhattan. I'm on the phone with the Senior Vice-President for Information Technology making the appointment and he said 'Where you coming from again?' 'Nashville,' I said."

"Grab any table you want," the waitress called from behind the counter.

Alex led the way and we took a table in the far corner. We set our helmets and leather jackets on the chairs next to us.

"So when I said Nashville, this guy squealed. Literally

squealed. *Nashville! Oh, man, can you drive out to Center Point and bring me some barbecue? I'll pay you for it!*"

The waitress, who wore a tight pair of jeans and a red flannel shirt, even though it was July, came over to our table and set two glasses of ice water down and a pair of menus.

"I'm Shirl," she said. "I'll be taking care of you today. Can I get you something to drink?"

"I'll have a Coke," Alex said.

"Iced tea, please, half-and-half."

Shirl nodded and walked off. I leaned in toward Alex.

"So needless to say, two days later, Lonnie and I showed up in his office with twenty-five pounds of Center Point, along with a quart of baked beans, slaw, and two pans of cornbread, all on dry ice in a huge rollaway insulated cooler. The guy offered to pay us and we *aw-shucked* him right outta that notion."

Alex smiled. "And did it work?"

I leaned back. "A week later, we had a signed, multi-year lease agreement in the high six-figures. Saved the company..."

Alex laughed out loud this time. "Saved by the barbecue. Okay, I'm ready to try me some Center Point."

ෆ

An hour later, we were both leaning back in our chairs ready for a nap.

"Well?" I asked.

She yawned and stretched her arms out in front of her. "As advertised, Daddy," she said. "The best I ever had. I'm stuffed, though. I think maybe just a snack for dinner."

"We can carry some home," I said. "Put it in the fridge."

She nodded. Then she stared off over my shoulder and her eyes seemed to drift.

"You okay?"

She turned her gaze back to me. "Momma would have loved this day," she said quietly.

I nodded. "Yeah, she would have."

We got back on the bike, a sack of carryout tucked into the sidecar beside her, and began the drive back home. By the time we pulled into the driveway, it was near five o'clock and the sun was low in the west. We parked the Ural, then went inside and stowed the barbecue away.

I went up to the media room and turned on the flat screen and started channel surfing. Alex disappeared into her bedroom for a few minutes and then stuck her head in just as I was pulling up the cable guide.

"Hey!" I said. "*Alfred Hitchcock's The Birds* starts on TCM in five minutes! You ever seen it?"

She sat down on the leather sofa next to me. "No," she answered. "Is it good?"

"Oh, it's incredible. It's one of the essentials. If you're up for a movie, you'll love it"

She shrugged. "Sure, go for it."

So I turned down the lights and fired up Turner Classic Movies and sat there with my daughter and watched Tippi Hedren fight off swarms of killer raptors while Rod Taylor tried to resolve the raging conflict between his aching desire for Melanie Daniels and the pull of his needy, neurotic smothering mother.

It was the nicest day I'd had in years. I'm glad I didn't know then that it would be the last relaxed, carefree day I'd have for a long time.

Chapter Fifteen

I parked the Tesla in my spot in the underground garage and powered it down. Next to me, Alexis twisted around and grabbed her backpack from the back seat, then eased out of the car. The fit was a little tight, but she managed to slide out while I plugged in the charging cable. I snatched my backpack up and we headed for the elevators.

She'd been quiet the whole drive downtown. I assumed it was because I'd gotten her out of bed about three hours earlier than usual. We'd both swilled down a mug of coffee without saying much, then she'd loaded up her stuff and we'd taken off.

We were going to have to figure out how all this was going to work. In another four weeks, she'd be in school at Bealesworth and we'd both be up by 7 or 7:30 in the morning for the cross-town commute. I was dreading that probably almost as much as Alex was, but I saw the advantage in it as well. Lately, I'd taken to sleeping later than I should. Having a schedule and structure would get me going earlier.

It's always good to have to be somewhere.

The next four weeks were another matter, though. I couldn't very well take her to work every day. Unless, of course, we found a job for her and that might be something I take up with Ashley. We could call it an internship, although internships usually have some kind of educational component to them. Dusting furniture in the conference room hardly qualified.

Today, though, she was going with me. She wanted to see

Ashley and I'm sure the feeling was returned. I could leave the two of them together while I took care of a few things.

We stepped into an empty elevator and I pressed 12. The door closed with a soft whooshing sound and we started up. Alex leaned against the side, her head cocked and her eyes half-closed.

"There's a comfy sofa in my office," I commented. "You can take a nap."

She smiled. "I'm sorry, Daddy. I'm still having trouble sleeping and I'm not used to being up so early."

"So I gathered…"

The door opened on the main lobby and a crowd of people herded in. We both backed up to the rear wall of the elevator and watched as a flurry of hands pushed buttons on the elevator panel, lighting it up like a Christmas tree.

I glanced over at Alex. "Guess we got the local."

She smiled back. "I was hoping for the express," she whispered.

After a vertical stop-and-go lurching elevator ride, the doors finally opened on the 12th floor. We walked down the hall and pushed open the door, with the DENTON & ASSOCIATES name and logo painted at eye height.

As soon as we entered the lobby, Ashley was out from behind the desk and bounding over to us. There was mutual squealing all around as Alex and Ashley jumped into each other's arms.

Ashley was the first one to speak. "It's so good to see you! I'm just so sorry it's like this…"

Alex looked for a second like she might break out into sobs, but managed to hold it all in. "It's okay," she said softly. "It's good to see you."

Ashley pulled away and gave me a quick hug. "How are you, Harry?"

"Okay. Glad to be home. I just want to get back to some kind of routine. How are things around here? Catch us up while we go stow our stuff."

I led the way into my office and dropped the backpack on the floor behind my desk. Alex followed and plopped down on the sofa, with Ashley trailing.

"You want coffee?" she asked.

Alex raised up a bit. "That sounds great."

"I'll put some on," Ashley said. "And everything's chugging along here. Pat told me to tell you she's got the June spreadsheet ready for your review. Donald's put together a proposal for you to look at on upgrading the servers. We had a record high number of outage minutes last month and he's not happy. And Hugh's working on the new app demo. He says he'll have something for you by the end of the week."

"Oh," I said, looking through the small stack of unopened mail on my desk. "Is that what you guys were working on this weekend?"

Ashley looked away for a second. "Yeah, he just wanted me to go over some things with him."

Then she switched gears in a way that made me think there was something she wasn't telling me.

"And the folks over at C&S are balking at renewing their contract. They said they don't need any more hand-holding. What's probably really going on is that the trucking industry has taken it on the chin the last couple of years."

I thought for a second. C&S was a regional trucking company that had signed on as an Asfáleia Technologies client about two years before Lonnie sold the company. When the Europeans bought us out, all of the Asfáleia clients were grandfathered in as

Denton & Associates clients. We knew that most of them would either break or not renew their contracts over time.

C&S was just one of the first to say goodbye. That's okay. We knew Denton & Associates had an expiration date.

"They probably don't need any more hand-holding," I said. "When does their contract expire?"

"End of August. Renewal date's first of September."

"I don't feel like busting my chops to keep 'em at the party if they don't want to be here anymore. Let's just ride it out and see what they decide. Do they seem pretty determined?"

"Intractable," Ashley said as she walked out of my office.

Alex got up from the sofa and walked over to the floor-to-ceiling glass that was the exterior wall of my office. She stared down at the river and across to Nissan Stadium.

"Wow, what a view. I'd forgotten."

I walked over next to her and put my arm around her shoulder. "Well, you were only here once before…"

She nodded. "Yeah, before Momma got too sick."

I pulled her to me and gave her a hug. "Listen, what works for you? You want to set up your laptop in here where you've got the view or you want the conference room? Fewer distractions in the conference room, but I can tell you in advance that the walls sometimes feel like they're closing in on you."

She looked up. "I don't know. What are you going to do? I don't want to disturb you if you're working."

"Don't worry about that," I said. "I've got some paperwork to take care of and then I've got some business to attend to outside the office."

"Maybe I'll hang around with Ashley until you take off and then use your desk."

I leaned down and kissed the top of her head. "Sounds like a plan."

Behind us, Ashley came back in. "Coffee'll be up in a minute."

We both turned. "Thanks," I said. "Look, Ashley, I brought Alex into the office today 'cause I didn't want her sitting alone in the house so soon after getting back here. We're going to be settling in, though, and it won't be every day."

Ashley smiled. "S'okay by me if it is."

"That's sweet of you," I said. "Thanks. But for today, I've got some things to take care of this afternoon."

I reached for my wallet and pulled out a fifty-dollar bill. "Why don't you guys go get a nice lunch, maybe take a walk and enjoy the day."

Ashley looked over at Alex. "There's a new place on Fourth Avenue I've been wanting to try. I forgot what it's called, but it's supposed to be an absolutely faithful recreation of a New York deli. They even insult you, like the Soup Nazi on *Seinfeld*."

"Soup Nazi?" Alex asked, looking back and forth from me to Ashley.

I looked at Ashley and grinned. "Something tells me for the first time in your life, you just felt old…"

I turned to Alex. "Try the Reuben."

"Then we can go up Third from Commerce," Ashley said, ignoring the "old" remark, "and go to that place that has the ten dollar milkshakes."

I pulled another couple of twenties out of my wallet. "Ten dollar milkshakes? Here, just in case."

Ashley took the bills and folded them in half. "Oh, by the way," she said. "Pat wanted to talk to you. I think she needs some signatures. You know, paperwork."

"Okay," I said. "I'll head to her office."

"And I'll get your coffee," Ashley said in Alex's direction. "If I remember, cream, one sugar. Right?"

Alex piped up. "Oh, I can get it."

"No worries." Ashley motioned to her to sit down. "Happy to do it. I'll grab some myself and we'll take a break."

Ashley followed me out of my office and down the hall toward Pat McClellan's office, where our Chief Financial Officer was no doubt crunching numbers for breakfast and waiting for me to sign stuff. As we passed the break room, Ashley cleared her throat and stopped.

I turned. "Yeah?"

She looked at me suspiciously. "If anyone should ask," she said quietly, "where should I say you're going this afternoon?"

I stared at her for a beat. "I'm going to a funeral home," I said. "Visitation's from 11-2."

~

I met with our Chief Financial Officer, then did the executive patrol through the rest of the company. Executives do that, they patrol around from time-to-time, just checking on the troops. Only in my case, there were only three troops besides me and Ashley, so it didn't take very long.

Then there was about an hour's worth of email to go through—most of it junk—then I packed up my backpack and headed for the elevators.

"Daddy, what are you gonna do for lunch?"

I turned and walked back over to my desk, where Alex had her laptop open and was sitting in my tall leather chair. I leaned down and gave her a hug.

"You're sweet to worry about your old man," I said. "I'll grab something later. You and Ashley have a good time."

It was a bit hellish getting out of the downtown area. Nashville's got about four rush hours a day: the morning rush hour, the lunch rush hour, that window between 3 and 4:30 when the state civil service workers head for home, and the full-blown rush hour that now goes past 7 o'clock most nights.

I made my way down Broadway, then turned left past Division Street onto the freeway entrance ramp. I juked my way back and forth, crossing lanes like a fighter pilot, and made my way to I-40 East toward the airport. It was a typical day in Music City: tractor-trailer rigs blew past me at 70, then locked up their smoking, squealing brakes when they hit the logjam.

I got off the interstate at Stewart's Ferry Pike, then turned left and went back over the freeway past the old state mental hospital and the Tennessee School for the Blind. I turned right onto Lebanon Road, then out past the strip malls with the Kohl's and the Target, then over the Stones River.

I'd read Leo Walsh's obituary on my iPad while drinking coffee this morning. For the second time in a week I was headed to a funeral home. I thought back over the years.

Yep, this was my personal best. Two funerals in a week.

The Riley & Boscombe funeral home was on the right side of Lebanon Road, tucked in between a decaying strip mall with an abandoned Shoney's restaurant on one side and a massive mega-church on the other. It was catty-cornered across Lebanon Road from a Captain D's, a bakery, and yet another discount tobacco and vaping outlet, one of the dozens of which seem to be cropping up everywhere in this city.

I pulled into the lot and parked the car in a far corner. The front that came in Saturday night was still hanging around, so the temperature was only in the upper-80s, without the sweltering humidity that made you feel like you could whip out a knife and cut yourself a slice of air.

I walked across the parking lot and through the double front doors, into the funeral home lobby.

An eclectic crowd milled about. There were the traditional men in black suits, women in subdued, somber dresses. But there were younger kids wearing jeans and pullover shirts, T-shirts, and denim work shirts as well. There was a middle-aged man who had to be 6'5" or better in jeans and cowboy boots, with a denim jacket over a black silk shirt, with a long grey ponytail down the middle of his back.

I eased around the edge of the crowd to where a black sign with plug-in white letters read "Mr. Walsh" with an arrow to the left.

The crowd thickened as I went down the hall. If these folks were all here for Leo, he pulled a good crowd. I think this probably would have surprised him. There was a line of people waiting to get into the viewing room. I joined it, just wanting to silently observe for awhile.

I only caught snatches of conversation—a word here and there—as people went by. A strange mix of shock and curiosity seemed to be the common denominator in most people's thoughts.

The line crawled slowly along for twenty minutes until I got to the guest book that was parked on a podium next to the door. When I got within arm's reach, I picked up the gold pen out of its holder and signed my name, then scanned down the list of names.

Didn't recognize any of them.

I flipped back a few pages, then turned to the first page. There

I saw some names I recognized: Ursula Gilbért, avec *L'accent aigu* over the *e*, followed by Raisa Petrov, then Jack McEwen.

All names I remembered off the Nashville Academy of Cinema Arts website.

A couple of minutes later, I passed through the doorway into the packed viewing parlor. Clumps of people jammed in next to each other at various spots throughout. There was a group of obvious NACA students gathered in the corner farthest from the front of the room and away from the door. In the middle of the room, groups of people milled around producing a mindless drone of murmuring.

At the front of the room, surrounded by funeral sprays—one of which was about an eight-foot-tall old-fashioned movie camera on a tripod done in white and red carnations—a massive, bronze closed casket sat on a stand, surrounded by mourners. A single framed picture of Leo Walsh stood on display in the center of the casket.

I stayed in the receiving line to pay my respects, but also to meet the woman whom I thought was Leo's third wife, Aileen. He hadn't mentioned her name during our conversation, but it was in the obit, along with his single remaining survivor, his sister Madeline. As I got closer, step-by-slow step, to the front of the room, the two women came into view.

Leo Walsh's wife was a thin woman, maybe 5'5" and a hundred pounds, attractive with a thick head of jet black hair and large brown eyes. She looked like she spent a lot of time either in the sun or had a membership in a tanning salon.

Next to her, a stern, gray-haired woman who looked like she hadn't smiled since the last century stood grimly shaking hands and nodding at small talk.

As I got closer to the casket, I got a better view of the framed picture on top of the casket. The photo was taken a good twenty years ago, at least, and the longer I stared at it, the more I began to think it was the author photo from one of Leo's books.

Better to remember him that way, I supposed.

Then I got to the head of the line. The older woman with the gray hair pulled back in a tight bun took my hand. Her hand felt cold and dry.

"Thank you for coming," she said. "I'm Madeline Walsh, Leo's sister."

We shook hands for the mandatory two pumps, then disengaged. "Ms. Walsh, I'm so sorry for your loss. My name's Harry Denton. I was a fan of your brother and I met him a couple of times, just casually. Many years ago, I went to his first book signing. He was a great writer and such a nice man."

"Thank you," she said stiffly. "We very much appreciate you coming by."

She glanced to my right, to the next person in line. I took that as a cue and took two steps past her.

Aileen Walsh was even prettier as I stood there in front of her. She offered her hand and I took it. Her hand was warm and felt like real human flesh.

"You must be Mrs. Walsh," I said. "I'm Harry Denton."

"Thank you so much for coming, Mr. Denton." Her voice was slight, a bit shaky. Her eyes were bloodshot, the kind of bloodshot that comes from crying and lack of sleep.

"I'm so sorry for your loss. I was a huge fan of your husband's, and while I only had the opportunity to have one real conversation with him, I felt on some level like I knew him."

She smiled. "If you had a real conversation with him," she

said, "you were lucky. He was a man of few words when they weren't on a page."

I smiled back. "But he knew how to put them on a page, didn't he?"

She nodded and for a second, her eyes started to fill. "Yes," she said so low I could barely hear her. "He could do that."

Her grief seemed genuine, as if she were barely holding it together. I learned a long, long time ago that instincts can be wrong and one should never reach any conclusions based on a hunch, but I had a hard time imagining this woman beating her husband to death with her bare hands and then abandoning his body behind a dumpster.

I don't normally shoot from the hip like this, but I thought it was time to take a chance.

I leaned in to her. "Mrs. Walsh, I know this is a difficult time. And it's certainly not the place. But is there some way you and I could have a private conversation in the next day or so? I know you've got a lot going on and this is kind of an odd request, but I think you may want to hear what I have to say."

She studied me for a moment. "Who are you?" she asked.

I studied her for a moment as well, then decided to take the next leap. "I spoke with your husband a few days before his…"

I hesitated for a moment.

"Murder?" she said.

I nodded. "Yes, a few days before his murder. And I think you should know what we talked about. Is there a way we could get together?"

She hesitated again, but not for long this time. "Have you got a cell phone?"

I nodded.

"Then save this number," she said. She rattled off the 615 area code and a string of numbers.

"Got that?"

"Yes, I'll save it on my phone."

"Visitation's over at one," she said. "I'll be home by three. Call me later."

"Okay," I whispered. "Thank you."

She looked to her left, where the next person was waiting. We shook hands again and I walked away from her.

As I walked away, I typed her number into my mobile and stored her as a contact. On a table pushed against the wall adjacent to the casket, there was a display of Leo's books and more framed photographs of him, of him and his students, of Leo and Aileen, of Leo in London and Paris and Barcelona, of Leo when he was younger and happier and more successful and not dead.

Above the table, a high-definition monitor played a recording of Leo signing books before a huge throng of people in a bookstore I recognized as the old Davis-Kidd, back in the days before it went under. Then the display changed and it was a video of Leo teaching one of his classes. He stood before the class, animated and full of energy and passion. The students all looked up, paying close attention, enthralled even.

The volume was turned down so low I could barely hear it. I stepped closer and leaned in, wondering if his voice sounded much different from the exhausted, worn voice that sat across from me in my conference room less than a week ago.

"Remember!" Leo said in the recording. "There are no new stories!" His arms flapped as he spoke. "Human beings have been telling each other stories since the beginning of time, when they were trying to keep each other awake to tend to the fire so the sabre-tooth tigers didn't come in and eat the babies!"

Then he held up his right index finger. "There are no new stories, but there are new voices. Each one of you has a distinct, unique voice. All stories have been told, but all voices have not been heard. That's what you must find and that is what you must run with!"

I suddenly felt weighted down. What Leo didn't tell his students was that you could find your voice and then lose it.

He would know.

I turned away from the monitor, not wanting to see or hear any more. In the center of the room was a long sofa with two heavily upholstered wing chairs on either side, all occupied by people focused on the center of the sofa. Ursula Gilbert held court in the center of the couch, her long salt-and-pepper hair perched on top of her head in an elaborately swirled French bun.

She wore a cashmere sweater despite it being July in Nashville, and a long black pencil skirt that ended mid-calf. Her hip European eyeglasses were a fashion statement in blazing cranberry. Her legs were crossed, revealing a pair of black leather riding boots with about a two-inch heel. Her arms were crossed in front of her and she leaned forward.

"I simply do not know what we are going to do without him," she said, her French accent heavy, pronounced, to the six people surrounding her. To Ursula's right, almost in her shadow, sat the diminutive Raisa Petrov, nodding in time to Ursula's soliloquy.

"He was ze 'eart and soul of ze program," she continued. "We will never find another like him!"

The tall guy with the long gray ponytail sat in one of the wing chairs on the left side of the sofa. He stared at Ursula, nodding in agreement. The others sat around her, sycophantizing in some kind of obsequious Greek chorus.

I suddenly felt almost sick at my stomach. Maybe it was time to get out of there.

Chapter Sixteen

Years ago, before Alex was born and things went south between me and her mother, long before Lonnie dreamed up the idea of starting a computer security company that made us all stinking rich, I took on a really minor case. There was an old guy who ran a junkyard out in Mount Juliet and he had five or six guys who worked for him on a regular basis. Out of nowhere, cash started disappearing, expensive wrecked cars were suddenly missing parts that could have been sold for a nice chunk of salvage change, and this guy just figured something wasn't right.

So he hired me to find out what was going on. I became an undercover junkyard employee, which I guess was even worse than being an undercover maintenance man in a brothel in Reno, Nevada. There was no murder involved in this case, though, so it wasn't anywhere near as memorable. Just a couple of IQ-challenged rednecks, a condition we refer to down south as *ignernt.*

It took me about three days to find out who the culprits were and how they were scamming the junkyard owner. The owner fired these two dumbasses and decided not to press charges. I later heard he sent a couple of his boys over to beat the dog shit out of them, but by then I'd long moved on.

Anyway, it was a few hundred bucks at a time when that made a big difference in my lifestyle. The only other memorable thing about it was that these boys who worked at the junkyard ate at the same restaurant every day, a run-down little place on a side street just off Lebanon Road on the other side of Mt. Juliet called Molly's.

Molly's was a classic, old-school Southern meat 'n three. For the uninitiated, a meat 'n three is where you get one meat entrée and three side dishes (usually with a *co-cola* to drink or iced tea as sweet and thick as pancake syrup). A lot of people think it means a meat and three vegetables, but that's a misnomer unless you think of macaroni and cheese as a vegetable. And it's hard to consider okra still a vegetable after it's been breaded, salted, and deep-fat fried in bacon grease, which is how Molly cooked it.

And it's a pretty good bet that part of the breading was cigarette ash that fell off one of the thirty or forty Marlboros that Molly smoked every day. In the four days in a row that I had lunch at her restaurant, I never once saw her when she didn't have a butt hanging out the side of her mouth.

With all that, the single most memorable thing about Molly's meat 'n three was that she made the best country fried steak I've ever had in my life. So when I walked out of Leo Walsh's visitation back into the hot July sun, I decided to turn right and head out of town. Thirty minutes or so later, I pulled off Lebanon Road onto a side street and parked in the gravel lot next to a battered Chevy Silverado with a Confederate flag decal in the back window.

Turns out Molly passed on a few years earlier, the five-year survival rate for small cell carcinoma of the lung being precisely *zero*, but her son and daughter-in-law were carrying on her culinary legacy. While I waited for my country fried steak, white beans, fried okra, candied yams and hot water cornbread, I texted Aileen Walsh because I forgot to ask her where we were supposed to meet.

Less than ten minutes later, she texted back: If you're okay coming to the apartment, meet me at 2375 Lincoya Bay Drive, Apartment 3-A. I'll text you when I get there.

That worked for me, so I texted her back just as Molly's daughter-in-law—whose name tag read "Earlene"—set two plates down. I thanked her and dug in. Whoever was running the kitchen now had taken Molly's lessons well.

Thirty minutes later, I needed a nap.

I GPS'd Aileen Walsh's address, which was an apartment complex off Stewart's Ferry Pike, about two minutes past the Bell Road cutoff to Percy Priest Dam. I had to laugh; twenty-five years or so ago, my long professional and personal relationship with Lonnie Smith began when we repo'd a car together from that very same apartment complex. I knew exactly where it was.

I had some time to kill. It wasn't worth going back to the office or heading back to East Nashville, just to turn around and fight the traffic back out here. So I made my way over to I-40, back to Stewart's Ferry Pike, and drove past the Lincoya Bay complex all the way to Hamilton Creek.

Hamilton Creek was one of the inlets off of Percy Priest Lake. Decades ago, the city had built a sailboat marina there. No powerboats allowed… And you can't put thirty or forty sailboats in one place without somebody calling it a yacht club, which in this case became the Percy Priest Yacht Club.

On a lark a few years ago, I drove out here to watch their annual summer sailboat races and regatta. Sometimes I thought of buying a sailboat, but for many years that was an unaffordable luxury, even though you could pick up a pretty decent used boat for about five grand. Now that I can afford it, there's not enough time and I have too many toys anyway.

So I took a drive down memory lane and parked in the lot next to the clubhouse. The rustic wooden building was built into the side of a hill overlooking the marina. The marina manager was the only one in the building. He nodded as I walked by, crossed the lobby, and walked out on the back deck. I stood on the cedar plank deck for a while in the hot July sun, the wind gently bouncing rigging off of aluminum masts like bells ringing. It was a calm, serene, summer day.

Maybe I need to rethink this. Wonder if Alex would like to take sailing lessons.

Suddenly, I felt very alone again.

❧

I only had about twenty minutes to stare out over the lake when my mobile buzzed with an incoming text. Aileen Walsh was back at her apartment and I could come on over any time that was convenient. I texted her back that I was on my way.

Ten minutes later, I pulled up to a row of grey apartment buildings that made up the Lincoya Bay complex. Between the buildings, I could see the lake less than a half-mile away. I took a guess that the rent included a premium for such a wonderful view.

I parked in front of Leo's building—only I guess it wasn't Leo's anymore—and climbed three flights of open-air stairs to the third floor. The building was actually similar in design to an interstate highway motel, like a Red Roof Inn or a Motel 6, with poured concrete floors and the wrought-iron stairs with rust spots blossoming through the faded black paint.

I stopped in front of the door labeled 3-A and knocked. A moment later, the door cracked open a foot and Aileen Walsh stood there in a pair of jeans, sandals, and a white blouse. She stared at me a moment, then pulled the door all the way open.

"Please, Mr. Denton, come in."

I stepped into the living room and looked around. It was a typical apartment complex apartment, with a living room on one side and the kitchen/dining area on the other. Between the two, a hallway ran down toward a series of closed doors.

The place was simply furnished, with a sofa and recliner, a flat-screen TV on a media center against the wall closest to the door. Generic brown carpet, cheap to replace and easy to reinstall after every tenant, covered the floor. There was a sliding glass door that opened onto a tiny concrete and wrought-iron balcony and I could see through the closed sheers the faint blue of the lake.

"Thanks, Mrs. Walsh," I said. "I appreciate your seeing me, especially during this terrible time."

"Please," she said, closing the door. "Call me Aileen."

I turned, gave a little smile. "Only if you call me Harry."

She walked past me over to the kitchen area. "Something to drink?" she asked. "It's awfully hot out there."

"I'm fine," I answered. "Had a late lunch."

"Oh, okay," she said. She reversed course and came back into the living room. "Have a seat," she instructed, pointing to the couch. I sat at the end of the couch near the hallway; she sat at the other end as far away as she could get.

I sat there for a second, a combination of gathering my thoughts and trying to get a read on her. My first instincts were holding, that she didn't seem like the beat-you-to-death type. What I didn't know was if she was the type to pay someone else to beat you to death.

"As I said at the funeral home," I began, "Leo came to see me last week."

She leaned back, settling herself against the arm of the couch. "And why would Leo come to see you?"

"I own a consulting firm," I said. "We specialize in a niche area of computer security. We work with high-end corporate clients, S&P 500 companies and the like. But before I went into that line of work, I was involved in much lower level security work."

She looked at me, her brow knitting in confusion. "So why—"

"I used to be a private detective," I said, interrupting her.

She let that sit for a few moments. "And my husband came to see you?"

I nodded. "He stopped by my office Monday afternoon."

"So let me get this straight," she said. "You used to be a private detective, only you're not anymore. You don't advertise, you're not looking for clients. So how did he even find you?"

"I'm not sure I know the answer to that, but I have kept my license current over the years, as well as my memberships in the state professional associations. So all he had to do was scrub down into a few websites."

She eyed me suspiciously. "But why you?"

"The only reason I can come up with is that twenty or twenty-five years ago, I was involved in a couple of very high profile cases that got in the news just about the time your husband was breaking out as a writer. Maybe Leo remembered my name or one of those cases. Beyond that, I simply don't know."

"What did my husband want from you, Harry?"

I took a breath and let it out.

"Leo told me he knew he was going to be killed," I said. "He wanted to hire me to investigate his own murder."

Okay, you can Google image the word *stunned* right now and

there would be Aileen Walsh's picture.

Her jaw moved for a few seconds but nothing came out. Her eyes unfocused and she seemed to be staring at something way off in the distance.

"My god," she whispered. "He knew..."

"Aileen," I said after a moment, "do you know anyone would want to do this to your husband? Is there anyone who would want to hurt Leo like this?"

She stood up from the couch, turned away from me, and stepped over to the sliding glass door. She pulled the curtains aside and stared out at the lake.

"Thank you for not assuming I did it," she said quietly. "You gave me more benefit of the doubt than the police did."

I sat on the couch, not moving. "Were they hard on you?"

She turned and crossed her arms. "Not really," she answered. "But whenever a person's killed, the spouse automatically becomes the prime suspect. A lot of the time, it's a good bet..."

I nodded. "Not this time, though. Right?"

She shook her head. "I didn't kill my husband, Harry. We had our problems, yes, and Leo was hard to live with. He was depressed and drank too much, and the last couple of decades he'd just had one disappointment after the other. But he was a good man on the inside and I loved him. Despite what everyone thought..."

That caught my attention. "And what did everyone think?"

She let a couple of beats go by before answering. "Leo's twenty-two years older than me," she said. "Everyone thought I married him because he was some kinda famous writer and had a lot of money, all that shit. A younger woman out to snag herself a little rich and famous."

She uncrossed her arms and raised them to the sides of her head and rubbed her temples.

"And, of course," she continued, "everybody assumed they knew why he married me. Old guy trying to get one last run at some fresh young pussy."

I cringed. I never got used to batting the *p-word* around so casually among guys, let alone hearing it tossed out by somebody who had one.

"Although God knows I'm not that young anymore."

"Tell me what happened the night he was killed."

"There's nothing to tell," she said. "It was a normal day. He had a six o'clock screenwriting class that went until nine. After that, there was paperwork. Scripts to grade, attendance to enter into the computer. On Thursday, that was his only class so he didn't go in until right before dinner, which meant there were always emails to answer, emails to write, just stuff to take care of. By the time he finished up, it was often ten or even a little after. I was always nervous about him being in that part of town so late at night, but he'd been doing it for several years and he said it was safe."

"So what time did he usually get home?" I asked.

"I didn't like it," she answered. "But I got used to it. I'd learned not to look for him before 10:30."

"And last Thursday?"

She moved over and sat back down on the couch. "By eleven, I was starting to get nervous. I called his cell and it went to voicemail. I called the school but no one answers the phones after nine. So I left him a note in case he got home, then got in my car and drove over there. His car was in the lot, but there was no sign of him. The building front door was locked. I went around the side to the equipment room doors and they were locked."

"Weren't you a little nervous being there by yourself? That's not exactly the greatest part of town."

"I was terrified," she admitted. "But I'm also no fool. I have a carry permit and I keep Little Miss Ruger with me at all times."

She reached around and patted the end table on her side of the couch. "In fact, she's right here."

She started to open the drawer.

"That's okay. I believe you."

She smiled and pulled her arm back.

"What next? What next when you couldn't find him?'

The smile went away. "I knew there was something wrong. I started to drive up Murfreesboro Road to the police station, but they won't do anything until somebody's missing for a while. So I drove around the block, thinking maybe something had happened and he'd be out walking around. But no sign of him."

She seemed to drift off again, maybe still in some kind of shock.

"I drove around for nearly an hour. Finally, I headed home. There was no one to call, no one to help me. I figured I'd wait until the school opened and get right over there. Maybe he fell asleep in his office. Maybe he tripped and hit his head. So I lay awake the rest of the night. Around 7:30, I got dressed and was walking out the door and ran right into the police officer and chaplain who were bringing me the news."

"Jesus, Aileen, I'm so sorry," I said. I sat there silently, thinking for a second. "Can you tell me how you came to be married?"

She leaned back and rested her head on the back of the couch. "Leo and I met when he moved in across the hallway. My boyfriend and I had a, let's just say, *volatile* relationship. One night a couple months after Leo moved in, the boyfriend and I got into it big time. Lots of yelling and screaming and then he flew out of here like his hair was on fire. Leo knocked on my door later, just to see if I was okay. I was a mess, sobbing, hysterical."

She sat back up, then nervously got to her feet again, walked over to the sliding glass door and leaned against it with her left shoulder. "I was vulnerable. He could have pretended to give a shit and taken advantage of me. I was ripe for the taking. But he didn't. He talked to me for awhile, gave me his number if I needed anything, told me to dump the boyfriend with the bad temper, that I was a nice girl and deserved better."

She laughed. "Yeah, *nice girl*... Hadn't been called that in awhile."

"So you started hanging out," I said.

She nodded. "We'd have a glass of wine on the balcony, watch the boats go by on the lake. Leo was a novelist, a screenwriter, published in twenty languages, a university visiting writer, a film school professor. And you know what he liked to do most?"

I shook my head.

"He liked to grab a pole and walk down to the lake and throw a line in Percy Priest and catch dinner. After we married and moved in together, sometimes we'd do that three or four nights a week in the spring and summer. Whenever it wasn't too hot. Take a bottle of wine down to the lake. Fish off the shore, bring home a bass or a mess of crappie. Leo'd clean 'em and we'd fry 'em up."

I smiled. "Sounds like fun."

"It was great. We just became friends and hung out and then, I guess..." She looked like she was trying to hold something in. "And then, I guess, we fell in love."

Her voice trailed off.

She leaned forward, her shoulders slumping, and looked down at the rug. She stared quietly for a few moments.

"We eloped one night, drove across the state line just outside of Huntsville. It's not like either of us had a bunch of friends and family for a big wedding. We were basically alone."

She was real still for a moment, like somebody looking way off into the distance. "I like to think I made him happy," she said real low. "At least for a little while."

I could see her eyes glistening. "I'm sure you did," I said.

She cleared her throat, then stood back up straight, squared her shoulders and looked me directly in the eye.

"You know, he was writing again," she said.

"Really? What was he working on?"

"He started a novel about ten months ago, right after we got married. He hadn't written anything in years. The awful, conflicted, expensive divorces, the rejections, having to take a series of crappy teaching jobs just to get by. It took a toll. But something happened a few weeks after we got married and moved in together. He started this book. And then six months ago, he started working on a screenplay."

"A screenplay?" I asked. "Really…"

She nodded. "Yeah, I think he was working on it with one of the other teachers over at NACA. He was kind of closed-mouth about it."

She stopped talking for a moment, looked away as if pondering something, then turned back to me.

"Want to see his office?"

I nodded. "Sure. You mean, here? He worked at home?"

She crossed the living room as I stood up. "When we got

married and he moved across the hall into this apartment, that obviously cut our living expenses in half. But we still couldn't afford for him to have a separate office. I used the second bedroom as a storeroom and I did some craft stuff in there occasionally. It was pretty easy to clear it all out for him."

I followed her down the hallway and she opened the first door on the right. She reached over and flicked the light switch.

Leo Walsh's office was about what you would expect from someone who spent his life generating and processing paper. A massive wooden desk was stacked high with books and three-ring binders, stacks of manuscript paper, trinkets, and clutter everywhere. There was a layer of dust on everything and the acrid smell of way too many smoked cigarettes. I'd noticed the smell a little bit in the living room, but it was overpowering here. An ancient computer monitor that was as big as a portable television dominated the center of the desk, with a keyboard shoehorned onto a shelf below it, and a huge, bulky printer off to the side. Leo Walsh was about a decade behind the high-tech curve.

Framed yellowing book covers filled what little space on the walls wasn't dominated by floor-to-ceiling cheap pressboard bookcases. Bankers boxes, hundreds of books and magazines, and what the hoarder thinks of as valued mementos—but what most people would just call *junk*—filled the rest of the room.

Leo Walsh didn't know that when he got up Thursday morning, drank his coffee, read his email, and smoked his first cigarette of the day that this would be the last time he'd ever see this room. A wave of sadness washed over me. Life can be gone so suddenly and unexpectedly, and we leave such a mess behind for others to clean up.

"Wow," I said. "So this is what a real writer's office looks like."

She snaked her way in between the piles on the floor. "I don't know how I'm ever going to get this cleaned out," she said.

"I was just thinking something along the same line."

"At some point, I'll have to go over to his office at NACA and clean that out, too."

I walked over behind the desk, just looking everything over and trying to take it in.

"What was the novel about?" I asked.

"It was a story about a fallen ideologue, an aging, cynical man who's lost his ideals and his integrity and is trying to find himself again."

I looked up at her. "In other words, an autobiography."

She smiled and nodded. "Pretty much"

"What's it called?" I asked.

"*In Too Deep*."

"Wow," I said. "Great title for an autobiographical novel. Is it going to be published?"

"It's with an agent in New York right now," she answered. "Leo told me that when his career went down the dumper he couldn't even get an agent to return his calls. But that was so long ago. The agents he dealt with back then have either forgotten about him, retired, or passed on themselves. Anyway, he found this young woman agent who decided to take him on."

"I just want to ask you one last thing," I said. Aileen Walsh looked at me, a question on her face.

"Okay," she said.

"When Leo came to my office, he gave me a thumbnail history of his three marriages. He told me that he thought you married him because he was a famous author and when you found out he didn't have any money you were quite angry and distressed."

Her jaw tightened almost imperceptibly. "We had a fight one night," she said, her voice tense. "We'd been drinking, both of us, but he'd been hitting it especially hard. Sometimes I'd drink with him to just not be left behind. But it got especially ugly that night. He said all that, that I'd married him for fame and status and money, just like everyone else thought. That I was no different from the others… And I was fairly hammered by then myself, so I started yelling at him. *So what if I did? What's wrong with that? Everybody wants that, even you!*"

She turned away for a moment, gazing at the tower of Leo's own novels stacked on top of the filing cabinet.

"The next morning, we were both hungover, spent. I swore to him I didn't mean that, that I really loved him, and could he please forget I ever said that."

Then she turned around again and faced me.

"He said he would, but I don't think he ever completely let go of it. For a long time, things weren't the same. But I loved him and I would have done anything to prove it to him. Anything! Shouldn't that mean something? Wouldn't that mean something to you?"

I gazed at her a second.

"I don't know, Aileen. Nobody ever loved me that much."

Chapter Seventeen

By the time I got Alex up, caffeinated, and reasonably functional, we were already running at least a half-hour late. From East Nashville, it could easily take an hour to get across town if there were any problems at all. We were due at the Bealesworth School by 11 and it was already 10:20.

I cut over to Shelby Avenue, then toward town until we got to the freeway entrance ramp. I gunned the Tesla and we slipped into the space between two semis doing about seventy-five. I merged into the center lane, and when an opening showed up in the next lane, I grabbed it fast enough to cause Alex to grab the door handle to keep from sliding over.

"Sorry," I said. "Didn't mean to act like a NASCAR driver."

I glanced over at her. She had on black pants and a beige silk blouse, pearls, makeup, and a gold bracelet that belonged to Aunt Marty. I'm not normally one to offer fashion advice to anybody, which believe me, is a good thing. But I thought she looked about ten years older than her actual age, very sophisticated and on point.

"You're awfully quiet this morning," I said as we curved left over the river and out toward the west side of town. So far, the traffic was moving steadily and uninterrupted. With a little luck, we'd make our 11 AM.

She kept her eyes forward and didn't say anything.

I shifted into the right lane so the idiot coming up behind us in a black Escalade wouldn't wind up in the back seat.

"Alex, is there something wrong?" I asked as the guy blew by us doing at least ninety.

"I'm sorry, Daddy," she said after a moment. "I guess I'm kinda nervous. I didn't sleep much last night."

"Sweetie, you haven't slept much ever since you got here."

She turned to me. "Well, the last couple of weeks have been a lot to take in."

"I know that. I know how hard it's been on you. I just thought maybe the best thing to do is just take care of what we need to take care of, get you settled into this new life of yours as quickly as possible."

"I know that's your way," she said, suddenly sounding like a woman wise beyond her years. "But I'm not sure it's mine, at least not right now."

Neither of us spoke for a few moments. Ahead of us, the crazy concrete multi-layered ribbon that was the White Bridge Road interchange seemed jammed up and slowing down. I eased off the pedal and the Tesla slowed quickly. I barely had to tap the brakes to get us back in the flow.

"I'm sorry if I'm pushing you," I said. "We can ease off if you want to. Take our time…"

She turned to me. "Do we really have to do this today?"

"Well, I made the appointment," I answered. "And these folks have been really understanding from the get-go. Given the situation with your mother, they've already let a lot of things slide. We were supposed to visit the campus in April and I was supposed to make the deposit by mid-June. It's over a month past that."

Alex shifted back around and stared out the windshield.

"How about this?" I said. "No pressure. Let's just go check

the place out, meet a few people, get a tour. Get a feel for the place. If you don't like it, we'll put together a Plan B."

"And what happens if they don't like me?" she said.

I turned back to her. "Are you worried about that?"

A couple of hundred yards ahead of us, a yellow mini-van swerved to the right to change lanes, oblivious to the fact that another vehicle already occupied that particular space. There was the grinding crunch of metal impacting metal. The old Toyota that got hit by the van then juked to the right and scraped into a little tiny compact car, one of those little Fiat 500s that was punching way above its weight. The Fiat slammed on its brakes and did a 180, then spiraled off the road and down into a ditch just as we drove by in the far left-hand lane.

"Seriously," I said. "You're not worried about that, are you? You've got the grades. Your SSAT scores were, what, in the 98th percentile? You know you're in."

She looked down at her hands, which were crossed in her lap. "Maybe it's not that. What if it's just a bad fit?"

I reached over with my right hand and laid it on top of hers.

"Alex, I promise you. If this doesn't work for you, we'll find something else."

She squeezed my hand and smiled. "Thanks, Daddy."

We left I-40 West at McCrory Lane and started up the winding hill that felt more like the country than the outskirts of Nashville. I'd entered the location on the GPS before we left and now the moving map was tracing our progress as we made our way through the roller coaster ride.

In a few minutes, we were at the intersection of McCrory Lane and Highway 100, which was also the entrance to the

Natchez Trace Parkway, a 444-mile long, two-lane road that followed the old Natchez Trace all the way from Nashville to, not surprisingly, Natchez, Mississippi. The wonderful thing about it was that there were no traffic lights, few side roads, and the speed limit was 50 miles an hour. I once drove about 150 miles on it one weekend on the Ural and it was the single best ride I'd ever had in my life.

I turned left, away from the Parkway, and drove down not quite a half-mile past the Loveless Cafe, and turned right into the grand brick and iron gates of the Bealesworth School.

The Bealesworth School looked more like an old New England Ivy League college than a private high school in Tennessee. There was a long winding drive that led to the main administration building on the far side of a great expanse of lawn, with a majestic four-story library dominating the right side of the quadrangle. The grass was immaculately manicured, the landscaping perfect. On the left side of the quadrangle was the science building and, next to it, the music building. I knew from searching the website that the theater building, the math building, the IT and computer complex, the athletic center, and the student services center with its immense formal dining hall were all beyond this first ring of buildings. On the outermost ring, on the right side, were the three dormitories, a chapel, and the infirmary. Somewhere toward the back of campus was the soccer field, the track, and fields for lacrosse, field hockey, and, I imagined, anything else they could come up with.

The Bealesworth School was all-girls, with 450 of the brightest, most promising young women in residence, most of whom boarded. The school bragged that it had a 100 percent college placement rate and had for an unbroken chain of years stretching back to the early seventies. The underachievers went to state schools and the smaller, private liberal arts colleges. The best hit the majors: Harvard, Yale, Stanford, MIT, Columbia, Vanderbilt, Tulane, Duke, on and on and on.

And this ticket to the big time only cost $46,000 a year.

For high school.

Unpack that if you can—forty-six grand a year for high school.

I say again: *shit's changed.*

I parked the car in front of Hampton Hall, the main administrative building, and Alex and I climbed the massive stone staircase to the front entrance. We were met by a blast of icy air as we entered and approached the reception desk.

"Harry and Alexis Denton," I said to the woman. "We have an eleven o'clock with Admissions. Ms. McGowan, I believe." The clock on the wall read 10:58.

Not bad, I thought. *We made it.*

The receptionist picked up the phone and punched four numbers. "Elsie, your eleven is here."

A moment later, she hung up and pointed behind her. "Down that hall to the third door on your left."

We walked down the cavernous hallway, our footsteps echoing off the marble floor, and went through a door marked "Admissions." There was a reception area with a couple of young women behind desks, and offices off to the right and left.

"Mr. Denton?" the young woman closest to us asked. She stood up and approached us. She was tall, thin, with thick black hair and prominent cheekbones. She wore tight skinny jeans and a pullover shirt that looked expensive. The pair of espadrilles added another couple of inches to her already impressive height.

"I'm Bitsy Wray," she said in one of those patrician Southern accents you often encounter in Belle Meade. She extended her hand.

I took it. "Hello, Ms. Wray, I'm glad to meet you. This is my daughter, Alexis."

Bitsy let go of my hand and reached for Alex's. Alex smiled shyly. "Glad to meet you," she said.

"Elsie's been waiting to meet you," she said, shaking Alex's hand. She turned and pointed to the other young woman. "That's Cricket Mortenson over there. Say hello, Cricket!"

The other young woman looked up from her laptop and waved. "Hello, Cricket."

Bitsy smiled again. "Cricket's a rising senior, figures that gives her a license to be a smart-aleck. C'mon, let's go meet Elsie."

She walked over to the far corner office, with Alex and me in tow. She knocked on the white wooden door with the brass nameplate on it and opened it. "Elsie, the Dentons are here."

"Send them in," a loud British voice announced. Bitsy held the door for us. We walked in to find a tall, slightly matronly red-haired woman who bore a creepy resemblance to Margaret Thatcher standing up for us.

"Thank you, Bitsy," she announced, her English accent even thicker now that we were actually in her presence. She extended her hand. "I'm Elspeth McGowan, the Director of Admissions here at Bealesworth."

Alex took her hand first. "Pleased to meet you, Ms. McGowan."

"Oh, we go by first names around here, Alexis," she said. "Most of these women have never heard the name 'Elspeth,' so I'm mostly just Elsie."

We completed the formalities and then all took seats.

"First of all, Alexis," Elsie McGowan announced, "I want to extend my most sincere condolences on the loss of your mother. I know how difficult this must be for you and how much an adjustment moving here from out West must be. Please know that we want to do everything we can to welcome you to Bealesworth and to make your time here as valuable to you as possible. For nearly fifty years now, this institution has been sending young women out into the world who are strong, independent, educated, and ready to take on the world."

"Thank you," Alex said quietly. "I appreciate that."

And then the conversation began. It wasn't actually an interview. There were no probing inquiries, no trick questions designed to trip her up. They'd seen Alex's test scores, her recommendations, her transcripts, and most importantly, her admissions essay, which was all the more amazing because Marsha and I had both vetted it. When Marsha's cancer came back after her first round of chemotherapy and she knew, as a doctor, that she had only a few months left, she came to me with a plan. Alex would come live with me and she would go to an all-girls private preparatory school. There were only a couple in this area and Bealesworth got the nod.

Our talk went on for twenty minutes, then Elspeth McGowan announced that Alex was going on a tour.

"Your father and I have some last-minute paperwork to complete," she said, "so Bitsy and Cricket are going to give you the tour. Now, it is July out there and already hitting ninety degrees, so they aren't going to take you on the ninety-minute death march. But you'll see the main academic buildings, the labs, a quick tour of one of the dorms—even though you are going to be a day student—and then the student center and the athletic complex. That work for you?"

Alex nodded. "Sure. I'd like to see it."

"Bitsy, Cricket!" she called. Bitsy came to the door. "You can start the tour with Alexis now."

Bitsy looked at Alex and grinned. "Let's do it."

"Don't forget," Elsie instructed, "we have a 12:15 with Dr. Livingston. Have her back by five after."

Alex followed Bitsy out and the three of them took off for the grand tour. Elsie McGowan watched them leave, then turned to me.

"She seems like a very bright young girl," she said. "But terribly sad."

I nodded. "That's a fair assessment. She's been through a lot. I'm trying to take as good care of her as I can, but truth is she's never actually lived with me."

"I rather imagine it's quite an adjustment."

I nodded again and there was an almost awkward moment of silence; then Elsie McGowan sat back down and extracted a thick file folder from a stack on her desk.

"Now," she said. "We have some paperwork to take care of…"

~

Forty minutes later, Alex returned with her two tour guides. She was smiling, while Bitsy and Cricket were positively giggling. I took that as a sign the tour went well. It was lunchtime in July, though, and they'd walked a good portion of the campus, so all three girls looked like they'd worked up a bit of a sweat.

Then I remembered what my mother told me many years ago: nice girls don't sweat, they *glisten*.

Elsie McGowan and I were in the reception area when they came in.

"So it went well?" I asked.

Alex smiled. "Yes."

We walked down the hall to the main offices.

"So Dr. Livingston is the… what?" I asked. "Headmistress?"

Elsie McGowan turned and smiled at me as we walked. "That was a term we did away with in the last century. Headmaster, headmistress, it all sounds so patrician and 18th-century English. We're trying to move away from that."

"Okay," I said.

We came to the a frosted glass door with the words DR. LUCILLE LIVINGSTON, HEAD OF SCHOOL painted across the glass.

"Head of school," I said to Alex. "Make a note."

We entered an even larger office than the one we'd just left. There were two large desks in the reception area, a lot of fresh flowers, some lovely art on the wall, and a row of framed portraits of previous Heads of School, or whatever they were called then.

Elsie led us in to Dr. Livingston's office. Lucille Livingston was patrician and full of aristocratic Southern grace. She welcomed us warmly and seemed genuinely glad to meet Alex. We sat in her office and it was clear that all this was just small-talk informality. My daughter would be welcomed into the Bealesworth community with open arms.

We stayed about fifteen minutes and that was it. I'd written a check for the first semester's tuition and left it with Elsie McGowan. All the paperwork was complete, with the exception of some health and vaccination forms that had to be filed before school started. Alex would be a day student, which meant I was doing daddy taxicab duty for the foreseeable future. Alex turned sixteen in a month-and-a-half. I'd get her enrolled in driver's ed and then when that got squared away, we'd get her a first car, something safe and economical but still cool enough that she wouldn't be ashamed to park in the Bealesworth student lot.

It had been a crazy time, I thought as we walked out of Hampton Hall into the steaming July sun and toward the car, but we're about to get it all together. I felt pretty good right now; in fact, I was rather impressed with myself.

I held the door for Alex, then crossed around and got in on the driver's side. I booted the car up, backed out of the spot, and as we pulled away, I looked over at Alex.

"So how are you, Sweetie?" I asked. "What do you think about all this?"

She sat there, looking straight ahead through the windshield, stone-faced for a few moments. Then her lip began to tremble.

And then her shoulders began to shake…

We were still on the long driveway through campus, so I pulled over to the curb and stopped.

"Alex, are you okay?"

Suddenly, she burst into tears and bent over at the waist, pulling against the seatbelt. She buried her head in her hands and sobbed uncontrollably, her whole body shaking in the car seat.

"Alex, honey, what's wrong?" I asked. I put my hand on her left shoulder.

"Oh, daddy," she sobbed, almost choking. "I hate it. I just hate it."

Chapter Eighteen

I pulled into a Dairy Queen down the street from Bealesworth, hoping that something cold, sweet, and slathered in hot fudge might help. The worst of the storm had passed by pretty quickly. My daughter was not the kind of person to lose her composure for long. We drove in silence for the ninety seconds it took us to get to the DQ. She blew her nose and dried her eyes, and by the time we got the car stopped she was over the worst of it.

We realized when we got inside that we were actually hungry, so we ordered burgers and fries. We took a booth while we waited for our number to be called.

"Okay," I said. "Talk to me. What's going on?"

She leaned back against the side of the booth and hitched her legs under her on the seat. "Daddy, it's just not me. I don't care a thing about homecoming or cotillions. I'm never going to be a debutante and I'm never going to join a sorority."

"Sororities? They have sororities?"

"Yeah," she said, shaking her head. "It's high school, for God's sake. Who has sororities in high school?"

Her voice tightened and went up a notch. "And for that matter," she demanded. "Who the hell names their daughter *Cricket*? What, is her sister named *Cockroach*? Oh, and her brother, *Centipede*, is a tailback on the football team!"

I had to laugh.

"And how do you go through life with a name like *Bitsy*? I mean, it's cute when you're sixteen, but what happens if she decides to go to law school? I can see her in court twenty years from now, when the Judge announces *And as counsel for the plaintiff, we have… ugh, Bitsy*."

I was trying hard not to laugh any harder than I already was. Over the loudspeaker, our number was called. I got up, grabbed the tray, straws, napkins, ketchup packets, and sat back down.

"And Daddy," Alex asked, unwrapping her burger, "what is MBA? All they talked about was so-and-so from MBA and did you know *Libby* was dating *Chad* from MBA and Cricket thinks they actually *did it* in the back of Chad's Beemer."

I looked down, grinning, almost embarrassed. "MBA," I said, "Montgomery Bell Academy. The most exclusive all-boys private preparatory school in Nashville. They've churned out generations of gentlemen-scholar-athletes."

"Yeah," Alex said, mumbling through a mouth full of burger, "gentlemen-scholar-athletes who'll do ya' in the back of a Beemer."

"Hey, I almost went there," I said. "Your grandfather wanted me to, but I didn't get in. Seems I was a bit deficient in the 'athlete' department."

"It was their loss," she offered.

"Hey, you know that movie *Dead Poets Society*?"

"What?" she asked. "The Robin Williams film?"

"Yeah, it was written by a guy who went to MBA and was based on a teacher he had there."

"Groovy," she said, ripping open a ketchup packet with her teeth and squirting it all over her fries.

We finished eating and ordered sundaes. We were mostly quiet for a few minutes. Alex seemed way off, somewhere else.

"Sweetie," I finally said, "what are we going to do about this?

You've got to go to school somewhere. There's only one other private girls school in Nashville, and while it may be a bit less Southern and a little more progressive than Bealesworth, I'm not sure that's going to work for you either."

Alex looked up from her sundae. "I'm sorry," she said. "I don't mean to be so much trouble. I don't know what to do."

"No need to be sorry," I said. "If it's not the right place for you, it's not the right place. I don't want you to be miserable. You've had enough of that."

"What about just going to public school?"

I pursed my lips. "Okay, there's no way I'm gonna come out looking good after saying this, but I don't care. I don't mean to sound like an elitist, but the truth is the Metro Nashville public schools are pretty rough. I'm not sure I'm comfortable sending you to one."

She smiled. "Oh, that's not elitist," she said. "Racist as hell, but not elitist."

"Hey, c'mon," I countered. "Cut your old man a little slack here. I'm only interested in what's best for you."

She looked at me a moment, then reached over and patted my hand. "I know."

I squeezed her hand back. "Maybe we should just sit on this one for a while," I said. "We've probably got a couple of weeks before we pass the window for a tuition refund."

"If that's okay," Alex said.

I smiled at her. "Done deal. So what are you up for the rest of the day? I've got a few things to take care of at the office. You can park there for a while, but I may have to run out. I guess I can drop you off at the house. I'll have to get used to that, I suppose. You're too old for a babysitter."

"You know what I'd really like to do?"

"What?"

Alex smiled and leaned toward me. "What I'd really like to do is hang with Aunt Sheba for awhile. You think that'd be okay?"

That was the first genuine smile I'd seen her have all day. "You've got her number," I said. "Give her a call."

⁂

Sheba was waiting for us in the lobby when I dropped Alex off at The Travertine. I pulled into the cutoff and a uniformed doorman opened her door. She gave me a hug and darted off. She and Sheba were headed to the mall and I would pick her up around dinnertime. With a little luck, we'd get an invitation.

It was just past two when I got to the office. Ashley was at her desk, with Hugh standing behind her, They were huddled together, laughing and staring at her monitor.

"Hey, guys," I called. Hugh stood up quickly.

"Hey, Harry," he said. "How are you? Haven't seen you in awhile."

"Yeah," I answered, walking past them and into my office. "Been in and out. Got a lot going on."

I dropped my backpack and went back out into the reception area.

"How'd it go at Bealesworth?" Ashley asked.

"Let's just say not like I expected." I picked up a stack of mail on the edge of the counter. "How are things around here? Everything reasonably stable?"

"Everything's fine," Ashley said.

"We're chugging along," Hugh added. "We're going to have a beta demo for you to see by Friday, I hope. In fact, I need to get back to it."

"Great," I said, thumbing through the envelopes. Nothing of any importance...

I turned to go back into my office. Ashley grabbed a printout and followed me in.

"Okay, I got the intel you wanted."

I sat down at my desk. When I looked up, she was standing there right in front of me. She wore a pair of tight jeans and a men's Oxford cloth, button-down collar shirt. Her hair was pulled back in a ponytail. None of it was very business-like, but we're pretty casual around here. I stared at her a moment, trying not to contemplate how simply pretty she was.

"The two ex-Mrs. Walshes, right?" she asked as she laid the papers facedown on my desk. I picked them up. "Walsh," she continued, "as in the guy who dropped in last week and then got murdered."

I scanned the first page, which was a Whitepages.com printout on Vivienne Walsh, wife number one. "Hmm, Burton Hills," I said. "Some toney real estate here."

"Yes, it is. And if you don't mind my asking, why would you be looking into the background of Leo Walsh's ex-wives?"

I scanned the next couple of pages, just to see if anything jumped off the page at me. I looked up and Ashley had her hands on her hips.

"What?"

"Harry," she said quietly. "We're used to you being a little distracted, but lately even when you're around here, you're not around here."

I set the papers down on my desk and leaned back in my chair. Every once in a while, I thought to myself, maybe I should remind these people who the boss is.

"I'm not trying to get in your face here, Harry, but frankly, I'm kinda worried about you."

"Why would you be worried about me?" I said, trying not to sound as annoyed as I was becoming.

"This has not been a great few months for you," Ashley said. "I get it, that you'd want to find anything to distract you from your problems. But this whole thing with Leo Walsh, you chatted with him ninety minutes and now it's like you're on a mission. You've got a business to run, Harry. We need you here. Alex needs you here."

I didn't say anything for a few seconds, trying to sort through this swell of frustration.

"Look, Ashley, I'm not going off the deep end on this. I'm just curious more than anything else, curious and a little guilty. The guy wanted my help and I blew him off. He knew this was going to happen and I didn't take him seriously. I'm partly responsible for this."

Ashley held out a hand, palm toward me. "Wait a minute, Harry, that's a little over the top. A stranger walks in and tells this crazy story. I thought the guy was off his rocker myself. No sane person would hold you responsible for this."

I glared at her a moment, then stood up. "So now I'm not sane."

"That's not what I meant," she said. "I just don't want you to lose yourself in this."

I jogged the papers into a neat stack and folded them into my palm.

"Maybe I'm trying to find myself," I said. "I'll be back in a couple of hours."

I walked past her and out of the office.

❧

I maneuvered out of the downtown area over to Music Row, then crossed Wedgewood at the Belmont University campus, and continued on to Hillsboro Road just past the Village. I turned left and went over I-440, which was still in its usual state of perpetual construction, then settled into the slow-moving herd of traffic moving toward Green Hills.

I always tried to avoid this part of town. After a few decades of life in Nashville, you eventually learn where the hopeless spots are. My radar failed me this time, though. I was thick in the weeds when it hit me that I could have taken I-65 south and gotten off at Harding Place.

So it took twice as long to get to Burton Hills, but that only gave me more time to think. Ashley had gotten under my skin, but I knew on some level she was right. I really didn't have any business trying to figure out who murdered Leo Walsh. I saw nothing that made me think the police were taking this any more seriously than a drug deal gone sour or a hookup gone bad. Even the news media had dropped the story. I hadn't seen a mention of it in three days.

Was I the only one taking this seriously?

"Don't flatter yourself," I said out loud. And then it hit me. The offhanded remark I'd made to Ashley before I left—that crack about finding myself—maybe had more truth in it than I was willing to face. I'd spent the last fifteen years trying to meet my responsibilities, to become successful at something—*anything*—so I didn't have to eat cat food in my old age and leave nothing to my daughter.

I'd been lucky and more successful than I ever dared imagine. Along the way, though, I'd lost something. That time over twenty years ago when my first and only wife dumped me, I lost a job and a career in the newspaper business and my fancy apartment and car and had to move basically into somebody's attic in East Nashville was, in retrospect, the happiest time of my life.

I'd lost everything and, as a result, life had more potential, more possibilities, than it ever had before. I'd spent my life trying to follow in the upper-middle class respectable footsteps of my father, who'd served his country in World War II, come home and gone into the insurance business, built his own successful company, retired to Hawaii, and been married to the same woman fifty-five years when he passed away from congestive heart failure.

And what was his son? A divorced, disgraced newspaper reporter who'd stooped to becoming a *private detective*—one of those smarmy, little greasy men who hung around outside cheap motel rooms with a camera, waiting to catch a cheating spouse.

And yet I'd never been happier, more excited, more glad to be alive.

Bob Dylan was right: *when you ain't got nothing, you got nothing to lose...*

I pushed these thoughts out of my head as I finally got through the massive jam at the Green Hills mall. This was an area that had once been great farms run by the descendants of Revolutionary War soldiers who'd been given massive land grants for their service during the war. One of them, William Compton—who had served under Andrew Jackson in New Orleans during the War of 1812—owned about a thousand acres that was passed down from one generation to the next and was eventually, almost a couple of centuries later, developed into a pricey, exclusive area called Burton Hills.

Burton Hills was where Vivienne Walsh migrated after burning Leo Walsh down in their own private War of 1812.

The development she lived in was called, pretentiously, Blackberry Manor. The homes there started in the 750k range and went up from there. The houses were all custom built, designed and constructed on tiny lots that were just a couple of feet shy of zero lot line. Blackberry Manor was a private development with its own tennis courts, community clubhouse, beautifully landscaped gardens, and three separate pools.

But at least, I thought as I turned off Hillsboro Road and entered the development, it wasn't a gated community. I didn't have to ring for permission to enter.

I kept an eye on the moving map on the dashboard screen as it instructed me to turn left, then right, then left again two blocks up, as I entered what felt like a maze. Most of the streets were cul-de-sacs, quiet streets with few pedestrians and literally nothing out of place. This was not a part of Nashville where you were going to see old beaters in the driveway or cheap lawn furniture, broken toys, or rusted-out gas grills in the front yard.

I turned right into a short street that went up a hill called Blackberry Winter Court. Vivienne Walsh lived at 805, which came up on my right. The house was built into the side of a hill and had the steepest driveway I'd ever seen. I wondered how they got up it during the winter snows; then I remembered that since the global warming hit it rarely snows in Nashville.

I parked on the side of the street, then walked up the driveway like I was walking into a stiff wind. I got to the half-flight of the brick stairway leading up to the front door, stepped into an alcove, and pressed the doorbell.

A moment later, a light on a security camera above me and

to the left lit up red. A hidden speaker crackled and a voice came on.

"May I help you?" a woman's voice said.

I looked around, trying to figure out where the voice came from, then finally raised my head toward the camera.

"Ms. Walsh, my name is Harry Denton. I'm sorry to show up unannounced like this, but if I could have just a couple moments of your time, I'd really appreciate it."

The speaker crackled again. "What's this about?"

I reached into my coat pocket and pulled out the leather wallet holding my license, unfolded it, and held it up toward the camera.

"Ms. Walsh, I'm a private investigator," I said.

Then I stopped for a moment. It hit me that this was the first time in a decade or more that I'd said that to someone.

"I'm looking into the death of your ex-husband," I continued. "And I just had a few questions I wanted to ask. I promise it won't take much of your time."

I stood there for a few beats before she spoke again. "I've already been interviewed by the police."

"I understand that, Ms. Walsh, but I'm not with the police. I'm a private investigator."

"Who are you working for?" she demanded. Her voice sounded stern, almost angry.

"Actually, ma'am, I'm working for Leo. That's who I'm working for. Leo."

There was a staticky, scratchy noise over the loudspeaker and the red light on the security camera went dark. I stood there for a full minute, shifting my weight from one foot to the other, feeling the sweat trickling down my sides under my shirt in the awful heat.

I figured she'd just decided to blow me off, just as I had Leo. I was about to give up when I heard the metallic sounds of locks being unlocked and then the front door opened.

Vivienne Walsh unlocked the tempered glass, probably bulletproof, storm door and pushed it open. "C'mon in," she said. "You had me when you said you were working for Leo."

Chapter Nineteen

I walked past Vivienne Walsh into the entrance foyer of her mini-McMansion and the first thought that ran through my mind was something along the lines of *holy crap*…

This place was like a feature out of *Southern Living*. The foyer ran two stories high, with an antique chandelier hanging overhead that definitely did not come out of the lighting section at Home Depot or Lowe's. Polished hardwood floors reflected the light above; a row of contemporary paintings lined the walls. A grand parlor was off to the left, and further down the hallway, a small but exquisitely formal dining room was dominated by a beautiful antique walnut dining table with delicate Queen Anne legs.

Vivienne Walsh was a work of art herself and could probably have slotted right into the "antique" category as well. She was an inch or two taller than me, with dark piercing eyes and a shiny, stiff jet-black wig modelled after a hairstyle last seen during the *Mad Men* heyday of the sixties. It was the middle of the day and she was home alone, but she'd gone full makeup and jewelry, with strings of what I'd be willing to guess were real pearls down the front of her beige silk blouse, which perfectly matched her sand-colored trousers. She'd obviously spent a lot of time in the sun in her younger days, her dark brown skin on its way to being leathery and wrinkled.

Another few years, and she'd be a dowager like her former sister-in-law. Seems Leo was surrounded by dowagers for much of his life.

Leo was about to turn 68 when he was murdered. I hadn't done a deep enough dive into this yet, but my guess was she was a few years older than him.

"C'mon in, Mr.—" she said. "What was it?"

"Denton," I answered. "Harry Denton."

She led the way down the hallway into a great room dominated by a fireplace with a grand mantle that ran two stories up. Built-in bookcases held rows of leather bound books that looked more like decorations than reading material, framed pictures and a large flat-screen in the center.

In the far corner of the room, a tall fountain surrounded by fake greenery gently gurgled.

"Please, Mr. Denton, have a seat."

She gestured to a chair next to the fireplace, across from the large glass-topped coffee table in the center of the room. She took the middle of the sofa opposite me.

I eased down in the chair and tried not to listen to the fountain. Too many minutes of that and I'd be asking Vivienne Walsh where the guest bathroom was.

"Now tell me how you came to be working for a dead man."

I stared at her for a second, just trying to take her all in. She was clearly wealthy, refined, intelligent. But there was an air of coldness about her, a sense that what you were seeing was her presence and not her real self.

The way she said *dead man* without a trace of emotion…

I was tired of repeating the story of how Leo came to my office, but there seemed to be no getting around it. I'd had lots of practice, though; it only took a few minutes and then she stared at me for a second.

"So why are you here?" she asked after a few moments. "The

police came and talked to me. I know nothing about his murder. He hasn't been a part of my life for years."

"How long has it been since you last saw him?"

She shrugged. "Years," she answered. "Can't even remember the last time."

I looked around this seven-figure house and did a mental comparison of it with the tiny apartment in Antioch where Leo had spent the last years of his life. I wondered if he even knew what he'd lost.

"Do you have any idea of who would have wanted to do something like this? The police said it was a rage killing. Terribly violent…"

Even my description of Leo's murder didn't seem to faze her.

"Mr. Denton," she said sternly, "Leo and I had very little contact over the years after our divorce. About five years ago, he paid an attorney to contact me. He claimed he couldn't continue his alimony payments anymore. He offered to transfer copyright and ownership of two of his books to me."

"Did you take that deal?"

For a moment, it seemed like the faintest trace of a smile crossed her face.

"One of the books was unpublished, the other long out of print. I accepted the deal as a way to offer Leo the chance to save face. I could have gone after him in court, but what would've been the point? Besides, I don't need it."

I looked around the room. No, she didn't need it. I don't know what Leo was paying her, but I doubt it paid for this.

"You have a very nice home," I said. "If you don't mind my asking, did the divorce settlement make this possible? From what Leo told me, when you two divorced there was still something worth splitting up."

"Leo grew up very poor," she said, "so I suppose to him it was a lot."

Not that I liked this woman very much to begin with, but I was liking her less by the minute. "So I gather you did not grow up poor."

"My father was a farmer in West Tennessee," she said. "And I grew up an only child. But we were lucky. The gas company discovered a natural gas field and paid my father a substantial royalty starting in the late 1960s. It enabled him to have a very nice retirement, and when my parents passed there was something left for me. I'm a pretty savvy investor, so between what my parents left me and the settlement from Leo, I've had a good life."

So that's how you measure a good life... I thought.

"What was life with Leo like then?" I asked.

"Oh, for years we were getting by, but only getting by. Leo had dreams but he didn't seem to be able to make any of them come true. You see, some men are driven by the desire to accumulate wealth, to accomplish great things, to prove something to the world. Other men are driven by something much darker."

She was quiet for a moment. "Like what?" I asked.

"Leo was driven by a sense of inadequacy. He felt like a failure from his earliest days. He used to say that no matter how hard he worked, how hard he tried, nothing ever worked out for him. Whatever success he had came late in life and by then he was struggling with his own demons, not to mention a love affair with the bottle. In the end, that's what got him. He finally made it and then he made sure he self-destructed."

I bit my tongue. What I really wanted to say was *Damn, that's a little harsh and judgmental.*

"I spoke with Leo's wife after the funeral," I said, almost offhandedly. That seemed to get a reaction out of her.

"Oh, *her*," she sniffed. "The one with the retail job. Where was it? Walmart? Dollar General?"

"Actually, Ms. Walsh, I didn't ask. But she described Leo as being very kind."

Vivienne Walsh's eyes narrowed. "Leo was very weak," she said coldly. "If he'd listened to me and done what I told him, he wouldn't have wound up living in a dumpy apartment in Antioch."

I shifted forward in the chair and stood up. "Well, Ms. Walsh, I think I've taken enough of your time. I appreciate you talking to me."

She stood up as well and walked toward the hallway, with me a couple of footsteps behind.

"There is one more thing I'm curious about," I said. She stopped in the hallway and turned back to me.

"Leo's wife said that despite what people thought of her, she loved him very much."

"Yes?" she said, more ice in her voice.

"Tell me," I said. "Did you love him?"

She looked over the top of my head, off into the distance. "Oh," she said after a moment, "I suppose I was fond of him. At times..."

I nodded. She led me to the front door. I thanked her again for her time and walked out of the house as she held the door open for me.

I turned as she was closing the door. "By the way," I said.

She glared at me, annoyed. "Yes, what is it now?"

"If you didn't have any contact with Leo for years, how'd you know he lived in a dumpy apartment in Antioch?"

She glared at me and closed the door. Metallic clicks followed as she locked herself in tight.

ꕥ

I felt like I'd spent twenty minutes in a refrigerator as I pulled out of Vivienne Walsh's driveway and gunned the Tesla out of her neighborhood. I swung right and followed the road down to the light at Hillsboro Pike. I took a left, then a right on Harding Place and drove through Belle Meade, past the Belle Meade Country Club and its perfectly manicured golf course.

Then I got to one of those exquisitely surreal intersections the likes of which I'd only ever seen in my beloved hometown: the intersection of Harding Place and Harding Pike. Whoever came up with that idea deserves a place in the pantheon.

I pulled into the parking lot of a tiny strip mall containing a dry cleaning business and a Japanese restaurant, across the street from a used car dealership that specialized in luxury cars. I guess when a used car costs sixty grand, it's not so much used as *pre-owned*.

I pulled open the file that I'd stuffed all that paperwork into and scanned through the pages one last time.

Sometimes you just have to go with your gut. And as cold as Vivienne Walsh the Ice Queen was, I didn't figure her for being a murderer. As far as I could tell, she wouldn't dirty her hands by having anything to do with anything that messy.

So that left the middle wife of the Leo Walsh alumna society. I thumbed through the stack of papers Ashley had pulled together for me.

Leo's second wife was Dr. Nancy Shannon, the "Dr." part being a Vanderbilt Ph.D. in English, her specialty being Victorian literature. When she and Leo met at the Community College where they were both teaching, neither of them realized at the time where they were. For her, it was a starter job that years from now she probably wouldn't even put on her *curriculum vitae.*

For Leo, it was the end of the line.

So she'd written a novel about an independent woman in charge of her own life in the mid-nineteenth century who defies custom and culture to rise above all the horrible men putting women down and abusing them in that era. Leo helped her; his Dashiell Hammett to her Lillian Hellman. It had become a success, so she and Leo got married, she published a couple more novels, and that got her a plum job with the English Department at Rhodes College down in Memphis.

And as he had so many other women, Leo let her down.

Only from what he told me, this one wasn't just resentful and disappointed. This one was downright pissed and determined to ruin him, which she did a pretty good job of. When somebody hates you enough to get you fired from a crappy job, that says something.

But she lived in Memphis now. She was far away from Leo and maybe absence really did make the heart grow fonder, or at least less furious. And as Leo said, probably with some credence, there was no way Dr. Nancy Shannon was going to kill him as long as his life was so freaking miserable.

That would be too kind, the easy way out.

I scanned the last of the printouts on Nancy Shannon, which included her bio on the Rhodes English Department website (which neglected to mention her previous marriage to a Pulitzer-nominated author), her growing list of publications, awards, and honors, and her own personal website, with glamour shots of her and links to her novels on Amazon, Barnes & Noble, Kobo, Apple Books, and about a half-dozen other outlets.

Ashley had made printouts of her entire website for me. On the "Latest News/Blog" page, she'd posted an entry about how she was spending the first week of July in England at a conference at St. Hilda's. She was spending the rest of the month motoring around the Cotswolds researching her next novel.

Well, I thought, it's a dirty job but somebody's gotta do it.

I shook my head. This lady's got a serious career and a serious alibi. Talk about upward trajectories… Okay, maybe she was pissed enough to murder Leo, but my guess was she had too much to lose.

Besides, if she really wanted to get back at Leo for all the distress he caused her, all she had to do was fall back on the advice of that old Limey poet she probably studied in graduate school, the one who said that living well is the best revenge.

Alex called me maybe half-an-hour later. She and Sheba were back at The Travertine and Sheba was ordering Chinese. Could we stay for dinner?

"I was hoping we'd get an invite," I said, relieved. "I haven't been to the store and the cupboard's a little bare."

By six, Lonnie and I were sitting on the rooftop garden watching the sun set over I-40 West toward Bellevue, then on to Kingston Springs and Dickson in a relentless march to night. A front had moved in, the temperature had dropped to the mid-80s, and the humidity had dropped to bearable. Sheba and Alex had gone to pick up the Chinese. Lonnie was on his third Yazoo as I opened my second. All seemed right with the world.

"So I'm stumped," I admitted. "You'd think that a murder

victim with that kind of marriage history would have a whole laundry list of pissed-off ex-wives. It's the most natural place to look, but I swear I just don't think any of them did it."

Lonnie was reclining in a chaise lounge, his long legs extended over the end of the chair. "I still can't figure out what the hell you're trying to do," he said. "But we'll let that slide. The fact is you're doing it. So the question becomes 'What's the next step?'"

I took a long swallow of the cold Yazoo. It was one of their summer seasonals, a light unfiltered Hefeweizen that was as cold and hoppy as it was cloudy.

"I don't know," I confessed. "As far as I can tell, Leo's world had really shrunk in the last couple of decades. He didn't party, he didn't have a whole lot of friends. He didn't do drugs, buy drugs, make drugs, or sell drugs. I don't buy for a second the police theory that this was a some kind of hooker hookup gone wrong. From everything I can figure, he worked, went home to his wife, wrote a little bit, and then drank 'til bedtime. He was almost boring."

Lonnie swung around on the chair and planted his feet on the deck in front of me.

"Then why the fuck did somebody kill him?"

My jaw tightened. "That's what's driving me crazy."

"I haven't seen you this animated by anything in a long time."

I looked away from him for a second, toward the horizon. "Maybe it's just a distraction from all my problems."

Lonnie snorted. "What problems? You're an old, rich, white guy. You haven't got any problems."

"Yeah, that's what everybody tells me."

Behind us, the sliding glass door hissed as Sheba opened it. "Chow's up, boys. Come and get it."

Alex had set the table and set out the cartons of Chinese. Kung pao chicken, beef broccoli stir-fry, and my favorite, moo shu pork, which is only my favorite Chinese food because I like to slather everything in hoisin. I was in New York on business a couple of years ago and our client took me to a real Chinese restaurant down on Mott Street. I asked for some hoisin sauce and the waiter looked at me like I'd dropped my pants and taken a dump on the table.

Who knew?

"Another Yazoo?" Sheba asked. "Or are you switching to a nice Pinot Grigio like a civilized person?"

"Yazoo," Lonnie stage-whispered, cracking open a crab rangoon. "Yazoo!"

"Or you could have some iced tea," Alex added.

"I probably should go with the tea," I said. "But white wine and Chinese food is too good to pass up. Just one, though."

We settled down and dug in. We mostly made small talk and avoided any mention of either murder or private girls' schools. Sheba and Lonnie were thinking about flying down to their beach house in the Florida panhandle next week. Alys Beach was postcard-Florida beautiful this time of year, but searing hot and full of tourists.

"Thinking about going diving," he said, looking at Alex. "There's a great little dive shop down there. We could sign you up for a resort course, get you certified in three days. Then you and I could dive the Navy barges they sunk off the coast. Not the best diving you'll ever do. No real reefs or anything. But it's good visibility and not deep. About sixty feet down is all you'll ever go."

Alex grinned, then turned to me. "What do you think, Daddy?"

"Thought you had to be sixteen to get your C card," I said.

"Officially," Lonnie said. "But she's turning sixteen in a month or so. As long as she gets signed off by an instructor and dives with a buddy, she's good to go."

I shrugged. "Sure, why not? If it's what you want to do. As long as Uncle Lon, here, keeps an eye on you."

"We'll probably be on a dive boat with a bunch of people," he said. "I know the dive master. He'll go with us. She'll be fine."

"Yes," Alex said, reaching out to high-five Lonnie. "Let's do it!"

The rest of the evening went on like that. A pleasant, conflict-free, remarkably ordinary summer evening. Alex and I headed home around nine. We agreed that she would have her first day alone in the house tomorrow while I went to work, as long as she checked in with me a couple of times during the day.

Alex went upstairs to take a shower and I grabbed another glass of wine, then flicked on the television. There wasn't much on; there usually isn't these days. I didn't have the energy or the attention span to start a movie on Netflix or Hulu. Alex came down in a pair of sleeping shorts and a T-shirt, a towel wrapped around her wet hair. She seemed quiet all of a sudden.

I started to ask what was going on, then decided maybe the best thing I could do was dial it back a little and give her some space. I was beginning to see that my constantly checking in on her was more a reflection of my own anxiety than anything else.

Just relax, I thought. It'll be okay.

We watched the local news, then about half of Colbert. Alex went up to bed and I headed off to my room. I took a shower, then walked into the kitchen to grab one last glass of wine. As I crossed the living room, the house was dark except for the light spilling out from under Alex's bedroom door. Curious, I padded quietly about halfway up the steps. I stood there for a moment, wondering whether I should check on her one last time.

That's when I heard the faint crying again.

It wasn't a wailing, tearing-out-your-hair kind of crying, just a sad kind of phlegmatic snarfling. I set the glass of wine down on the step and started up the stairs. I'm her parent; if she's upset, it's on me to try and figure out why, to find some way to help her, to fix it.

Then I heard her talking.

Spanish.

Chapter Twenty

Mt. Olivet is one of Nashville's oldest and most prestigious cemeteries. It's also the most stratified. There's a portion of the cemetery marked by grand monuments and mausoleums where famous celebrities, politicians, genuinely rich aristocrats, and, of course, nearly 1500 fallen Civil War soldiers in the area known as "Confederate Circle" are buried.

Then there was the other side, the resting place for regular old middle-class working folks, tourists who died while in Nashville, and the outright paupers. Their graves were largely marked by bronze plaques flush with the ground so as not to impede the grass cutters.

That's where all my people are buried.

And that's where they were burying Leo Walsh this afternoon.

Alex was still asleep when I pulled out of the driveway Wednesday morning and headed for the freeway. I laid awake half the night thinking about all this and trying to figure out what to do with this day.

I didn't even know if going to Leo Walsh's funeral would accomplish much. Of course there was always the chance that something unexpected would happen that might break this case wide open, but that usually happens only in movies and TV crime shows. The murderer shows up at the gravesite and in an overwhelming tsunami of guilt and grief decides to confess and beg forgiveness of the survivors. Or some brilliant detective figures out that only the murderer could have known the white carnation boutonnière on the corpse's suitcoat was *the same one on the victim's dresser the night he was killed!*

Yeah, in my dreams. I only know if I'd beaten somebody to death and tossed their body between two Dumpsters in the back of a restaurant parking lot, I damn sure wouldn't bother to show up for the funeral.

So I was going to hold off on deciding about Leo Walsh's funeral. But I also figured the morning of his funeral might be a good time to start noodling around the other side of Leo's life.

I exited the freeway at Fesslers Lane, then turned left and crossed back over the interstate. A couple of turns later, I was pulling into a visitor's space at the Nashville Academy of Cinema Arts. The lot was nearly full now, unlike Saturday afternoon. I pulled out my mobile and Googled "Best Film Schools." I read down the list, memorized a few of the names, and pocketed the phone.

The front that had pushed out the worst of the heat and humidity the last few days was itself being shoved aside by a new heat wave. It was just after 10 in the morning, though, so we were still a few hours away from the worst of it. I crossed the parking lot and opened the front door.

The Nashville Academy of Cinema Arts lobby was filled with movie posters and huge photographs of eager young students on film sets. There was a large semicircle of a desk in the center of the lobby with a faux wall behind it. There were more bright, cheery photographs on the wall and a sign above that read:

"*Welcome To THE Nashville Film School!*"

And below that:

"*Dreams Begin HERE!*"

I walked up to the large reception desk where a young

woman with blazing red hair who looked like she should have been a student sat staring into her laptop. I cleared my throat as I approached.

She looked up. "May I help you?"

I gave her my best innocent smile. "I hope it's okay for me to just drop in like this. Maybe I should have phoned the Admissions Office for an appointment, but I was in the neighborhood and had some free time before my next appointment and just thought I'd take a chance."

"No," the young woman said, "this is fine. Would you like to speak to someone?"

A group of students emerged from a hallway on the right side of the lobby, chattering and laughing. They crossed through the gallery behind the lobby and disappeared down another hallway.

"Well, I've got a senior in high school who thinks he wants to get into film. He's got good ACT scores and a great GPA, but his mother and I are just not sure we want him to go to New York or Los Angeles. I thought we'd take a look at a local program and see if we could convince him to stay close to home."

She reached for the phone and tapped a few keys. "Yes, is Ms. Gilbert there?"

She pronounced it *Jeel-bear*, just like Leo had.

"Great, I've got a parent who's interested in the school. I thought Ms. Gilbert might want to meet him, perhaps a tour if he has time."

There was a pause on the phone, then the young woman looked up at me. "And what was your name, sir?"

"Northrup," I answered. "Dr. Henry Northrup."

She turned back to the phone. "It's Dr. Northrup… Yes, he's in the lobby."

She hung up. "Dr. Northrup, Ms. Gilbert will be right out."

"Great," I said. "Is she the admissions person?"

The young woman smiled. "No, Ms. Gilbert is the president of the college. She's on her way."

So the president of the Nashville Academy of Cinema Arts was going to give me a personal guided tour. I wondered if Ms. Gilbert was this accommodating to all parents or just ones whose name was preceded by the word "Dr."

I stepped away and looked around the lobby like any other curious parent. A few moments later, I heard the click of high heels approaching from the hallway to the left of the reception desk. I turned as Ursula Gilbert, wearing bronze-colored pants and an iridescent, almost shimmering, gold blouse came toward me. Her long, wavy salt-and-pepper hair was piled in a swirl atop her head, and her glasses were perched up high on her forehead. She seemed abuzz and aglow, all at the same time.

She held out her right hand. "Dr. Northrup," she exclaimed in the thick French accent, "I am so *please* to meet you."

I took her hand and shook it politely. For the briefest moment, she looked me in the eye and seemed to be examining me. I wondered if she remembered me from Leo's visitation, but not once when I'd seen her holding court had she looked in my direction.

"Thank you so much for your time," I said. "Perhaps I should have made an appointment."

"Oh, no no no," she said. "Parents of prospective students are always welcome at NACA."

"Well, I do appreciate your time," I said, laying on just the slightest hint of Southern drawl. "And I promise I won't take too much of it."

"It's my pleasure. Let me show you around our little arts community here." I followed as she turned and crossed behind the reception desk, through the gallery with more framed photographs from student film sets, and toward the hallway where the group of students had come from a couple of minutes earlier.

"Please keep in mind," she said. "This is the middle of July so we only have a very small student presence here now. We do have summer classes, but it's on a reduced schedule. There aren't as many students here then. Come next month, this place will be packed."

"How many students do you have here?"

"Our student census is approaching 250," she answered.

We walked on a little further and she went into her sales pitch. "The Nashville Academy of Cinema Arts has been an integral part of the local filmmaking community for over a decade," she began. "This is a two-year, full-time program, although some of our students choose to go part time, so it can take a little longer. We are fully accredited by the CFAAFP and our students are eligible for all federal aid programs."

We turned down another long hallway with classroom doors on either side. "I don't know how familiar you are with the filmmaking process, but there are five basic components of film. There is the writer, the director, a cinematographer, a producer, and an editor. Our students take foundation classes in each of these areas during their first year. In their second year, they can specialize in an area of their choice."

She opened a door and stepped into an empty classroom. There were rows of tables and plastic chairs and a large, flat-screen monitor mounted on the wall.

"This is a typical, more traditional classroom," Ursula announced. "Our students take a variety of classes in here, including critical studies classes. All of our students, for instance, take film history, and their Foundations of Production and Finance class is taught in here as well."

She flicked the light off and closed the door as we left. She continued with her spiel as we walked on, back to the main hallway, then left down to another, narrower hall. "To our left down here is our primary editing lab."

She cracked open the door. "There is a class going on right now," she whispered.

I looked over her shoulder. The editing lab was a square room with the walls painted flat black. There were four rows of tables on each side of the room, with four monitors on each table. There was a massive flat-screen monitor mounted on the wall at the front of the room and a phalanx of speakers surrounding it.

The monitor at the front was off and the room was largely silent. Each table had a row of students with their faces turned toward their desk monitors, large headphones atop their heads.

A small, thin woman in jeans and a white blouse at a desk off to the side, between the rows of tables, turned and spotted us. She stood up and came to the door.

"We don't mean to disturb you," Ursula Gilbert whispered.

The woman smiled. "It's okay," she said, with just a trace of an eastern European accent. "They're all buried in their dailies."

She turned to me. "Dr. Northrup, this is Professor Petrov, our senior editing and sound teacher."

The woman offered her hand. "Henry Northrup," I said, shaking it. "Glad to meet you, Professor Petrov."

"Please, call me Raisa." I guessed she was in her early 50s. I remembered her as the one sitting next to Ursula on the couch at the funeral home.

"Dr. Northrup's son is considering film school and wanted to come see our facility."

"Oh," she said. "What's he looking at?"

I recalled the list I'd just Googled back in the car. "Well, USC and NYU, of course, but they're very competitive. He's also looking at Florida State, Columbia College in Chicago, and a little closer to home, NCSA."

"North Carolina School of the Arts," she said. "Good school. Nearly as competitive as the others."

Ursula turned to me. "Where does your son go to school now?"

I smiled, remembering lunch the other day at the Dairy Queen. "He's a senior at MBA."

Both Raisa Petrov and Ursula Gilbert seemed impressed. "Good school," Ursula said.

"Thank you," I said. "He's done very well there and would do just fine at any program, I think. But, well… frankly, it's his mother."

Ursula and Raisa glanced at each other for just a beat, then Raisa lifted an eyebrow. "His mother?"

I hesitated. "His mother's, well… not well. And his leaving home and going that far away is going to be very hard on her. I was thinking if we could get him the kind of program he wants, without going so far away..."

Ursula Gilbert reached out and put her hand on my arm. "Say no more. I understand. Why don't we continue the tour and discuss how we might be able to help you."

Raisa Petrov reached out again and I took her hand. "Please, if you have any questions, my email address is on the website. Just let me know what I can do to help and please bring your son—what was his name?"

"Briggs," I said. "Briggs Northrup."

"Just tell Briggs to call us as well and let him know we want to get him over here as soon as possible for a tour."

"Thank you," I smiled. She turned and went back into the editing lab.

We walked on down and Ursula showed me the sound studio and a small mix room. There was a tiny voice-over booth and something she called a Foley studio, which she explained was where the students recorded sound effects. We walked down the faculty hallway and she introduced me to Justine Moye, whose picture I remembered from the website—the one with the row of piercings, the sleeve tattoos, and the brilliant scarlet red dye job. She also wore faded jeans, running shoes, and a blue, button-down Oxford cloth shirt. She taught producing and finance. I began to see that one of the real benefits of teaching in a film school was you didn't need to dress up.

"Our cinematography professor, Chris Weyreuth, is on a student shoot today. They're shooting an episode of our web series at a location in Germantown."

"You're shooting a web series?" I asked.

"Our students generate original content," she answered. "It gives them the chance to gain some actual credits and to leave here with a portfolio of their accomplishment."

That last word seemed to have an extra heavy layer of French on top: *ahh-com-pleesh-mahn…*

We turned left into an alcove and came to a set of double doors. She pulled one of the doors open and stepped aside for me to enter. There was a large area of bare concrete walls and concrete floor and at the end, a two-story-high freight door.

I drew a mental map as best I could for the turns we'd made and figured that we were now on the side of the building where I'd been Saturday afternoon. Two double doors to the left of the freight door were propped open, while the two double doors on the right were closed. A red strobe light just above the door frame flashed rhythmically, so bright it was hard to look at.

"I want to show you our main soundstage," Ursula Gilbert said, "but that flashing red light means they're shooting in there."

"Oh, well, it can wait for another time. I'm sure it's as impressive as everything else I've seen."

The red light suddenly stopped and about ten students poured out in a flurry of sound and movement. Ursula looked down at her watch.

"Break time," she said. "Most of our classes are three hours and we give the students a break halfway through."

When the crowd of students were out, she walked into the soundstage, with me following. The tall, rail-thin guy I remembered from Leo's visitation and the NACA webpage was over in one corner, staring at a monitor with a couple of other students.

The room itself was huge, cavernous, with black walls and a metal framework above containing rows of lights with those paper lanterns around them like you'd have at an outdoor party. There was equipment everywhere: cameras on dollies and tripods, boom mikes hanging down from above, and coils of thick extension cords. It looked like a small house had been built inside the soundstages, only it was smaller and flimsier and some of the walls were on rollers and had been pushed into weird, acute angles from the rest of the set.

"Jack," she called, only it came out *Jacques*. The guy turned to face us. He was even taller the closer we got. His thick salt-and-pepper hair was pulled back into a long ponytail and he was wearing a pair of jeans and a T-shirt. His bony shoulders seemed to protrude through the top of the shirt.

He looked even older now than he did on the website. Guy was easily close to my age or older, and if I may say so, not aging anywhere near as well. His face was crisscrossed with wrinkles, his jaw square and slightly jutting.

And there was a dark, intense look in his eyes.

"Yes, Ursula," he called out, his deep voice seeming to echo in the hollow space.

"I want you to meet someone," she said. He began walking toward us and we met in the middle of the set.

"This is Dr. Henry Northrup. His son, Briggs, is a senior at MBA and is considering film school. Dr. Northrup, this is Jack McEwen. He's our professor of directing."

"Well," he said, shaking my hand. "That's great. What does your son want to concentrate in?"

I smiled. "Knowing Briggs, my guess is he wants to be a director."

"They all do in the beginning," McEwen said. "My job is to beat that out of them. If I can, they shouldn't be directors in the first place. If I can't, then they might make it."

"*Jacques* is, of course, just kidding…"

"That's okay," I said. "This is what you expect out of a demanding program."

He stared at me for a moment and I saw something hard in his eyes. "Glad you feel that way."

We made small talk for another minute or so and then the students started filtering back from their break.

"It was a pleasure to meet you, Dr. Northrup," Jack McEwen said, shaking my hand again. I can't remember the last time I shook so many hands in such a short time; hope I still had that travel bottle of hand sanitizer in the glovebox.

"We'll stop by the equipment room," Ursula Gilbert said. "You can see what's available for our student film productions."

She led the way across the freight dock again and we went through the propped-open double doors. The equipment room seemed massive to me, although I'd never seen one before so I didn't have a lot to compare it with. Industrial metal shelving against three of the four walls went from the floor all the way up to the ceiling, which looked to be about fifteen feet high. Hard gray plastic cases were shelved like books in a library; pallets of sandbags rested in the corner. Giant racks on wheels held tripods and stands of some kind. Each shelf was crammed with gear, cables, lights…

I didn't recognize most of this stuff, but it looked damned impressive. There was a long workbench against one wall, with boxes of tools, soldering irons, vices, rows of plastic trays full of nuts and bolts and screws and other guy-type mechanical stuff splayed out in a confused mess. Next to it was a desk with a couple of computer monitors arranged at an angle from each other.

Seated at that desk was one of the largest young men I'd ever seen in my life. It wasn't just that he had to be a couple inches taller than Jack McEwen; it was that he was a couple of times wider as well. He had to weigh 300 pounds if he weighed ten and the massive, oversized office chair he was leaning back in looked like it was straining to stay in one piece.

"Bowen, I want you to meet someone," Ursula announced. The chair began to swivel as the young man swung around to face us. He was pasty white, with long red hair that, unlike the dyed red hair that was so popular these days, was completely natural. He was shaggy, needed a haircut, and had a thick, untamed growth of beard. He wore a short sleeve T-shirt, revealing a row of tattoos up both arms, all of them related to film.

There was an inked coil of 35 millimeter film that wrapped around his right arm like a snake, starting at his wrist and working its way all the way to his shoulder. On his left arm, there was a tattoo of an old-timey movie camera on a wooden tripod. Above that, there was a reproduction of the silhouette of Alfred Hitchcock that was used on the Hitchcock family Christmas cards and was also the logo for *Alfred Hitchcock Presents*.

His biceps were as big around as my thighs, bulging as he placed his hands on the chair armrests and pushed himself to a standing position. His skin was ruddy, freckled, and he looked like the effort of standing up may have taken more breath than he had.

"Dr. Northrup, this is Bowen Masterson," Ursula said. "He graduated from NACA four years ago and joined as us a staffer shortly after. He's our equipment room manager and media center director."

Bowen Masterson took a step toward us and stuck out his hand.

"Bowen, this is Dr. Northrup," Ursula continued. "His son may join us next year."

"Great," Bowen said. His voice was deep, husky, phlegmatic, as if he needed to clear his throat but couldn't quite swing it.

"Pleasure to meet you," I said as he took my hand in his and made it look like it had been swallowed up by a ham.

"I'd like you to give Dr. Northrup a quick tour of the room and give him an idea of what kind of equipment we have."

"Keeping in mind," I said, "I won't have any idea what you're talking about."

"Well, we can give you an idea of what our capabilities are," Bowen said, turning and walking over to one of the shelves with suitcases lined up on it. He pulled one off and unsnapped the buckles, then raised the lid.

"Our beginners start off with the Panasonic GH5," he explained. Then he went into a recitation of the camera's specs, most of which meant nothing to me. I did recognize the term "high res" and a couple of others, but it all basically went in one ear and disappeared before it found its way out the other.

Then we went around and I got a quick lesson in field audio recorders, prime lens packages, and I learned that those wooden crates that came in various sizes were called "apple boxes." It was fascinating and made me wish I knew more about all this stuff.

"Got any questions?" he asked when we circled back around to his desk after about ten minutes.

"Not about equipment, but I'm sure Briggs will," I said. "But there is one thing I am curious about."

Ursula perked up at that. "Yes?"

"You told me about the five different components of filmmaking," I said. "I've met your producing teacher, editing teacher, and directing teacher. You said your cinematography teacher was in the field."

I hesitated for just a beat. "So where's the writing teacher? He's probably the only one I could talk to and understand."

Ursula Gilbert's face went completely blank, as if I'd just

committed a *faux pas* so unbelievable that she couldn't believe her ears. To her left, Bowen Masterson seemed to lose an inch in height.

"What?" I said after a moment. "Did I say something wrong?"

"I am so sorry, Dr. Northrup, but we have suffered a terrible tragedy here at the Nashville Academy of Cinema Arts. It's been in the news many times. Our screenwriting professor, a beloved member of our NACA family, died under terrible circumstances and we are all still in shock..."

"What happened?" I said somberly.

"Professor Walsh was murdered," Bowen said darkly.

"Oh, Bowen!" Ursula Gilbert squealed, waving her hands. "*Please...*"

I looked at them both, from one to the other, studying their faces. "I'm so sorry," I said quietly. "That's terrible."

"Have you not seen it in the papers?" she asked.

"No, I'm terribly busy these days. I simply haven't the time to watch much news."

Bowen Masterson turned and went back to his desk and sat down. He stared into his computer, then took a pen and huddled over to write something.

"It has been a terrible experience," she said, stifling a sob. "None of us have ever seen anything like this and we simply don't know what to do next. His funeral is this afternoon and we are closing the school. We are all going..."

"I'm so sorry," I said. "Especially to have just dropped in like this at such a difficult time. Why don't I just let you get back to this and I'll be in touch later."

"Oh, it has been no bother," she said. "It has been a pleasure to talk with you. I don't mean to get so emotional."

"It's perfectly understandable."

"Why don't I walk you to the lobby. We'll pick up an admissions packet for Briggs."

I smiled. "Thank you," I said. "I'll make sure he reviews every bit of it."

I turned and gestured for her to lead the way. As she walked through the door, I heard the chair creak behind me as Bowen Masterson got to his feet again.

"Dr. Northrup," he said. "It was a pleasure to meet you and I hope you and your son will come back for another visit. I think he'd love it here."

The large young man stuck out his hand. Jeez, all the handshaking. I was going to need a hot arm soak by the time I got home. We shook hands, only this time I felt something scratchy and stiff rubbing against my palm.

"See you again soon," he said as he pulled his hand away. As he did, he left something behind. I opened my hand for just a moment, then quickly closed it back.

My hand held a small, sticky Post-it Note, folded in half.

I turned and followed Ursula Gilbert to the lobby.

Chapter Twenty-One

Ursula Gilbert ushered me to the front door, past the young woman at the reception desk who handed me a large manila envelope full of brochures she'd retrieved from a display case. There was a college catalogue inside and all the application forms, with information on Federal and State financial aid and the special scholarships and support available to veterans, minorities, and the challenged.

It was all beautifully designed and professionally printed. Definitely top shelf.

Everyone couldn't have been kinder or more accommodating and helpful. They went out of their way to make me feel welcome and assured me that my son, Briggs, would find a community of like-minded and supportive artists and teachers who would prepare him for a successful, rich, rewarding life.

Almost made me feel guilty for lying my ass off…

Almost.

Walking out into the searing heat and humidity made my head swim. When I opened the door to the Tesla, another wall of hot air smacked me right in the face.

I sat down, hit the start button, and waited for the car to boot up so I could crank the AC up to Warp Factor 12. While I waited in the car with the door still open, I shifted to the side to be out of the front door line of sight.

The folded Post-it Note was still nestled in the palm of my hand. I extracted it and folded it open.

I know who you are the note read. Text me.

There was a number scrawled across the bottom of the note.

The car came to life and I pushed the buttons for maximum air conditioning. I closed the door, put it in gear, and backed out of the parking space. I turned right onto the street, drove a few blocks, crossed back over the freeway and pulled into the parking lot of a convenience store on Elm Hill Pike.

Okay, I typed into my phone. You know who I am. Now what?

I sat there, sweaty and uncomfortable as the car struggled to bring down the interior temperature to bearable. Nothing, then more nothing.

I was trying to decide what to do next when my phone buzzed.

We need to talk. Going to lunch in 20 min

Where? I typed back.

Little place off Murf Rd. Pancake Palooza. Google map it.

I smiled and started typing: Don't need to. CU in 20.

The lunchtime traffic jam had already begun and I had a hell of a time turning left out of the convenience store onto Elm Hill Pike. Then I had to make another left onto Fesslers Lane, but at least there was a light. Then another left on Murfreesboro Road.

It occurred to me that this was becoming The Day of the Left Turns…

Once I maneuvered through that cluster-maze, it was a pretty straight shot. I crossed under the freeway, then past the light at Spence Lane. Three minutes later, I pulled into the parking lot of the supermercado and backed into a parking space under a tree as far as I could get from the little chrome and glass building that was the PP.

I slid down a little in the seat and hoped the sun was at the right angle so nobody could see through the windshield. I don't know whether it was my paranoia-radar or what, but I didn't want to be boxed in or surprised. Bowen—what was his last name?—oh, yeah, *Masterson* may or may not be a very dangerous person, but either way I was in no mood to find out.

I pulled out my mobile and shot off a quick text to Alex: Everything okay, sweetie? You up?

I sat there staring at the screen for a couple minutes. No answer. I kept the car on so I could keep the cold air coming. At least, I thought, I wasn't spewing exhaust out into the air.

A couple of minutes later, a massive jet black Ford pickup truck with a loud diesel engine and oversized tires turned into the parking lot. I read the chrome letters on the tailgate as it passed me: F350. The truck had a chrome exhaust stack behind the double-sized crew cab, tons of extra chrome and lights. It was spotlessly clean, polished to a sheen.

The driver did a sharp turn to the left, then put the truck in reverse and backed into a slot on the far side of the lot.

I say he parked it. My experience with vehicles that size is you don't park them; you *dock* them.

The driver's side door opened and Bowen Masterson's colossal bulk poured out of the truck. The truck was jacked high enough up that he had to plant one foot on the step rail that ran the length of the cab and then lower his other leg to the pavement.

He looked around the parking lot, his gaze stopping for just a moment in my direction, then he crossed the lot with surprising speed and entered Pancake Palooza. I couldn't tell if he'd recognized me or not.

I sat there for a few moments and checked my phone again.

No word from Alex; hope she's okay. Sometimes teenagers don't accommodate their anxious parents by actually answering the phone or acknowledging a text.

I pushed open the car door and stepped out into the heat, then crossed the parking lot and climbed the three steps into the restaurant. I wondered if Micki Hicks would be on duty this early, and then I wondered if she'd remember me.

That might not be a good thing under the circumstances.

Bowen Masterson was seated at the farthest table away, in the far right hand corner. His back was to me, his immense bulk spreading over both sides of the chrome chair with the red vinyl seat and back. I wondered how the chair was holding up.

The restaurant was nearly full, with a couple of servers weaving in and out with trays loaded with food. A thin woman with mousy brown hair and orange makeup lines on her jaw passed me with an open notebook in her hand.

"I think you'll have to sit at the counter," she said, almost breathless.

I nodded toward the corner. "Meeting somebody..."

"Go for it," she said over her shoulder.

I dodged and zigzagged my way across the crowded restaurant and came up behind Bowen, then circled the table and sat down opposite him. He seemed almost sleepy, his heavy hooded eyes staring out at me.

Neither of us said anything for a beat. Then I went first: "So you know who I am."

"I misspoke myself," he said. "I don't know who you are, but I know who you *aren't*."

"What? Tell me who I'm not."

"You're not some guy with a kid who wants to go to film

school. That's not why you were there today."

I leaned forward, rested my hands on the table. "And how do you know that?"

He leaned back and lowered his chin to his massive chest. "I saw you at the visitation."

I sat back up straight. "Oh," I said. "I don't remember seeing you, and if you don't mind my saying, you're a hard feller to miss."

"Well, I was there. And I saw you. I saw you go up to Mr. Walsh's wife and lean down and talk to her."

I thought for a second before speaking. "Okay. So I was there. And I talked to Aileen Walsh. Just giving her my condolences… Anything wrong with that?"

He shook his head just as the waitress with the orange line on her jaw walked up to the table. "Hey, Bo," she said, setting a large glass of iced tea on the table in front of him. "How's it hanging today?"

"Just fine, sweetie," he said. "You?"

"I'm making it. The usual?"

"Yep," he answered. I picked up a menu.

"So what's the usual?" I asked.

"Woodchopper Special," he said. I scanned down the menu. Woodchopper Special: four eggs over easy, slab of ham, four slices of bacon, two hot sausage patties, grits, hash browns scattered and smothered, biscuits and gravy, and a side of baked apples for dessert.

I started laughing. "Holy crap," I stage-whispered.

"What?" he said.

"Nothing," I answered, folding the menu. "Short stack and a side of bacon, crisp please. And a coffee…"

The waitress scribbled down our order and backed away through the crowd.

"So you said we need to talk."

"Yeah," he answered. "But first, who the hell are you?"

I sat back and crossed my arms, just thinking for a moment. I may as well come clean with him; hell, all he had to do was sit on me and I'd be begging for mercy and giving him the password to my Merrill-Lynch account.

"I'm a private detective," I said softly. "I'm looking into Leo Walsh's murder."

His eyes opened wider and a tremor of excitement seemed to run through him. "Really? You're a real P.I.?"

I reached into my front pocket and pulled out my license case, then flipped it open. He looked it over and broke into a wide grin.

"Wow, cool."

"Not really," I said. "So what do we need to talk about?"

"Well, Harry Denton, what did you think of the Nashville Academy of Cinema Arts?" he asked back. "After your first visit, I mean."

"Well," I answered. "Seems like an okay place. The people who work there seem to get along, to be pretty happy, in fact. I've seen worse workplaces. And the students must be happy. You graduated and never left. Two years to finish the program and four years as a staffer. I'd take that as a good sign."

"There's a lot of alums who've worked there over the years," Bowen said. "Ursula can hire 'em cheap because steady jobs are hard to come by in this business unless you move to L.A. or Atlanta. The joke is that on the back of every NACA diploma, there's an employment application."

"Okay, but it's still a pretty impressive place."

He shook his head and grinned. "Yeah, that's what everybody thinks. But everybody don't know the real story."

"So, Bowen. Bo. Can I call you Bo?"

He nodded.

"Bo, tell me the real story."

He started to speak, but Makeup Line Lady showed up with an assistant in tow. It took an entire circular tray to bring Bowen Masterson his Woodchopper Special. There were three plates and two bowls, one jammed with baked apples and the other a good heaping cup full of that thick white sausage gravy that's endemic to the South, along with heart disease, hypertension, and adult-onset diabetes.

The assistant, with a tray a quarter the size of the other, held my small plate of pancakes and a side plate with bacon.

"Sure that's enough?" Bowen asked, eyeing my tiny plate.

I nodded. "I'm good. Not to worry…"

"I don't eat breakfast, man," he said. "By lunchtime, I'm starved."

He arranged the plates in front of him and attacked the food like a hungry wolf. I put half a teaspoon of sugar in my coffee and a dollop of half-and-half.

"So, again, Bo, what do we need to talk about?"

"That place is a joke," he said, the words muffled through his stuffed mouth. "Frickin' clown college…"

I remembered Leo Walsh deploying the same term to describe NACA in the one conversation we had.

"Yeah, there's lots of expensive-looking, shiny toys there, but the school don't own a piece of it. It's all leased, every bit of it. And the teachers? Every one of 'em is a failed fill-in-the-blank. Most of 'em don't give a shit about the students either. They're just on some kinda ego trip."

"So what if they lease equipment?" I said. "A lot of places lease equipment. It's easier to lease the latest and greatest. You don't tie up a bunch of capital and get stuck with stuff that's gonna be obsolete in six months."

"Yeah, it's okay to lease it if you can make the payments..." He took a huge spoon full of white gravy, smeared it across half a biscuit, and shoved the whole thing in his mouth.

"And what's this about the faculty?" I asked. "Ego tripping?"

"Every last one of them, except for Mr. Walsh."

"You keep calling him *Mister* Walsh."

Bowen nodded. "He didn't like being called Professor Walsh. He thought it was pretentious. In fact, he mostly wanted people to call him Leo. If we were talking alone, that's what I'd call him."

"Did you like him as a teacher?"

He folded a sausage patty into a split-open biscuit, then dipped the whole thing into the bowl of gravy and took a huge bite.

"He was the best teacher I ever had," he said after getting part of his mouth clear. "He was a no bullshit kinda guy, which is more than I can say for most of them. You got the sense that he understood what it was like to be young and struggling."

I nodded. "Maybe that's because he was old and struggling."

"I used to go by his office and just hang out and shoot the shit with him," Bowen continued. "I got this crazy family. My dad's a Tea Party wingnut who drinks too much, makes an ass out of himself in public. I'm embarrassed to be seen with him. Mr. Walsh would talk to me about it. Sometimes, he'd just listen."

"So he would—" I started, but Bowen interrupted me.

"I'm trying to get this feature off the ground," he said, his voice rising. "I wrote this script, and even though I wasn't in any of his classes anymore he'd read it anyway. Give me feedback and suggestions."

I thought for a second. "Okay, Bo, let's go in another direction here. Leo Walsh told me that he'd gotten wind of some problems at the school. That the Feds were investigating some financial goings-on, that there might be some real trouble."

I let that sit there for a second.

"And that he'd been contacted by the Feds and was cooperating," I said. "Tell me what you know about that."

He unfolded another biscuit and raked it across his plate, sopping up egg yolk and gravy and grits all in one motion.

"You got any idea who did this to him?" he asked as the biscuit was halfway to his mouth. "I'd sure love to get my hands on whoever did this."

"Well," I said, "he had a couple of ex-wives that he wasn't too friendly with and he and his current wife had their share of problems. But I looked into that and I don't think there's anything to it."

Bowen looked down and studied the nearly empty plates in front of and below him. "That place is falling apart…"

"What?" I asked. "Would you repeat that."

He looked up. "That place is falling apart," he repeated in a louder voice. "They're out of money. They can't pay the lease bills, can barely make payroll. They took out a massive loan six months ago and the balloon payment's coming due soon. The Fed's auditing the Financial Aid office. What they're finding ain't pretty. Yeah, it's all crashing down…"

"Bo, how do you know this?"

"I run the media center," he said. "I'm responsible for processing the lease payments on all the equipment. Plus I'm friends with the IT guys. Those guys know everything. And they've let me see some records, some emails, shit people ain't supposed to see."

I leaned in to him. "What have they shown you?"

"The Nashville Academy of Cinema Arts ain't a real college. It's one of those for-profit scams that keep showing up in the news. We don't have no endowment, no generous alumni base. We have rolling admissions and we literally pay the bills this month with the tuition that came in last month. Add to that about half our students are veterans, kids who survived Afghanistan and Iraq, and are living their dream of going to film school, all on their VA benefits."

"So when the Feds started investigating…"

He nodded. "Yeah, the Feds finally audited the last few years and discovered that our retention rate sucks, our graduation rate sucks, and our students who do graduate leave with a shitload of student loan debt."

"And yet the ads on local TV keep showing up every night during the local news," I said.

"It's one of those, what do you call it? *Ponzi schemes…* You have to take in successive waves of suckers. The money comes in one door and out the other, except for six-figure salaries in the front office and whatever they can skim off the top and hide."

"And the faculty and staff?"

He snorted and a big bacon crumb sprayed out and stuck in his beard. "*Shee-yit,*" he drawled. "Staff don't make shit and the faculty not much better. We haven't had raises ever. Ursula screws the staff out of overtime. The benefits suck. I passed on the health insurance. Can't afford the premium."

I suppressed the urge to tell my young friend that perhaps someone whose "usual" is the *Woodchopper Special* might want to consider keeping that health insurance current.

"So then the Feds put the brakes on," I said.

He nodded. "Damn right. The place is literally going to close unless the movie gets made. And now that Mr. Walsh is dead, that may be the end."

I took a sip of coffee, just thinking and trying to take it all in.

Then it hit me.

"Movie?" I said. "What movie?"

Bowen picked up his extra-large, Big Gulp-sized glass of sweet tea and downed half of it in one swallow.

"It finally hit 'em a year or so ago that the stars might lie, but the numbers never do," he said. "They're cutting faculty, staff, reducing the number of courses. Mr. Walsh tried to argue with them, told 'em you can't cut your way to growth."

"So what did he suggest?"

Bowen pulled a fistful of paper napkins out of the dispenser at the center of the table and started wiping the crumbs and egg yolk out of his beard.

"See, the problem is, when NACA opened, what? Ten years ago? When it opened, there were only a couple of film schools around. We were the only one where you didn't have to have test scores, or for that matter, even a high school diploma to get into. Now, there's like eight programs within driving distance of downtown. And all of them have more to offer and bigger ad budgets than we do."

"You said Leo Walsh argued with them," I said. "So what was his argument? What did he want them to do?"

"He said we needed to make a bold move. Needed to do something that'd put us on the map. Something that no other film program in this part of the country had ever done..."

He went silent for a second and I began to wonder if he was just effin' with me.

"So what did he want them to do?"

Bowen smiled. "Make a movie."

"Make a movie? They were going to bet the future of the institution on a *movie*?"

"Yeah, a movie. A movie that would get picked up for distribution, like a real movie from a real studio, and it would bring in some cash. Maybe lots of it. And it would be publicity like we'd never seen before. Mr. Walsh said we oughta go big or go home. If we went down, at least we went down in a blaze of glory."

And then I remembered, Aileen Walsh said Leo was working on a film script. He'd been closed-mouthed about it.

"So," I asked, "what happened?"

"They bought it," Bowen said. "Loved the idea. Ursula would EP it—"

"EP?"

"Executive produce," he explained. "Jack McEwen would direct it. Raisa would edit it and Chris would shoot it. Justine would line-produce it. All the faculty members would take key positions and the rest of the crew would be students."

"And," I said, "Leo Walsh would write it."

He nodded.

"So did he?"

"As far as I know," Bowen answered. "The thing was, they were getting it together when spring quarter ended. They were gonna spend the summer quarter location scouting, casting, all the pre-production. Shooting would start in the fall."

"Only now there's been a little hitch," I said, staring down to my plate. "The guy who wrote the script is dead."

There was a long beat of silence. I looked up. "Was the script finished?"

He shrugged. "I don't know."

"Who would?"

"Ursula or Jack, for sure. But I'd be very careful about asking them."

"Why is that?" I asked.

"Because those people are not what they seem," Bowen said. "They're real nice and warm and friendly when they're trying to get money or something else out of you, or when they're trying to convince you to send your kid there. But don't ever forget, this business is cutthroat. These guys can be very dangerous when they're cornered."

"You seem awfully young to be that jaded," I commented.

He leaned in toward the table and lowered his voice. "You wanna know how jaded I am?" he asked.

I leaned in toward him. "What?"

He shifted his chair around the table, so that he was almost sitting next to me rather than across from me. He looked around warily, then reached down to his waist, where his XXX-Large pullover shirt was tented over his waist. He lifted the shirt up and motioned with his head to look down.

The handle of a pistol was nestled down in the cloth, inside a leather holster attached to his belt.

"Don't worry," he said. "It's legal. I got a carry permit."

I reached up and rubbed my chin. "You carry even on

campus?" I asked.

"In that neighborhood? Hell, yeah. Some nights I'm there 'til midnight. I ain't going out in that parking lot naked."

"Thought it was illegal to carry on a campus."

"Better to be tried by twelve than carried by six," he said, shifting his chair back around.

"So I'm told," I commented.

Makeup Line Lady showed up with separate checks. "Here you go, boys," she said as she set them on the table.

Bowen reached for his but I grabbed them first. "My treat."

"You don't have to do that," he said.

I shook my head. "I appreciate your time. I think we should stay in touch."

I pulled out my wallet and folded a fifty-dollar bill around the two checks and handed them off. "Keep it. Say, Micki Hicks isn't working today, is she?"

Makeup Line Lady smiled. "She comes on at four."

"Tell her Harry said hi..."

I looked down at the array of plates and debris on the table in front of us. "You didn't eat your apples," I said.

Bowen Masterson stretched and yawned. "Aw, I'm full," he said. "Besides, I'm trying to lose a few."

Chapter Twenty-Two

The roar of Bowen Masterson's pickup echoed through the parking lot as he gunned the truck out of there. I sat there for a second, running the air-conditioning full blast on the Tesla to try and cool it down. I also needed a moment just to process what I'd learned over lunch.

There are only a limited number of motivations for murder. Jealousy, hatred, greed, revenge, maybe a couple of others that I can't think of right now. All were reasons, even if unjustified, for killing. By far, though, the primary motivation for the ultimate undoable act was money. Whether it was robbery or embezzlement or blackmail or desperation, money was the number one catalyst in most murders.

Somebody has to die so somebody else can benefit.

But these things had to be weighed off against each other very carefully. More than anything else, murder is something you can't take back. Once you kill somebody, then that's who you are for the rest of your own life.

Believe me, I know. And the only thing that can take any of that weight off is if the killing was an act of self-defense or an attempt to save others. Or at least that's what I told myself during the nights when I couldn't sleep.

I pulled out my cell phone. Still no answer to my text to Alex. *Where the hell is she?* We're going to have to have a talk about this whole daddy/daughter communication thing.

"Hey, Siri," I said.

What now, Harry?

"Call Alex."

Oh, all right… Calling Alex.

A beat later, Alex's phone rang. And rang. And rang. Finally, it went to voicemail.

"Alex, it's me," I said after the prompt. "Give me a call, would you? I'm a little concerned."

I pulled the car out of the parking lot and drove to the light on Murfreesboro Road. When it turned green, I went left, up a block, and then right on the long hill up Spence Lane. Curiosity had gotten the better of me; I was less than twenty minutes away from Mt. Olivet cemetery. Leo Walsh's funeral was at one. I didn't think it was a good idea to attend the funeral; the NACA folks might wonder why a prospective parent would show up for something like that.

On the other hand, I wondered what kind of a crowd he was going to draw.

Spence Lane dead-ended into Lebanon Road. I turned left and drove down about a half-mile to the entrance to Mt. Olivet, which was a sprawling, huge cemetery that seemed even sprawlier because it butted right up against the Catholic Cavalry Cemetery. When you round the corner on Lebanon Road and begin the downhill run to Mt. Olivet, it seems like the entire left-hand side of Lebanon Road is nothing but graveyard as far as you can see.

I made the turn into the cemetery, the funeral home itself off to my left just inside the gates. It was a good half-hour before the funeral was scheduled to start, but the parking lot was already close to full. There were even a couple of news vans there, so maybe Leo hadn't been entirely forgotten so quickly.

I drove down the entranceway and came to another road that ran both ways. There was a black sign with a circle, an arrow pointing left, and the word "Funeral" etched on it in silver letters. Below that, the word "Walsh" had been spelled out in smaller letters.

There was no way I was going to join the crowd, so I turned left and drove past the funeral home. The road curved around to the right. I followed it into the cemetery, which was subdivided into plots that were almost like neighborhoods. One sign read "Garden of Gethsemane," while a little farther down, another read "Garden of the Gospel."

Another funeral sign directed people to turn left to get to Leo's graveside service. I stopped at that sign and looked over to my left, where a large tent was set up in front of a freshly opened grave. There were rows of folding chairs, lots of them, and a huge pile of dirt covered in purple blankets. A truck was off to the side, with a couple of groundskeepers in green coveralls standing around smoking.

I drove past them without making the turn, to the end of the road, then made a right and went up a hill. I was getting into the older and more prestigious part of the cemetery now, where the famous, the historically significant, and the well-off slept in what one hoped was eternal peace. There was a little side street. I turned into it, drove down to the end, turned the car around, and parked beneath a large tree with a lot of overhang that gave a little shade from the blistering sun. I was on a hill overlooking the plot of ground where Leo would be buried. The tent was plainly visible, although it blocked some of the folding chairs.

I checked my watch. Leo's funeral would start in about fifteen minutes. I cranked the AC up and pulled up a web browser on the instrument panel screen and started checking my email. As usual, most of it was either junk or newsletters and ezines I subscribed to. I'd gotten to where I was a sucker for clickbait. If somebody posted a link to a video of a rodeo clown having sex with a mountain goat, I wouldn't click it but I'd probably stare at it for a moment.

Nothing of substance here, so I pulled up the website for the local ABC affiliate and, sure enough, there was a live feed from Mt. Olivet on the daily lunchtime show. A young woman with a microphone was in the lobby of the funeral home interviewing, of all people, Ursula Gilbert. Ursula had changed into all funereal black for the occasion, with black slacks and a black suit jacket over a black silk blouse.

There was a crowd gathered round her, all listening to her answer the question of how much Leo Walsh had meant to the Nashville Academy of Cinema Arts and how he was the heart and soul of the Nashville creative community and how much he would be missed.

Blah, blah, blah…

I really didn't feel like listening to this crap and was about to hit the touchscreen to go to the CNN feed when I noticed a movement in the back of the shot. I leaned in close, squinting to try and get a better view. I touched a couple of buttons on the screen and blew the picture up.

Yeah, there she was, in the back of the crowded lobby, turning to go into the room where the funeral would be held.

Aileen Walsh.

She looked frail and shaky as she stood there alone. I wondered where her friends and family were, the folks who would help her get through this. And then I realized the truth for Aileen Walsh, a truth I'd only guessed at the afternoon I met her.

Aileen Walsh was truly alone.

I switched over to MSNBC Live on the satellite radio and listened to the latest craziness going on in the world. I tried to avoid politics as much as possible and national news even more than that. It was bad enough being in this unhinged world without having to listen to a daily update.

I got out of the car, hit the front trunk button on my fob, and lifted the "frunk" lid. I had a kit bag in there with road flares, a first aid kit, the usual auto emergency stuff. I'd also stashed a pair of binoculars in a black case. I pulled the binoculars out, carefully replaced the hood, and got back in the car. Having the car under a tree had cooled it off just a bit and, as often happened in Nashville in July, the afternoon sky had become thick with clouds.

I sat in the driver's seat and lowered the passenger window. I'd positioned the car so I had a good line of sight on the gravesite. By pivoting around and looking through the windshield, I could get an angle through the trees on the funeral home. Just as I turned the knob to bring it into focus, people started spilling out of the front of the building.

And from the side entrance, the pall bearers carried Leo Walsh's casket to the back of a hearse.

I sat there and watched this unfold as the cars lined up. In a few more minutes, the hearse pulled away from the funeral home and turned onto the road I'd just been on, then started the procession to Leo's grave. I stopped counting after thirty cars.

At the grave, the cars lined up for a hundred yards down the side of the road. The Nikon Monarch binoculars—the kind of toy I yearned for in my early days as a P.I. and could never afford—put me right in the middle of the crowd. As the pallbearers carried Leo to his final resting place, Aileen Walsh was accompanied by a guy in a black suit to the front row. He got her seated, then backed away.

There was a good crowd; Leo would have been surprised and he would have appreciated it. I spotted Ursula Gilbert with Jack McEwen, and behind them Raisa Petrov. Justine Moye was there as well and there were a bunch of other people around, some in jeans and T-shirts, whom I took to be students. The NACA group stood off to one side, near the back of the tent, but they were the biggest group there.

Then I saw it… At the rear of the procession, an immense Ford F350, all chrome and shiny black. The truck pulled over and parked behind the last car in line, and seconds later Bowen Masterson climbed down and plodded across the street, then stepped up onto the grass. He walked the hundred feet or so of sod to where the tent had been erected and stood there, by himself, in the back, away from everyone else.

I suddenly realized I'd seen everything I needed to see. I laid the binoculars on the seat next to me, raised the passenger window, then put the car in gear and left Mt. Olivet by the back way, so I wouldn't have to pass the crowd gathered to say goodbye to Leo Walsh.

❧

I plugged the car into the charger and took the elevator up to my office. Ashley sat behind her desk typing furiously away at something as I opened the door.

"Have you heard from Alex?" I asked, skipping the niceties. "I've been texting and trying to call."

Ashley looked up, shook her head. "Where is she?"

I stopped in front of her desk and pulled my backpack off my shoulder. "This was the first day I was leaving her alone at home. I told her I'd be checking in."

"She hasn't called here," Ashley said.

I let out a long, frustrated sigh. "Okay, I'm going to try again and if I can't get her, I'll head to the house."

I started toward my office. "How're things going today?"

"Thanks for asking," she said, with just a hint of smart-ass. "Everything's cooking along just fine."

I sat down at my desk and pulled up the Nashville Academy of Cinema Arts website, then went to the faculty page. I dumped the faculty page to my printer, then pulled up each bio and dumped those. By the time I finished, I had about twenty pages. I jogged them into a neat stack and then walked out to the front office.

"I've got a little assignment here for you," I said. Ashley looked up, curious.

"I need you to start digging into all these folks," I said. "You still have that file I gave you with the logins and passwords for those databases?"

"Yeah," she said, "the ones we never use."

"Never mind that," I said. "They don't cost that much. I kept the subscriptions current because you never know when you might be in the private detecting business again."

Ashley opened up a bottom drawer and pulled out a file folder. She thumbed through a stack of paper.

"Okay, we're still current with Intelius, PeopleFinders, US Search, and BeenVerified. Oh, and we let the TruthFinder sub expire, but I can restart it with no problem."

"Great," I said. "Now you get to play detective."

She smiled. "It'll be fun. Anything in particular you're looking for?"

"I'm especially interested in credit histories," I answered. "Employment and criminal history if anything unusual gets pinged. I highlighted the names I want you to check. Dig especially deep into Ursula Gilbert. I want to know everything there is to know about her."

Ashley nodded.

"And start digging into the Nashville Academy of Cinema Arts. I don't think they're a nonprofit, so they won't be on that website where the tax returns are… Uh, what the hell is it? What's its name? I can't remember."

"GuideStar?" she asked.

I snapped my fingers. "Yeah, GuideStar. See if they're on there, but I doubt it. So if it's not a 501(c)(3), then I want to know what it is. Is it a C Corp or an LLC?"

"It's almost got to be one of those," she said. "I don't see it as an S Corp or an LLP."

"Yeah, agreed. So get everything you can from the Secretary of State's office. And run a credit history on NACA, whatever structure it's got."

"Right," she said, picking up the stack of printouts and scanning the first page. "So when you need all this?"

I thought for a second. "Would sometime tomorrow afternoon work?"

Ashley smiled. "It'll be on your desk when you come in."

"Great." I turned and walked back into my office, closing the door behind me. I needed a minute.

I stared out the smoked glass that was the floor-to-ceiling exterior wall of my office. The river wound lazily by a dozen stories below me. Upriver, a tugboat pushed a row of barges that were probably too hot to touch in the searing July sun. Watching that somehow seemed soothing and made me wish I was standing on the banks of the river, staring out even closer.

I reached into my pocket and pulled out my mobile, then pushed the number to call Alex's cell again. It rang four times and I was about to hang up when she answered.

"Yes," she said, very quietly and subdued.

"Alex," I said. "I've been trying to call. Are you okay?"

There was a beat or two of eerie, dead silence and then a burst of sobbing.

"Alex, what's wrong, sweetie? Tell me."

The sobbing went on uncontrollably.

"Alex, honey, you've got to tell me what's wrong. I can't help if I don't know what's going on. Please, tell me."

She dialed it down just a bit and I heard her sniffling. "Daddy," she said softly. "I don't mean to keep saying this, but I hate it. I just hate it."

"Hate what, honey?"

"Everything," she said. "All this. I hate it. I'm miserable. I want to go home."

I hate to deploy a cliché here, but sometimes there's an element of truth at work in clichés: I honestly felt like I'd been punched in the gut.

"Alex, I'm coming home. I'll be there in twenty, twenty-five minutes tops. Can you just fix yourself a cup of tea or something and give me time to get there?"

"Okay," she whispered.

"I'll be there in a few minutes. Just sit tight."

She clicked the phone on her end and left me hanging in silence.

I stuffed my phone back in my shirt pocket.

Damn it.

Chapter Twenty-Three

Alex was sitting at the kitchen table when I walked into the house, nursing a cup of herbal tea and staring ahead. It was nearly three o'clock in the afternoon and she was still in the sweatpants and T-shirt she'd worn to bed the night before. Her eyes were red and bloodshot, her hair uncombed.

I sat down across from her. She looked up at me and we just stared at each other for a second. Then her eyes began to fill.

"I'm sorry, Daddy," she whispered.

I reached across the table and took her hand. "Look, you don't have anything to be sorry about. You've been through hell the past few months. It'd get to anybody."

She smiled, kind of, through gritted teeth.

"We've got our first, full-blown crisis on our hands, Sweetie," I said. "We've got to figure out what to do about this. We can't have you this miserable and upset all the time."

"Daddy, I don't know what to do," she whispered. "I just hate it here."

"Is it Nashville? Living here?" I asked. "I know this is a different world from the one you're used to, and truthfully, I'm not as fond of the place as I used to be. So I get it."

She laughed, again, kind of.

"Is it this house? Is there something about it you don't like, something we could change?"

"No," she said, shaking her head. "The house is fine."

I thought for a moment, then looked down at the table. "Is it me, then? Have I done something?"

She squeezed my hand. "No, it's not you. I don't know what it is."

"You know," I said. "This really is different. When you were younger, I'd fly to Reno and stay a couple days, maybe longer. Then we'd get on a plane and come back here. At first, you stayed a few days. Then a week or two. The last couple of years, it's been the whole month of July. But we always knew it was time-stamped. We always knew that on such-and-such a date, you'd go back home."

She teared up again and nodded her head.

"And we knew that our time together was special, so we'd try to work in as much fun as we could. We drove to Florida that one time, remember? A few days in that beachside condo that was pink flamingo all over the place. We drove up to Virginia, saw Appomattox, then came back through Dollywood…"

She laughed. "God, Dollywood…" Then she sniffed and reached for a napkin and wiped her nose.

"Yeah, and Gatlinburg. It was so kitschy you couldn't help but love it. But we always knew that you'd go back home. Now we don't know that."

"Yeah," she whispered.

"Now you are home," I said quietly. "And this is real life. Real life isn't road trips and Dollywood. It's the grind of school and work and day-to-day living."

She started to tear up again. "I miss her so much," she said. "I miss Aunt Marty's house and Estella and I miss the dry air and the beautiful clear nights. I want this to be home, I want to feel good about it, but I just—"

She stopped for a moment and wiped her nose again.

"I just can't."

"Alex, I'll do whatever I can to make this better, to make it tolerable. Maybe we should think about getting you in to see somebody. Somebody you can talk to and who can help you resolve all this stuff."

She stared at me for a moment. "You mean a shrink?"

"I mean a therapist," I said. "Nobody's saying you're crazy or anything like that. The world gets to everybody eventually. Sometimes, you just gotta put in a little couch time. God knows, I have."

"Really?" she asked.

I nodded. "Sure. I went through a bad time a long time ago and I needed some help. I resisted getting it at first. Your mother encouraged me and I eventually did. Never regretted it. Sometimes I think I could use a tune-up."

She laughed. I took that as a good sign.

"The truth is," I went on, "we've never lived together. I'll be sixty-years-old in another eighteen months. I came to parenthood pretty late in life. I'm trying to adjust myself, but at a certain point in life you're just not as flexible as you used to be. But I want this to work, more than anything."

She looked up at me, teary but smiling. "I know. I love you, too."

"If it has to be, we'll figure out a way to make it work with you back in Reno. The company pretty much runs itself. I could telecommute from Reno if need be. And if I have to let go of the company, I will."

"I don't want you to do that," she said. "It's your work, your company."

"And you're my daughter, so you're more important. Besides,

speaking of time-stamped, we all knew the company was going to come to an end when the European contracts expired. We can just move up the timetable a little bit."

She leaned back and ran her hands through her hair. "I guess I should get cleaned up," she said. "I've never laid around in my pajamas all day."

"Why don't we do this?" I said. "The Florida trip is still on this weekend. You fly down to Panama City with Lonnie and Sheba and spend a lot of time walking on the beach by yourself. You really ponder this. You're old enough to know what's right for you, and you're smart enough to figure it out. So why don't we put everything else on hold."

"Me fly down?" she asked. "You're not going?"

I leaned back in my chair. "I don't think so," I answered. "I think you need a little time away from me and this house and everything it means. Take a little Alex time and try to get some clarity. Let Uncle Lonnie teach you how to scuba dive. Have some one-on-one girl time with Sheba. Then when you guys get back, whatever plan you've put together, we'll get to work on it."

She stood up from the table. I stood up as well and we came into each other's arms. It felt good to hug her, to hold her, even if she did still smell like sleep.

"Thanks, Daddy," she said. "I love you."

"I love you, too. Go take a shower and figure out where you want to go for dinner tonight."

❧

The rest of the night went a lot calmer. We jumped on the freeway and drove over to Wedgewood Avenue on I-65 South, then into the Melrose area, where Alex got her first taste of Nashville hot chicken at Hattie B's. I warned her not to let her ego write checks that her taste buds couldn't cash, but she went a level or two above me anyway. She handled it like a pro and I was proud of her.

We settled into the sofa in the media room later that night and turned on Turner Classic Movies just in time to catch one of my favorite black-and-white Warner Bros. swashbucklers, Errol Flynn in *Captain Blood*. Unlike a lot of kids her age, Alex was perfectly comfortable with old movies; in fact, she'd been exposed to them and developed a love for them at an early age. She hadn't seen this one, though, and I was delighted she loved it.

After that, she headed for bed. When I went to the kitchen around one in the morning for a last glass of wine, I noticed her light was off. It was the earliest I'd seen her get to bed since she got here.

The next morning, she got up just as I was headed to the office and we had a chance to have a cup of coffee together before I left. They were leaving for Florida the next afternoon, so Alex was going to start packing. She assured me she was feeling a little better, a little more grounded, so I headed for the office with her promise that she'd answer my texts or call me if she needed anything.

Ashley was already at her desk by the time I got to the office just after 9:30. She had several piles of paper jogged into neat stacks on her desk. She looked tired, though. I went into my office and dropped my backpack behind my desk.

"You okay?" I asked when I came back out into the lobby.

Ashley yawned widely and stretched in her chair. She wore a pair of khakis and a loose blouse that was an homage to the paisley-powered sixties.

"I was here until almost midnight last night," she sighed. "You opened up quite a can of worms, sir."

"Wait a minute," I snapped. "Nobody said stay here 'til midnight. I don't like the idea of you being alone in this building that late at night. I mean, it's pretty safe and all, but this is Nashville."

"Don't worry," she said. "Hugh was working late as well. He's in a bit of a panic over our Friday meeting. He walked me to my car. I was perfectly safe."

"Well, all right," I said. "Is he back in already?"

She shook her head. "Haven't seen or heard from him. My guess is he slept late."

"Fair enough. Now what about this can of worms?"

She looked up at me for a second. "It's a lot to go through. And I'm going to need to explain some of it. Why don't we go sit in the conference room? I'll get us some coffee."

"No," I said. "I'll get the coffee. You should be waited on after all this extra work."

Ashley smiled. "It'll be interesting to see if you even know where the coffee is, but give it a try. I'll set everything up in the conference room."

I went into the breakroom and, sure enough, it had been so long since I made a pot of office coffee I had to dig around. I wasn't going to give Ashley the pleasure of recognizing that she'd spoiled us all, so I was determined to find the damn coffee and eventually I did. By the time I got back to the conference room, she had everything set up on the same side of the table that Leo Walsh had sat on.

"Coffee'll be up in just a minute," I said. I scanned the tabletop. "Jeez, you have been busy."

"Yeah, it's a fair amount to take in. I got you a pen and a legal pad out of the supply closet so you can take notes."

I sat down and tried to get comfortable. It looked like we were going to be here for awhile.

"Let's start with NACA," she said, grabbing a stack of papers, turning them around to face me and spreading them out across the table. "The Nashville Academy of Cinema Arts is, as we guessed, a Limited Liability Corporation. It was set up in the State of Tennessee just over a decade ago."

As she talked, Ashley pulled out sheet after sheet and pointed to pertinent places on the page. She'd highlighted specific places for me to take note of.

"The structure of the LLC is pretty standard. Now I'm simplifying it a bit here, but the reason to form an LLC is, as you know, it doesn't cost a ton of money and it's much less complex. The reporting requirements are way less stringent and there are some pretty significant tax advantages, depending on each person's individual tax situation. And perhaps best of all, the main reporting requirement in Tennessee is that you file annual paperwork with the Secretary of State's office. If the LLC becomes inactive and you don't file the paperwork, then the LLC simply self-dissolves. Easy peasy, lemon squeezy."

"Okay," I said.

"And unlike a C Corp, there aren't 'directors,' per se," she continued. "There are 'members,' and in the case of NACA, there are three of them. Ursula Gilbert is the majority member. She controls 55 percent of the corporation, with Jack McEwen controlling 30 percent. Raisi Petrov controls the remaining 15 percent."

"That's interesting," I said. "A school that's owned by its

faculty members. Not something you see every day."

She nodded. "For real," she said. "So that's how the company is set up."

She shuffled through the stack and pulled out another sheet of paper. "Now Ursula and her buddies actually set the company up at an interesting time. They filed the papers right after the 2008 election. During the Bush years, the regulations controlling for-profit schools were really lax. It was kind of wild west in those days. You had massive, nationwide chains of for-profit technical schools, business schools, even places that tried to pretend they were real colleges that were owned and acquired by hedge funds, venture capitalists. It was easy pickings because there was so much Fed scholarship money. Pell Grants, VA benefits, federal loans… It was like picking money off a tree. At one point, even Goldman Sachs had a hand in it."

"Really?"

"Yeah, they owned the Art Institute chain. There was one out on I-40 off Stewart's Ferry Pike, the Art Institute of Tennessee. It went under a few years ago, leaving hundreds—if not thousands—of students with worthless diplomas or no diplomas, and tons of student loan debt."

"So Ursula got in at a good time."

"When the Obama administration came in, they started taking a hard look at these guys. But NACA was already established and was, frankly, small enough to slide under the radar. It was companies like ITT Tech, the Art Institutes, a few others that drew the majority of flack. The local Art Institute even shared a building with another for-profit, Argosy University, that's rumored to be going under any time now. And in a complete ripoff of our own Hospital Corporation of America, one of the biggest chains is called the Education Corporation of America. There are rumors going on about them, too."

"So?"

"It's a different story now, a different world, but we're getting ahead of ourselves. All of these guys, even in the wild west days, had to have some kind of regulation. Are you familiar with accrediting agencies?"

I stared at her a moment. "If we're gonna get this bogged down in the weeds, I need some coffee."

I stood up. "How do you take yours?"

Ashley grinned at me, a smile that made me want to, for just a brief moment, melt.

"Cream, one sugar."

I made the coffee and carried two cups back to the conference room.

"It's not going to be as good as yours," I said. "But I hope it's drinkable."

She took a sip. "It's fine."

"Now to get back to your question," I said. "I don't know much about college accrediting, but I know you need it. I can't just rent a building and open up Harry James Denton's College of Advanced Philosophical Inquiry."

"Well, actually, you could," Ashley said. "But what you couldn't do was have access to federal financial aid. And in the end, that's what it's all about."

"So NACA was accredited?"

"In a manner of speaking," Ashley said, setting her cup down. "Without getting any more bogged down, there are basically six regional accrediting agencies throughout the country who establish standards for academia. All conventional colleges are accredited by one of these agencies. In this part of the country, it's SACS, the Southern Association of Colleges and Schools. Vanderbilt's accredited by SACS, Belmont's accredited by SACS. Blah, blah, blah…"

"So the Nashville Academy of Cinema Arts was SACS accredited?"

"Hah," she snorted. "Not on your Great Aunt Sadie's life. No, all these for-profits and fly-by-nights had to come up with something else to get access to the federal trough. Now there's one exception to what I said earlier. Art colleges, and that's 'art' with a pretty broad definition, are accredited by NASAD, the National Association of Schools of Art and Design. They're a legitimate, and in fact, quite demanding accrediting agency."

"So NACA went with NASAD?" I asked. "Try saying that three times without fumbling."

"No, NACA couldn't come anywhere near meeting those standards."

I suddenly felt exasperated. "So if NACA was able to get federal funding, who the hell accredited them?"

"Ever heard of the CFAAFP?" Ashley asked.

I scrubbed my memory. I had heard that before.

"Wait," I said. "When I got that tour of NACA…"

She nodded. "Yep, it's on the website as well. The Nashville Academy of Cinema Arts is fully accredited by CFAAFP."

"And what, pray-friggin'-tell, is the CFAAFP?"

Ashley pulled out another sheet from the stack and slid it in front of me. "The Council for Accreditation of Alternative Film Programs."

I scanned the sheet she'd put in front of me, which was a printout of the CFAAFP website home page.

"This looks like," I said slowly, reading the page, "the biggest load of horseshit I've seen in a long time."

"It is," Ashley said, pulling out another few pages and shoving them in front of me, "and as this article from *The Chronicle of Higher Education* reveals, the United States Department of Education was about to come to the same conclusion."

I picked up the printout.

"No need to read it," she said. "I can give you the bullet points. The Feds have finally worked their way down through the for-profit swamp to the level where NACA resides. Every quote-unquote college that's claiming this accreditation is being audited. They're not only at risk of losing their Federal funding, if they're found to have embezzled funds or inflated numbers or anything else not kosher, they could be forced to pay back every penny they ever got…"

"Holy shite," I said. "So it really is all about to collapse."

She nodded. "And that's just from the Fed side."

Ashley turned back to her stacks of papers, shuffled through another stack and spread it out in front of me.

"Look at this," she instructed. "I scrubbed down through the County Clerk's office and the Secretary of State's office. Six different companies have slapped liens on NACA for nonpayment of leases, debts, and they're behind on some business taxes. Sixteen individuals have taken them to small claims court for nonpayment of bills.

"Check this out," she said, pointing to one line. "They didn't pay their roofing contractor for repairs after the tornados in April."

A line of spring tornados had gone through the area a few months ago and shaken everybody around a bit. Nothing out of the ordinary for Nashville, though. Climate change has shifted Tornado Alley down and over a bit; some people speculate we're right in the middle of it now.

"And you know what FICO is, right?"

"Sure," I answered, "that's your credit score."

She nodded. "Right. Well, small businesses have FICO scores as well, the FICO SBSS."

"SBSS?"

"Small business scoring system. It ranges from 0-300. Lenders like to see at least something north of midway between the two."

"And NACA's credit score was?"

Ashley yanked out another sheet and pointed to a highlighted number at the bottom of the page.

"*Forty-five*?" I asked, incredulous.

"These people don't have a credit score good enough to pawn a car title," she said, "which they couldn't have done anyway since the cars for all their key personnel are leased. And about to be repossessed..."

I stared at the paperwork scattered all over the table for a few moments, then looked back up at Ashley.

"Bottom line, cut-to-the-chase," Ashley said, "the Nashville Academy of Cinema Arts was well and truly eff'd."

I sat there quietly for a moment, just taking it all in. Then I looked up at Ashley and felt this pang as I remembered the last time I'd sat in that conference room.

"And Leo Walsh knew about it," I said, my voice low. "He knew it and he came to me for help."

Ashley gave me a sympathetic look, but only for a beat. Then she reached for the next stack of paper.

"Oh," she said. "We're not done yet. Not anywhere near done."

Chapter Twenty-Four

An hour later, we took a break and I made another pot. We were both going through coffee like it had some kind of magical properties. Ashley had done an incredible job of pulling together this mass of data and molding it into something that we could both get our heads around. Between the caffeine and the revelations, we were both getting energized.

In diving down deep into the Secretary of State website, Ashley had located several other business entities that Ursula Gilbert had her fingers in. The first was another LLC that had been set up a couple of years ago and looked like some kind of leasing pass-through. I don't know whether this was something legitimate or some other scheme to try and save NACA. In any case, not much money had ever gone through and the LLC dissolved in year two.

There was another LLC that Ursula had formed with Jack McEwen, this one to provide location services and gear rentals to the local film community. Other than the public filings with the Secretary of State's office, there wasn't much other information available.

"You know what it looks like to me?" Ashley asked at one point.

I shook my head. "No idea."

"Location services and gear rental to the local film community," she said. "Now who's the local film community? The networks and the studios who come into Nashville have their own equipment or long-established partnerships. Tennessee's a right-to-work state, so it can't be a union thing."

"So?"

"I think she set the company up to rent gear and trucks and stuff like that to her own students."

"You're kidding," I said, after the few moments I needed to let that sink in. I scanned the documents. Damn, she was right. "Ursula *Jeel-bear* was charging students for tuition and then turning around and zapping them again to rent the stuff they needed to make the student movies she was requiring them to make?"

"Why not?" Ashley asked. "The students didn't know she owned the company they were renting from. There wouldn't be any blowback from them. It's a secondary income stream that has some really good tax advantages. Amortization, write-offs, the twenty-percent pass-through deduction. If I'm right, it was actually quite smart."

"Except she was ripping off her own students," I said.

Ashley shrugged. "It's the movie business. They need to get used to it."

We poured fresh cups of coffee and headed back to the conference room. She shuffled through an entirely new set of pages and set them in front of me.

"Now here's the one I can't figure out," she said. "To begin with, it's not an LLC. It's an LLP, which is a Limited Liability Partnership."

"Okay," I said, "is it necessary for me to understand the specific differences between the two forms?"

"Only in one respect," she said, spreading out the paperwork she'd downloaded from the Secretary of State's office. "An LLC is a company and while you can elect to have a member-managed LLC, usually you have one person in charge. With an LLP, you actually have a true partnership. The management of the partnership is determined by the partnership agreement, which can designate one partner as managing partner if everyone agrees, or not. The business, though, is run as a *partnership*, not a company."

I looked at her. "You should go to law school."

"I'm thinking about it," she said, pointing down to a line on the page. "Now look…"

I scanned the lines Ashley was pointing to. "Blue Moon Films, LLP," I said.

She nodded. "And look at the partners. Ursula Gilbert, Jack McEwen, Raisa Petrov, Justine Moye, Christopher Weyreuth, Katy Lederberg, and this one right here."

She ran her finger under the last name on the list.

I looked up at her. "Leo Walsh," I whispered.

She nodded again. "Yep, our old buddy, Leo Walsh."

I looked down again at the list of names. "Who's Katy Lederberg?"

She pulled another sheet of paper out of the stack. "She doesn't have a spot on the NACA website, but I pulled her up on the staff/faculty directory. She's the CFO."

"The Chief Financial Officer for the Nashville Academy of Cinema Arts," I said, "is involved in an outside LLP with the president of the college and the senior faculty members. Okay, next question. What is this partnership trying to accomplish?"

"The actual partnership agreement is not required to be filed with the Secretary of State. It's maintained by the partnership itself. But with a name like 'Blue Moon Films,' my guess is it's got something to do with the movie business."

I looked up from the paper. Ashley had a big grin on her face. "Good guess, Sherlock," I said.

"Just for shits and grins, I Googled 'Blue Moon Films.' There's no website set up, but the domain name's been purchased."

Then I remembered lunch with Bowen Masterson. "That's what the kid was talking about."

"What kid?"

"This kid I was introduced to when I took the tour at NACA. He graduated a few years ago and now he works there. Runs the equipment room. He slipped me his number, told me to text him. We wound up having lunch together and he told me this was Leo's idea, this plan to save the college by making a movie."

Ashley raised an eyebrow and tilted her head. "They were gonna make a movie to save the college?"

"Yeah," I said. "That was my reaction."

"Why didn't they just take every penny they had and buy Powerball tickets? Their chances would've been better."

I leaned back in my chair and stared down at the chaotic piles of paper in front of me, just trying to take it all in.

"How does this work?" I asked. "So Leo writes a script. They form an LLP and all the key players are partners. So the next step is what? Raising money, right?"

"You'd think so," Ashley said.

"Is there any way of knowing if they did that?"

She shook her head. "Not from this stuff. They're not required to file any financial papers with the state, at least not until their end-of-year deadline."

"So let's assume, just for the sake of argument, that they were going to try and raise the money. What would be the next step?"

"Well, first they'd have to have a business plan," she said. "And business plans for prospective movie projects are a little different than your ordinary run-of-the-mill mom-and-pop establishment. You have a treatment for the script—the script's usually too long to include in a business plan—and then you have a professional bio, credits and all that, of the key players. Then you usually have a wish list of who you'd like to star in the movie. And if you're able to approach actors with some firepower and get them interested, an LOI really helps."

"LOI?" I asked.

"Letter of Intent," she answered. "You get a Letter of Intent from Tom Hanks, it means he's aware of the project, probably read the script or at least one of his people has, and he's expressed an interest to his agent and is allowing you to use his name in connection with the project to raise money."

"But not committed."

"Right. But you get Tom Hanks' name attached to a script, you'll find the freakin' money. Then you put in the rest of your wish list, the other stars, principal parts, featured players, etc. And then you have to work up a projected budget, or sometimes several budgets. We can do this for 200k, we can do that for 600k, and for five mil we can blow this much stuff up."

She reached for her coffee cup and took another long sip. This was an intense pursuit, requiring frequent priming.

"And then you do your comps," she said. "You find other movies that are similar to the one you're trying to make and you list box office, foreign sales, rentals, streaming, and VOD. And you put all that stuff in there to make it attractive to potential investors. Show 'em how much money they're gonna make, although in truth what they're probably looking at is a great big tax loss."

"Who would they approach? Where would they get that kind of money?"

Ashley threw up her hands in the classic *who knows?* position. "I went to the main crowdfunding sites, Indiegogo and the like. No pings there. Nothing on the web search for Blue Moon Films either. Which means one of two things: either they haven't started the fundraising yet or they've already got it sewed up."

"It's a slice, isn't it?" I said. "Clearly, Ursula Gilbert and the rest of her crew went to a lot of trouble. And there was a lot at stake. The question is *was it enough to commit murder?*"

Ashley stared at me for a few moments. "I guess that's what you have to figure out, Sam Spade."

"And if this whole scheme had nothing to do with Leo Walsh's murder," I said. "Then what effect is his death going to have on the project? Could it go on?"

"That depends on a lot of things," Ashley said. "From the terms of the partnership to the question of ownership of the script. A script has the potential to be valuable intellectual property, and the laws related to IP are complicated and involved. And, of course, we start to venture into estate law as well. One could make the case that if the project goes forward, Walsh's widow is entitled to something. Maybe a lot… And if Leo Walsh was in the Writers Guild, then there's a whole ripple effect there. Residuals and death benefits and future payouts. Harry, this is a mess that's hard to describe without using the word *cluster* somewhere in the sentence."

I looked at Ashley. "How'd you get to know so much about the movie business?"

"Did two separate modules on the entertainment industry in MBA school."

"Well," I said, "it took."

Back in my office, I sat down at my desk and tried to calm my racing heartbeat. Too much caffeine, I guess.

Or maybe it was something else. A couple of decades ago, when I first started out in this crazy business, my heart rate used to go up when that first thread unraveled. You look at the same piece of fabric over and over and over until you think you've seen every pattern, every stitch, and it's all the same and nothing changes and you feel that frustration.

And then something happens. The light hits it at a certain angle it's never hit before, or you hold it a certain way and a fold appears that you never would have guessed was there.

Suddenly, you're looking at it differently.

That first little thread sticks up from the pattern and, at first glance, it appears harmless, insignificant. But you scrape your fingernail across it and it stands up just a little bit. So you scrape some more and it pulls a little bit looser and then suddenly you can get your index finger and thumb on it at the same time. You can get a grip.

So you pull.

The thread comes loose, so you pull some more and it pulls out even longer and you realize for the first time that the first thread's connected to another thread, woven into a pattern of many threads.

And if you just stick with it, just keep pulling and don't give up, the whole damn thing'll come apart.

We had just gotten to that first little whisper of a thread. We'd scraped a couple of times and gotten it a little looser. Now it was time to take two fingers and apply some pressure.

I sat in my office chair, my back to the desk, facing out over the Nashville skyline and the river and the Titans stadium, just pondering what I'd learned from Ashley this morning. Ashley, who by the way was due a hefty bonus check when this was all over, had found the right piece of cloth and scratched around until the first thread came loose.

I picked up my mobile and scrambled down through the text messages until I found the right one, then touched the screen and the call went through. It rang four times and she picked up.

"Hello."

"Aileen, this is Harry Denton again. I hope I didn't get you at a bad time."

"No, it's a good time. What's up?"

"Remember when we were talking back in your apartment and you told me Leo'd been working on a new script?"

"Yeah, I remember."

I held off for a beat, just wondering if this was such a great idea. What the hell, go for it.

"You wouldn't happen to have a copy of that script, would you?"

There was a long silence over the phone. Finally, Aileen Walsh made a kind of sighing sound, sort of a hiss.

"Why do you ask?"

"Curiosity, Aileen. I'd just love to see the last thing Leo wrote. I'm sure it's good and maybe, just maybe, we'd get some answers out of it."

"Everybody seems to want a copy of that script," she said.

"What? Has somebody else asked for it?"

"Jack McEwen called this morning," she said. "He asked if I had a copy. I told him the truth, that I'd found a three-ring binder in Leo's office with several drafts of the script."

"Did you give it to him?" I felt my heartrate going back up.

"I told him I'd drop it by the school the next time I was over there. I've still got to collect Leo's things from his office."

"Okay," I muttered. "What's next..."

"What?" she asked, her voice tightening. "Is there some reason I shouldn't give it to him?"

"No," I said. "None at all. But can I ask one thing?"

"What?"

"Let me come by and make a copy of it first, okay? I don't want the original, but let me make a copy."

She hesitated, but only a moment. "All right. I suppose it's okay."

"If it's convenient, I could even pick it up in an hour."

"I'm home," she said. "I've got two more days before I have to go back to work."

"Thanks, Aileen," I said. "I really appreciate it. I'm on my way."

I grabbed my backpack and headed for the elevator, then texted Bowen Masterson before I pulled out of the garage: Call me when you can talk. I was just pulling onto the freeway entrance ramp when the hands-free went off in the car.

"Bo," I said. "I'm in the car. Can you hear me?"

"Sure."

I gunned the Tesla to get past a tractor-trailer and the car silently shot up to 75 in about two seconds. "Are you somewhere where you can talk?"

"I'm in the equipment room alone," he said. "The doors are closed."

"Okay, listen, we've been doing some digging and it turns

out that what you were telling me about Leo's idea of making a movie was true."

He made a noise like a bull snorting. "What, you think I was lying?"

"No," I said. "Of course not, but I needed more specifics. And we've got them. It turns out all the key people at NACA are involved in this."

"Wow," he said. "Okay, so what can I do to help?"

"You're there late a lot of nights, right?"

"At least two or three a week."

"So what access do you have to the building?"

"I've got a C6 key. It's the master to the whole building."

"Great," I said. "Ursula and Jack and all the others formed a Limited Liability Partnership, with Mr. Walsh as one of the members. I need a copy of that partnership agreement. And as part of this, they'd put together some kind of a business plan or prospectus. If we could lay our hands on either one of these, then we might be able to get some answers."

There was a long beat of silence, and for a moment I thought the call had dropped. I switched two lanes over and got into the far left passing lane just past Briley Parkway.

"Bo?"

"I'm here," he said. "So you think somebody here might have had something to do with Mr. Walsh's murder?"

"I don't know," I answered. "Probably not. Good God, I hope not. But there's only one way to find out. When we know what was really going on there, then we can eliminate that as a possibility."

"Tonight, there's a production class that goes 'til nine," he said. "I have to stay at least that late to get the gear checked in and then I have to get the soundstage squared away for tomorrow morning's classes. I'll see what I can find tonight."

I smiled. "Great. And I'll be up late tonight. Call me or text me with what you've found, okay?"

"Okay, Harry," he said. "I will. I just hope nobody here's involved."

"Me, too," I said. "And Bo?"

"Yeah?"

"Be careful, okay. Watch your ass."

❧

Aileen Walsh said barely two words to me when I stopped by her apartment to pick up Leo's script. It was in a thick, three-ring binder with a red vinyl cover. I flipped through it briefly. It looked like four drafts of the script, three-hole punched and bound one after the other, with a whole section of handwritten notes. The earlier drafts were marked up in red pen to the point where it looked like Leo had taped the pages to a wall and fired a shotgun full of red ink at them.

I walked back out to the car. Siri reluctantly, and with a great deal of attitude, GPS'd me to the nearest copy center on Lebanon Road. I pulled the notebook apart and started feeding the pages into a document feeder. The whole notebook ran 450 pages or so and it took awhile to make the two copies I wanted. I'd take one copy for myself and I'd lock the other one away, for what I didn't know. It was just an instinct.

I'd actually never read a film script before, so I wouldn't know whether Leo's script was any good or not from a filmmaker's viewpoint. But I read a lot of novels and see a lot of movies, so I figured I could probably assess whether the story was at least engaging to a layman.

I took the box full of copies and set it on the backseat floor of the car, then drove back to Aileen Walsh's apartment. I made it back just before two. I thanked her and asked how she was coming along. She spoke in one or two word answers, clipped and terse.

I wished her well, then got back in the car, which was beginning to feel more like my living space than just a device to get me from one place to the next. I had to get back to the office, then plow through my email and correspondence. I was, after all, still running a business.

Well, sort of.

Chapter Twenty-Five

By five that afternoon, I was back home. I'd stashed my copies of Leo's script in my backpack and dumped them off in my home office. Alex had packed and pulled herself together quite nicely. She seemed a little more relaxed, easygoing. I won't say happy or upbeat yet, but at least we didn't appear to be in crisis right now.

"Are you sure you're okay with me staying the night with Aunt Sheba and Uncle Lonnie?" she asked as we were setting her bags near the back door. She had a suitcase, her backpack and laptop, and a soft duffle bag.

"Sure," I said. "I'll miss you, but this way we don't have to fight the morning traffic to get to the airport. I just hope you can sleep."

"Sheba showed me the guest room the last time we were there," Alex said. "It's nice. It'll be fine. Are you going to be okay?"

I smiled at her. "Yes, I'll be fine. I've actually got a busy day tomorrow. The IT guys have been killing themselves the last couple of months developing this new software package and we're meeting Friday so I can see it for the first time."

"What does the app do?"

I cocked my head and thought for a second. "I haven't the faintest idea," I confessed. "But it's got something to do with cybersecurity, analytics, whatever."

Alex laughed. "Daddy, you're a Luddite."

"I'm amazed that at your age," I said, picking up her suitcase and duffle bag, "you know what a Luddite is."

She grabbed her laptop and backpack and followed me out the door. "Oh, that's easy. A Luddite is every baby boomer who thinks they know what technology is all about but resents it anyway."

"Hey, lighten up," I chided. "You forget that my generation is the only generation in human history that was born into a world without computers and a third of the way through their lives were drowning in them."

We loaded her stuff into the car. I pulled up the app on my mobile and activated the security system, then hit the button on my key fob and opened the gate. We pulled out of the driveway, turned left and headed toward Shelby Street. Ten minutes later, I was across the bridge and into the downtown area. We were due at Lonnie and Sheba's for dinner at six.

"So how did your day go?" I asked. "Spend most of it packing?"

She turned, looked at me funny. "How long do you think it takes to pack?"

I shrugged. "I don't know. I think it's different for guys. I've never needed more than about twenty minutes for any trip that was less than a month. I think it's a little more complicated for women."

"Only a little," she said. "It took about a half-hour. But I did have one weird thing happen today."

"Yeah? Tell me."

"I got an email from Bitsy and Cricket at Bealesworth," she said. "Which was weird in itself, because nobody emails anymore. But there's a weekend-long new student orientation next weekend."

"This coming weekend?"

"No, next weekend, the weekend after we get back from Florida. We'll be back Thursday and the retreat starts Friday afternoon."

I turned. She had a blank look on her face, one I didn't know how to interpret.

"So what's involved in all this?"

I turned onto Charlotte Avenue and got in a long line of traffic crawling past the state capitol.

"They sent me a link to a page on the website," Alex explained. "We'll stay in the dorms all weekend and there's a big welcome dinner Friday night, then games on Saturday and a dance on Saturday night. There's like some orientation meetings, we can meet the teachers, stuff like that."

Legislative Plaza came up on our left. There was some kind of festival or something going on. I couldn't tell what it was, but it was a good-sized crowd and that was probably what was slowing the traffic up even worse than usual.

"So what do you think?" I asked. "Are you even thinking about going? I thought you couldn't stand Bitsy and Cricket."

"Oh, I never said I couldn't stand them," she countered. "I just meant they… Well, I'm not sure what I meant. But they followed me on Snapchat and Instagram and I followed them back and, really, they're not so bad. I guess."

I smiled. "Have you decided to do it?"

She hesitated. "Well, I guess it won't hurt…"

We were silent for a few moments. I came to the stop light just past the capitol. We sat there, quiet, until the light changed.

"I'm glad," I said, as we drove on down the hill. "I'm glad you're going to do it and I hope it turns out to be a good thing.

But there's no commitment still. If you don't want to go to Bealesworth, we'll do something else."

She smiled at me. "Thanks, Daddy."

ᯓ

Sheba had a dish full of lemon and garlic baked chicken breasts in the oven when we got there. Alex peeled off and left me like she'd just spotted Zac Efron in a mall food court. I grabbed a cold one and walked out onto the terrace, feeling a little left in the dust. Lonnie was already out there nursing one, a couple of empties on the deck beside him, as I sat down in a patio chair.

"Everything squared away on the plane?" I asked.

He turned to me. "You nervous about her going?"

I took a sip of the beer and stared off into the horizon. The sky was especially glowing and colorful today, which meant, of course, the pollution was worse than usual. Nashville was notorious for getting trapped under heat inversions in July.

"Of course I am," I said. "And it's got nothing to do with you. I'd be scared if Chuck Yeager were flying the plane."

"Well," he laughed. "You should be. Chuck Yeager's, like, fuckin' ancient."

"Smartass," I said. "You know what I mean."

"Why don't you go with us?" he asked. "I'm going to need a little extra testosterone to survive this estrogen tsunami. I'll take you deep-sea fishing."

"I would," I said, truthfully. "Except I'm in the middle of something right now and just can't get my head out of it."

"Let's not speculate on what you can't get your head out of, okay?" he said. "So, The Case of the Famous Murdered Author. What's going on with that?"

"It's getting interesting," I said.

Lonnie winced, then groaned. "Oh, man, I remember how you used to use that word in the old days. It usually meant things were about to go to smash."

I laughed. "I hope not. But it does look like our buddy Mr. Leo Walsh had a lot of complicated shit going on in his life."

"Spare me the details, okay? I just hope you know what you're doing."

"I will admit," I said after a long pull on the Yazoo bottle, "it feels good to be back in the game. I was afraid that muscle had completely atrophied from misuse."

I turned the chair to face him as he lay stretched out on his favorite chaise lounge. "I know this sounds crazy," I said, "but since Alex came here and this whole Leo Walsh-thing just kind of fell in my lap, I almost feel more… more…"

"Alive?" he said.

"Yeah, alive. That's it. More so than in a long time."

Lonnie looked for a second as if he were studying me. "Yeah," he said. "You seem more alive. Just make sure you stay that way."

"Oh, don't worry. I intend to. This is just a really interesting intellectual exercise."

"Hey, dumbass. You forget that somebody killed somebody over this intellectual exercise. Remember the old saying: *It's all fun and games until somebody loses an eye…*"

He tipped his beer bottle toward me. "*Then it's frickin' hilarious.*"

⁂

Dinner was delicious, the conversation relaxed, convivial. Alex laughed along with the rest of us and it seemed for a little while like the chaos and upheaval we'd gone through in the past couple of weeks was on its way to being behind us. We finished off a bottle of really nice Spanish white wine and then opened another. By 8:30, the world had cooled off. We moved outside and had ice cream on the terrace. There was a slight breeze blowing in from the west and the traffic noise far below us was just a faint buzz. The Gulch was packed with traffic, tourists, and locals out enjoying the summer night.

"Has this always been such a party town?" Alex asked in the middle of a discussion about how the city had changed over the years.

"The simple answer is *yes*," Lonnie said. "It's the music business. You can't have country music without honkytonks and you can't have honkytonks without a lot of cold beer."

"It goes back farther than that," I offered. "If you look at it historically, this city's always had a certain *laissez-faire* approach to life. During the Civil War, Nashville was the first Confederate state capitol to surrender to the Yankees. And what effect did that have on the city?"

"If I remember my history," Sheba said, "there was an explosion of prostitution."

"It was regulated and licensed," I added. "One of the earliest instances of legalized prostitution in America. In one sense, this city's more like New Orleans than any other place in the South."

"Maybe that's why I like it so much," Lonnie said, grinning.

I looked at my watch. It was nearly ten o'clock.

"So when are you guys taking off tomorrow?"

"I told Compact to have the plane fueled and ready by eleven."

I turned to Alex. "You excited?"

She smiled, nodded. "I'm a little nervous about the whole scuba thing."

"You'll love it," Lonnie said. "It'll change the way you look at everything."

I stretched my legs out in front of me and let loose with a loud yawn. "I should get out of here, let you guys get some sleep. I'm pooped myself."

"I get it," Lonnie said. "You okay for driving?"

"I cut myself off over an hour ago. Sheebs, that was a wonderful meal. Thanks."

I stood up and held my hand out to Alex. "Why don't you walk me to the door?"

She took my hand. "Love to."

I said goodnight to Lonnie and Sheba, and Alex and I walked through the coop to the elevator door.

"You'll call me when you get there, right?"

"Sure. I won't forget," she said. "I promise."

"And you be careful down there in the water," I said. "Stick close to Lonnie and Sheba, okay?"

She smiled. "I will," she said. "Don't worry."

"Don't mean to be a helicopter parent," I said. "I'm still new at this."

We hugged and said we loved each other, then hugged again. I'd gotten used to having her around all the time in a remarkably short period. Now it was hard to let go.

The traffic through The Gulch was still at a *party-time-battalion-style* level. I had to slam on the brakes once when a couple of drunk frat-boy types stumbled out into the street without bothering to glance one way or the other. They staggered across the street without even acknowledging that I'd just saved their lives by not mowing them down.

Once I got back to Charlotte Avenue, the traffic lightened up tremendously. In about fifteen minutes I turned off the main drag in East Nashville and onto my side street. As I approached the house, I fumbled with my key fob to hit the button and open the gate.

As the gate began swinging open, a pair of headlights just past the driveway on the same side of the street as me blazed on, blinding me. The glare filled my windshield; it was impossible to see anything. I jumped on the brakes in the middle of the street.

"Damn it," I hissed. I flicked my high beams once to try and alert the other driver to turn his blasted lights off.

No luck.

I eased up on the brakes and moved forward a few feet, then turned the wheel to pull into the driveway. Suddenly, the glare in front of me was partially blocked by this hulk stepping into the street. I ducked down and squinted hard, tried to focus.

Bo Masterson came into view. He stopped right in front of the Tesla.

I opened the door and practically jumped out of the car. "You scared the shit out of me," I barked. "What the hell are you doing?"

"I didn't think you'd ever get home," he said, looming over me. "I've been sitting here almost an hour."

"Why didn't you just text me?"

"I did. You never texted back."

It was then I remembered. I'd silenced my phone when we started dinner and forgotten to turn it back on. I pulled my mobile out of my pocket and tapped the button. The little text icon had a "1" above it.

"Sorry," I said. "I was at dinner. How'd you find out where I lived?"

He sneered and literally looked down his nose at me.

"I get it," I said. "Stupid question. Nobody's off the grid anymore."

"Took me exactly four mouse clicks."

"So what do you want?" I demanded. "It's late."

He reached into his pocket. "You asked me to dig around, see what I could find. Well, here it is."

He pulled his hand out of his pocket and extended it to me. When he opened his hand, a small USB drive with the Nashville Academy of Cinema Arts logo printed on it was in his palm. He handed it to me.

"What's on it?" I asked.

"A lot. I didn't even have time to read it all. Emails, a bunch of Word files, and a PDF of Mr. Walsh's script."

I took the drive from him without mentioning I already had the script. "How'd you get all this?"

"A little birdie gave me the administrator's password to the network drives," he said. "I just went into everybody's Gmail account and did a bunch of keyword searches. Didn't have time to read much. Just download it all and scram."

"You didn't leave anything behind, did you? No bread crumbs to trace you or anything like that?"

He shook his head. "No, it's clean."

"What happens if they find out?"

"What do you think? I'm history. But it's a good chance my job's going away anyway."

"I'm not worried about your job," I said. "You can always find another job. I'm worried about something happening to you if the wrong person finds out."

He reached down, patted the holster under his pullover shirt. "I can take care of myself."

I nodded. "Good. When do you need this back?"

"I don't. I made a copy."

I stared down at the little red-and-white plastic doohickey in my hand. I wondered what kind of trouble we'd just bought ourselves.

"Okay," I said. "I'll dig down through all this and touch base with you tomorrow."

He nodded. "You watch your ass, too. Okay?"

"All the time, my friend. Thanks."

Bo Masterson turned and walked toward the light. He climbed into his massive Ford pickup, turned the wheel hard to the right and roared past me, leaving me on the side of the road. I got back in the car and pulled into the driveway, making extra sure the gate closed behind me.

As I parked the car and plugged it in to charge, I suddenly felt a knot growing in my stomach.

"So much for nice, relaxed evenings," I said out loud.

Chapter Twenty-Six

The house seemed creepily quiet with Alex gone. She'd been here a week and I was already used to having her around. The next few days, I feared, were going to drag by like sludge.

I stacked up a couple of pillows behind me and settled into bed with a glass of white wine and my laptop. I had a hard copy of Leo's script on the bed next to me as well. I sensed it might be a long night.

I slipped the thumb drive into the USB port on my laptop. A couple seconds later, an icon appeared on the screen. I double-clicked that and a series of folders appeared. Each folder was labeled with the name of the person who had the account. There was one for Ursula Gilbert, another for Jack McEwen, and so on down the faculty and staff list. There were also a couple of folders with names I didn't recognize.

I double-clicked Ursula's folder. A long list of emails appeared, way too many to take in right now. I closed that folder, then opened every other folder and did a quick scan. Bo Masterson had bootlegged copies of hundreds of emails off the NACA servers. I don't know how he did it, but it must have taken hours.

There were also some other folders on the drive. One was labeled Blue Moon, with another labeled Spreadsheets. I clicked on the Blue Moon folder and saw a long list of emails, and along with them, a bunch of subfolders. There was a subfolder labeled Budgets, another labeled Business Plan, and another labeled Pre-Production.

One was labeled DoE.

Department of Education I whispered.

I opened the pre-production subfolder and unveiled another group of folders, which I guess were *sub-subfolders*, with names like Casts, Locations, and Props.

All the minutiae and machinations of making a movie…

I took a long sip of wine and leaned back against the pillows. I felt overwhelmed, as if by opening up this thumb drive I was risking going down a rabbit hole that was going to be awfully hard to come back out of. I'd been bogged down in the weeds before and I knew how tough it could be to try and keep a clear head under these kinds of circumstances.

And now I knew why Leo Walsh had struggled so hard to explain his story to me. Leo Walsh's life, both personal and professional, was *complicated*, in every sense of the word.

I looked over at the clock on my bedside table. It was just past eleven and I hadn't slept much the last few nights, at least not the kind of good sleep that's restful and restorative. Everything's so fitful and unsettled these days…

I set the laptop aside and picked up the stack of papers next to me. The top page of the script had a title:

YOUNG AGAIN

centered on the page, and below that:

Written By

Leo Walsh

At the bottom of the page, the words "Registered WGAW" appeared, with Leo's contact information typed in the far left-hand corner. I set the title page aside and turned to page one.

FADE IN:

was typed at the top of the first page on the far left-hand

corner, and below that:

EXT. BACKYARD – DAY (DECEMBER, 1962)

I started reading Leo's script, wondering if I was going to encounter movie terms and weird stuff I wouldn't understand. I'd never seen a film script before.

As I read, though, I realized that what I was reading was a fairly conventional story just laid out differently on a page than a short story or a novel. There were some terms that I'd never heard of, but they seemed pretty intuitive. Some were obvious abbreviations. Inside shots were abbreviated "INT." and outside shots "EXT."

I also noticed that everything in the script was visual. There was no interior monologue for the characters, nothing about what they were thinking or feeling, and as I continued reading, that began to make sense. Since movies could only present stuff visually and through recorded sound, there's no way for us to know what characters are thinking or feeling or planning.

No way to capture the endless stream-of-consciousness narrative that goes through most of our heads in real life during every waking moment.

The story started off simply enough, with the portrait of a middle-aged man in a boring office job, with a wife who probably kind of still loves him but is pretty bored with him after nearly twenty years of marriage. He has three kids: a teenaged daughter showing signs of real rebellion, a middle son who likes him okay but doesn't have time for him, and a younger son who still adores him the way only six-year-old boys can adore their fathers.

The middle-aged protagonist cares for his widowed mother, but she's in a nursing home, needy and broken and fading into her own twilight. He's also haunted by the death of his father, who was killed in a freak accident when he was ten. His father was a mechanic who was working on his car Christmas day when the jacks collapsed and crushed him.

Yeah, I guess having your father die on Christmas Day would result in a little baggage.

The one thing the protagonist has to remember his father by is the Chevy that killed him. He's restored the car to pristine condition and now it's a collector's item. One night, he's driving and a railroad crossing gate malfunctions just as a train approaches. There's a horrible accident. The protagonist lies unconscious in the wreck.

When he comes to, it's November, 1963. The protagonist is a little boy again, only he's got the consciousness of a middle-aged man and all the memories he's collected over the decades. He sees his parents again, when they were young and beautiful. He has his beloved pet dog back again.

And two weeks to change history and save his father's life…

He had me by page five. The writing was simple and visual, but vivid and alive and eloquent. Leo Walsh's writing was almost lyrical in places, moving and fluid. It flowed and was easy to read and follow, yet at the same time never felt like it was pandering or talking down to readers.

At the end of the script, the protagonist-as-young-boy does save his father by diving under the car just as the jacks collapse and save him. But the car falls on him. When he wakes up, he's middle-aged again, in a hospital bed after the train wreck.

And his whole world is different…

By the time I hit the last page, with `FADE OUT.` typed against the right-hand margin, it was nearly one AM.

There were tears in my eyes as I read the broken Leo Walsh's tale of redemption and healing and changing history. It was what we all want in life: a do-over, a chance to go back and fix everything that went wrong in our lives. It was magic, a fairy tale, of course, and it could never really happen. But it was also written in a way that made you think maybe, just maybe, it *could* happen and, in the process, give us a little hope that we might all get out of this shitty mess with a little of our souls left.

Okay, I'm not a movie critic and certainly don't have any real knowledge of what makes a script or a movie great, but this stack of paper piled next to me on my rumpled sheets spoke to me in a way that not much had in a long time. Maybe Leo tapped into some kind of old-guy zeitgeist and I, basically being an old guy carrying around more regret than I ever thought I would, bought into it.

In any case, it was something special. But what were they going to do with it? How were they going to take this stack of paper and turn it into something that would literally save a school that was within weeks of going under?

Suddenly, Scarlett O'Hara flashed through my brain: *I can't think about that right now. If I do, I'll go crazy. I'll think about that tomorrow.*

I reached up, turned off my lamp, and slid into an uneasy, restless sleep.

❧

My cell went off just as I was loading my laptop into my backpack, along with the usual pile of stuff I carried into the office every day. Sometimes I felt like I was carrying a mobile office with me everywhere I went.

"Hi, Sweetheart," I said as I slid the button across the screen to take the call.

"Daddy, I just wanted to say goodbye. We're headed to the airport in a few minutes."

I smiled. When a teenager calls a parent without prompting, that's a minor victory. "How'd you sleep last night?"

"I had a hard time settling down," she said. "But Sheba and I stayed up and watched a movie together."

"Yeah? What'd you watch?"

"The ultimate chick flick," she answered. "*Twilight*."

"I never saw that one," I confessed. "Had you seen it before?"

She laughed. "About twenty times," she said. "And Sheba and I had a real serious discussion. She's Team Jacob and I am *so* Team Edward."

It was my turn to laugh. "When you get back," I said, "you'll have to explain to me exactly what that means."

"C'mon, Daddy, it's kind of like in Harry Potter, where you figure out which house you are."

"Say what?" I asked, fumbling for my keys.

"C'mon, you know. Like I'm definitely a Ravenclaw."

"Okay, you'll have to add that to the list of things you're going to explain to me when you get back."

"Daddy, are you saying you never read *Harry Potter*? I gave you the first one three years ago and told you to read it. I said it would change your life."

"Yeah," I said. "Middle-aged corporate types always depend on thirteen-year-olds to give them something to change their lives."

"So did it?"

I had my backpack over my shoulder and was about to go out the door. I stopped for a moment.

"The truth?" I asked. "I read the first 25 pages and fell asleep.

Bored the crap out of me."

She made a noise like a kitten reacting to having its tail stepped on.

"I'm sorry," I said. "So what house am I?"

She was silent for a moment, then her voice sounded like a pout. "You're probably a Hufflepuff. But you might be a Gryffindor."

We were both silent for a long beat. "I'll have to Google that when I get to the office. I hope it's a compliment."

"It is," she said. "At least you're not a Slytherin."

"Be careful," I said. "I love you."

ᘛ

When I got to the office, Ashley was nowhere to be seen. The reception area was empty and silent. I walked into my office and unloaded my gear, then fired up my laptop. I started to drill down deep into the thumb drive, but the silence began to get to me.

I walked back out into the empty reception area, past the conference room and the break room, down the hall toward IT. Don Hazzard, our network server guy, was behind a wall of oversized HD monitors parked next to each other on his massive desk. Don's one of those people you just never quite figure out. He was a large, heavy guy who usually dressed in jeans, suspenders, and flannel shirts. He shaved his head but had a neatly trimmed beard and piercing blue eyes. He was also, I'd been told in confidence, gay.

The hard part to figure out, though, was that he was an arch-conservative, ultra-right-wing Republican. I don't mean he was a gay Republican like those Log Cabin Republican folks. He was a Rush Limbaugh, Glenn Beck, Ann Coulter-type wingnut. He had a framed Rush Limbaugh poster on the wall behind his desk and a framed, autographed photo of Antonin Scalia on his desk next to the monitors.

Yeah, never could figure him out. But he was the best damn network server guy any of us had ever met. Each one of those terminals on his desk monitored network and server activity from all over the globe—six monitors, six continents. We didn't have any customers in Antarctica yet, but when we got some, Don could wire them in and take good care of them.

Back before the acquisition, he and Lonnie used to get into it big-time and, on occasion, I had to step in between them. Now that Lonnie was out, though, Don had gotten a lot less vocal and in-your-face. He and I had a talk; I respected his opinions even if I didn't understand them, and as long as it didn't interfere with any work or cause any disruptions among the team, we were good to go.

"Don," I said, leaning into his open door. "Morning, buddy. Where is everybody?"

His shiny bald head popped up from behind the bank of monitors. "Not sure," he said. "Pat's in her office, I think. Ashley was here earlier. I guess Hugh's around. He's in a panic over the demonstration tomorrow."

I shook my head. "He don't have to worry about that," I said. "There's no pressure. If he wants to push it out, I'm good with that. We're not under any contractual deadlines or anything."

"He'll be glad to hear that."

"I'll go talk to him," I said, backing out of his doorway.

I went on down the hall. Pat McClellan was on a call in her office to the left, so I just lifted a hand and waved to her. Hugh Caulfield's office was at the end of the hallway, the door to the right. As head of IT, he was sort of second-in-command and I fully admitted he knew more about the tech side of the business than I ever would. He had an office that was about the size of mine, with a great view of the river as well.

His door was closed. Without thinking, I knocked twice, grabbed the doorknob, and pushed the door open.

And there they were, Ashley and Hugh, standing in the far right corner of his office, with their arms wrapped around each other and their faces in a world-class, Olympic gold medal, *ooh* and *aah* liplock…

I sucked in a gulp of air so quick it sounded like a burst from a blowgun. Ashley's eyes shot open and she broke the kiss with a squeal that was not a squeal of pleasure. Hugh pulled away with a look of shock that quickly transitioned to something along the lines of *holy shit*.

I held out my hands in the classic pose of apologetic supplication, like when you think you're home alone so you just open the bathroom door without hesitation, only to find there's somebody sitting on the toilet with their pajamas around their knees.

"Sorry," I squeaked. "Shoulda knocked."

I backed away and jerked the door to, then turned and fast-walked down the hallway to my office. I shut the door and retreated behind my desk.

Okay, I whispered to myself, *just go on with your day*…

I opened the thumb drive. I'm pretty good with reading stuff on a computer screen, but when I'm really doing some serious study, I've got to have a hard copy. So I methodically and mindlessly started dumping emails to the private printer in my office. I started with Ursula Gilbert's folder. She had separate folders for correspondence, reports, and a separate folder as well for the Blue Moon project.

When we set up the offices, we had a too-generous budget for office supplies and equipment, so I told everybody to go all-out. I took Hugh's recommendation and bought a high-speed, dedicated, top-of-the-line color laser printer for my own personal use. The printer whirred now as I dumped the emails as fast as the queue could spool them.

Twenty minutes into this little whirlwind, there was a quiet tap on my office door.

"Yeah?" I said, loud enough to be heard.

The door opened slowly and Ashley stuck her head in, but just barely.

"Bad time?" She sounded tentative, nervous.

"No," I said. "Please, c'mon in." I motioned to the visitor's chair in front of my desk.

Ashley slipped in and closed the door behind her, then stepped over and sat down without making even a footstep sound on the carpet. She folded her hands in her lap and looked down at them a moment, then looked up at me.

"Listen, Harry," she said. "I'm sorry."

I smiled at her. "It's me that owes you an apology," I said. "I should learn to knock."

She smiled back at me, which I was suddenly grateful for. "Are we okay? Hugh says you're probably gonna fire us."

"Don't be ridiculous," I said. "I couldn't run this place without you. In fact, I'm not sure I run it with you. You guys keep this place going more than I do."

"C'mon," she said, teasing. "You're our fearless leader."

"Yeah," I said, curling my lip, "it's been my experience that fearless leaders usually don't do much."

"I am sorry, though," she said. "It was a breach of professional protocol."

"Oh, hell, don't worry about it. We're a small group of people, working odd and long hours in an intensely close environment. Hey, *effluent occurs*."

"Besides," I added. "It's not like we caught you huffing spray paint in the supply closet."

She grinned. "No, that's next on the list."

I looked at her for just a moment and she stopped smiling. Maybe I looked a little serious.

"I just hope you know what you're doing."

She looked away for just a second. "Harry, he's a really nice guy. You know he went through this terrible divorce and he's got custody of a six-year-old boy."

"I remember," I said. Hugh Caulfield's divorce had been about as ugly and drawn-out as any one I'd ever seen. Made me glad I never remarried after my own.

"And after something like that, you'd think he'd hate women or be terrified of ever getting involved with anyone ever again. But it seems to have had the opposite effect. He's a gentle guy, kind and loving."

I tilted my head toward her. "Not trying to pry. But is it serious?"

"We're taking it a day at a time," Ashley said. "Harry, it's scary to say this, but I think I may kinda love him."

I felt a twinge in my chest.

"Why didn't he come down here with you?"

"If he knew I was here, he would have."

I sat up and nervously jogged a pile of papers into a neat stack. "Tell him everything's fine. Oh, and tell him there's no pressure on the demo of that new app. We haven't made any announcement about it or anything else. This is something we're doing on a time-available basis."

She watched me stacking the papers, then looked behind me to the printer on my office credenza. It was borderline running over with printouts.

"What are you doing?" she asked, puzzled.

"Well," I said, hesitating. "To deploy a term I used to use a couple of careers ago, I'm trying to crack a case."

Ashley looked at me funny, as if she were confused and trying to figure something out.

"Want some help?"

Chapter Twenty-Seven

I burned a quick copy of the USB drive to my laptop, then handed it off to Ashley. We split the folders up and she began dumping copy to the main printer in the breakroom.

"You sure you're up for this?" I asked before she headed to her desk. "It's not part of your job description."

"C'mon, Harry, you know me. I'm always up for an adventure."

"I appreciate it," I said. "And look, you want some DoorDash for lunch, just have it sent up. My treat."

"Great. What've you got a hankerin' for?"

I looked up from my laptop. "I'm easy. Why don't you poll the rest of the crew and we'll just feed everybody today. Too hot to go out anyway."

It took almost an hour to dump everything from my half of the thumb drive. I had a stack of paper close to six inches high, a couple of reams anyway. It was just after noon by now and the DoorDash guy showed up just as I was wrapping it all up.

Ashley was finishing her printouts, so I helped the delivery guy unload in the breakroom. I signed the chit for the bill and handed him a twenty as he left. I stepped out in the hallway.

"Lunch," I yelled. "Come and get it."

Pat McClellan hobbled out of her office on the cane she'd been using ever since she took a fall off her bicycle a few weeks ago. Pat was nearly my age, short and struggling to avoid becoming any more matronly than she already was. She probably didn't have any business biking through Warner Park, but we tail-end baby boomers just don't seem to want to let go.

Don followed her. "Where's Hugh?" I asked as he walked by. He shrugged, pointing behind him.

I walked to the end of the hallway. This time, his door was open and I stuck my head in.

"Ashley ordered lunch," I said. "That new Mediterranean place over near 4th and Commerce. Supposed to be pretty good."

He looked up nervously from behind his computer terminal, struggling to make eye contact.

"C'mon," I said. "Ya' gotta be hungry."

"If you're sure," he said, standing up.

"About this Friday," I said as we walked down the hall. "Would it be possible to put off the demo a week? I'm kind of jammed up and I'd really like for Lonnie to see the demo as well, if you don't object."

Hugh Caulfield tried, largely unsuccessfully, to hide his relief at having an extra week and at knowing things were okay with us. "Sure, Harry, if you're okay with that. And I'd be happy to have Lonnie here."

"Great," I said. "He's down in Florida right now with Sheba and Alex. But they'll be back Thursday night. So Friday afternoon?"

"Sure, that works."

We all stood around the table in the breakroom, dishing up Mediterranean salad with goat cheese and olives, healthy stuff that I wasn't used to. We made small talk and joked around, politics and the weather and the traffic and all the craziness that seemed to be going on in Nashville and the world these days.

About ten minutes into it, Ashley walked into the breakroom.

"Grab a plate," I said. Ashley smiled at me, but she looked over at Hugh, sitting at the far end of the table. Their eyes met and I saw something for just a second. Maybe it was just my imagination.

Maybe I was wishing I could share a look like that with somebody.

I pressed that pesky thought out of my head very quickly and turned back to my gyro smothered in yogurt sauce.

"Have you been reading any of these?" Ashley asked, her voice low as she walked up to the corner where I was standing with a plastic plate in my hand.

"I've scanned some of them," I answered. "Not enough to have a sense of what they all mean."

She leaned into me. "Let's not make a big thing of it," she whispered. "But we need to get this stuff into the conference room and have a behind-closed-doors talk."

I nodded. "Okay. Right after chow."

❧

We cleaned up the wreckage from lunch and stowed the leftovers in the breakroom refrigerator. Everybody migrated back to their offices and the place became deadly silent again. I loaded up my stack of paper, with red sticky notes dividing the pile by folders, and walked it down to the conference room. Ashley was already there, with her piles neatly arranged in front of her.

"You seemed very cautious at lunch," I said.

"I've seen enough and read enough of this to get the feeling that there's some pretty explosive stuff here."

"You're a step ahead of me," I said. "Why don't we each sit down and just take a bit of time to scan through these and see what we come up with. I don't mean thoroughly read each page.

That'll take forever. But just a quick scan…"

She nodded.

I had a red pen and a legal pad with me and started with Ursula Gilbert's folder. It was pretty easy to scan the subject line of each email and scan the text. Like most people, Ursula Gilbert's emails were far too long and badly written.

What emerged as I scanned the documents was nothing new: a portrait of a business on the verge of collapse. There was even an air of desperation as she pleaded with updates each day on incoming revenue, which bills had to be paid and which ones could be put off. It turns out that their bogus accrediting agency required some pretty hefty payments to keep their accreditation current. Somehow I doubted that Vanderbilt and Harvard had to make monthly payoffs.

Then there was an exchange between all the faculty members over this possible movie project. I began to see that a lot of what Ashley and I printed off was going to wind up as duplicates. Ursula would get an email from Jack McEwen and reply to it, then he'd reply, and she'd reply back, and pretty soon you had an email chain that no doubt existed in both their accounts.

Ashley had Jack McEwen's folder. We were probably reading the same emails.

There was a long email chain between Ursula and the NACA Chief Financial Officer, Katy Lederberg. These also portrayed a desperate cash flow situation.

Clearly, things were not good.

Ashley looked up. "Have you started digging down into the emails about the movie project?"

I nodded. "Yeah. And I didn't mention to you that I read Leo Walsh's script last night. His wife gave me a copy."

"Was it any good?" she asked.

I stopped for a second and stared off behind her. "It was brilliant," I said. "It's everything these guys all say it was. If they'd made the movie and done it right, it might have saved the place."

She looked down. "So whatever went wrong is buried here."

I nodded and went back to work.

Forty-five minutes later, I looked up at Ashley. "Did you find the email chain between Ursula, Jack, and Leo from late last May?"

She shuffled through some papers and extracted a short pile, heavily marked in red.

"Yeah," she said. "The tone's pretty strident."

"It seems like everything was moving along just fine and then suddenly it all went off the rails. Some minor disagreements, then some back-and-forth… Creative differences, maybe. But then it looked like it was starting to get nasty."

Ashley shuffled through a stack of printouts and pulled one out. "Go to May 25th," she said. "Not quite two months ago."

I started fumbling through my stack. She reached for a blue highlighter and ran it across a few lines and then slipped the paper across the table to me.

"Here it is," she said. "Formal notice that Leo Walsh was pulling out of the deal. He officially withdrew himself and his script from the project."

I read the lines and felt my forehead knotting up.

"But why?" I asked. "Did he show it to somebody and get a better deal? Were Ursula and Jack trying to screw him out of something? I mean, I don't even know if he was getting anything out of the deal anyway."

Ashley shuffled through another set of papers. "Here's the

LLP agreement," she said. "The formal instrument that created the project. It was attached to one of the emails from March."

She turned a few pages, then pointed. "Leo was in the Writers Guild," she said. "And he was determined to keep his membership valid and adhere to the union terms."

"I've heard of the Writers Guild," I said. "Every few years they show up in the news when they go on strike and then there's no new TV for a while."

Ashley smiled. "It's a little more involved than that. I did a paper in MBA school on the early days of the movie business in Hollywood. The earliest screenwriters would often get screwed out of money and credit. Louis B. Mayer or Jack Warner or one of those other movie moguls would get pissed off at a writer and take his name off the movie, or else give screenwriting credit to his mistress because she'd given him an especially good blow job the night before."

I smiled. "Okay."

"So the writers got together and formed a union and for the traditional Hollywood studios and production companies who sign on—what they called *signatories*—the contract is as binding as a straitjacket."

Ashley shuffled through a stack of pages she'd set off to the side and pulled out a couple that were stapled together. "I went to the Guild website and printed off a few pages that summarize what they call the MBA, the Minimum Basic Agreement."

She gave the pages a 180 and slid them over to me.

"See," she said, pointing to a highlighted place on the page, "even if Ursula and Jack and the others made the movie at the smallest possible, micro-budget level, they still had to pay Leo just over forty grand.

"And," she added with a bit of a flourish, "sole credit."

I stared at the highlighted chart on the page in front of me. "Holy crap," I said. "Leo Walsh, who was so broke he could barely make rent, was willing to walk away from forty grand and a screen credit."

"My guess is the credit meant more to him than the money."

"Probably," I agreed. "So the question is *what the hell did they do to him that made him willing to walk away from that*?"

"That's question number one," Ashley said. "And here's question number two…"

She stared at me a moment.

"Did Leo walking away from this deal make somebody, somewhere, mad enough to kill him?"

I sat there for a second, then suddenly jumped to my feet. I pushed the chair back against the wall and started pacing back and forth on the carpet.

"Yes, this is it," I said. "I knew there was more to this than a disgruntled ex-wife or a pissed off current wife. And it sure as hell wasn't the case of a middle-aged guy trolling Murfreesboro Road for a hooker and having it go sideways. That was just the cops being lazy."

I paced down the table to the end of the conference room, then turned, folded my arms and leaned against the wall. Ashley sat there, watching me.

"It's in there," I said, pointing to the piles of paper. "We've only gone through a small percentage of all this junk. But it's in there. The answers. We keep digging and we'll find it."

"Why do you think Leo didn't just come out and tell you this the first time you met him?" Ashley asked.

I tucked my head into my chest, then reached up and started

massaging my temples. I was getting one of those tension/stress headaches that sneaks up on you sometimes.

"Maybe because I was in such a hurry to get to a fucking funeral," I said.

"Or maybe he didn't think you'd believe him," Ashley offered. "And maybe he realized that even if he had explained it all, there was nothing you could have done. Remember, he didn't say he wanted you to *stop* his murder. Just solve it..."

"What'd they have to kill him for?" I said. "If he was buggering up the deal, sue him. Hell, fire him. Don't beat him to death and throw him between a couple of fucking Dumpsters."

I stood there thinking for a moment. I wasn't sure what the next move should be, and then it hit me.

"I think we've cracked this, Ashley," I said. "But now it's outside our wheelhouse. The next step is to get all this paper organized, write up a summary report, and get it to Lieutenant Akers at Metro. And maybe to the District Attorney. Let them take it from here."

I stared at Ashley for few seconds as the color drained from her face.

"What?" I asked.

"Harry," she said quietly. "Sit back down."

I narrowed my eyes. "Why?"

"Please." She motioned toward the chair. "Sit down."

I eased back over to the table and sat down. "What?" I said again.

She took a deep breath and let it out slowly. "I don't know where you got all this stuff—" She held out her hands, palms toward me, as if warding something off. "And for God's sakes, don't tell me. I'm in deep enough already."

"What are you talking about?" I demanded. "I've got one nerve left and this is getting on it."

"Thirty years ago the Feds enacted an amendment to a 1984 federal law called the Comprehensive Crime Control Act of 1984. The law is called the CFAA, the Computer Fraud and Abuse Act. This law made it a crime to hack into anyone's email. Not just the government's, not just a corporation's, but *anyone's*. It's a federal crime, Harry. Whoever took these emails committed a federal crime, and by taking possession of them, you've become an accessory."

I was stunned, and the look on my face must have conveyed that.

"And by sitting here reading them with you and having this discussion, I've joined the conspiracy."

"That's crazy," I said. "We're investigating a murder, for chrissakes."

"Law enforcement agencies investigating a murder can go before a judge and get a warrant," she said. "You can't."

"Okay," I said. "Federal crimes. Don't federal crimes usually have some interstate component to them? Don't we have to carry these emails across state lines."

Ashley shook her head. "Look at this stack here, a series of emails between Ursula Gilbert and that fake accrediting agency, whatever the hell it was. Their offices are in Chicago. And look at all those emails between Leo and the Writers Guild in L.A."

I felt the color draining out of my face this time. "Oh, shit…" I muttered.

"Remember when Sarah Palin was running for vice president in 2008?" she asked.

"What the hell has Sarah Palin got to do with this?" I asked, feeling like I was in a thick fog.

"In 2008, this kid down in Memphis—Germantown, I think it was—hacked into Sarah Palin's email account. He frickin' guessed her password and got it right. He was just pranking her. He changed her password so she couldn't get into her own account. He posted some personal shit on a couple of websites, then posted the new password so everybody could read her email."

"So what happened?" I whispered.

"He was only twenty years old and from a well-off family. His father was a state senator. When he got busted, he went in front of a jury and confessed, said it was all a joke, a prank. The jury laughed their asses off and sent him to prison for a year and a day..."

I let out a long sigh.

"Harry, if we went to the cops and managed to somehow avoid the hoosegow, the evidence couldn't be used in court anyway. It's tainted. Fruit of the poisonous tree. We not only cannot go to the cops with this, we can't tell anybody else about it either. If any of these guys in the office find out, they're as liable as we are. We're all in a world of hurt then. What we need to do is run this stuff through the shredder and then drop that thumb drive down a sewer grate."

"Yeah," I muttered after a few moments. "Yeah, you're right."

Then it hit me.

"Wait," I said.

"Wait on what?" Ashley demanded. "This stuff's hotter'n a two-peckered billy goat. If somebody walks in here in the next five minutes and asks us what it is, we're screwed."

I started laughing. "Okay, you can take the girl out of the

holler, but you can't take the holler out of the girl. Look, nobody at NACA knows we've got this stuff. And if they find out, they're not going to the law on it because then the hacked emails become evidence, and therefore open to discovery."

I sat back and thought for a moment.

"As bad as this is, they've got more to hide than we have. Even if there's no evidence of murder in this paper, if it got out it'd be a P.R. disaster they could never come back from. Try recruiting students with this stuff hanging all over you. No, we lock this away in my desk drawer. You forget that you've seen it. I certainly won't rat you out, given that I'm the one that got you into this in the first place. Let's just sit tight and keep digging…"

"Are you sure?" she asked.

Just then, my mobile buzzed. I pulled it out of my shirt pocket and touched the screen.

A text message, from Bo Masterson.

"Oh, shit," I muttered.

"What? Who is it?"

I looked up at Ashley. "I can't tell you."

Chapter Twenty-Eight

I left Ashley alone in the conference room with the piles of paper that could, under just the right circumstances, send us both to Federal sleepaway camp for awhile. She was going to box it all up and tape it securely, then I'd find a place to stash it until we figured out what to do next.

One thing was for sure, though. We might not know *who* murdered Leo Walsh, but we had a pretty good guess as to *why*.

There are details to be filled in, specifics yet to be explained, and to paraphrase a former useless politician who dragged us into yet another stupid war, there are the things we know, the things we know we don't know, and the things we don't know we don't know.

The known unknowns and the unknown unknowns…

It would come together, though. It was just a matter of when.

I ducked into my office and closed the door behind me. I reached into my shirt pocket and pulled out my mobile, then tapped the screen to get the incoming text message. I hate to fall back on an old cliché, but as I read Bo Masterson's text, my breath literally caught in my throat.

THEY KNOW. EVERYTHING. INCLUDING YOU.
I DON'T KNOW HOW, BUT I'M OUTTA HERE.

I don't know how many *oh, shit* moments in a row I can take. First, I find out why Leo Walsh was killed. Then I find out that by finding out, I can go to prison. Then I find out I've been found out.

I closed the text message screen. "Hey, Siri," I said.

What, Harry?

"I'm not in the damn mood right now, Siri," I barked. "Call Bo Masterson."

Jesus, Harry, chill... Calling Bo Masterson.

The phone rang three or four times, then Bo picked up. The signal had a ton of ambient noise, almost like a whooshing sound, with an engine roaring in the background.

"Yeah!"

"Take me off hands-free," I said.

"I can't," Bo Masterson snapped. "I'm in the truck." The state legislature passed a law that says you can only use a cell phone in a car if it's on hands-free. As far as I knew, Bo Masterson and I were the only two people in the entire state aware of that law.

"At least roll the windows up," I said.

There was another whirring sound and then the noise level dropped about fifty percent.

"Thanks," I said. "Now I can hear you. Listen, Bo, you can't just drop a bomb like that in a text message. How the hell did they find out?"

He didn't say anything for a long time. Just ambient noise and traffic noise filtering into the closed cabin of the truck.

"How was I supposed to know the offices had security cameras?" he asked, his voice low.

"Oh, no," I said. "You didn't tell me you actually broke into their offices. I thought you just got access to their email accounts."

"And the safest way to do it was to do it from their desktops," he said. "That way, they'd know somebody hacked their accounts but there wouldn't be an IP address or a MAC identifier to trace back to who did it."

"I think I understood about half of that," I said. "So they've got security footage of you sitting at their desks late at night typing away on their computers. But you said they knew about me. How the hell did that happen?"

"Harry," he said. "I think somebody must've followed me when I went to your house last night."

My jaw clenched so hard my teeth hurt.

"Okay," I said. "This is not good."

"Yeah, tell me about it."

"So what happened. Did you quit?"

"Hell, no," he said. "I didn't tell nobody nothing. I left at lunch and I ain't going back. Didn't even clean out my desk."

"Where are you going?" I asked.

"Home right now, to pack a bag. Then I'm headed out of town."

I thought for a second. Mike Tyson once famously said *everybody has a plan until they get punched in the mouth.*

Well, we have officially been punched.

"Something stinks here, my friend." I said. "I've had things go off the rails before, but this was too easy for them to figure out. You told me your IT guy was the one who gave you the passwords, right?"

"Yeah, it was Brent. Brent Haggerty. He slipped me the passwords."

"Well, wouldn't Brent Haggerty have known about the individual security cameras in all the offices? In this company and my last one, it's the IT guys who install the cameras and maintain them."

There was a long pause and then a spewing sound erupted like somebody snapping a pop top on a warm beer can.

"*Son of a bitch,*" Bo said.

"You've been set up, my friend," I said. "No, we've been set up. What was that IT guy's name again?"

"Brent Haggerty," Bo yelled over the roar of the engine. God knows how fast he was going. "And I'm gonna beat his ass."

"No, you're not," I said. "These guys are playing for real, Bo. They're not screwing around here. I think one of them killed Leo Walsh, and it's a funny thing about killing…"

"What?"

"In for a penny, in for a pound," I said. "If they've killed once, they'll do it again."

"So what do we do?"

"You do exactly what you're doing now. Go to ground and stay there. Keep your cell phone close, though, and take my calls. Okay?"

"All right, Harry. I'll do what you say, for the time being. But if one of them did kill Mr. Walsh, I'm gonna take it out on their ass."

"You just lay low for the time being. Let's check in in a day or so."

I hung up, slipped the phone back into my pocket, then left my office and went down to the conference room. Ashley had gotten all the printouts into a single cardboard bankers box and was sealing it up with a tape gun.

"I've always thought the best place to hide something was in plain sight," she said as I sat down at the table. "I'll just slip this onto a shelf with the two dozen other bankers boxes in the storeroom and nobody'll ever notice."

I looked up at her. I hoped I hadn't done anything that would put her in jeopardy. I was ready to kick myself to begin with. My stomach was in a knot and my thoughts seemed scrambled.

Suddenly, I was struggling to think clearly and filled with something that felt an awful lot like dread. How do you back out of something like this?

"No," I said after a moment. "I don't want it in the office. If I had known the problems this was gonna cause, I would've never involved you. Nobody's seen you with this stuff except me, and like I said, I ain't talking to nobody. If I take that box and put it somewhere where you don't know where it is, then at least you've got… What do they call it?"

"Plausible deniability?" Ashley said.

I nodded. "Yeah."

I reached into my pants pocket and pulled out the original thumb drive from Bo. I pulled my shirtsleeve down over the drive and rubbed both sides and both ends of it on my pants.

"Before you seal that thing up," I said. "Let me drop this in the box."

Ashley lifted a corner of the box and I slid the thumb drive under the top and let go of it. It made a plopping sound as it landed.

"Are you okay?" she asked, the tape gun screeching as she layered tape over the top, sealing the box tight.

I thought for a second. That's a complicated question right now.

"Yeah," I said. "Everything's fine. Let me have that thing and I'll get it out of here."

~

I carried the box back to my office and started searching on my laptop. I needed to get this as far away from my office as possible, and I couldn't take it home either. I didn't want it anywhere near the house.

I found one of those self-storage places out in Bellevue, on the west side of town, just off I-40 at the Highway 70 South exit. You could rent a storage unit totally online, fill out a contract, pick out a unit, and get the access code to the main gate without ever talking to a human being.

Which was good, because I wasn't in the mood to talk to anyone right now.

I filled out the forms, typed in my credit card number, and rented the smallest unit they had on the corner farthest from the entrance. By the time I got it all squared away, it was nearly three o'clock.

I loaded up my backpack and carried the white cardboard box out into the lobby.

"I found a place to stash this where it'll be safe," I said to Ashley. "And you can truthfully say you don't have any idea where it is. That is, if anybody ever asks…"

"Harry, they probably won't," she said. "Maybe the best thing to do is just lay low for a little while. Maybe the cops'll figure this out on their own. They won't need us or the emails."

"Yeah," I answered, "and maybe monkeys'll fly out of my butt."

This look of confusion crossed her face. "What?"

"*Wayne's World*," I said. "*Saturday Night Live*? Movie?"

She shook her head. "Little before my time."

"Great," I muttered. "Make me feel even older than I already do."

She smiled. "Sorry."

"I'm headed out of here," I said. "Won't be back tonight."

"Harry," she said as I was about to go out the door. I turned and faced her.

"Be careful."

I got on an elevator, not knowing that it was going to stop on nearly every floor. Every time someone stepped in, my paranoia levels rose even higher. When the car hit the main lobby floor, most people got off, but then five more got on for the underground parking garage.

Glad it wasn't cold or flu season…

I got off at the Parking 1 level, along with two other people, and we all went off in different directions. As I approached the Tesla, in the section of the garage reserved for plug-in electrics, my anxiety ratcheted up even further. Electric cars that have to be disconnected from wall cables aren't the best vehicles for fast getaways. If there was somebody hiding nearby, that fifteen seconds or so it took to unplug a car and stow the charging cable was a perfect time to strike.

I hit the key fob and unlocked the car a good twenty feet away. I threw my backpack and the bankers box into the backseat and did a complete 360, scanning the whole area. It looked like I was alone. I unplugged the car, then jumped in and locked the doors.

I backed the car out of its spot and drove through the underground parking garage with my head on a swivel. As I got to the garage exit onto Fourth Avenue a couple blocks up from Commerce, the afternoon traffic was already so thick you had to wait your turn to wait. The thought suddenly occurred to me that the car in front of me and the one behind me trying to leave the garage effectively had me boxed in.

Now I know how Sonny Corleone felt at the tollbooth…

No gunfire erupted, though, and after about five minutes, I managed to squeeze out into the traffic. I wound my way over to Charlotte and then hit I-40 Westbound toward Memphis. The traffic was *speed up—slam on your brakes—speed up again* all the way to the White Bridge Road interchange, then it spread out and lightened up. I pulled off at Exit 196, where I-40 intersected 70S, and went left up the hill.

There was a Home Depot on the right. I pulled in and bought a Master combination lock, like one of those you used to have on your locker in high school. I folded the sheet of paper that had the combination on it and tucked it into my wallet.

I crossed back over Highway 70S and went into the entrance of a small strip mall. Behind it, almost hidden from the street, was the Bellevue Self-Storage lot. I stopped at the keypad right before the closed chain-link gate. I grabbed my backpack out of the back seat and retrieved the printout with the access code on it.

A few seconds later, I was in the lot with the gate sliding shut behind me. According to the paperwork, my storage unit was to the right and all the way down to the back of the lot. Thankfully, there was nobody else around.

I pulled down to the end of the lot and then scanned my paperwork. My unit was J-25. I looked up and there was a big J on the building next to me. I turned the car around so I wouldn't have to back out, then got out and pulled the bankers box out of the back seat.

I carried it over to Unit 25, a 5x7 storage locker. The door was a metal shutter that raised up like the front of a Manhattan deli. The inside of the unit was like an oven in the hot July sun. The buildings on the outside of the facility were not temperature controlled, so you better not store anything perishable. The temperature-controlled inner units were almost as expensive as an apartment used to be.

I slid the box into the corner of the unit, then went back and got the lock out of the car. It had been a while since I fumbled with one of these things, but after a couple of tries I got it to work. I lowered the shutter door, then slid the lock into the gate and snapped it shut.

I looked around quickly, still paranoid. I was alone. Maybe, I thought, I'd managed to pull this off.

Just as I climbed back in the front seat of the Tesla, my cell phone went off. Probably Alex, I thought, phoning me to let me know they'd settled into the condo okay. I swept a finger across the screen without looking at it and raised the mobile to my ear.

"Hey, how—" I said. Then stopped, mid-sentence. There was no one there.

Just music.

Only it wasn't music like you'd get if you were on hold with someone. That annoying *Muzak* everybody hates.

No, it was… *circus music*. There was a calliope playing that familiar circus music from when we were kids.

Dat dat datta-datta, dat dat dah dah, Dat dat datta-datta, dat dat dah dah, Dat dat datta-datta, dat dat dah dah, dat dat datta-datta, dadda dadda dadda…

"What the hell?" I said out loud.

Then this voice came on, masculine, deep, gravelly, loud, and decidedly angry.

"*Hey, Dr. Northrup! How's that kid of yours? Briggs?*"

"Who is this?" I said, the calliope music still blaring in my ears.

"*Does he still want to go to film school? Are you gonna bring him by for a tour?*"

There was something mechanical about the voice, something not human. "Who is this?" I demanded again.

"*Cut the bullshit,*" he yelled. "*We know you ain't no doctor and we know you ain't got no son. We know who you are, Harry, and we know where you fuckin' live! So if you don't stop digging around and start minding your own business, you're gonna be real sorry*!"

"All right," I said, "this is crazy. Who are you?"

"*And those emails you stole better not ever see the light of day, you little prick*!"

The calliope music got even louder and more chaotic. "For the last time," I yelled into the phone, "who is this?"

Then the music stopped cold. I thought for a second that whoever it was had hung up. Then he came back on.

"*Who do you think it is, Harry*?" he growled into the phone. "*It's me, Krusty the Clown! And I'm coming after you if you don't back the fuck off.*"

Chapter Twenty-Nine

So I'm standing here alone in the back end of the parking lot at a self-storage facility on a July afternoon when the temperature's approaching 98 degrees and the humidity is thick enough to slice yourself a chunk of air, and I'm absolutely freezing.

Literally, I'm shaking.

There's sweat running down my back beneath my shirt and it feels like ice water. My knees feel shaky and weak. I leaned against the side of the car and put my face up toward the sun, closing my eyes and just trying to get my heart rate down.

There was a burning in my gut and I had goosebumps on my arms.

Krusty the Clown.

Who the hell is Krusty the Clown?

I tapped the button on my mobile.

"Hey, Siri," I said.

What now, Harry?

"Who the hell is Krusty the Clown?"

I stood there for a few seconds.

"Okay," Siri said. "I found this on the web for *Who the hell is Krusty the Clown?* Check it out."

The first citation was Krusty the Clown's Wikipedia page. I tapped the screen, read a few lines, then realized I was wasting time and operating out of panic. Of course, a character from *The Simpsons* had not just threatened my life. There were apps that could disguise a voice and turn it into anything. You can have Frank Sinatra do the outgoing message on your voicemail. Yogi Bear could be the intro message on your answering machine. You could sing "Happy Birthday" into a phone on your end and have it come out as Marilyn Monroe singing to JFK on the other.

I tapped the phone again and went to the "recent calls" screen. Just as I imagined; the call was a blocked number, probably a burner. I raised my hand to slip the phone back into my pocket when it went off again. I jumped like I'd accidentally walked into an electric fence.

This time I checked first; the number on the screen was Alex's. "Hi, Sweetheart," I said.

"Daddy, we made it." I could hear the ocean in the background.

"How was the flight?"

"As smooth as could be," she answered. "No problems at all. We got to the airport and grabbed a rental, then drove to the condo. It's beautiful here. Lonnie and Sheba's place is right on the beach and it's just gorgeous. The beaches are like sugar."

Alex sounded happier and more relaxed than I'd heard her any time since her mother's funeral. "I wish I was there with you," I said, in one of the truer statements I'd made in awhile.

"How are you?"

"Fine, Alex," I said, trying to keep my voice steady. "Just a normal day at the office. So what are you guys up to tonight?"

"Lonnie says we have to go to his favorite restaurant."

I smiled. "Café Thirty-A."

"Yeah, he says it's really good."

"It is," I said. "Great seafood, steaks to die for."

"Lonnie says they have their own separate martini menu."

"Yeah, well, you stick to the Shirley Temples, okay?"

"I will. I miss you," she said.

"I miss you. Can we talk later?"

"Of course. We shouldn't be out too late tonight. We're going into Seaside tomorrow night for their Friday night concert."

"You'll love that," I said. "It'll be fabulous."

"Okay, Daddy, gotta run." she said. "Sheba says we're hitting the beach. I'll call you later."

"Lots of sunblock," I said. "I love you, Alex."

"I love you, too."

We rang off and I stood there a moment, just baking in the hot July sun, the shivers gone for now. I realized that I was in a state of cognitive dissonance; standing here making small talk with my daughter about a restaurant in Florida while Krusty the Clown is threatening to come after me.

I don't think I remembered much of the drive home. Years ago, in another life when I was a full-time private investigator, I got myself into a few scrapes. I even got the crap pounded out of me a couple of times. But that was a long time ago, when I was young and broke and didn't have much to lose.

Before Alex came along…

I won't say I was ever foolish enough to consider myself bulletproof. I was never *that* stupid. But I do remember having a sense of being able to come back from just about anything that happened to me. Maybe I was more resilient back then. Maybe I was just a lot younger.

Now I wasn't so sure. A nearly sixty-year-old man doesn't come back so quick from a good old-fashioned ass whoopin'.

This was the first time I'd been threatened, really threatened, in about fifteen years. My last real case back in Reno, right before

Alex was born, got pretty dicey. By the time it was over, there were some people involved who would have been delighted to see me flat on a morgue slab.

Nothing like that has ever happened to me since then.

So, more than anything else, I was just stunned. I don't remember feeling fear in the traditional sense of the word. It was more than that. It was a really profound sense of doubt.

If they came after me, could I handle it? Would I survive it?

As I turned into my street in East Nashville, my head went back on a swivel and I scanned from one side to another, constantly checking out the space around me. People in East Nashville park on the street all the time. My house was one of only two on the block that had a conventional driveway big enough for more than one car.

I recognized most of the cars parked on the street. The ones I didn't looked empty. I pressed the button and the gate started opening. I jetted in as fast as I could, then hit the button again to close it as fast as possible.

The house seemed dark and empty. I'd come home to this house for years, and up until Alex moved in, it was always empty. It never felt empty like this, though. It was empty down in its bones.

Like me.

I flicked all the lights on and armed the security system. I went into the kitchen and poured myself a tall glass of white wine, then sat at the table and stared out over the empty surface.

Damn, I thought. *Forgot to get the mail.*

I'd never felt the silence of a silent house more deeply.

I missed Alex, but I was glad she wasn't here. I needed to get a handle on myself before she got back.

I went into the living room and turned on the television. The national news was on and I turned it down low. Hearing about the day's insanity and the blatherings of our elected assclowns wasn't going to help.

As I sat there, though, staring off at the wall just above the television, I started to settle down. Maybe it was the half-glass of wine I'd slammed down in three sips, but I began to relax a little and savor that glow that starts in your mid-torso, then radiates outward from your core.

"Okay," I said out loud. "They've gotten to you. You're scared. Own it. Embrace it. The fear itself isn't going to hurt you. Just park it over there and let it perk while you ponder what to do next."

The longer I sat there, the calmer I got. In fact, after getting over the initial shock of the threatening phone call, I began to see it in a different light.

If somebody's willing to run their voice through a voice disguiser and threaten to hurt you very badly, it says as much about them as it does about you. So I started to see that there were some things I'd learned as a result of that phone call that might come in very handy.

First, they mentioned the emails. That meant they knew how dangerous the emails were to them and how valuable they would be to whomever was investigating Leo's murder, whether it was me or the cops. And since those emails were obtained through email accounts owned by the administration of the Nashville Academy of Cinema Arts, they had to be involved.

Which meant, in a sense, I now knew who killed Leo Walsh. I didn't know which one of them did the actual, physical act.

But I knew it was them.

The second big thing I'd learned was that they were more scared than I was. They wouldn't have taken the risk they did otherwise.

I went into the kitchen and refilled my glass. The television droned on in the background, but I wasn't listening. I just needed some ambient noise to cover up the deafening silence.

I opened the freezer door and played frozen meal roulette by pulling a box out without even looking at it and drew a single serving lasagna. I set it in the microwave and pushed the buttons.

So the question was, now that I'd learned something pretty damn valuable from what was probably a strategic error on the part of my enemies—and that's what I was beginning to think of them as—what was I going to do with it?

This had all started to crack when Bo Masterson took a chance and slipped me a note as I was leaving NACA the day that now seemed so long ago. He became my inside guy. But now he was gone, in hiding.

He wasn't high enough up anyway.

I needed somebody from the administrative hallway, somebody who was part of the plan and was scared shitless themselves now that this had ramped up to murder. Somebody in the front office knew what was going on and was a willing partner.

But who?

While my frozen lasagna was nuking, I went into my bedroom and grabbed my MacBook Pro. I set it on the table and booted it up just as the microwave went off. I opened the door and gingerly took out the hot tray and set it on the stove to cool.

I went to the NACA website again and started scouring through the pages. Ursula Gilbert, Jack McEwen and the rest of the faculty were probably not good candidates. Raisa Petrov seemed completely subservient to Ursula, and Jack didn't look the type to be afraid of much of anything. Besides, they were principals in the Blue Moon LLP, so they probably had the wagons circled. Even Katy Lederberg, the Chief Financial Officer for the school, was too inner-circled to break.

No, I needed somebody out on the second ring from the sun. I had a pretty good idea that the head of IT, Brent Haggerty, was probably not going to break either. It had to be somebody else.

But the website didn't list anybody else. There were no flashy pages, glowing bios, and glamorous pictures of the regular people. In the upper-right hand corner of the home page, though, next to the button that said Contribute To NACA, was a button labeled Faculty/Staff Directory. It was a tiny little button on the web page; you had to be consciously looking for it.

I brought the page up and it was a web page full of simple text, numbers, and email addresses, organized by department. Not surprisingly, the largest two departments in the "college" were the Admissions Department and the Financial Aid Department.

That made sense: *get 'em in and fleece 'em as quick as possible.*

I poured another glass of wine and started drilling down into the directory. There were five names, all male, in the Maintenance Department. There was only one name listed in the Equipment Room: Bowen Masterson. He probably had student workers, but they didn't count.

There was one person in Media Relations and one person in the Development Office. That struck me as odd; development people raise money, and in most academic institutions the Development Office is one of the largest. They write grant requests, research rich people and how to get their money, and organize the alumni as a fundraising force.

But then I forced myself to remember, once again, that I wasn't dealing with a real college here. They weren't in this for the long term. They weren't out to get major foundation grants that would stretch out over years. I doubt most legitimate foundations would even give grants to a for-profit.

No, these folks were in it for the churn. Rake up as much short-term cash as possible, skim as much as you can off the top, then pay your bills so you can do it again next month.

Rinse and repeat.

I topped off my wineglass and continued digging through the faculty staff directory.

I got down to the "R"s, where the only office listed was the Registrar's Office. The Registrar of an academic institution of higher education is basically the keeper of the flame. The Registrar enters grades, keeps records, audits records and transcripts, makes sure all academic policies are followed so that the accrediting agencies—the legitimate ones, anyway—are forever satisfied. The Registrar coordinates class schedules, resolves the inevitable conflicts, does transfer credit evaluations, and keeps the students on the path to graduation and then makes sure they're rightfully there when they do.

The Registrar of a College is the guardian of the institution's integrity. It's a big job and requires a lot of experience, resources, and staff.

Which is why I was surprised when the Nashville Academy of Cinema Arts had precisely one person listed as being on staff in the Registrar's Office: Ms. Stacy Jones.

I sat back in my chair and stared down at the screen. Could one of the biggest jobs in the entire college be done by one person?

Damn, I said out loud, *think how stressed out she must be…*

I looked up at the clock on the microwave and realized I'd been sitting there nearly forty minutes. My nuked frozen lasagna that was supposed to sit for five minutes after coming out of the microwave was now room temperature, greasy and tasteless, tepid as hell.

I took two bites and poured myself another glass of wine.

Too late for a call? I typed into the text screen, then pressed the little blue arrow pointing up to send it.

I leaned back on the couch, staring mindlessly at the television. A moment later, my mobile went off. I swiped the screen to answer it.

"Hey," I said. "I could've called you."

"What difference does it make?" Bo Masterson said.

"You okay? Someplace safe?"

There was a moment's hesitation on the line. "Yeah, I'm at my—"

"Don't tell me where you're at," I said. "I don't need or want to know."

"Okay, what can I do for you?"

"Tell me about Stacy Jones," I said.

"Stacy Jones? What do you want to know about her?"

"What's she like? She one of the good guys or is she in with the villains?"

He laughed. "Stacy? No, Stacy's one of the good guys. Nice lady, black woman. She used to be in the Registrar's Office at Fisk, but they had some staff cutbacks and she got let go. She was working at Abercrombie & Fitch over in the mall when the NACA registrar quit about five years ago. Stacy applied for the job, been there ever since."

"Look," I said. "I wish we could dial this back a bit, but it ain't gonna happen right now. Those emails you hacked? It turns out, my friend, that you committed a federal crime and I'm in it with you since I took possession of them. I don't think they're going to turn us over to the Feds because of what's in the emails, but I think they're willing to do just about anything to make this go away."

"What did you do with the emails?" Bo asked. "The thumb drive?"

"Put 'em where nobody's going to find them," I said. "But there's more. This afternoon, I got a call from a blocked number. The person on the other end was running their voice through a disguiser. Whoever it was threatened me. It worked. I'm scared."

"Holy crap," Bo said. "Maybe it's time to bail on this. Just let it go."

"No," I said after a moment. "Leo deserves better than that."

"So what's Stacy Jones got to do with this?" he asked. "You don't think she's involved, do you?"

"I don't know. That's why I'm calling you. If she's one of the good guys, then maybe she wants to see Leo Walsh get some justice here. Maybe she'd be willing to talk to me. As the Registrar, she's one of the insiders in a way—and don't take this the wrong way—you're not."

"That's fair," Bo said. "I kept my eyes and ears open, but there's no way I was on the inside. I think she can probably be trusted. If she doesn't know anything, she'll be upfront about it."

"So you think it's worth taking a chance."

There was a long pause before Bo Masterson spoke again.

"Yeah," he said. "Go for it."

Chapter Thirty

Alex called later that night and we chatted for a while, with her doing most of the talking. They'd driven west on 30-A from Lonnie and Sheba's condo and had dinner at Café Thirty-A, which turned out to be as good as I described.

Then they'd taken a drive toward Seaside and Watercolor, two very posh developments on the Emerald Coast. Lonnie had rented a Lexus convertible, so they were driving around with the top down. The night had been beautiful and calm, the skies clear, the stars more brilliant than any Alex had seen since leaving Reno and the high desert, and she sounded about as happy as I'd ever heard her.

When we rang off, I was more miserable than I'd been in a long time. Not only did I miss Alex, but I had the distinct feeling that she was having a better time down there without me than she would have had with me.

Or maybe that was the wine talking. Maybe I'd had enough for the night.

I sat down in front of the laptop and started digging to find Stacy Jones. The company had a paid subscription to Whitepages.com, so I started there and had her pegged in under two minutes.

Stacy Jones, the Nashville Academy of Cinema Arts registrar, lived up Gallatin Road in Inglewood about ten minutes from me. She and two other women with Jones as a last name lived on a short little street called Solley Drive, just up Gallatin Pike right after Isaac Litton.

So, I thought, another adventure to look forward to tomorrow.

❧

I let myself sleep a little later on Saturday morning, then took a shower and drank a couple mugs of coffee. I started hunting Stacy Jones down on social media. I found her Facebook page and saw plenty of pictures of her and her friends. Apparently her mother and sister lived with her.

They liked cats. She liked gospel music and was active in her church. Mama was retired; sister worked in a doctor's office.

I found her LinkedIn profile and saw that she went to Fisk, graduated Class of 1999, majored in Religious Studies. That'd put her somewhere close to her 40s. She spent seven years in the Fisk registrar's office, then worked retail for a couple of years and was now in her sixth year at NACA.

No sign of a boyfriend, husband, kids…

I Google-imaged Stacy Jones' address on Solley Drive and saw pictures of her house. It was one of those faux Tudor cottages that you see so often in East Nashville. Built in the mid-to-late Fifties, they were usually two-bedroom, one-bath cottages, around 1400 square feet or so that went for under ten grand brand new.

Now people were snapping them up, remodeling them—usually a second bathroom, a totally renovated kitchen, and ripping up carpet to expose the original hardwood floors—and putting them on the market for upwards of $300,000. It was amazing to me. Even ten years ago, these houses were owned by plumbers and carpenters and electricians. Now you had to be a senior health care exec to afford one.

I've always been a proponent of the *it's easier to ask forgiveness than it is to ask permission* school of living. The proper thing would have been to call and introduce myself and ask if I could drop by to discuss a matter of some importance with her. You know, be a professional. My experience has been that you get about half that request out of your mouth before the phone slams down.

No, I've always found that the best thing is to just drop by. Catch 'em by surprise, get 'em with their guard down.

I put on a pair of jeans, a denim work shirt and a Predators ball cap. I started to get into the Tesla, then at the last moment, let the top down on the Mustang and climbed in. The car had been sitting idle for weeks; I hoped it would start.

It took a couple of tries and a good cough, but the Mustang eventually fired right up. I backed it out of the garage and turned it around, then headed for Gallatin Pike. It was a beautiful Saturday morning for July. A front had moved in with an unusual drop in the July temps. I pulled out my cell and lit up the weather app; it was only 85 degrees.

I guess you'd call Gallatin Pike the main drag through East Nashville. Like a lot of streets in Nashville, its name depends on where you are. To get into East Nashville, you cross over the river right by the courthouse at the Victory Memorial Bridge. Then you're on Main Street. You drive a while on Main Street and the same slab of asphalt becomes Gallatin Pike. Then when you go far enough north, leave the county and enter Hendersonville, it's Main Street again. A few miles farther along into Hendersonville and you're magically on the Johnny Cash Parkway.

Go figure. Nashville's the kind of place that would cause a GPS satellite to break down sobbing.

The traffic thinned out a bit and I found myself shifting up to third gear. I eased into the left-hand turn lane just past the old Isaac Litton High School, or at least that's what it was when I was high school age. Now it's an ancient building repurposed as a middle school, probably complete with the original lead paint and asbestos drywall.

I turned left onto Solley Drive and went up about a quarter of a mile, where Stacy Jones' house was on the right just past a house with a lot of plastic pink flamingoes in the front yard. This part of East Nashville—Inglewood—was a little less dense than the part I lived in. As a result, there were fewer cars on the street. As I approached the Jones house, I pulled over to the curb and stopped the car.

Stacy Jones was in the front yard, on all fours, weeding a flower bed. I stepped out of the car in the least threatening way possible and caught her eye just as she turned to look at me.

"Miss Jones," I called out, my voice morphing into a little more Southern drawl than it normally had. I smiled and waved with my right hand and kept my left hand in plain sight. People can't be too careful these days.

She shifted around, then leaned back and squatted on her heels. With some effort, she pulled herself into a standing position.

"Yes?"

She wore gardening gloves and held a spade in her right hand. She was short, 5'5" at the most, and was leaning toward heavy, although I wouldn't actually call her fat. Her hair was processed and pulled straight back into a bun. Even from the street, I could tell she was pretty, her skin glowing and reflecting the sunlight. She wore a pair of shorts, a T-shirt, and flip-flops. Standard summer day in the South.

"Miss Jones, my name's Harry Denton and I wonder if I could take just a minute of your time," I said, taking a couple of tentative steps off the sidewalk and into her yard.

She didn't stop me, so I walked a little closer.

"I just had a couple of questions," I said. "And I thought maybe you could help me."

"Who are you?" she asked, her eyes narrowing.

I reached into my back pocket and retrieved my license case. I held it out in front of me and opened it. "I'm actually a private detective, Miss Jones."

She had this confused look on her face. "Private detective? What would a private detective want with me?"

"I'm looking into the death of Leo Walsh."

Her face went solid stone. "You need to leave," she said coldly.

"Bo Masterson sent me," I said. "He said he thought it would be okay to talk to you."

She dropped the spade. "Bo?" she asked. "Where is he? Is he all right?"

I took a few more steps toward her and she didn't back off. "He's fine, Stacy. He's away right now. But he's okay. Listen, can we talk for a minute or two?"

Stacy Jones looked to her right, then to her left, then centered her focus back on me.

"You'd better come inside," she said. "We can talk on the back porch. But don't you do anything to upset my mama, you hear? This's all been hard on her."

I folded my license case shut and slid it back into my pocket.

"Don't worry, Miss Jones," I said. "I won't."

I followed her up the few stairs to her front porch. She stopped at the door and kicked off her shoes. I leaned down, untied my hiking boots, and followed her into the house in my sock feet.

The house that Stacy Jones shared with her mother and sister was neat and orderly, not much clutter, and looked like it had been decorated sometime in the late seventies and not touched since. A large couch upholstered in bright green fabric covered most of the far wall, with a large coffee table with Queen Anne legs in front of it. Tables on either side of the sofa were covered in doilies, with hurricane lamps that looked like genuine antiques. There was a large oval braided rug in the center of the room, with two comfortable easy chairs placed at angles to the couch.

It was a house of women who lived without men. They were, I imagined, quite content.

"Mama, I'm back inside," Stacy called. "I've got somebody with me."

"Who?" the voice of an older woman called from down the hallway.

"A friend of Bo's, Mama. He just came by for a visit. We're going out on the back porch."

Stacy Jones led me through the living room and into the kitchen, which was definitely a kitchen from the late Sixties, early Seventies. I hadn't seen pastel appliances in ages. The hipsters love this stuff, along with polyester plaid pants.

Hold on to anything long enough, I thought, it becomes cool again.

There was a door on the left side of the kitchen that led to a screened-in sun porch with four white wicker chairs around a patio table with a glass top.

Stacy pulled out a chair and sat down, motioning to me to take a seat opposite.

"Thanks for seeing me," I said, my voice subdued, as a I sat down. "I talked to Bo last night and he thought it would be a good idea to talk to you."

"I don't want no trouble," she said. "My sister and I take care of Mama. I don't want no trouble."

"I understand. But you seem like a good person, Miss Jones, and I'm sure you want some kind of justice for Leo Walsh as well."

She looked away and her eyes started to fill.

"I liked Mr. Walsh," she said. "He was a kind, gentle man. Real nice. Never had any trouble getting along with people. For the most part the students liked him. He was always doing extra for them."

"Bo felt the same way. Is that how you and Bo got to be friends?"

She nodded. "Partly. Bo spent a lot of time in my office when he was a student. Every time I turned around, he had some kind of problem he needed me to solve. But he wasn't like a lot of these kids. So many students these days feel like they just *entitled*. Anything bad happens, it's your fault for not fixing it. When Bo had a problem, he owned up to it, took responsibility."

Stacy sat there a moment. "Where is Bo? Is he okay? Mama liked him a lot. We had him over for dinner a couple of times. Man, that boy likes to eat."

"I don't know where he is," I answered. "I know he's taken off, he's in hiding. And that means he's scared, too."

Stacy grinned and her voice went up about half an octave. "And that's saying something. That boy's so big, it'd take a lot to scare him."

I grinned and nodded back at her. "So what do you think happened to Mr. Walsh?"

She looked down at her lap and fidgeted with her hands for a moment. "I can't lose my job, Mr. Denton. When I lost my last job, I had to take a retail job working in the mall. Nine-fifty an hour. You could only get part-time, no health insurance, no sick leave. It took me almost four years to get this job at NACA."

I leaned forward in the chair and rested my arms on the table. "Stacy," I said, "you know how much trouble that school is in, don't you? I've done a lot of digging. If something doesn't turn that place around, it's going to close, anyway. And soon."

She sighed and brought her hands to her face and rubbed her eyes. "I know. We all knew. But Jack McEwen and Ursula were telling everybody there was a plan in place. Everything was going to be okay."

I nodded again. "Yeah, they were going to make a movie. But something happened, didn't it? Something went wrong."

"I know that Mr. Walsh was really upset. He used to come by my office, almost like he was looking for a place to hide. The week before he died, he came and sat in my office. Told me that Ursula and Jack were up to something, but he wasn't sure what. But he said it was crooked and he didn't want any part of it."

Now that's interesting, I thought.

"Did he say anything more, any details?"

She shook her head. "Only that he was pulling out of it. He said they could go to prison if they weren't careful. Then a day or so later, the three of them, along with Katy Lederberg, met in the conference room next to my office. They closed the door and I heard a lot of yelling. Somebody was pounding on a table. It went on for almost an hour and then I heard the door slam open, then slam shut. I peeked out my door and saw Mr. Walsh stomping down the hallway like he was really mad."

Stacy Jones spoke softly, almost tenderly.

"Mr. Walsh's office was at the end of the faculty hallway," she continued. "I stayed late that day, after everybody else in the front office was gone. I went down to his office on the pretext of needing some papers signed. He was sitting there alone…"

She stopped and stared off almost wistfully, then smiled. "His office was a mess. You should've seen it. Framed movies posters on the wall all cockeyed, broken down pasteboard bookcases full of books and DVDs and VHS tapes. About half-a-dozen dirty coffee mugs scattered around."

"And let me guess," I said, "an overflowing ashtray."

"Oh, no. There was no smoking in the building. He had to smoke in the parking lot beside the building. We had a smoking section down from the freight dock."

"So what happened that day? That day you went down to his office."

"He looked about as beat up as I've ever seen a man," she said. "I mean, he really looked like he couldn't think straight. He said that Ursula and Jack were evil, that they were about to bring the whole house down. He'd made up his mind to go see somebody, get some help, no matter how dangerous it was."

"*Dangerous*," I said. "He used the word dangerous?"

She nodded. "Yeah, but he didn't sound scared. He sounded almost, I don't know… resigned to it, to whatever happened."

"When was this?" I asked.

She leaned back in her chair and thought for a moment. "Let me see, it was a few days before he… When was it? Yeah, that's it. It was Monday night. Like I said, the night classes had started. Most of the faculty were gone. There wouldn't be many people around, we could talk. Yeah, it was definitely the Monday night before he was… killed."

I sat back in my chair, stunned. The Monday night before he was killed. He decided to get some help. The Monday night before he was killed…

I was that help. Leo Walsh was in my office that morning. Only he hadn't gotten the help he needed.

"Stacy," I said after a few moments, "did you tell the police any of this?"

She shrugged. "What was I gonna tell them, that there was a screaming match between some faculty members? Guess you haven't spent a lot of time around film school people. Somebody's always screaming at somebody."

"Besides," she added a moment later, "the police never even questioned me. And I wasn't going to volunteer. I can't lose my job. My sister and me, we take care of Mama."

I stared at Stacy Jones. She was a good woman, a woman who wanted to live her life and take care of her family and go to church every Sunday and Wednesday. She didn't deserve any of this crap.

"I know," I said. "I know."

Chapter Thirty-One

Okay, I admit it. I'm stuck.

The conversation with Stacy Jones left me feeling leaden, even depressed. I'm not normally the kind of person who easily gets beaten down, but this seemed like I'd learned just enough to feel like the truth was out there in front of me, but not enough to actually get there.

And now the rest of the weekend stretched out in front of me, with nothing to do and nobody to do it with. For years, I was used to spending weekends alone. Usually, I worked. That's what I do.

Work.

All those years, Alex was in Reno with her mother. For most of those years, I wasn't dating anyone or spending much time with anyone outside of work. Lonnie and Sheba were the center of my social circle and there were plenty of Saturday nights where I served as their third wheel.

Now everything's different.

Having Alex living in my home now flipped some kind of switch for me. I was worried when we first started talking about her living with me that I wouldn't be able to make the adjustment. The exact opposite happened. I got so used to having her around that the place felt unbearably empty without her.

Which only made me feel even guiltier and emptier. A parent's not supposed to need a child that way.

I said goodbye to Stacy Jones and wished her well, then drove back to the house and picked up my laptop. I snaked my way through the East Nashville side streets and got back on the highway again, headed to the west side. I wanted to have another look into those emails.

I'd leave the printouts locked in the storage unit. In a pinch, I wouldn't be able to dump them quickly or effectively. That thumb drive, though, was smaller and thinner than a pack of chewing gum. If need be, I could always ditch it.

I stopped for lunch at a fast-food place right off the freeway, then went over to the storage unit. I lifted the metal gate and found the bankers box tucked in the corner, right where I left it. I slipped the thumb drive into my pocket, then backed out and locked everything up.

Say what you will about Nashville and all its problems in the last decade, we have got one hell of a public library system, one of the finest in the country. The Bellevue branch library, so new it still had that new library smell, was tucked away in a residential neighborhood right next to a middle school about five minutes away.

I parked, then pulled the top up on the Mustang; the July heat had crossed over into searing in about the last hour. A blast of cold air hit me as I entered the library and found a quiet place to sit in the far corner. A group of kids who looked to be about thirteen years old were in a conference room, sitting around a table engaged in what appeared to be actual study. I settled into a comfortable chair in the farthest corner and booted the laptop, then plugged the thumb drive into a USB port.

I looked around, nervous and paranoid, to make sure no one had followed me, and then started bringing up the emails one by one. I wasn't even sure what I was looking for other than what we'd already found.

An email from last May, from Ursula to Jack McEwen, no CCs: *Have we heard anything from our friends in NYC yet? KL and I met this morning and we are at DC5 in the accounting department.*

Jack McEwen's reply: *Spoke with the office last night. One last signature needed on their end and the funds will be released from escrow…*

Ursula's next in the chain: *What about the problem on this end?*

Jack: *No movement. I'm going to meet w/him tonight. He needs to understand what we, and he, are up against. If we're unable to come to a MOTMs, the consequences will be severe.*

Ursula's last in the chain: *Stay on him. There's an invoice in from the party rental place in Antioch that's due Friday. Without that check from NYC, we can meet payroll or have graduation. Not both…*

"Friends from NYC?" I whispered. "Met with KL? Who's KL?"

Then it hit me: Katy Lederberg, the Chief Financial Officer. And what's DC5 in the accounting department?

I stared off into space, out the window overlooking the street that ran in front of the library. My mind went blank and I let it drift for a few moments.

DC5? DC5?

DEFCON 5. That's it.

I tapped a few keys on the laptop and got to a Wikipedia page. Yeah, that's what I thought. DEFCON 5 is the least critical state; DEFCON 5 means relax and stand down.

That doesn't sound like the situation at the Nashville Academy of Cinema Arts.

Then I saw another note on the Google search findings and had to smile. "Screenwriters," it read, "often get the scale wrong, so begin with this fact: the lower the number, the higher the worry."

That was it, I realized. Ursula Gilbert had just gotten it wrong. What she meant was Defcon 1, which puts one in mind of the old pirate joke: *Bring me my brown pants!*

I turned back to the emails. There were funds that were going to be released from escrow, and if they weren't, some hard choices were going to have to be made. It was literally a case of making payroll or paying for their commencement ceremony.

I went to the Nashville Academy of Cinema Arts website again. I noodled around from one page to the next and saw pictures from the June graduation. And I hadn't heard anyone complain about not getting paid, so obviously they managed to find some cash.

Ursula had asked about "the problem on their end." What was the problem on their end and what were the severe consequences if they were unable to come to a MOTM, which I took to be a meeting of the minds?

I turned back to the laptop and dug further into the emails. Over the next couple of hours, I read through hundreds of them. The middle school study group eroded into a bunch of chattering, laughing teenagers who had to be shushed a few times by the librarian. The sun started to set outside and the shadows began to deepen. At a quarter to five, an announcement came over the loudspeaker telling people the library would close in fifteen minutes. But by that time, I'd finished drilling down into this mountainous stack of digital paper, and I knew.

Like Barton Keyes in *Double Indemnity… Papa has it all figured out, figured out and wrapped up in tissue paper with pink ribbons on it.*

I knew who killed Leo Walsh, and why.

I was the last one out of the library, with my laptop bag over my shoulder and the thumb drive in my pocket. As I walked out of the building, I noticed the temperature had dropped into the almost-bearable range. I felt a rumbling in my gut. Guess that fast-food cheeseburger didn't stay with me very long.

I pulled out of the library parking lot, then turned on Old Harding Road and made my way over to Highway 100. A mile or so down, I passed the Bealesworth campus and thirty seconds later, pulled into the parking lot of the Loveless Café. I parked across from a bank of Harleys. The Loveless had become a regular weekend haunt of bikers from all over this part of the state, who chowed down at the Loveless and then hit the Natchez Trace Parkway for one of the best rides in this part of the country.

I made a mental note to bring Alex out here on the Ural someday.

I ordered a breakfast that seemed huge to me but was nowhere near the Woodchopper's Special, or whatever it was that Bo Masterson had ordered at Pancake Palooza. I wondered where Bo was, and while he didn't appear to be the kind of person one would waste much time worrying about, I hoped he was okay.

And I thought about Alex and Lonnie and Sheba down on the beach on a gorgeous summer night and I felt a pang. I held up a finger and asked the waitress to bring me a glass of Chardonnay. Nothing like white wine with a Southern omelet from the Loveless.

I sat there thinking about everything I'd figured out today. There were still a few pieces missing, but almost everything had fallen into place. Ursula Gilbert was a scam artist par excellence. I'll bet if you did a deep enough dig into her background, you'd discover that the Nashville Academy of Cinema Arts wasn't the first grift she'd pulled. Maybe not even the biggest...

As Bo Masterson said, though, it was a variation on the classic Ponzi scheme. Only instead of paying off investors with the money new investors gave you, you paid yourself this month with the tuition money that came in last month.

But when it all started to dry up and the walls were closing in on her, she had to find a workaround. So she and Jack McEwen, who'd definitely thrown in with her years ago, came up with another Ponzi scheme: scam investors with a movie deal.

Only it's not a bogus movie deal because you've got one hell of a script, courtesy of Leo Walsh. Leo had written a script that would probably sell anywhere if he could have just gotten it into the right hands. Then Leo found out Ursula and Jack had no intention of making a movie, or at least not a real one. Anyone who's ever invested in movies knows you do it for the tax loss. Very few movie projects ever return anything to the investors. There's just a lot of cachet and ego-massaging in being in the movie business, and the scammers depend on that to keep the suckers reeled in.

So you take their money and keep the movie "in development" for as long as you can. Skim off as much cash as you can, then maybe you make a crappy movie that goes nowhere and you declare a loss and the investors walk away with a huge tax write-off.

In the meantime, you've had a pretty good ride on somebody else's money. Over fifty years ago, Mel Brooks wrote the instruction book for this kind of scam in *The Producers*. Only what went wrong there was the totally crappy project turned out to be a masterpiece.

In Ursula's case, the guy who made the scam possible discovered it was a scam, pulled out of the deal, and threatened to expose them.

So they killed him.

ళ

I left a nice tip for the server at the Loveless, then walked out into what was shaping up to be a beautiful summer evening. There was nobody waiting for me at home, nothing to do but have a couple more glasses of wine and try to find a movie on TV. Neither of those options had much appeal, so I put the top back down on the Mustang and turned right out of the Loveless parking lot.

The entrance to the Natchez Trace Parkway was about an eighth of a mile up on the right. I slid onto the entrance ramp, which did a climbing loop to the right onto the Natchez Trace.

As beautiful a drive as it is, though, as seems more and more common these days, there's a dark side. A few miles down the parkway, right after crossing into Williamson County, there's a bridge over State Route 96. It's a beautiful, concrete double-arched bridge with the most amazing, spectacular view spanning a valley about 145 feet down. The valley below is heavily wooded, dotted by farms and incredibly expensive homes owned by country music stars and the like.

The locals call it the *suicide bridge*. At last count, over thirty people had taken a header off it…

I needed a place to think and that seemed as good a place as any.

I pulled the Mustang into the car park right before the bridge. As always, there were a dozen or so cars there, with people strolling around in the slowly darkening and cooling summer evening. I walked down to the bridge, sat in the grass right next to it, and gazed down into the valley below. The sun was striking it in just such a way that it looked like one of those luminist paintings from the mid-19th century. The colors seemed more vivid and alive, almost vibrating, and as I stared out over the landscape, I felt calmer and more centered than I had in weeks.

I knew the truth now. If life is a movie, then this particular film was in the third act.

Chapter Thirty-Two

It was nearly ten before I got home. I sat in the grass beside the parkway bridge over Highway 96 for almost two hours. The sun went down; the night sky was cloudless and clear, the humidity lower than normal. The black dome over me was like being under a tent of sparkles.

Alex texted and we went back and forth a few times. Lonnie got her into a resort course at the local scuba place and she'd made her first ocean dive that afternoon, just off the beach maybe twenty-five feet down. As I expected, she took to it and loved it. She shot me a bunch of pictures Lonnie had taken with his underwater GoPro and in one she was staring straight into the camera, hovering weightlessly in the water like an astronaut in outer space, giving me a thumbs up.

This only made me miss her more.

For a moment, I thought of just catching a plane tomorrow. I could be there in time for dinner and I didn't have to worry about buying a 21-day advance ticket anymore. I could do it.

No, I thought. This is her time to have an adventure.

Besides, I had plenty of other fish to fry. This was going to be a busy week.

❧

I had a meeting first thing Monday morning with Pat McClellan and the auditors from our accounting firm. I was there mostly to review the second quarter books and to sign off on a bunch of paperwork. Denton & Associates was, so far, still a profitable firm. Our contract with the consortium that bought out Asfáleia Technologies had another eighteen months to go. After that, the company would dissolve with every employee walking away with fat stacks of severance cash.

Ashley could pay cash for law school…

And I'd be done with it. I'd be in my sixties by then. Maybe it was time to retire. Maybe it was time to do something else with my life.

As I signed one form after another, with discussion going on around me constantly, in the back of my mind I was still wondering what to do with all this stuff. Should I go to the police? I could tell them everything I knew, but unless I wanted to spend my first few retirement years wearing the minimum security all-khaki ensemble, I couldn't tell them how I knew. I'm not even sure if the emails were enough to convict them, especially since they were obtained in a, *harrumph*, questionable fashion. Unless the cops had something I didn't know about, there was still no physical evidence to connect Jack McEwen and Ursula Gilbert to Leo Walsh's murder.

Still, I couldn't sit on this. And I couldn't go bursting into the NACA offices and tell everybody to put their hands in the air.

Nearly twenty years ago, when I did this sort of thing all the time, I don't remember ever feeling this stuck. Maybe this is all just a byproduct of getting older. Or maybe it's just a muscle that hasn't been used in over a decade.

After the accountants and auditors left, I was in my office going through some records and trying to get some office clutter cleared away when Ashley came in.

"You happy with the way that went?" she asked. I motioned for her to sit down.

"Yeah, these guys always make it easy," I said. "You and Pat keep everything in order and I'm grateful."

"We'll only do this about six more times," Ashley said.

"Yeah, a year and a half… Six quarters."

She leaned back in the chair and crossed her legs. "What are you going to do after this is all over?"

"I don't know," I answered truthfully. "How about you? Law school?"

"I'm thinking about it. It's three years and that feels like a real commitment. I'd be in my thirties by the time I finished."

I grinned at her and made a *whew* sound. "Ooh, your thirties," I said. "You'll be *ancient*."

"C'mon, Harry," she scolded. "Have a little empathy here."

"Empathy, *schempathy*," I said. "Girl, I got socks older than you."

She grinned and shook her head. "You're hopeless."

"Don't think you're the first woman who ever said that to me."

The grin disappeared. "What would you think if something were to happen that made it possible to keep the company going?"

I felt my forehead furrowing. "Like what?"

"We've still got this demonstration Friday," she said.

"What are you talking about?" I asked.

She shook her head again. "I've said too much already. This is Hugh's rodeo, not mine. But I'll tell you this much, Harry. He's gonna rock some shit up. He's a visionary. Smartest guy I ever met."

"That's something coming from you."

"What'd you do with those emails?" she said, suddenly switching gears. Sometimes she was hard to keep up with.

"They're locked away safe," I answered. "That's all you need to know. I want you as far away from this Charlie Foxtrot as possible. But I will tell you this, Ashley. I spent the weekend going through all those emails. I think I know how and why this happened, why Leo Walsh was murdered. And I have to go to the police. I just have to figure out how."

"Harry, you know you can't do that," Ashley said, her voice somber.

"They can't just get away with it," I said.

"If you go to the police, that's precisely what might happen."

I spun in my chair and faced the glass wall. Outside, the city was baking under a July sun. "What if I didn't mention the emails? What if I just told them that I'd been nosing around and I think this is what happened?"

I spun back around. "What then?"

She stared at me a few moments. I felt like I was being studied. "Well, since you clearly aren't going to just let go of this, if you absolutely never mentioned the emails… Maybe it would work."

I turned to my keyboard and Googled the number for the South Precinct.

⁂

Two hours later, I was on the other side of town pulling once again into the parking lot of the Metro Nashville Police Department's South Precinct. This time, the guys at the reception booth were waiting for me and led me right back to Lieutenant Akers's office.

"I thought I told you to stay out of this," Akers growled when the uniform who escorted me left.

"Yeah, well, I don't always do like I'm told. I know, it's a character flaw. Keeps me awake at night. But it's a good thing

I didn't. If you guys think Leo Walsh was murdered by a Murfreesboro Road trick gone sour, you're as full of crap as a Christmas turkey."

Akers motioned for me to take a seat. This time, we were in his office, but it wouldn't surprise me if before this was over he had me back in a witness interview room. I sat down across the desk from him as he glared at me.

"After you left here Saturday afternoon a week ago," he said, "I got a little curious myself. Started doing a little digging into your background, even wound up in a conversation with Howard Spellman down in Florida."

"Great," I said. "How's the fishing boat business?"

"He says he's making a living. And he also says you're a complete pain in the ass."

I smiled. "Sounds like Howard. Once you get to know him, you realize that insulting you is how he shows affection."

Akers did not return the smile. "In your case, I think he's telling the truth. Look, Denton, I told you to back off. Interfering with a criminal investigation is nothing to take lightly. Being a smartass is no defense against obstruction of justice."

"Doing nothing to solve a murder is an obstruction of justice as well," I said. "C'mon, Lieutenant, don't you guys want to catch who did this?"

I could see the steam rising in Akers's face. "You realize how many current homicide investigations I've got going on right now? You know how many homicides were committed in this precinct since you were here just a week ago Saturday? *Nine*..."

I sat back in the chair and took a deep breath. "Look, Lieutenant, nobody says you guys don't work hard. But Leo Walsh's murder wasn't a mugging or a domestic case or a drug deal gone sour. This case is as complicated and involved as anything I've ever heard of. I have the luxury of time that you guys don't. I've just been doing some digging and I'm pretty sure I know what happened. Only I can't do anything about it. It's really up to you."

Akers glared at me.

"Now," I said after a moment, "you want to hear what I've found out or not? If I tell you what I think happened and then later I'm wrong, then it's on me. I get to be the dumbass who let his imagination run wild."

Akers picked up a Bic pen off his desk and twiddled it nervously between his thumb and index finger. "All right," he said quietly. "I'm listening."

I launched into the whole thing, of the imminent demise of the Nashville Academy of Cinema Arts, the danger of having the whole scheme exposed and collapsing in on them. I told him about the plan to save the school with a blockbuster movie and of how the plan was subverted into another scam, another chance to rip off a bundle. And of how when Leo Walsh found out what was really going on and tried to stop it he paid for it with his life.

"So how do you know it would have been a good movie?" he asked when I finished.

"His widow let me read the script," I said. "It was amazing. They needed a bad script so they could make a bad movie. They needed some hack piece of crap. Leo messed up. He gave them a fantastic script and then he figured out what they were going to do with it."

"And you think that was enough to kill him?" Akers asked.

"People have killed for a lot less."

"How did you find all this out?" he demanded.

I sat there silently for a beat. "I managed to get a couple of people on the inside to talk to me. One person knew a little bit, another person knew a little bit that was different. You get a piece here, a piece there, and you spin them around like pieces of a jigsaw puzzle and damn if they don't fit. Then I started digging into public records and what I found only made it clearer. The Nashville Academy of Cinema Arts was about to go under and there was more to it than just people losing their jobs. The people at the top were going to be financially ruined, their reputations shot. Maybe even some jail time."

Now it was Akers's turn to stare off into space for a bit. "It's not enough to secure a conviction, not by a long shot."

I shook my head. "No, it's not. But it's enough to take to the D.A., have him convene a Grand Jury, start issuing some subpoenas, signing some search warrants. Seize their files, email accounts. There's a paper trail there. There's got to be."

Email accounts, I thought. *Email accounts… Okay, are lies of omission as bad as any other lie?*

Lieutenant Akers took his Bic pen and made a few quick notes on a legal pad. "So you think they've already taken the mark?"

"The word I got was that cash was so short, they might have to cancel graduation. If you look at the website, they had graduation…"

"So you put two-and-two together," he said.

I nodded. "One draws inferences, doesn't one?"

This time, Akers did smile.

"Want to know what else Spellman said about you?"

"What, besides the fact that I'm a pain in the ass?"

"Actually, the term he used was *first-class* pain in the ass."

"Well, coming from Howard, that's high praise. What other

verbal slurs did he deploy against me?"

"He said you were about as straight a shooter as he'd ever encountered in his whole career. And that was a big part of what made you a pain in the ass. You had integrity and you were relentless, and that made for a difficult combination at times."

I stared across the table at Lieutenant Garrett Akers for what felt like a long moment. Then I stood up.

"Good luck, Lieutenant," I said, extending my hand across his desk. "Let me know how this all works out."

Chapter Thirty-Three

I walked out into the hot July sun, thinking this was finally over. I had jumped back into the game and exercised a set of muscles that had long atrophied. The truth is a bitch to find sometimes, but I'd dug and tunneled and maneuvered until I finally found it, and then I'd turned it over to the powers that be without managing to snare myself or anybody else. In very short order, Ursula Gilbert and Jack McEwen would get what was finally coming to them and the ring of secondary players who had enabled them would pay a price as well.

So I was feeling a bit puffed up as I pulled the Tesla out of the parking lot onto Harding Place and started running the gauntlet up to I-24, then back to the office. Life could get back to normal now. I had a business to run, a daughter to take care of, friends to see, investments to watch.

Places to be, things to do. Something vaguely resembling a life.

As I pulled onto the freeway entrance ramp behind a battered Dodge Ram pickup billowing blue smoke, the hands-free went off in the car. It was Alex, so I tapped the touch screen.

"Hello, Sweetheart," I said happily.

"Daddy, how are you?"

"I'm great now. I'm on the phone with you."

She laughed. "It's good to hear your voice. We just got in from the beach and I thought I'd call. Hope I didn't get you at a bad time."

"Just finished running an errand and headed back to the office. So what are you guys up to for the rest of the day?"

"Aunt Sheba wants to drive over to Rosemary Beach. There's an artist who has a studio there, makes beachy stuff out of driftwood and old surfboards. She's still trying to figure out how she wants to furnish the beach house."

"So what's Lonnie up to?"

"He's got his laptop open on the balcony and just opened his first beer of the day."

"Well," I said. "It's five o'clock somewhere."

She laughed again. "Yeah, but not here. That doesn't seem to matter, though."

"Have you guys figured out when you're coming home?" I asked.

"Lonnie said he got an email from you about a meeting Friday and he wants to be there. So it looks like Thursday afternoon."

"Plus, you've got your weekend orientation at Bealesworth," I reminded her. "I have to have you there by two, right?"

She sighed. "I guess so."

"You guess so?" I asked. "I thought you'd kind of gotten around to looking forward to it."

"I don't know," she said, drawing out the last two words. "Cricket and Bitsy have been all over me on Snapchat and Instagram. I'm not used to it. I didn't have that many followers back in Reno. They expect me to respond and comment and all that. They even let me follow their Finsta."

I hit the bottom of the exit ramp, checked the side mirror, then jammed the pedal to the floor. I juked two lanes over and shot past the smoking Ram pickup and settled into one of the middle lanes.

"Finsta?" I asked. "What's Finsta?"

"It's short for fake Instagram," Alex explained. "You have your public Instagram account where you post all the perfect selfies and family celebrations and incredible parties and all that stuff. How great your life is… Then you have your behind-the-curtains, invitation-only account where you post selfies of what you look like when you just woke up."

"Why would anybody do that?" I asked.

There was a long pause.

"Seriously, why would anybody do that?" I repeated.

"Daddy, I don't understand the question."

"No, I guess you wouldn't. And I guess I just don't understand all this stuff."

"Okay, boomer," she said, teasing. "It'll be okay. Listen, Sheba's calling for me."

"I'll see you Thursday afternoon," I said. "I'll arrange my day so I can pick you up. And I'll take the rest of the day off so we can hang out. You're gone to Florida, then home one night, then gone for the weekend at Bealesworth. I hope I can remember what you look like."

"I know. I'm gonna need a vacation from summer vacation."

I grinned. "Maybe we can get out of here over the Labor Day weekend. Just you and me. So text me Thursday morning, okay? Let me know when you'll be boots on the ground."

"I will," she said. "See you Thursday. I miss you."

"I miss you, too. Be careful. I love you."

"Love you, too."

Then silence, just as a tractor-trailer roared by me so fast and so close his wake threw the car around. I countersteered to keep it in the lane.

Life felt good.

ঌ৩

The rest of the week was pretty routine, almost humdrum in comparison to the last couple of months. This had been a year of transition and adjustment, some of it difficult and painful, other parts of it difficult and not so painful. I was glad to have Alex in my life on a full-time basis, with all the changes that had entailed. Alex reminded me of how stale I had become, how much inertia I'd accumulated through that difficult passage of life we humans call *middle-age*. She'd shaken things up just by being here.

And this whole thing with Leo Walsh had been almost serendipitous, although admittedly it didn't work out so well for Leo. Who could have guessed that just when Alex was shaking up one side of my life, the universe presented me with the chance to get back to what might actually be my true calling, if that's not an over-the-top and melodramatic way to put it. The years when I was an investigative reporter who morphed into a private detective were years when I discovered something about myself that I didn't know.

I'm an ordinary, almost lackluster commonplace kind of fellow not given to much in the way of self-reflection or self-aggrandizement. I feel things passionately and deeply, but I rarely put it on public display. To my friends, acquaintances, and fellow professionals, I appear to be laid back to the point of lethargy at times, and I think most people perceive me to be an amiable enough, low-maintenance kind of guy who occasionally cops a bit of a smart-assed attitude.

Inside, though, I am relentless.

Almost twenty-five years ago, in one of the last fights my one-and-only wife and I ever had—long before I met Marsha and so long ago I can barely remember her—she absolutely lost it.

"Of all the things I hate about you, you know what I hate the most?" she screamed. "*You never quit!*"

And she was right.

So I went back to the office and I called Bo Masterson, who was still safely gone-to-ground somewhere in one of the many rural areas of Tennessee. I told him what I'd discovered and that I'd been to the police and I expected this to all explode any day now. Just stay tuned to the local news outlets and in a matter of a very few days, he'd be able to watch Ursula *Jeel-bear* and Jack McEwen do the traditional perp walk past the television cameras.

And then it would be safe to stick his head up again.

Later, I called Aileen Walsh and, without going into any specifics, told her I thought something would be breaking on this case soon and that I had every reason to believe that there would still be justice for Leo Walsh. That wouldn't bring him back but it would at least give her that most vaunted of clichés in this most violent society: *closure*.

Meanwhile, Ashley and Hugh and the rest of the team were setting up the big app rollout for Friday afternoon. I made an executive decision and booked us a reservation at Jimmy Kelly's, the finest steakhouse in Nashville by a country mile. Seriously, there's no competition. As hard as everyone had worked on this, I figured a blowout reward was in order. The demo was at four, so I booked the restaurant for seven. Everybody would have time to go home, change clothes, de-stress a little, then we'd all meet at the restaurant, which was over on Louise Avenue a few blocks away from the Vanderbilt campus.

I took a quick poll to see how big a table we needed and decided the best thing to do was book a private room. Ashley and

Hugh had dropped all pretense of covering up their relationship, so they'd be there as a couple. Donnie Hazard would bring his latest boyfriend. Pat McClellan said she'd bring a plus-one, and Lonnie and Sheba would be there as well.

Which made me the lone solo…

I would have brought Alex, but she'd be at The Bealesworth School, getting herself orientated. No matter, I thought. It was just a celebratory dinner, one that was going to set Denton & Associates back a couple of grand and worth every penny.

Alex texted me Thursday morning just before 10 AM. They were loading up the rental and heading for Panama City. They'd stop for lunch at a seafood place Lonnie loved near the airport and be back on the Citation by about one. Flying time from Panama City to Nashville was a little less than an hour, so I'd make sure I was at John Tune airport by two o'clock.

I went ahead and drove to the office, mainly because I was getting itchy sitting around the house. For some reason or other, I found myself increasingly unsettled and uneasy the last couple of days. It was hard to focus, hard to get anything done. Was it because I missed Alex? The big upcoming meeting on Friday? I kept getting distracted, like a dog being walked who suddenly sees a squirrel out of the corner of his eye and takes off without thinking. I've always been a sucker for clickbait, but increasingly I couldn't even read an article on the web without being distracted by the chance to see what celebrities from the eighties look like today…

Then, as I was going through my backpack trying to make sure I'd remembered everything I needed for the day, it hit me.

Radio silence…

That's what it was. The silence. I'd been checking my local

news apps even more than usual, compulsively running through each one a couple of times an hour. I rarely watch local news on television anymore, but suddenly I'm making sure I'm in front of the tube for the Fox news at nine, then surfing ABC, NBC, and CBS at ten.

And there was nothing.

No arrests, no perp walks, no *Breaking News*…

How long was it supposed to take? I'd laid it all out for Akers. He had everything he needed: the backstory, the characters, the conflict, the driving desire and underlying need.

And more importantly, the motive. The pieces were all there.

So where the hell was he?

At the office, Ashley had a stack of reports for me to go through. I had a hard time focusing on them, just like everything else in the last couple of days, but managed to wade through, along with a couple hundred emails. By then, it was lunchtime. I told Ashley to hold down the fort and I'd see her tomorrow afternoon after dropping Alex off at Bealesworth.

I made my way down Broadway past Union Station hotel and jumped on I-40 West. I remembered a little Mexican place on White Bridge Road I hadn't eaten at in years, so stopped in and grabbed the ubiquitous daily lunch special offered in every Mexican restaurant I'd ever been in, known as the *Speedy Gonzales*: two tacos, rice and beans. As I sat there scarfing down my quick lunch, I pondered why in this day of increased sensitivity and awareness of cultural prejudices and baggage the term "Speedy Gonzales" was still somehow politically correct and acceptable.

It was like walking into a soul food restaurant and ordering the Stepin Fetchit.

An hour later, I was standing in the pilot's lounge of Compact Aviation staring out onto the tarmac. John Tune airport doesn't have a control tower, so airplanes communicate on a common frequency. A speaker overhead was tuned to the frequency and I smiled as I heard Lonnie's voice come through the static.

"*John Tune traffic, Citation Niner-Alpha-Tango is on final to two-zero, full-stop.*"

I leaned and looked out the window as far to the right as I could see and in a couple of seconds, the Citation came into view, slightly nose-high in its approach attitude, the gear extended. A hangar obstructed part of my vision and the jet disappeared behind it, then reappeared a moment later fully on the ground. A couple of minutes later, Lonnie taxied the jet to a stop and the engines began to spool down.

I walked out into the lobby. "Is it okay if I go out and help Mr. Smith unload the baggage?"

The cheerful young woman who manned the counter smiled at me. "Sure. As long as Captain Smith is out there with you."

Captain Smith… I kept flashing on Lonnie when he lived in a trailer in East Nashville.

I walked out into the hottest-part-of-a-July-afternoon sun and trotted over to the jet just as Lonnie dropped the air-stair door.

"Howdy!" I yelled.

"Yo, Harry!" Lonnie wore a pair of jeans and cowboy boots and a white, long-sleeved pilot's shirt with epaulettes. He looked tanned, ruddy, and even a bit slimmer. Lonnie wasn't a big vacation kind of guy, but he wore this well.

"Damn, man," I said, the two of us going into a guy hug at the bottom of the steps, "I think Florida agrees with you."

Behind him, Alex stepped out of the jet wearing a pair of

white shorts and a graphic tee advertising something called The Sugar Shack. She'd tanned as well and her hair was a shade lighter from the sun and salt water.

I pushed Lonnie aside as she came into my arms and we hugged like we hadn't seen each other in years. "So good to have you home," I whispered.

"I missed you, Daddy," she said, smiling. "Uncle Lonnie let me ride up front in the right seat!"

"Great!" I said. I looked over at Lonnie and he winked.

Sheba followed her and we all had a grand reunion on the hot asphalt. I helped Lonnie unload the bags and sort everything out. The four of us talked about getting dinner together, but I suspect everyone was a little tired and could use some down time. Plus, Alex had to do a quick turnaround in the laundry room and repack for the weekend.

Alex and I loaded up the car and left while Lonnie made arrangements to have the plane cleaned and serviced and towed to its hangar. I was relieved that we weren't going out for dinner tonight.

On the way home, I had Alex tell me everything about the trip. She loved scuba diving and had made six dives in their time down there. She'd gone down almost 80 feet, to where the Navy had sunk a series of decommissioned barges a few decades ago as diver attractions. She'd seen schools of grouper and a few stingrays, a bunch of colorful tropical fish she couldn't identify, and even a couple of small nurse sharks.

They'd restaurant-hopped and shopped, gone to a couple of outdoor concerts, and walked miles of beach.

"It all sounds wonderful," I said, as we pulled off the freeway and headed into East Nashville. "Next time, can I go?"

Alex poked me, teasing. "You could have gone this time," she chided.

"I know. Just a lot going on right now. But things'll calm down soon. In fact, they already are."

We got to the house and Alex split off to her room to unpack and sort out the dirty laundry from the rest of it.

"I stopped by the store last night and picked up the makings of a pot roast. That sound okay?"

She poked her head over the stair rail on the second floor. "You know how to make pot roast? Doesn't that take hours?"

I raised my head to see her, bending my neck into an uncomfortable position. "I've got a pressure cooker, believe it or not, and I know how to use it."

She grinned. "Sure, go for it."

I went into the kitchen and dug the pressure cooker out of a cabinet and set it up on the stove, then pulled the roast and vegetables out of the refrigerator. It had been awhile since I'd used the cooker; I mainly bought it because I went through this phase where I was bored and decided to take up cooking as a hobby. I'd hit a triple or two and a few singles and doubles, but a whole lot of strike-outs as well. I made a mental note of a few quirks I'd discovered about using a pressure cooker.

I opened a nice everyday merlot and poured myself a glass. I felt very centered and domestic as I started cooking. I browned the roast, then pulled it out of the pot and set it aside. I cheated on the broth, using a canned onion soup mixed with wine instead of making it from scratch. I used a wooden spoon to scrape off the fond, those crunchy little brown bits left in the bottom of the pan, then added the liquid and deglazed the pot. I added garlic, bay leaves and a few spices, then set the roast and the vegetables into the pressure cooker, basted everything with the liquid, then sealed it and gave it the heat. A few minutes later, steam started hissing out of the escape valve and filled the whole kitchen with an aroma that made you feel like you were starving.

"What in heaven's name is that?" I heard Alex call from upstairs.

"What's what?" I yelled back.

"That smell? It's heavenly. The whole upstairs smells like a gourmet restaurant!"

I raised my glass of wine and took a sip. "I'll take that as a compliment!" I yelled again.

Alex came into the kitchen carrying a bundle of dirty laundry and crossed to the laundry room, which was about the only room in the house that was pretty much the same as when Mrs. Hawkins lived here almost twenty years ago.

"That's incredible," she said as she passed me. "Where did you learn to do that?"

"Where you learn everything these days," I answered. "YouTube videos."

"What is it?" she said from the laundry room.

"I call it my French country pot roast."

She stuck her head out of the laundry room. "What makes it French?"

"You put thyme in it," I answered. "You put thyme on anything, it's French. You put thyme on a peanut butter sandwich, it's now a *French* peanut butter sandwich and you charge ten bucks for it."

She laughed. "I'll remember that when I open my restaurant."

An hour later, we sat at the kitchen table and dug into what I had to admit was as close to a home run as I'd ever hit in the kitchen. Alex was clearly ravenous and ate with a relish that only an adolescent metabolism could handle. I ate a little slower and sipped wine as I went along.

"So have you talked to Estella lately?" I asked.

Alex looked up at me with, surprisingly, a bit of discomfort. "Uh, yeah," she answered.

"How is she? How are things in Reno."

She looked down at her plate and pushed a couple of carrot pieces around a potato. "Things are fine."

I felt my forehead scrunching up as I put down my fork. "Okay," I said. "What's going on? I asked what I thought was a simple question and now all of a sudden we've got a side dish of awkward on the table."

She looked up at me, the look on her face all serious. "Daddy, I talk to Estella almost every day."

"Okay," I said after a moment. "You act like that's something you didn't want to tell me."

"It's not that," she said. "It's just that… well, I thought it might make you uncomfortable."

"Uncomfortable?" I asked. "Or is what you mean you were afraid it would make me jealous?"

She looked me directly in the eye. "I just didn't want to hurt your feelings."

I smiled at her, reached across the table and took her hand. "My hide's a little thicker than that. Look, I know you're close to Estella. She practically raised you. I know you love her. I also know the two of you speak what sounds to me like pretty fluent Spanish."

She pulled her hand back. "Wha— How did you know?"

"I wasn't eavesdropping," I said. "But I came downstairs the night of Momma's funeral and overheard the two of you in the kitchen. And I've overheard you a couple of times on the phone with her. Look, Alex, it's okay."

Her eyes started to fill. "She spoke Spanish to me as a baby. I was basically raised bilingual. I miss her so much," she said. "And I'm so worried about her being out there in that house all alone."

I leaned back in my chair and watched her for a few moments. "Listen, you start school in what, ten days? We go a couple of weeks and then we've got the Labor Day weekend. Why don't we fly out to Reno and see her? Or if you want, I'll put you on a plane and you can have some alone time with her."

She brightened. "Oh, Daddy, could we?"

"Sure," I answered. "And then you can see her again on Fall break. The Titans are playing by then. She's always wanted to go to an NFL game. We'll fly her out here."

"That's great!" she said, almost giddy. "And maybe Christmas."

I nodded. "Absolutely, Christmas. You and Estella talk. She can come here or we can go there."

Alex turned back to her food, smiling.

"Let's finish up here and see what's on Netflix," I said.

Chapter Thirty-Four

I let myself sleep a little later Friday morning since I wasn't going to the office until early afternoon. It was just before ten when I walked out into the living room in a bathrobe with a mug of coffee and looked upstairs. Alex's door was closed and there was no light peeking out from underneath.

I went up the flight of stairs and tapped gently on her door. "Hey, you," I said softly, "time to get moving."

A long groan wafted from behind the door. "Okay."

I grinned and started back down the stairs. If I tried real hard, I could sort of remember what it was like to be almost sixteen and asleep. I slept like the happiest baby in the world during my teenaged years. I didn't have the heart to tell Alex that it all goes downhill from there and that by the time she was my age she'd be lucky to get more than three or four uninterrupted hours of sleep at a stretch.

She wouldn't believe me anyway.

Twenty minutes later, Alex came downstairs after a shower with her hair turbaned up in a thick bath towel. I was sitting at the kitchen table nursing my second mug of coffee and reading the *New York Times* on my laptop. She grabbed a mug out of the cupboard and poured herself a cup, then sat down across from me.

"Bad night?" I asked.

She took a long sip. "Anxiety's up a little bit. I'm not thrilled about this weekend."

"Maybe we could take it this way," I offered. "Let's call this weekend the *determinator*. If it goes well, then you can slide into Bealesworth and see how it goes. If it sucks, then we can drop back and punt."

She looked at me across the top of her mug for a moment. "I don't mean to be so much trouble."

"You're not. This is a big step. Given what you've been through, I'd say you were pretty low maintenance so far."

She grinned. "I don't want to cost you any money, either."

"I've only put down a deposit and we can probably get it back. If we can't, we'll write it off to experience. A life lesson."

"Thanks, Daddy."

I winked at her. "Not to worry…"

Alex finished packing and getting dressed and I made her the offer of either getting lunch out or making something in the house. Her call. She rustled around in the refrigerator and decided grilled cheese sandwiches and chips sounded the best, so she dug out the skillet and went to work.

I called the office and checked in with Ashley. Everything was still moving forward with the demo this afternoon.

"Hey," she said as we were about to hang up, "the restaurant called to confirm tonight. I've never been to Jimmy Kelley's before so I looked it up on the web. Holy cow, Harry."

"I know, it's an indulgence. But everybody's worked so hard and things have been going so well that I thought we all deserved a celebration."

"What if the demo's a disaster?"

"Then we'll all need a little comforting, won't we?"

❧

Alex was mostly quiet as we pulled out of East Nashville onto the freeway and headed for I-40 West. She plugged her playlist into the Tesla's sound system and stared out the windows. This time, she seemed drawn to lighter, more pop stuff than the brutal, aggressive rap she'd hit me with that first time: Lana Del Rey, Ariana Grande, Taylor Swift, even an old Jewel hit I kind of recognized.

Earlier in the morning, the sky had been cloudy and overcast, as if threatening rain or even a pop-up thunderstorm. By lunchtime, though, the clouds had boiled off and the sky was a brilliant, harshly lit blue. I cranked up the A/C and listened along with Alex, neither of us saying much.

I took the Old Hickory Boulevard exit off the freeway, then wound my way over to Highway 100. A few miles further on, I pulled into the Bealesworth campus, which had been decorated with signs and balloons welcoming everyone to new student orientation. There were tents and tables on the quad and throngs of teenagers and their parents. Off to one side, there were a half-dozen guys in khaki pants, seersucker jackets, and straw boaters playing loud, happy New Orleans jazz.

"Wow," she said, staring out the car window.

"Yeah, I guess this is kind of a big deal."

There was a tent near the center of the campus with a big sign out front that said Registration. I parked the car and Alex started to pull her bag out of the back seat.

"Why don't we get you registered first and find out where you're gonna be staying," I said. "It's too hot to lug this stuff around if we don't have to."

We walked over to the Registration tent, where a team of young women sat behind tables with lettered signs. We shifted over to the D-E-F table and were second in line. Off to one side, Elspeth McGowan, the Director of Admissions who'd interviewed us on our first visit, spotted us and came over.

"So good to see you, Alex," she said brightly, taking Alex's hand. "And you, Mr. Denton, welcome back to Bealesworth. This is all so exciting. I'm always glad to see another year get started."

"Yes," I said, shaking her hand. "We're excited, too."

Alex smiled.

"So how does all this work?" I asked.

Elspeth McGowan turned and pointed toward the table. "You'll register here. There's a little bit of paperwork, but not too much. Then we'll get someone to escort Alex to the dorm room where she'll be staying for the weekend."

She turned to Alex, smiling warmly. "I'll text Bitsy and get her and Cricket over here. They told me you've all been keeping in touch."

Alex nodded. "Oh, yes. All the time."

"I'm so pleased. Oh, look, you're next." She stepped aside so we could approach the table.

"They'll have a schedule of events for you and a packet of material," she said. "That'll explain how the weekend's going to go. I'll text Bitsy right now."

We thanked her, then stood there and filled out paperwork for a few minutes. As I signed the last form, which was basically a liability waiver, we heard a squeal from behind us.

"*Alex!*" the two yelled as they ran up to us and swept Alex into a group hug. I stood back a few paces, smiling, hoping this was all going to work out. I sensed that both Bitsy and Cricket were well-intentioned and that their affection for Alex was genuine, although as I've proven many times in my life, I know *bupkis* about women. For all I know, they could be setting her up for a rerun of *Mean Girls*.

The joyous shrieking went on for another fifteen seconds or so and then they were all three chattering away. The next step was to get her to her dorm, so I volunteered to go back to the car to get Alex's backpack and rollaway suitcase. Afterward, I followed them across campus to the main dorm, Bealesworth Hall, which was a three-story, modern version of a 19th-century Georgian residence hall. Half of the first floor was the school's formal dining room, where the girls had to wear uniform jackets and skirts, and the other half was a huge common room with fireplace at one end, a grand piano tucked into the corner, and overstuffed sofas and chairs scattered about. Portraits of long-retired faculty members lined the walls, along with a few paintings that looked like they might really be worth something.

The two floors above were the dormitory, where the girls slept two-to-a-room, with a common bathroom at each end of the hall. The rooms were spartan but adequate, and with some posters on the walls and a couple of throw rugs, might even seem homey.

Alex's room was on the third floor. Bitsy and Cricket explained that her roommate hadn't checked in yet, but they expected her any minute. I saw the look on Alex's face and realized the prospect of sleeping in a small room with a stranger was not something she expected.

There wasn't much left for me to do after that. We all headed back to the quad, where there were snow cone and cotton candy machines and county fair-type games. The first thing on the program was a school-wide assembly in the auditorium, followed by dinner, a movie, and then some free time before bed. Things would start up the next morning when breakfast would be served promptly at 8:30.

Alex walked me back to the car after we got her settled into her dorm room.

"You gonna be okay?" I asked.

She shrugged. "Yeah, it'll be fine. Not wild about that whole *breakfast-at-8:30* thing…"

"You'll just have to power down some coffee."

She stopped, grabbed my elbow. "Oh, god, Daddy, you don't think this is the kind of place where they think coffee's not good for teenagers, do you?" She shook her head. "Honest to God, if it is, I don't know if I can take it."

"You are definitely your father's daughter," I said. "But you need to cool your jets a little. Just dial it down. I'm sure you can get coffee."

We got to the car and she gave me a hug.

"Why don't we leave it this way," I said. "I'll resist my urge to be a helicopter parent and check in with you every two hours. You just go about your business and call if you need me. I'm supposed to pick you up after breakfast on Sunday, right?"

She pulled the schedule out of her pocket and scanned it quickly. "Yeah, we're supposed to be out of the dorm by 10."

I pulled her into my arms and gave her a hug. "I'll be here by 9:45."

She hugged me back. When she pulled away, her face looked tight.

"C'mon," I said. "Let's give it a chance. It'll be okay."

Alex nodded. "I know. Thanks, Daddy."

I opened the car door and gave the blast of hot air from inside a chance to escape. "Have a good time. I love you."

She smiled. "I love you, too."

❧

I was in my office pretending to work, as I so often do, when

I heard Lonnie enter the lobby. I'd been staring out the window again after going over a spreadsheet that had a bunch of numbers on it. That's the entire amount of attention I paid to it: it was a bunch of numbers.

My office door was cracked a couple of inches and Ashley pushed it open with a big smile on her face and Lonnie standing behind her.

"Looks like trouble's landed."

I stood up. "Yep, that's what it usually means."

She held the door open as he entered and then started to pull it closed. "I'll let you two have some privacy," she said, teasing. "Either of you want coffee, water or a soda?"

"I'm fine," I said. "Lonnie?"

Lonnie turned and eyed Ashley for a moment. "No, I'm good. Thanks."

She closed the door and Lonnie sat down in the chair across from my desk.

"Good to see you, man," I said. "You haven't been here in months."

Lonnie turned, stared at my closed office door for a moment. "Yeah, it's been a while, and I don't remember her being quite as strikingly beautiful as she really is."

"Yeah. She's something else. A very special young woman."

He turned to me. "Oh, cut the crap."

"What?"

"She's a gorgeous babe, smart as a whip, and as sweet as can be," he said. "She also seems to be fond of you, although God knows why. And you are, in case you've forgotten, a very lonely old man with a staggering amount of money. Seems like a natural match to me."

"Yeah," I said. "Except I'm old enough to be her father."

"Oh, you're being entirely too easy on yourself. You're actually old enough to be her grandfather."

"Thanks, Ace. I feel better already."

"Oh, c'mon, don't tell you haven't thought about it."

"Well," I answered, uncomfortable with the direction this conversation was taking, "one thinks about a lot of things."

"And thinking about it is apparently all you've done."

"It's a moot point, anyway," I said. "She's quite spoken for."

He leaned back in the chair and crossed one leg over the other. "Damn, that's a shame. A real shame."

I leaned back in my office chair, pulled my bottom drawer open with my foot, and used it as a footstool. "You know, I have absolutely no idea what we're going to be looking at this afternoon. Everybody's been really closed-mouthed about it. I guess I could have pulled rank and demanded a first look, but I've been a little distracted."

"Yeah, you're back wearing that snap-brim fedora cocked over one eye. Next thing you know, you'll be smoking unfiltered Chesterfields and keeping a bottle of rye in your desk drawer."

"Not a chance," I said. "Cigarette smoke makes me nauseous and white wine's about the extent of it for me."

"Ooh," he said, grinning, "you're a manly man."

"Yeah, well, I'm done with it. I've turned this stuff all over to the cops. I expect to see the news break any day now. In fact, I'm a little worried that it hasn't already."

"You know how these things go," Lonnie said. "Wheels of justice grinding slowly and all that."

"I guess so." I looked down at my desk. The clock on my laptop read 3:55. "Why don't we head for the conference room?

Sure you don't want a coffee or something?"

"Nah," he said, standing up. "It'll make me have to pee in the middle of the presentation."

We walked down the hall to the conference room. "How'd it go this morning at that private school?" Lonnie asked.

"Fine. Alex's a little anxious about it all. It'll work out."

We walked into the conference room, where Ashley and Hugh were standing at a podium in the corner under the monitor. Ashley had a stack of handouts and Hugh was testing the wireless connection to the monitor, which already had the first slide of a PowerPoint presentation on the screen.

"Hello, Hugh," Lonnie called as he entered. "How the hell are you?"

Hugh looked up and smiled, then crossed the long narrow room and shook Lonnie's hand. They hadn't always been on such friendly terms, but apparently time had greased that over a little.

"It's good to see you Lonnie," Hugh said. "Thanks for coming. Hope it'll be worth your time."

"I hope it's worth a hell of a lot more than that," Lonnie said. "My time goes cheap these days."

"You guys sure you don't want anything to drink?" Ashley asked. Lonnie turned around and looked at me, this goofy grin on his face.

"Do I look desiccated?" he demanded. "Everybody keeps offering me liquid."

"Don't mind him, Ashley," I said, grabbing a seat near the back of the table. "It's his old man prostate. If we give him something to drink, he'll have to go to the men's room."

Lonnie pulled a seat out next to me. "You could have gone all day without mentioning that."

We settled down, and a couple of minutes later Donnie Hazzard and Pat McClellan came in. Donnie had a look on his face like he knew what was about to happen and couldn't wait for it to launch. Pat had her usual accountant's poker face on.

Ashley slid a copy of the quarter-inch thick handout across the table to each of us, then sat down. Hugh Caulfield stood at the head of the room, beneath the monitor.

"Let's get started, shall we?" He pointed up to the monitor, where the words DENTON & ASSOCIATES were centered in bold on the slide, with today's date below.

"Lonnie, you and the rest of the OGs who started Asfáleia Technologies had one goal in mind, one mission," he began. "To develop the most effective, even lethal, cyber-protective defense against spyware, malware, and hacking of all kinds. Thanks to your forward-thinking vision and creative efforts, Asfáleia Technologies became one of the most successful companies in this entire industry. Your efforts have made the internet a safer and more orderly environment in which to do business and moved the internet from its early Wild West days to where it is now, the safest and most profitable platform for doing business in the world."

Hugh paused and looked down at his notes for a moment. He seemed a bit nervous.

"That, however," he continued, "was the first generation of cybersecurity. Protecting individual users from having their credit card numbers hacked, their passwords, their bank accounts. That was the era of hackers and pirates trying to phish people, to lure them into hitting links that would put malware or spyware on their computers. Or to break past firewalls and get into databases of credit card numbers, passwords, Social Security numbers, anything the bad guys could resell or use to get money. That was the first evolution of cybercrime."

He looked up from his notes and crossed his arms. He was settling down now, getting into his rhythm. I'd worked with Hugh Caulfield long enough to know this was his *modus operandi*, this initial nervousness at having to interact with people. But when his rapid-fire brain took over, the anxiety was pushed aside.

"What made Asfáleia Technologies' approach to cybersecurity unique was Lonnie Smith's foundational, conceptual approach to the initial problem. Software engineers, coders, anyone trying to protect a database, an email account, a website, a server, whatever, would approach the problem in a defensive manner. Like a mugging victim trying to fend off an attacker's blows, the victims of cyber assault were grateful that they could hold off the blows enough to where they didn't cause too much damage.

"Lonnie took the opposite approach. Don't defend; *attack.* Turn the hackers' and the pirates' attempts back on them. Hurt *them*. Destroy *their servers*. Beat down *their firewalls*! Expose *their IPs* so law enforcement could track them down no matter what cave or basement they hid in."

I looked over at Ashley. She stared at Hugh, a smile on her face, enraptured. I had to admit he had me as well.

"Now we come to the next generation of cyber threats." Hugh turned to the monitor and clicked the next slide up.

A PowerPoint slide appeared emblazoned with the words:

THE INTERNET OF THINGS (IOT)

THE CHANGING LANDSCAPE OF CYBERSECURITY

"This is where we're headed, folks," Hugh said. "The internet of things, a worldwide network of physical objects and devices that can identify themselves to other physical objects and devices to use embedded code, automated algorithms, and artificial intelligence to interact with each other."

I turned to Lonnie, who seemed absolutely mesmerized.

"The internet of things is the automated thermostat in your house that recognizes when no one is home and lowers the temperature in the winter to 67 degrees to save on your electric bill. It's the doorbell camera that you buy on Amazon.com for $150 that will ring on your smartphone twenty miles away in your office when a package arrives. It's the app on your garage door that talks to your smartphone and will let you know you forgot to close it."

Hugh paused for a second to let this all sink in.

"It's the latest evolution of the internet," he said. "It's where the world's headed. Experts predict conservatively that within the next three years, there will be six internet-connected devices for every individual on the planet. Other estimates suggest the number will be much higher, maybe on the order of 50 billion."

He paused for another dramatic beat. "The Koreans have marketed a smart refrigerator with a touch screen and voice recognition. When you're out of mayonnaise, you touch the screen and say 'Mayonnaise' and the refrigerator remembers it. In the premium model, you just scan the barcode on the empty jar. Then you're out of milk and butter, salad dressing, and eggs. When the list gets long enough, you punch another button on the touch screen and the refrigerator sends your grocery list to servers at the Kroger, Publix, wherever you choose. If you want, you can set it up for the refrigerator to do this automatically, say, when the list reaches fifteen items or every two weeks when the refrigerator talks to the bank's servers and knows your paycheck was electronically deposited, or when an algorithm predetermines something crucial is running short. Then, for a slight convenience fee, you can have the groceries delivered to your door or drive by the shopping center for curbside pickup."

"Wait a minute," I interrupted. "So we're at a place now that the refrigerator knows when I'm out of mayonnaise and sends off an order to the grocery and I don't have to do *anything*?"

"Not only that, the refrigerator knows, based on the analytics of your past usage and a predetermined algorithm, to order the quart jar of Hellman's rather than the pint jar of Kraft. And never, ever, ever, order Miracle Whip."

I turned to Lonnie. He nodded and raised an eyebrow.

"And the real corollary to all this is that while the refrigerator is putting your grocery list together, while the automated garage door opener and the AI thermostat and the app on your water heater are talking to each other and compiling data on when you're home and when you're not, how much electricity you're using, how much water, a database is being created. A database that can be mined and sifted, analyzed and dissected."

He stopped for a moment and clicked onto the next PowerPoint slide. "And as we all know, data is king."

The PowerPoint slide had a bar graph on it depicting the growth in analytical data mining over the last three years.

"Data today is what oil was in the last century, whale oil in the century before that, and Dutch tulips in the 17th century," Hugh continued. "It's the life's blood of our economy, the medium by which we all do business. I don't have to tell you that on the smallest, most micro level, that if you Google search user reviews for a pair of Timberland hiking boots in size 9½, a week later when you load CNN.com to check the latest headlines, there'll be an ad and a free shipping coupon for Timberland boots on the landing page. This isn't a coincidence. Data has enormous value, and anything with enormous value can be stolen."

A silence melted over the room for a few seconds as we all sat there stunned. I knew some of this stuff. I'd read a few articles, hit a few clickbait pieces, but never anything like this.

"Experts estimate that up to 70 percent of all devices on the Internet of Things are inadequately protected from hacking, spyware, and malware. And since on the Internet of Things, virtually all human interaction has been removed, there's no way any of us will know it until it's too late."

Lonnie leaned back in his chair and laced his fingers behind his head. "Something tells me you've not only isolated a problem, but that you have some idea how that problem can be solved."

Hugh smiled. "The mission of securing the Internet of Things is currently about where the first generation of internet security was when you started Asfáleia. *Asfáleia*, the Greek word for *security*. Now, what we're proposing is that Asfáleia go to the next level."

Hugh turned back to the monitor and pointed his little bug at the monitor and clicked it. The next slide came up.

"Ladies and gentlemen," Hugh announced with a flourish, "I give you Project Prostatévo."

Lonnie turned to me, leaned in and whispered: "Okay, what is this obsession with prostates today?"

"Prostatévo," Hugh said, "the Greek word for safeguard or protect. Project Prostatévo will be the most significant leap forward the world has ever seen in providing bulletproof cybersecurity for the Internet of Things."

Chapter Thirty-Five

For the next hour, Hugh Caulfield regaled us with his plans for making the internet safe for refrigerators. On the surface, it sounded very nerdy, even geeky, but there, in that small conference room with a half-dozen people in attendance, I had the feeling we were on the brink of something that might be bigger than any of us ever imagined.

Lonnie must have thought so, too.

"How long is this going to take?" he asked when Hugh sat down and turned the monitor off. "We can't be the only ones having this discussion right now."

Hugh nodded. "Absolutely. We've got to get going on this right now. I think this is the project that's going to keep Denton & Associates going after our contract with the Germans expires."

Lonnie and I turned to each other. The look on his face said the same thing as mine.

"So how much do you need?" I asked. "How many people, how much money, how long to gear up?"

"In the proposal you've got in front of you," Hugh said, "there's a detailed budget. But to hit the high points, I think a dozen of the best ISE's in the business would be a great place to start."

"ISE?" Pat asked. It was the first thing she'd said in the entire meeting.

"Information security engineers," Hugh answered. "Software

developers that specialize in cybersecurity."

"It's a rarefied environment," Donnie Hazzard added. "There aren't a lot of the best and they're very expensive."

"Can you two get the best?" Lonnie asked.

Donnie and Hugh looked at each other for a moment. Donnie nodded and Hugh spoke up: "It'll take some doing, but between us we know a good dozen or so top-notch people. Good mix of backgrounds and experience, men and women both. One guy I'd really like to have on the team, we'll have to move him from Mumbai. Another one's a Chinese Ph.D. student at Vanderbilt. She's insanely good and she wants to stay in this country."

"Time?" I asked. "And money?"

"Well, we think about six months to get up and running. There'll be hiring and acquisition expenses, more office space, lots of equipment. Expanded servers and massive increases in network power, product testing. But I think we can get rolling in six months and I'd think somewhere between seven and ten-million would get us started."

"Market-ready by?" Lonnie asked, his face as serious as I've ever seen it.

Hugh and Donnie looked at each other again, then Hugh turned to us. "Eighteen months," he said. "Best case scenario. Of course, we still have to meet our responsibilities to the Germans, so that may be a factor as well."

"Don't worry about the Germans," I said. "We can get a crew of rookies in to take care of them."

Lonnie leaned forward and put his elbows on the table, stared off at a spot on the wall somewhere above everybody's head. I'd seen him like this before, lots of times. I could tell the wheels were spinning hyper-speed.

Then he leaned into me and whispered something no one else could hear. I nodded. "Yes, I agree."

He leaned back in his chair, pushed back almost to the wall, stretched out his blue jean-clad legs and cowboy boots, then rested them on the table.

"Hugh," I said, "the plan was to dissolve Denton & Associates at the expiration of the German contract. Those wheels are in motion. That train's not stopping. Besides, this is a project so large, with so much potential, that we don't want to contaminate it with D&A baggage. My suggestion is we set up a separate entity. Basically start from scratch with a new company. The lawyers and the accountants can untangle that."

"And we don't have eighteen months," Lonnie said. "We're looking more like half that."

Hugh and Donnie looked at each other, as if they couldn't decide whether to squeal or faint.

"And how about we do a little riff on the company that started this," Lonnie said. "What would you think of *Prostatévo Technologies*? With all of you on the ground floor..."

Literally everyone in the room stopped, stunned and silent. Hugh and Donnie and Pat all knew what happened to the guys who got in on the ground floor of Asfáleia Technologies. Ashley wasn't around in those days, but she knew what this meant. Inside of three years, she could buy that hollow in East Tennessee.

"And ten million is way short," Lonnie said. "After the acquisition by the Germans, I set up a company, Shadow Venture Capital Management."

Shadow... Lonnie's beloved German shepherd. The night she died nearly twenty years ago back in that trailer in Inglewood was probably the lowest point of his life. It was a long, slow comeback after that.

"If we're going to do Prostatévo Technologies right, then let's do it right. I'm talking Manhattan Project, all-hands-on-deck here."

He turned to me. "Harry, if you want in on this, let's go. I'm thinking we need 100 mil to get started. What do you think?"

I nodded. "Sounds about right. Count me in."

Lonnie turned from me and scanned the rest of the room.

"Well?" he said, loud. "What do you think?"

There was silence all around. Hugh Caulfield looked like he was about to burst into tears. Pat sat there in shock, numb. Donnie Hazzard was sitting back in his chair, his hands across his huge stomach, an effluent-eating grin spread across his massive jowls.

Finally, in the softest voice I'd ever heard her use, Ashley spoke up.

"I think I'm gonna be getting another tattoo."

❧

If we'd had a bottle of champagne in the office, I would've opened it. By the time we adjourned, though, there wasn't time. It was 5:30 on a Friday afternoon and the rush hour traffic outside was going to be hellacious. For the folks who wanted to go home and change, there was barely time to make our seven o'clock reservation at Jimmy Kelly's. Everyone took off, with the exception of me and Lonnie. I'd dressed in slacks and a dress shirt this morning, with a jacket and tie downstairs in the car, in anticipation of not going home before dinner. As a result, I had a little time to kill. Lonnie was going to dash home, pick up Sheba, change, and go straight to the restaurant.

He stepped into my office just before heading for the elevator. "Well, this turned into a hell of a day, didn't it?"

I leaned back in my office chair and shook my head slowly. "I was wondering what I was gonna do next."

He grinned. "You know, I was bored with the company for a long time before we sold it. But hell, man, you can't go flying every day. I was getting sick of having so much time on my hands and I'm starting to get on Sheba's nerves. If this hadn't come along, I was thinking of going back to repo'ing cars and bounty hunting."

"You're too old," I said. "I can say that because I'm too old to go with you. So you want to be actively involved in this, not just the VC guy?"

"Hell, yeah. It'll be fun. I like building shit. It's running it after it's already built that bores the tits off me."

I stared at him for a beat. "Yeah, I get it. Me, too."

"I'll call Charly over at Fallon, McKenzie, and Dillingham. I'll set up a meeting as early as possible next week. Who should be there?"

Fallon, McKenzie, and Dillingham was the top corporate law firm in Nashville, maybe the whole Southeast. The senior partner, Charly Fallon, was a long way away from when our lawyer used to be a guy named Marvin Shapiro, whom everybody called "Marvelous Marvin." Marvelous Marvin told me once he had a client who passed so many bad checks he had a book of them printed up with the workhouse address on them.

"Well, if we're all going to be principals, then I guess we should all be there."

"Even the babe?" Lonnie said, with a grin that stopped just the right amount of being a leer.

"Especially her," I said. "She may look like a teenager with a bad attitude, but I *guaran-damn-tee* you she was the smartest person in the room."

His face settled into something very quiet. "Good for her," he said softly, stepping toward my office door. "See you in an hour."

"I'll be there."

Then I was alone.

I checked my phone again to see if there was any word from Alex.

Nothing.

I thought of calling or texting her, then did a mental self-scold. Gotta stop being the helicopter parent. She's almost sixteen. She'd be driving in a couple months; two years after that old enough to vote and join the army. Time to let go, give her some space…

I was surfing the web, reading the news, getting distracted by more clickbait, when my phone went off. I looked down, didn't recognize the number. I swiped the screen.

"Hello."

"Harry Denton?" I tried to place the voice.

"You got him."

"This is Lieutenant Akers, South Precinct."

"Oh, hi, Lieutenant. I've been thinking about calling you. I've been watching the news lately. Doesn't seem like there's much going on."

"And there won't be," he said, his voice stern. "We brought in four or five of those folks at the film school and interviewed them."

"You did what?" I barked.

"We had to," he shot back. "You didn't give us enough to nail 'em without it. They all had alibis, airtight ones I might add, and solid answers for every other question. We went to the D.A., took everything you gave us and everything we got from them and all the evidence from the crime scene. We even had DNA results back from the lab. No witnesses, no physical evidence to tie any of them to the victim or the crime scene. There was no *there* there. We pushed the D.A. as hard as we could. There ain't gonna be no grand jury. We're back to square one."

I felt my pulse racing. "This is bullshit, Akers! You can't just let 'em get away with it."

"I don't like this any better than you do, *Denton*," he snapped, barely concealing his own anger. "You think I like having one more unsolved homicide on my desk? But there's this little thing called the Constitution, right? I can't just tie 'em to a chair and beat it out of 'em!"

"Why not?" I demanded. "Wouldn't be the first time. Remember back in the old Criminal Justice Center? There were two elevators. If you got on the left one, you were going straight upstairs to the cells. If you got on the right one, you knew that elevator was gonna stop between floors and you were gonna get an ass-whipping."

"That was a long time ago," Akers said. "That shit won't go anywhere these days. Listen, Denton, I called you as a courtesy, not to get my own ass chewed. This is what it is and I'm telling you right now to stay the hell away. That is *not* a request. We clear?"

"We are clear, Lieutenant Akers," I said as coldly as I could. "Thank you for your consideration."

Then I hung up on him.

In retrospect, hanging up on a Metro Nashville Police Department Lieutenant may not have been exactly the best move, but my frustration had gotten the best of me. I was way too agitated to sit around this empty office anymore, so decided to just take my time heading to Jimmy Kelly's Steakhouse.

Down in the largely empty parking garage, I retrieved my tie and put it on, then checked myself in the side mirror. I put on the Navy blue blazer, then climbed into the car. The drive from downtown out to Louise Avenue near the Vanderbilt campus would probably take the better part of forty-five minutes during Friday rush hour anyway. I cranked up the AC and headed out into the traffic.

Jimmy Kelly's Steakhouse was about as old-school Southern as you could get. Housed in a corner lot mansion, the place had been around since the Thirties and passed down from one generation to the next. White-coated waiters in stiff, starched shirts and pressed black pants made you feel like you'd been transported back to the Gilded Age. They served up the best steaks and the finest whiskey this side of Chicago or New York.

I gave the key fob to the valet and, without thinking, asked him if he knew how to run a Tesla. He looked down his nose at me and smiled.

"Fourth one tonight, sir."

Well, I guess this is just my day to be an asshole. Note to self: *tip well.*

I walked up the steps under the red canopy and checked in at the desk. I was twenty minutes early and the first one here, so I headed back to the bar, which was all oak and mahogany and grand mirrors like something out of a movie.

I found a place and wedged in between two groups of businessmen who seemed well on their way to a lubricated Friday night. An older black man with salt-and-pepper hair in a white coat walked up and asked what I'd like.

"A Gibson, please, Bombay Sapphire and extra pearl onions."

"Neat or on the rocks?"

"Straight up," I said. "It's been a day."

My stomach churned. I wish I hadn't gotten that damn call from Lieutenant Akers. Here I was all primed to have an especially good night and now this was settling in on me like a dark cloud.

Sometimes, life just has a way of ruining life.

The waiter brought my drink in one of those classic long-stemmed martini glasses. I looked at myself in the immense 19th-century mirror across the bar. A late middle-aged man in a coat and tie with a slightly weary look on his face stared back at me. Sometimes I didn't recognize that guy and had to stare back a bit: *that's me*.

The Gibson martini was ice-cold and I sipped it the way an old friend of mine taught me to drink martinis over thirty years ago. I was in my late twenties, had never had a martini, and he explained to me that what was needed in martini drinking was persistence and determination.

The first sip, he explained, would taste like you were siphoning gas out of a lawnmower. The second would be just as bad, so you just had to push on through. Then a couple of sips later, it wouldn't be so bad. Sometime in the middle of the second martini, it would start to taste like the coldest, sweetest spring water you'd ever had in your life.

That, he explained, was when you had to watch out.

I finished the Gibson just as Ashley and Hugh came in, followed a couple of minutes later by Pat McClellan with her plus-one, who turned out to be an amiable enough fellow who was retired faculty from the Vanderbilt philosophy department. I forgot his name as soon as we were introduced.

Then Donnie Hazzard and his date showed up, who was a drop-dead gorgeous guy about half his age and half his weight. He was buff and tanned and later proved, despite appearances, to be able to carry on an intelligent conversation about both politics and movies. What he saw in Donnie I couldn't imagine, but these things are such a mystery to me.

We ordered drinks for everyone except me. One martini was my limit if I was going to have a glass of wine or two with dinner. Lonnie and Sheba walked in last, a few minutes after seven, and the hostess took us back to one of the private dining rooms, which was like a grand parlor with a fireplace at one end and Victorian-era wallpaper throughout. It was heavy oak and walnut and mahogany, just like the rest of the house.

We sat down and for some reason or other, I got elected to sit at the head of the table, with Lonnie and Sheba on my left, Ashley and Hugh on my right. Having an odd number of us made the seating arrangements a little complicated, but the staff made it work.

Ashley leaned in to me close. She was dressed in a black, square neck, three-quarter length sleeve, body-hugging dress that made you want to bite right through your lower lip. Her hair was pulled back and she wore simple, elegant jewelry, just a hint of makeup, and a soft perfume that wafted toward me as she scooted in close. As she came close to me, her left sleeve shifted up, exposing her Asfáleia Technologies tattoo. Soon, there'd be another one on her right forearm.

Ashley, I thought, was going to enjoy being rich.

"I've never seen anything like this," she whispered.

I leaned in toward her. "Yeah, it's pretty heady. I've only been here a couple of times myself."

I smiled and scrunched up my face. "Enjoy it!"

Our waiter came and introduced himself and assured us he would take the best care of us imaginable. A couple of backup guys set down plates of hot corn cakes, a Jimmy Kelly's staple you didn't even have to ask for and would remember all your life. There was laughter and chatter as drinks were brought and food was ordered. Appetizers—blackened Cajun catfish, barbecued prawns, fried calamari—were spread around and shared.

Sheba and Ashley both ordered the grilled salmon, and the thought occurred to me that the two of them plus Alex would make quite a trio. I felt a little twinge of missing her.

Lonnie ordered the Cowboy Steak, a 20-ounce bone-in ribeye that would have put me in the hospital, but wouldn't put a pound on him. Not to be outdone, Donnie and Young Gorgeous Boy ordered the Chateaubriand for two. Everyone was having a hell of a time.

I ordered the small filet smothered in Sauce Béarnaise, fresh asparagus, a twice-baked potato, and a glass of the MacMurray Ranch 16 pinot noir. Halfway through the first glass of wine, my spirits started to lift a little and I managed to push Leo Walsh out of my head.

The evening seemed to go on forever, with laughter to the point of giddiness. Ashley and Sheba got along famously, while at the other end of the table, Donnie and YGB held hands and flirted and delighted everyone with their double entendres. At any given point there were at least three separate cross-table conversations going on at once, with none of them seeming to interfere with each other. Lonnie was as animated as I've ever seen him, clearly thrilled at the prospect of another new business adventure.

I sat at the head of the table, largely watching it all. I tried not to feel left out, being the only solo act at the table, but it was a hard sentiment to dodge. Most of the time, I just rolled along from one day to the next, taking care of my business and trying to enjoy every day as much as possible.

Occasionally, though, it hit me. I'm alone.

A team of white-coated guys came and cleared the table, laid out dessert menus, and took after-dinner drink and coffee orders. Ashley leaned in again. "I'm stuffed," she said, *sotto voce*, "but it's too good to pass up. I'm glad tomorrow's Saturday."

"I know. I think I'll sleep 'til noon."

She held up the dessert menu and pointed. "So what do you think?"

I grinned at her. "You look like a Chocolate Decadence kinda gal to me."

She looked down at the menu and her eyes opened even wider. "Oh my God, double fudge chocolate brownie topped with French vanilla ice cream and drizzled with…"

Her voice trailed off. "Go for it," I said. "You can handle it."

Sheba leaned across the table. "Split it?"

Ashley beamed. "Perfect, thank you."

I ordered a crème brûlée, coffee and a Drambuie on the rocks. What the hell, it was a celebration.

Another hour later and the celebration was over. It was close to ten and the laughter and conversation was just beginning to die down a little, probably as a result of digestive systems kicking in and pulling blood supplies off brains. We were satiated and tired and ready to call it a night.

Our waiter came and the whole table gave him a round of applause. He handed me the check, which with a generous tip came to just short of $1500.00 It had been a grand night and worth every penny.

I fully expected, and hoped, that company morale would be at an all-time high. These were all good people, smart people, motivated and determined people, and I was lucky to work with them.

Outside, we all waited for the valet guys to get our car, with the exception of Ashley and Hugh, who'd parked down the street curbside. They strolled off under a clear, cloudless beautiful summer night arm-in-arm.

Sheba and Lonnie and I were the last ones to get our cars. Sheba sidled over to me on the sidewalk and laced her arm into mine.

"You were kind of quiet tonight," she said.

"Was I?"

She nodded. "I can't help but worry about you."

"Oh, c'mon, sweetie. I'm all right. Just got a lot on my mind, that's all."

"Lonnie told me all about this new venture. There's every reason to believe it's going to make the both of you even richer than you are now. And you're disgustingly rich as it is."

"It looks very promising. And if it's as successful as we think, it's going to do a lot of good. You're right, I've got more than I ever needed or wanted. Alex is never going to want for anything. I think I'll slice off enough to take care of her and any children she has for the next generation and then I'm going to start giving it away."

She squeezed my arm just as the valet brought her Mercedes

SUV up to the curb. Lonnie, who'd been standing a few feet off checking his phone, walked over.

"I'm pooped, baby," he said brightly. "Tired and stuffed. Take me home and put me to bed."

"You okay?" she said to me. "I mean, for driving?"

I nodded. "I'm alright," I said. "I didn't hit it too hard."

"Hey, man," Lonnie said, "we can call you a Lyft if you want."

"Not to worry," I said. "Go on home, you two."

"Talk to you tomorrow?"

"Sure."

They climbed into the Mercedes and drove off just as the valet brought my car around. It was the same guy who took the car earlier in the evening. He gave me his smart-assed smile as he handed me the fob.

"Your Tesla, sir, safe and sound."

I handed him a couple of folded Benjamins. He looked down and this time his smile was genuine.

"Thanks," he said.

"Just to prove I'm not a complete asshole," I said as I climbed into the car.

As I pulled away from the curb, the hands-free went off. I smiled; Alex calling to say goodnight. I hit the connect button on the steering wheel.

"Hey," I said happily.

"Mr. Denton?"

I'd heard that voice before. I looked down at the screen, didn't recognize the number. I pulled to a stop at the traffic light to turn left onto Elliston Place.

"Yes, this is Harry Denton."

"Mr. Denton, this is Elspeth MacGowan over at Bealesworth Academy."

As soon as she said that, I recognized the Scottish accent.

"Yes, Ms. MacGowan, is everything okay?"

She hesitated, clearing her throat over the phone. "Well, not exactly. I don't quite know how to say this. We've never had anything like this happen before."

"What's going on?" I demanded.

"Well, Mr. Denton, it's Alex," she said. "You see, sir, we can't find her."

Chapter Thirty-Six

"What the hell you mean, you can't find her?"

Elspeth MacGowan was clearly trying not to sound as distraught as she must be. "I don't know what to say," she stammered. "At ten o'clock, the girls were supposed to return to their dorms. We had a bonfire. That was the last scheduled event of the day. Everything was fine. The girls generally gather in their dorm rooms and stay up way too late, but we know they're in safe."

The light changed from red to green, but I didn't notice. Behind me, a guy laid on his horn. I looked up, made my left turn onto Elliston Place. The plan was to take Elliston Place down to where it turned into Church Street, then onto the freeway and home.

"So about 9:30, Bitsy and Cricket and a few of the other girls were in a room having a bull session and somebody said, 'Where's Alex?' Bitsy texted her and didn't get an answer, so they went up to the third floor. Her room was empty. All her things were there, but the room was empty. The girl who was supposed to be her roommate was already downstairs with the other girls."

I made the right turn onto 21st Avenue and headed to West End. No way I was going home until they'd located Alex.

"Have you tried calling her?"

"Of course, Bitsy texted her again and then tried to call her directly. The call went to voicemail."

I tried not to speed as I approached the intersection on West

End, catty-cornered across from the Vanderbilt campus. I was pretty sure I could pass a field sobriety test, but I didn't need the hassle right now.

"Okay," I said. "I'm on West End by the Vanderbilt campus. I'll be there in twenty minutes."

⁂

It's a straight shot out West End Avenue to Bealesworth Academy, although as with many Nashville streets, the same strip of asphalt changes names several times. The traffic was light this late on a Friday night and, for once, the lights cooperated. I made it to Bealesworth in about fifteen minutes and pulled to a stop in front of the main administration building.

I was working with sense memory alone at this point, but my inner compass worked and I trotted across campus to Bealesworth Hall, the dormitory where I'd left Alex only a little over eight hours ago. Elspeth MacGowan, in a pair of jeans and a Bealesworth sweatshirt, paced the lobby as I yanked open the front door.

A brief flash of terror shot across her face; guess I looked a little manic. I made a mental note to not look like a crazy person as I walked up to her.

"Any sign of her?"

"No, I'm afraid not."

I took a deep breath and let it out slowly. "Okay, how do you lose a nearly sixteen-year-old girl?"

"Mr. Denton, please, I don't know how this happened. I've got all the girls out scouring the campus now. If she's around, they'll find her. Are you sure you haven't heard from her?"

I pulled out my mobile and checked again. "No, nothing."

"Do you think she might have decided to go home? Maybe

she was upset about something." Elspeth MacGowan turned just a few degrees and the light from the overhead hit her in a different way. Her face was red and flushed.

"Look, Ms. MacGowan, no one's blaming you for any of this. If I sounded like I was, I apologize. I'm just concerned. If she decided to go home, why didn't she call me? I'd have come pick her up."

"Plus," she said, "she left her things in her dorm room."

I pulled out my mobile again and swiped the screen to wake it up. I've got an app on my phone that talks to the cameras around the house. I lit up the app and six tiny frames appeared on the screen, one for each of the four corners of the house, the front door and back door. I blew each one up, one at a time.

Nothing. No sign of movement anywhere. If Alex had gone in one of the doors, I would've gotten an alert on my phone.

Elspeth MacGowan's phone went off. She pulled it out, looked down.

"It's Bitsy," she said, swiping the screen and holding the phone to her ear. "Any luck?"

She nodded her head as a muddled voice came through the phone. "All right, you and the other girls go search the area behind the soccer field. There's a tree line on the east side of the field. Check and see if there's any sign of her out that way."

She nodded again, her head bobbing nervously. "All right. Check in with me in another ten or fifteen minutes."

"Have you checked the security tapes?"

Elspeth MacGowan stared at me for a moment, her lips pursed. "We don't have security tapes."

"What?" I demanded.

"We have some CCTV cameras in the academic buildings,

but not in the dorms. Privacy issues. And we don't have the external part of the campus under surveillance."

I rubbed my forehead, where a stress headache was just beginning to light up. "I should go out there and join them," I said.

"Should we call the police?" she asked.

"Good Lord, I hadn't even thought of that." My brain went into overdrive. "I don't know. Let's give it a little bit longer. My sense is the police won't even do much except take a report for a set amount of time. A teenager who's not where she's supposed to be when she's supposed to be there is probably not a major urban crisis these days."

Elspeth MacGowan's voice lowered. "Mr. Denton, I have to ask this…"

She hesitated, uncomfortable, not wanting to look me in the eye. "Alex doesn't have a boyfriend or anything like that, has she? We've never had a girl disappear during a summer orientation, but it's not at all uncommon to see them miss a bed check during the regular year. Boys sneak onto campus, girls sneak out to meet them. Do you think?"

I started to flare, then realized from her perspective, it was a perfectly valid question.

"Alex has only been in Nashville a couple of weeks," I said. "She hasn't met anyone since she got here. I don't think she had a boyfriend back in Reno."

She looked at me a moment as if studying me. "I hope you don't mind my saying this and I certainly don't mean anything by it. I don't even know Alex, but if there's one thing I do know in this day and age, it's teenage girls. It's not like when you and I were that age. If we were going on a date, our parents would know who it was with and when we would be back. Kids today, with social media and their own passcode-protected smart phones, and social media sites we haven't even heard of, can have a whole secret life we don't know about. It's not a reflection on your or anyone else's parenting. It's just the way it is."

I stood there silently for a moment and flashed back on all those times in the past couple of weeks when Alex had surprised me, when I'd had this sense that I didn't know her anywhere near as well as I thought I did. Elspeth MacGowan was right; she could have an entirely secret life I knew nothing about.

"I don't know," I said. "I don't believe so, but I can't guarantee it."

We stood there awkwardly, neither of us knowing what to do next.

"Would it be all right if I went up to her room?" I asked. "I could go through her things, see if there's some note, some clue, as to where she might have gone off to."

"All the new girls are in the common room. They're understandably upset, so we left them with two senior prefects and had them put on a movie. The common room is at the north end of the second floor…"

Elspeth MacGowan pointed to my right, toward the far end of the building.

"Alex's room is on the third floor, Room 320. It's on the right side of the hall at the opposite end of the dorm. Her door should be open."

I nodded. "All right, I won't bother anyone else's things."

"I'll wait down here for when the girls get back."

I turned and took the stairs two at a time. The staircase was steep and curved back in on itself like the bight of a rope. I hit the second floor landing, then went onto the third, by now panting, and through the double doors into the dorm hallway. I stopped for a moment to get my bearings, then turned left and went down the long hallway.

I hadn't noticed this afternoon that the dorm hallways were a lot more bare and spartan than the first floor. The walls were cracked-plaster painted over in some kind of green pastel paint the color of watered down pea soup. The carpet was institutional, bare and simple, with basic overhead lights lighting the way.

Room 320 was the last door on the right, near the entrance to the communal bathroom. I pushed the door open and flicked the bare overhead light on. I'd seen the room earlier, when I first brought Alex here, but that was in the light of day.

Now, late at night with no sun streaming in through the sole window, the room seemed completely depressing. The floor was red tile, the only furniture basic wooden twin beds with plain white sheets, a single pillow, and a gray blanket, a four-drawer chest of drawers, and a rudimentary desk and wooden chairs without cushions. It seemed almost military in its sparsity.

Alex's suitcase and backpack were on the twin bed. The suitcase was open, but otherwise untouched. Her backpack was still zipped. I crossed the room, grabbed the backpack, and sat on the bed. Inside was a paperback copy of a John Greene novel, her iPad, a leather-bound journal and a few other odds and ends. Nothing particularly revealing.

She clearly hadn't had time to get settled in. This meant that whatever happened to motivate her to leave had happened right after nine, which was the last time someone had seen her.

There wasn't much to see here. I kept scanning the room, hoping I'd see something the fourth time around I hadn't seen the first.

I was completely flummoxed. *Where the hell is she?*

My mobile buzzed in my pocket. I yanked it out without looking at the screen and answered it.

"Yes?" I said sternly.

And there it was again. *That damned calliope circus music…*

I stood up, stunned. The calliope music went on for maybe five seconds that felt like an hour. Then the gravelly, scratchy voice I'd heard once before.

"*We told you to mind your own fucking business, Harry! We told you. Why couldn't you mind your own fucking business?*"

"Where are you? Where's Alex?"

"*No questions, Harry! We told you to back the fuck off and you didn't. And now it's payback time!*"

More calliope music for a few seconds, then it faded away to silence.

"I want to talk to my daughter," I said, mustering as much iron in my voice as possible. Which wasn't much…

"*We don't care what you want,*" the voice growled. "*And we're asking the questions. Tell me right now, and tell me the truth, Harry. Where exactly the fuck are you?*"

"I'm in a dorm room at Bealesworth Academy," I answered. "The dorm room where my daughter's supposed to be asleep right now."

"*Don't you worry about your daughter's sleeping habits, Harry. If you don't do exactly as we tell you, she's going to have a nice long nap.*"

I bolt of lightning shot through my chest and for a moment, I wondered if I was having a heart attack. I felt light-headed and almost dizzy.

"What do you want me to do?"

"*First of all, have any of you fucks called the cops yet?*"

"No."

"*Good. You better not, and you better not be lying to me. Now, second, you're gonna gather up all your daughter's shit. Then you're going to tell all those snotty bitches that you've found your daughter. Make up something. She had an anxiety attack and took an Uber back to your house. Whatever… Then you go straight home and sit there until I call you again.*"

"Okay. I'll do that. But nothing better happen to my daughter. You understand? If something happens—"

Then the calliope music blared again so loud I jerked the phone away from my ear. Just as abruptly, it stopped.

"*Krusty hates it when you try to play hero, Harry. Just do what you're told. Go on, be a good boy.*"

Then there was silence, a silence as deep and empty as any silence I'd ever not heard before. A silence that hurt my ears and pounded through my chest.

My god, I thought, *if anything happens to her…*

There was only one thing to do. I folded Alex's suitcase shut and snapped it, then gathered all her things into her backpack. I did a quick look around the room. The drawers were empty, the closet as well. Clearly, Alex barely had time to even set her things down when they had done something—God only knew what—to lure her away.

Then they'd grabbed her.

Equally clearly, I had underestimated these people by a factor that was unimaginable. It's one thing to murder someone who had clearly become your enemy. But to threaten someone who was entirely innocent...

That was a mistake I wouldn't make again.

I dragged her suitcase behind me, her backpack on my back, down the three flights of stairs.

"Ms. MacGowan," I said loudly when I got to the first floor. I saw Elspeth MacGowan get up from one of the sofas in the common room.

"Yes," she called.

I hadn't thought of what I would say to her, hadn't had the time or the bandwidth to rehearse my lie. I'd have to wing it.

"Ms. MacGowan," I said as she approached. "I am so sorry for this. But Alex called me when I was upstairs in her room. She just got home. She was upset by something. I don't know what, but I'll find out. She called a Lyft. She's home safe."

She stared at me as if I had just told her aliens had landed on the Bealesworth Academy soccer field. "Why didn't she tell someone? Why did she just leave her things here?"

"Those are very good questions, ones I intend to get answers to as soon as I'm in the same room with her again. You said it yourself. Sometimes you just don't know what's going on with these kids. I am so sorry for the distress and disruption. If you want to rescind her acceptance, I'll understand."

"No," Elspeth MacGowan said, her voice softening. "We just want to make sure Alex is okay. That's all that matters."

"I agree. And she's going to be okay. I just need to get to her. You can call off the search now. Try and calm the girls down and everyone get some sleep."

I began backing away from her, eager to get to my car.

"Will you call me tomorrow and let me know how she is?"

I nodded. "I will. Thank you so much. I need to get going now."

Chapter Thirty-Seven

I don't remember much of the drive home. I was in shock, furious, terrified, gobsmacked, unbelieving…

All at once.

A literal tsunami of thoughts and emotions racing in all directions.

This can't be happening.

And then there was my old, dear, dark friend: *guilt.*

If I'd just minded my own goddamn business. If I'd just dialed it down, let it go. What business of mine was it if Leo Walsh went out and got himself beat to death because he got mixed up with the wrong people? It's not my job to right every wrong, bring the guilty to justice.

Hell, I am the guilty.

My mind raced to put a plan together. I couldn't just sit here and wait for this to unfold. I should call Lonnie; he'd know what to do.

No, not yet. What could he do? What could any of us do until those bastards got back in touch?

And I was sure they would. They wanted something, wanted something bad enough to take the biggest risks they'd ever taken. This was even bigger than murder. Clearly, the cops were willing to skate on Leo's murder and write it off to some lame excuse that would relieve them of the responsibility of really doing their jobs. Plus there was nobody around to stand up for Leo, nobody with any real firepower who could hold them accountable.

But this, this was different. There's no way they could get away with hurting—or worse, I forced myself to think—an innocent young girl. She had nothing to do with this. I hadn't even told her the Leo Walsh story and how I got involved with it trying to chase a long-gone life that had more purpose than just making money and accumulating shit I didn't need.

This only made me feel more guilty.

I raced inside and took Alex's things up to her room. It was the first time I'd really looked in her room in days. She'd moved some things around, set out a few framed pictures, managed to clutter the place up a little bit, just like a normal teenaged girl.

It was slowly becoming hers. And now it might be taken away.

Shut up! the voice in my head yelled.

I couldn't allow myself to think like that. I had to stay focused, keep my eye on the prize, and the prize was getting my daughter home any way I could.

I went downstairs, washed my face and changed into a pair of jeans and a T-shirt. You don't hear a lot about kidnappings these days; it's not exactly the commonplace crime it was back in the 1920s. I always imagined, though, that the worst part of it for the family was the waiting. The interminable, agonizing wait for someone to get back in touch with the instructions that would make this all work out right.

I kept my cell phone beside me, the ringer volume turned all the way up. There was no way I was going to sleep. I was still stuffed from dinner, and the effects of the alcohol had disappeared as soon as the call came from Elspeth MacGowan. I thought of pouring another glass of wine just to settle my nerves, calm the voice in my head.

No, I needed to keep my wits about me, to try and keep some

kind of edge.

I thought again of calling Lonnie, but I knew that he and Sheba had probably gone on to bed. Even after all this time, Sheba told me that the two of them still cuddled in bed at night, engaged in what used to be euphemistically referred to as *pillow talk*, and then drifted off to sleep, his spoon nestled against hers.

I'd slept alone for so long that having a warm body next to me would probably keep me up all night.

No, Lonnie wasn't the answer, not yet. I couldn't go running off to him for help like I used to in the old days, my Little Buddy Gilligan to his Skipper…

I was on my own for now.

I stared at the television, exhausted yet stressed, every nerve in my body on edge. There was an old Dick Powell movie on Turner Classic that would have ordinarily sucked me right in. I stared at the television, oblivious. After a while, I muted the TV and put my head back on the sofa. The leather was cool and slick, the cushion beneath it soft.

I drifted off into an uneasy, restless sleep. In my dream, I was in a dilapidated old house, one that literally seemed to be falling apart. And I was wandering from one room to the next, the house a rabbit's warren of interconnecting rooms, long musty dark hallways heavily in shadow. What little illumination there was came from low-watt, unshaded bulbs suspended by frayed wires from the ceiling.

In the background, far away, a distant crying sound. In my dream, I didn't know what it was but I instinctively felt drawn to it. As I wandered from one room to another—each of them filled with broken, dusty furniture, collapsed beds, peeling rotten wallpaper, garbage stuffed in the corner—the crying would get louder and louder until it sounded like it was just in the next room, if only I could get there.

And just as I got to the room, I recognized the crying. I'd heard it before, inside that funeral home in Reno when Alex and I stood in front of her mother's casket and she sobbed into my shoulder. Alex was in the next room and if I could only cross this room full of detritus, I'd find her.

Then I'd step through the doorway out of the room and into the next and it would be empty.

And the crying sound would be further away again.

In my dream, I yelled for her, but my voice came out muffled, as if I were calling to her from inside a barrel. But I kept going.

Suddenly, Alex's sobs became crystal clear, sharp and pointed, and from very close by. I stepped into a room where a dim yellow light bulb exposed an old plaster wall spider-webbed with cracks and holes, the rotten strips of exposed lath moldy and green in the faded light. Across from me was a door into another room, and from that room, Alex's sobs were clear.

I crossed the room quickly, the floor creaking and giving way under my feet but not buckling completely. I stepped into the doorway and looked into the room, which was painted purple and gold and was clean and well-put together compared to the rest of the house.

In the center of the room was an elaborate, wooden catafalque decorated in purple velvet, with a candelabra on either side illuminating the open casket that sat on it. In front of the bier, Alex stood with her back to me, her shoulders hunched as she bent over, her head in her hands, sobbing. I stepped into the room and toward her. I started to speak, but nothing came out.

I stepped on a floorboard and a loud squeak erupted.

Alex raised up and turned toward me. Her eyes were red and wet, with great dark circles underneath all the way to her cheekbones. Her cheeks were gray and sunken and she had a pallor over her whole face and hands that was the color of cement.

She looked up at me. "Daddy," she said, "I'm ready to go be with Momma."

I tried to speak again, but nothing came out. "No," I mouthed. "Alex, honey, it's not time."

Then there was a siren, a piercing blast next to my ear. I didn't know where it came from and what it was, but I knew it was pulling me out of the dream and I didn't want to go, not without Alex. But I rose toward the ceiling despite myself. Alex looked up at me in a death stare as she receded from my vision and the dream faded away.

And my mobile continued blaring from my shirt pocket.

I suddenly realized where I was and fumbled for the phone. "Yes," I snapped as I hit the red spot on the screen to take the call.

Calliope music again…

I was instantly wide awake, fully on point.

A few seconds of that awful organ screeching—I was never fond of circuses to begin with but I was damn sure never going to another one after this—and then the voice of Krusty the Clown again.

"*Well, Harry, we were beginning to wonder if you were going to bother picking up the phone. You haven't fallen asleep, have you? Did we disturb your nap?*"

I hit the guide button on the TV remote control to check the time: 1:58 on a Saturday morning.

"I'm here," I said. "I'd just stepped away from the phone for a moment. I've been waiting on your call."

"*Goody fucking goody for you, Harry. Now let's talk—*"

"Yes," I interrupted. "Let's talk. First, disable that ridiculous voice disguiser. You're not fooling anybody with it. I know who you are. If we're going to talk, let's do it like normal people."

A cackling Krusty the Clown laugh erupted. "*So you think you know who I am? Well, check out the brain on Harry James Denton.*"

I let that sit there for a moment, then spoke in the coldest, most detached manner I could muster under the circumstances.

"If you're not Jack McEwen, you're somebody working for him. So cut the crap, shall we?"

There was a long silence on the other end as my stomach clenched, hoping he wouldn't hang up. Then there was a rustling sound and a staticky crackling.

"Okay, Harry," a voice said, a normal, regular human voice, one that I recognized from my one conversation with him at the Nashville Academy of Cinema Arts.

"Hello, Jack," I said, a little more assurance in my voice. The final game had started; we met in the middle of the board and I'd taken my first pawn.

"You really fucked this up. You know that, don't you?"

"Did you really think you could get away with killing Leo Walsh because he backed out of your scheme to bilk a bunch of investors? It was a crazy idea in the first place, to gamble the whole college on a movie."

"I don't mind explaining this to you, Harry, because you're never going to have the chance to tell anybody anyway. I don't think the cops would believe you if you told them the sky was blue. But we were *never* going to save the school. We decided years ago the place was going down. There was no way this business model was ever sustainable, so we were just trying to—well, let's just say we're trying to enhance our 401(k)s."

"As long as we're on this subject, just exactly who is *we*?"

He hesitated. "It's not necessary for you to know that."

"C'mon, Jack. What difference does it make? As you said, I'm never going to say anything to anyone. As soon as I get Alex back, you'll never hear from me again. I know Ursula's in on it. Hell, it was probably her idea. And if the two of you are in on it, then Raisa Petrov can't be far behind. I think I'm most curious about the other two faculty members, that cute producing teacher, what's her name?"

"Justine Moye," he said. "Nah, she's not in the tent."

"And the cinematography teacher? The one I didn't meet."

"Chris Weyreuth. Not a chance. He's basically a hippie. Does yoga and meditates. Which is why he teaches. No one that laid back ever makes it in this business."

"And what's that other guy, the one in IT? The one that ratted out Bo Masterson for sniping the emails?"

"Haggerty, Brent Haggerty. Smart kid. Doesn't know shit about the world, though."

"So the one question mark is Katy Lederberg, your finance gal. I figure she's got to be right in the middle of it because you guys've been skimming tuition, cooking the books, and ripping off the Feds for years. She's the only one left with that wide a skill set."

Jack McEwen laughed, a soft kind of self-assured, smart-assed laugh that made me want to reach through the phone and yank his tonsils out. "Yeah, Katy's pretty talented."

"I want to talk to my daughter," I snapped. "I need to know she's okay."

"This isn't the movies, Harry. You don't get to be Mel Gibson and make demands. She's okay. You'll have to take my word for it because you don't have any other options."

"So how's this gonna play out, Jack? I want my daughter back."

"We know you do." His tone switched; he was on offense now. "We did a little digging on you, Harry James Denton. Turns out you're a rich motherfucker. Got in on the ground floor of a billion-dollar company."

I didn't bother to correct him; it was a *multi-billion* dollar company.

"So Katy's worked out a way for you to slice off just a little bit for us in return for getting your precious little princess back. Tomorrow morning, you're going to get a text. It's going to be a series of numbers. Those numbers are account numbers, routing numbers, everything you'll need to do a nice, quiet, tidy little electronic transfer of funds. Once that transfer is made, we'll set your daughter someplace safe and quiet while we're on our way out of the country. None of us will ever see each other again and we can all go on with our lives."

"Where you going, Jack? Not that I would ever come after you. After this is over, I never want to see your face again either. But I'm a curious kind of fella…"

"Why don't we just say it's a place that doesn't like being pushed around by the American government or the IRS. They don't extradite and they don't report. We'll all be just fine. Umbrella drinks and white sand beaches."

"You'll miss the business. You'll never make a movie again."

He laughed again. "I'll get over it."

"So just how big a slice are we talking here, Jack? Not that it matters. I want my daughter back and I'll pay whatever it takes. But I need a number."

There was a long few seconds of silence. I imagined Jack McEwen turning away from the phone, putting his hand over it, and asking Ursula: *Okay, how much did we say?*

"We're thinking that ten million ought to be the going market price for a prime piece of rich pretty white girl."

I let that one sit there for a few moments. Timing was everything in this sort of game, and for a few beats, I wanted him to sit and stew. When the moment felt right, I played my hand.

"You did some research, Jack, but not enough. Yes, ten million's a lot of money. Much more than that and you might draw some undue attention to yourself down on whatever third world Caribbean sand pile you decide to crawl under. So I'm happy to send your ten million wherever you want it."

I took a deep breath and let it out slowly.

"But you need to understand, my friend, that I have *a lot* more money than that. In the next couple of years, I'm going to give away more than that. And Alex's godfather has even more than I do. In fact, about fifty times more. He's got billions, Jack, and he loves Alex every bit as much as I do. And before we got rich, we repossessed cars together and worked as bounty hunters. Take a second to wrap your head around that."

He was quiet on the other end.

"So what this means for you, Jack, and your buddies, is that if anything happens to Alex, her godfather and I have enough money to track you down a hundred times over anywhere on this planet. We will devote our lives to hunting the four of you down and make no mistake, we will do it. We will find you. And when we do, I'm going to bring in *specialists*. I'm talking people who worked for Saddam Hussein. Guys who worked for the fucking Saudi royal family and were fired for being too extreme. Fellas who learned their trade with the Mexican cartels. People who can keep you alive indefinitely while putting you in places you've never been. And when I decide it's over, the last thing you'll ever see in this world will be my smiling face telling you that I'm going to track down everybody you ever loved and do the same thing to them."

That was it. I'd played the best gambit I knew.

"Nice speech, Harry," he said after a long pause. His voice was tense, tight. "You oughta write for the movies."

"This isn't a script, Jack. I mean every word of it."

The weird part was, I did.

"We'll get you those numbers tomorrow," he said. "It's a weekend, so we'll give you 'til noon Monday to make the transfer."

"I'll be waiting," I answered.

And then I hung up.

Chapter Thirty-Eight

As soon as I silenced my cell phone, an earthquake hit me.

I dropped the phone on the sofa and ran for the bathroom. I barely made it in time, on my knees in front of the toilet, slamming the toilet seat up with one hand while holding onto the porcelain rim with the other. My stomach convulsed and it felt like I was throwing up stuff I ate last week, let alone a few hours earlier.

So much for expensive steak dinners. May as well grab a basket of fast-food chicken next time if this is the end result.

I'd broken out in a cold sweat by the time the heaving was over. My torso felt like I'd just done 500 sit-ups in two minutes. I wiped up a couple of spots off the rim with a handful of toilet paper, then pulled the handle to make it all go away. I stood up, shaky as hell, and leaned against the bathroom counter.

The guy in the mirror staring back at me looked like he'd been pulled through a keyhole. Hair hanging limp and wet, eyes bloodshot, skin color a gray pallor. I turned on the cold water and let it run for a few seconds, then leaned down and splashed my face.

I thought of Alex, wherever she was, alone in the middle of the night, dark and terrified. Another surge of nausea swept over me and I started to head for the floor again, but then it passed.

Guess there was nothing else left to lose.

Then it hit me. *Nothing left to lose…*

Oh, no, there was plenty left to lose and those bastards knew it. As long as they had Alex, they had leverage. And leverage was something you used.

I had absolutely no reason to believe that if I cooperated with them that they'd let Alex go. In fact, it was probably not in their best interest to give her back to me. She was, after all, something that no other part of this rampant insanity could lay claim to: she was a *witness*.

I was sure they called me from a burner phone. If they were smart, they bought a bag full of them and destroyed each one after one call. Otherwise, they could track…

Track.

You can track cell phones. *Holy Jesus, you can track cell phones.*

I had a tracker app on my phone, but I'd never used it. I practically ran back into the living room and grabbed my mobile. I'd downloaded the app when I upgraded a few months ago. I'd installed it and never used it, so it went to sleep. I couldn't even remember which folder it was in. I scrambled around, found the app, hit the screen to light it up. I had to sit there staring as the little icon made circular motions until the app was active again.

I typed Alex's number, then tapped my foot, nervously waiting.

A minute later, nothing.

They're not stupid, I thought. When they found Alex's phone, they would have yanked the SIM card out and trashed it, then thrown the phone into a dumpster somewhere. It was the smart play; I'd have done that myself.

Another dead end, though.

I paced the floor, my mind racing, trying to figure out what to do next. I must have gone on for a long time. When I went into the kitchen, the clock on the microwave read 3:30.

I was starting to get that weird buzzing feeling you get when exhaustion finally hits, when adrenaline runs dry and the well is completely empty. I wasn't sure I could sleep and I felt guilty for even thinking of it when Alex was still…

Wherever she was.

But I also had enough sense left to know that I couldn't be of any help whatsoever in this situation if I let myself get reduced to pile of blubbering goo. I'd been in dicey situations before, and if I knew one thing it was that when the stress levels go above a certain point, people are apt to act in ways that are not necessarily in their own best interest.

So it's important to stand down periodically, to rest the body and let the batteries recharge. I went into the bathroom and ran more water on my face, then changed into a T-shirt and a pair of running shorts. I plugged my phone into the charger, set the ringer to its loudest setting, then laid down on the bed and flicked off the light.

Quicker than I expected, I settled into a restless, uneasy, and dreamless sleep that was like skipping a flat rock across a pond, then watching it disappear into the dark depths.

❧

Sunlight was straining to infiltrate the closed blinds when I came up from the darkness. I snatched my phone up to check the time and see if the text had come through.

Nothing.

It was 9:30 in the morning. I'd slept maybe five, five-and-a-half hours and it had gone by like twenty seconds.

I sat up and tried to rub the gravel out of my eyes, which only made it worse. I carried the phone into the bathroom with me; that thing wasn't going to be out of my sight. I stood there holding it in one hand as I peed like a racehorse, then scrubbed my teeth and my face. Somehow, my subconscious mind kept churning while my depleted body and conscious mind gave it up for a little while. And when I stepped into a hot shower, I realized I had the beginnings of a plan.

First, there were a couple of things I had to take care of. The thought occurred to me that if I could track Alex's phone, maybe they could track mine. After I dried off and got dressed, I made a pot of coffee and sat down with my phone and started Googling. I learned that if I untoggled "Location Services" in my phone settings, then it was not traceable unless you had some super-sophisticated app that only a real techie would have. So my phone, for now, was off the grid.

So if they couldn't trace me, where was I going to go?

That was the second question. I thought of getting everyone to my house, but realized that they could have a car down the street watching the place just like they did the night Bo Masterson came to see me.

No, the best bet was the office. This being a Saturday, weekend security was in effect. No one could get into the parking garage or on an elevator without an electronic ID to run through the scanner. There was a security guard in the lobby who was one of the best. No one would get past him.

Yeah, that's it. The office.

It was coming up on eleven in the morning by the time I realized I didn't yet have an answer to the third question, which was what the hell was I going to do after I got everyone together? Maybe the tribe could help me figure that part out.

As someone once said, it takes a village. Time to bring the village together. I typed out a group text to Lonnie, Ashley and Hugh, apologizing for the short notice, but explaining that it was absolutely crucial that they meet me at the office at noon. In the next five minutes, they all agreed.

I snarfed down a bagel and cream cheese and finished the rest of the coffee. As I got dressed, I pondered the one other person I'd considered bringing into the tribe and realized that he might be even more essential than the others. I hit a button on the phone and it rang three times before Bo Masterson answered.

"Where are you?"

He sounded tentative, confused. "I'm where I've been for the last week."

"Can you get to Nashville by noon?"

"If I haul ass," he answered.

"Don't get pulled over," I instructed. "We don't have time for that. But there are several of us that are gathering at my office downtown, Denton & Associates. I'll text you the address."

"Don't bother," he said. "I'll GPS it."

"Great. The traffic should be light downtown on a Saturday morning. Park anywhere you can and go in the front lobby of the building. Have the security guard call up and I'll get you in. Come up to the 12th floor."

"I'll be there by noon. Say, I've been watching the news. What happened to the cops and the big bust?"

"There ain't gonna be no big bust. That's why we're meeting."

On the way downtown, my cell phone chirped with an incoming text message. I was driving, so couldn't look at it too long, but it looked like a string of random letters and numbers, with nothing else. No instructions or anything.

I was in the office less than five minutes when Ashley and Hugh came in together. They were both in jeans, Ashley in a white top and Hugh in running shoes and a denim work shirt. Despite my shower and a few hours sleep, I must have still looked like hell. Ashley was especially solicitous, kept asking me if I was okay.

"We're waiting on two other folks," I said. "I'll explain it all when they get here."

"I'll go make a pot of coffee," Ashley offered.

"We may need it."

A few seconds later, Lonnie came through the front door. I'd given him a Denton & Associates ID when we moved into the new digs, so he didn't have to go through security.

I looked down at my watch. It was 12:10. *Where the hell was he?*

"I'm waiting on one other person," I said. "If you guys could just grab a seat in the conference room, we'll get going as soon as he gets here."

Just as I said that, the office phone on Ashley's desk sounded an incoming call. She started for it, but I got there first.

"Yeah."

"Lobby security here. I've got a Bowen Masterson who said he has an appointment with you."

"Send him up."

A minute or so later, I heard the elevator chime in the hallway. I stepped out of the office as the door slid open. Bo Masterson walked quickly out toward me. He wore a military green safari jacket buttoned and belted, with jeans and a pair of hiking boots. He looked like he'd put on some weight since I last saw him, which given his gastronomic habits, should not have been a surprise.

"Hey," he said. "Sorry I'm a few minutes late."

"Thanks for coming," I said, holding the door open.

Everyone else was settled around the conference table. All

heads turned as we entered. Bo Masterson towered over me and everyone else in the room. He was even bigger and taller than Lonnie, and he was probably twice the size of Ashley.

I motioned for him to take a seat. He settled into one of the desk chairs, which gave out a loud groan. I sat down in the chair next to him.

"Guys, this is Bowen Masterson," I began. "He works—or used to work—at the Nashville Academy of Cinema Arts. He's my guy on the inside."

Hugh Caulfield glanced at Ashley, then back at me, a confused look on his face.

"Hugh, you're probably the least in the loop on this, so let me give you short version of what's going on here. A little over two weeks ago—God, it seems like six months now—a guy came to the office trying to hire me as a private investigator. I used to be in that line of work, but it's been a couple of decades ago. Anyway, he wanted me to investigate a homicide. When I asked him whose murder he was talking about, he answered that it was his."

Hugh's eyes got wider and he shifted toward Ashley. "So that's what you were talking about."

She nodded. "Basically, I blew the guy off," I continued, "and three days later, he was murdered. The cops have been investigating, but to them it's either a street crime or a sex crime. I started looking into it and I believe—no, I know—he was murdered by his colleagues at the Nashville Academy of Cinema Arts, a local for-profit film school that's been scamming students and the Feds alike out of millions of dollars."

I stopped for a second, gathering my thoughts, trying to figure out how to explain this to everyone without getting tangled up in the minutiae and sounding like a whack job.

"Anyway, this guy, Leo Walsh, unknowingly became part of a scheme to rip off potential investors in a movie project. He wrote the script. It was supposed to be a crappy script that would never get made. Instead, he handed off what may be the best thing he ever wrote."

I turned to Bo. "As it turned out, there was never any intention of making a movie. They were gonna rake it in from the investors, then pull the plug on the project, abandon the college and the students, and retire to some nice beachy island. When Leo found out about it, he pulled out and threatened to blow the whistle on these folks. That's when they killed him."

"So the one thing I don't understand," Hugh Caulfield said, "is what this has to do with us, with you?"

"I started digging into the case because I felt guilty. The guy asked me for help and I blew him off. And also, I have to admit, because it seemed like an interesting intellectual exercise. Solving a murder, just like in the movies or a crime novel. Only now it's gone way beyond that."

Ashley looked at me, with a look on her face that was caring and concerned. "What's happened, Harry? You didn't bring us all together on a Saturday afternoon to have a nice chat."

"I stupidly went to the police and gave them everything I had. Only instead of getting warrants and seizing everything and busting these folks, they went and 'interviewed' them. In doing so, the bad guys figured out how the cops knew everything. I'd already been warned to keep my mouth shut and I didn't."

Lonnie, who'd sat quietly the whole time, glared at me and spoke up. "Get to the point, Harry."

I stared at him and felt the blood draining from my face.

"They've got Alex."

A chorus of gasps erupted. "Ohmigod," Ashley whispered.

"What?" Lonnie yelled. "She's at that fancy private school!"

"Who's Alex?" Bo Masterson whispered.

I turned to him. "My daughter."

"Oh, shit."

"After we left the restaurant last night," I went on, "I got a call from Bealesworth. Alex had disappeared from the dorm. Needless to say, I turned around and hauled ass out there. They had search parties all over the campus. I went up to her room to see if I could find anything that might help. While I was there, I got the call. They had her. I was to make excuses to the school and go home, then wait for further instructions."

"Why didn't you call me?" Lonnie demanded. "Sheba and I would've been there in a heartbeat."

"What could you've done? It was the middle of the night. There was nothing to do but wait."

"Did you hear from them?" Ashley asked.

I nodded. "They called about two this morning."

"Is she all right?"

I turned to Ashley, the skin on my face as tight as a drum. "I think so. They wouldn't let me talk to her."

"Okay," Lonnie snapped. "We need to settle down here. What do they want?"

I looked down at the table, where my hands were knotted into hard fists. I tried to relax, let some of the tension go.

"They want ten million dollars, wired to an overseas bank account. When they're safely on their way out of the country, they'll turn Alex loose."

Lonnie made a sound like a teakettle spewing boiling water.

"You're not thinking of paying 'em, are you?"

It was my turn to glare at him. "I can afford it and she's worth it."

"Harry, you know how this works. I don't like to think of this any more than you do, but once they've got their money there is absolutely no reason to believe they'll turn her loose."

"Don't you think I've thought of that," I snapped. "This is why I asked you guys to come here today. I want to explore all the options. We've got to get her home safe."

I turned to Bo. "You know these bastards. What do you think they're capable of?"

Bo looked down for a moment, thinking. "I gotta be honest with you, I always knew they were corrupt assholes. Even when I was a student, there were a bunch of us who thought something really stank about the place. But I never thought they'd do anything like what they did to Mr. Walsh."

He looked up. "But they did. And if they can do it to him, they could do it to anybody."

The bowling ball in my stomach took a hard lurch downward. I felt my pulse racing and I tried to ignore the little gold and silver sparkles that were dancing around in my peripheral vision.

"That settles it," Lonnie said. "We're going after these people."

I looked up and our eyes met. I'd seen that look in his eyes before, a long time ago, back in the old days when we worked cases together and things went sideways.

"What do you need us to do, Harry?" Hugh Caulfield asked. "I feel like I'm the least equipped person to be in this room right now, but I'll do what I can."

"No," I said. "Hugh, if we're not able to get Alex back and

I wind up having to pay the ransom, you may be the key to breaking this."

I pulled out my cell phone and brought up the text message I'd received. I handed the phone to Ashley and she leaned over to share the screen with Hugh.

"That's the text I got this morning on the way here. It's a string of letters and numbers, but I have no idea what they mean. There's no instructions, no guidance. We have to figure it out."

The two of them leaned in close and studied the cell for a few moments. "That's an IBAN, isn't it?" she whispered.

Hugh nodded. "Yeah."

"Okay, what's an IBAN?" I asked.

"It's the International Bank Account Number," Ashley answered. She pulled out her own smartphone and started tapping away.

"It's a unique number assigned to specific overseas bank accounts," Hugh continued. "We see them all the time when transfers are made from the Germans."

"Okay," Ashley said, pointing to her screen. "Here's the guide for decoding it. It's a two-letter country code."

She looked back at my phone, then back to hers. "The two-letter country code on this one is..." She paused, looking at something on her screen. "Belize."

"Belize?" I asked.

Hugh nodded. "Belize is one of the few countries left that won't cooperate with the IRS and the American government. Even Swiss banks cooperate now. There's no confidentiality left in most places in the world, but Belize is a holdout. It's a safe haven."

"Okay, the two-digit transaction code is generated on their

end, so they're already set up to receive the transfer. Let's see, the four-letter bank code…"

Ashley scanned down her phone, then swiped to bring up another screen. "Got it. It's the Banco Nacional de Belize. Headquartered in the capitol, Belmopan."

"Okay," I said, "we don't know where they're going, but we know where the money's going. So your job, Hugh, is to find out what our options are with that. Is there a way for us to track where the money goes, if it gets that far? Is there a way for us to head it off before they get it? Better yet, is there a way for us to ping their banking system so it looks like the money's there, but it's really not. If we can fool 'em for just long enough to let Alex go, we'll be clear."

"*If* they let Alex go," Lonnie snapped.

I nodded. "Yes, if. We have to at least keep open the idea that might happen. In the meantime, we need a Plan B. And that's why I asked Bowen here."

He looked at me with the earnestness only the young can muster, when you haven't lived long enough to become so disillusioned and cynical you never believe anything good can happen again.

"What can I do?"

"I've been beating my head against the wall, trying to figure out where they'd have her. They've done some stupid shit here, but I don't think they'd be stupid enough to hold her in one of their houses, apartments, whatever. Too many downsides to that. And they're not going to hold her in a motel room or any place like that. Too many chances they'd be spotted. And I know Alex, first chance she got she'd run for it in a parking lot, screaming her fool head off."

"So what are you thinking?"

"Where's the best place to hide something?" I asked. "In plain sight, right? The NACA building is huge. I only saw about ten percent of it."

Bo's head bobbed up and down. "Absolutely, that place is all tangled up. There's a million places to hide somebody. Locked closets on the soundstages, storerooms, equipment rooms with heavy security. Individual color correction suites that are just one workstation and a monitor, but the doors lock on each one. Plus conference rooms, offices, labs, there's even a locked file room behind Stacy Jones's office. That's where all the records are kept."

"What about other students? Would they inadvertently find her?"

He shook his head. "Not right now. We're between quarters. The building's not even open on weekends."

"So it's locked tight."

He nodded. "Yep."

I stood up and walked around to the front of the room. "And you've still got your master key, right?"

"Hell, yeah."

"And you know your way around the place?"

"I only spent seven years of my life there. I know the place, inside-out. I know places they don't even know."

I looked down at Lonnie and we made eye contact. He let loose with an almost imperceptible nod.

"And you'd be willing to get me and Lonnie into the building. And act as our guide?"

Bowen Masterson grinned, took a deep breath and seemed to swell up even larger.

"Hell, yeah!" he shouted. "Let's do it!"

Chapter Thirty-Nine

I squinted down at my watch and strained to see the time. The glow filtering through the Tesla's windshield from the underground parking garage lights was barely enough to see.

9:45—maybe ten more minutes.

Next to me in the passenger's seat, Bo Masterson had shifted his weight and was leaning against the door, his head resting on the passenger window. He'd drifted off and was breathing softly, his massive bulk rising and lowering in time with his breath. I've always been amazed that someone could sleep in circumstances like this. Guy'd probably do great in a foxhole.

I'd gone home in the afternoon, managed to snag a couple of hours sleep myself, and was feeling a little more rested. I think I slept more easily knowing that we'd made a decision, that wheels had been set in motion. That one way or another, this was coming to a head. Limbo is the worst. Or as a friend once said to me: *do something, even if it's wrong.*

I spent part of the afternoon doing more research online, then changed into black jeans and a dark blue denim work shirt, both a little loose. I'd be able to move quickly if need be, with a minimum of rustling. Bo went home and met me back here an hour ago, but he hadn't changed. He still wore the jeans and the olive drab safari jacket. He met me on the street, climbed in my car, and I'd gotten us into the garage.

Lonnie was supposed to meet us a little before ten.

I sat there a few more minutes, with Bo Masterson's rhythmic, soft breathing the only sound. Then, a level above us, I heard a car engine and the squeal of tires maneuvering around the hairpin turns of the underground garage.

A moment later, Sheba's black Mercedes SUV pulled into a slot across from us. I leaned over, nudged Bo.

"Hey," I said softly. Didn't want to startle him; he might be dangerous. "Showtime."

He came to quickly, rubbed his eyes. "They here?"

I motioned toward the windshield. "That's them."

We climbed out of the car just as Lonnie and Sheba got out of the Mercedes.

"No," I said. "This wasn't part of the deal."

We crossed and met in the middle between our two cars. "Don't even think about doing this without me," Sheba snapped.

"Lonnie," I said, looking at him. "This isn't a good idea. This could get ugly real quick."

Lonnie held his hands up. "I tried, man. She's made up her mind. And I'm with her on this one."

Sheba was clearly angrier than I'd ever seen her and I shivered to think it was directed at me.

"You weren't so worried about my coming along the night I met you, damn it. Remember that night? You and Lon and Jerry the Drill and I took down that badass Latino guy in the middle of a Mexican restaurant on a Friday night. You were glad to have me along then."

I looked at her, realized I'd hurt her deeply. Didn't mean to, but that didn't help much.

"You're right, Sheba," I said. "That was uncalled for. You can handle yourself better than I can. I wasn't trying to cut you out. I'm just scared."

"We all are, Harry." Her voice softened and I hoped she'd forgiven me at least a little bit. "Look, we get in there and find Alex, she's gonna need me. I can help."

"I just don't want anything to happen to you."

She smiled. "I'm not worried. You've got my back."

"And I'm glad you've got mine," I said, then turned to Bo. "Introductions are in order. Sheba, this is Bo. He's our inside guy at NACA. He's gonna get us in, find Alex, and cover us in the extraction."

Bo Masterson stared at Sheba, clearly taken by her. It was a common response. "Ma'am," he said, nodding.

She smiled at him. "Glad to meet you, Bo."

I nodded. "Okay, we all clear on the timetable?"

"There is one thing," Lonnie said. He pulled his jacket up and pointed to the handgun on his hip.

I shook my head. "No, not a good idea. We don't need to get in a frickin' gunfight with these people with Alex in the middle."

Bo lifted up his safari jacket, exposing the same handgun in the same holster I'd seen that day in the Pancake Palooza. "I'm not going in there naked," he said.

Lonnie nodded back to him. "Yeah, it's crazy."

Bo smiled. "Never leave home without it…"

I looked at him and cocked an eyebrow. "You're way too young to remember the American Express commercial."

"The what?"

"You know, the Karl Malden commercials for American Express?"

"Who?"

I shook my head. "Never mind."

"Harry," Sheba said, reaching into the bag slung over her

right shoulder. "I've even got my toy with me."

She pulled out a handgun. Bo let out a low whistle. "Sig P365," he said. "I'm impressed."

Sheba smiled. "You're good." It made his day.

"Okay, folks, if we've had enough of show-and-tell time here, can we get this party started?"

"Harry," Lonnie said, doing the worst Arnold Schwarzenegger impression I'd ever heard, "I've got a *lee-tul* girly gun just like Sheba's in the car if you *vant* it."

I narrowed my eyes, glaring at him. "I'm not comfortable with my skill level in that arena. I'm as liable to shoot you as much as what I'm aiming at. That is, unless I'm aiming at you…"

"C'mon, let's go."

We climbed into the Mercedes, Lonnie and Sheba in front, me and Bo in the back. The Saturday night traffic on Broadway in the summer was usually pretty thick and tonight was no exception. We got hung up at Broadway and 7th by one of those damn pedal taverns, with a dozen drunk bridesmaids screeching and sweating and howling at the moon. Finally, the poor guy steering it juked over into the turning lane, then veered onto 7th at First Baptist and got the hell out of our way.

We hit the entrance ramp on I-24 and Lonnie gunned the SUV up to about 75. We made the Fesslers Lane turnoff in about ninety seconds. Downtown Nashville was packed and rocking on a Saturday night, but this stretch of road was like a ghost town, completely empty, bathed in the sulfurous light of the crackling streetlights, and eerily quiet.

We drove past the Harley-Davidson dealer and turned left onto Calhoun, then about an eighth-of-a-mile down and made the right turn into the industrial park where the NACA campus was located.

Bo scooted forward on his seat and pointed out the windshield between Lonnie and Sheba. "Don't pull in there," he instructed. "If they're here, they'll see us on the CCTV."

"Okay, so where?"

Bo pointed again, further past the NACA building and to the right. "See that sign down there? That's Billy Potter's alignment shop. He doesn't have any cameras. Pull in there and nobody'll see us."

Lonnie pulled into the lot and parked. When he shut the engine down, the silence was a roar in my ears.

"We'll cross this parking lot, then there's a line of trees. We cut through those trees and come out the other side. That puts us in the back of campus. We cross that back parking lot and then there's a door next to the freight dock. That's where we'll go in. Any questions?"

"Seems like a lot of asphalt with no cover. Won't they see us on the cameras?" Lonnie asked.

"The light's not so good back there," Bo explained. "About half as bright as it is up front. Plus the security system is a cheap analog setup. Ursula wasn't going to spend top dollar on something hi-res. They'd notice a car driving in and parking up front, but to catch four people sneaking across a dark lot, they'd just have to be lucky."

"All right, that brings up another point," I said. "There's four of us now. I'm glad you're here, Sheba, but the plan was to deploy three. So how do we shift gears?"

"I'm not sitting in the car and waiting for the brave manly men to go rescue the damsel in distress. We're in this together."

"Yes," I said. "But *how* are we in this?"

"If I could make a suggestion," Bo said. "I'll go in point,

since I have the swipe card to get us in. We won't turn any lights on. I can disable the burglar alarm for the equipment room and we can base there. You guys can follow me in and we can either fan out in teams to start the search or stick together. Your call."

Lonnie turned to face me. "Ashley and Hugh are still at the office, right? If we get in a jam and there's no alternative but to pay them, we're set."

I nodded. "They're waiting on my call. As soon as they get the word, it's PTB. Push the button and these guys have ten mil waiting for 'em in Belize. I can hold up my cell and they can see for themselves."

"Then they'll have to let us all go, including Alex," Sheba said.

"From your mouth to God's ear," I answered.

We exited the car and walked wordlessly across the first parking lot. Lonnie handed out palm-sized Husky halogen flashlights to each of us. We flicked them on and held them low to transit the tree line, but once we were on the other side of that, we went dark again.

We padded across the back parking lot of the Nashville Academy of Cinema Arts, over to the freight door and the door next to it. Bo pulled out his wallet, extracted a smart card ID and swiped it through the reader. The red light on the reader changed to green.

Standing behind him, I heard him let out the breath he'd been holding.

He opened the metal door with a rusty squeal that sounded a lot louder than it actually was. We followed in, one by one, and Lonnie pulled the door closed, throwing us into the blackest black I'd ever experienced.

Bo flicked on his flashlight, held the beam low, and crossed over to an alarm panel on the wall. "I hope nobody's monitoring this at the front desk," he whispered, as he typed in a series of numbers to disable the system. The panel beeped as he typed the last numbers in.

He crossed a few steps past the panel, then swiped his ID again through a reader and got us access to the equipment room. Once we were all in, he closed the door behind us and locked it.

He switched on the overhead and we all squinted to adjust to the light. The NACA equipment room was as jammed with moviemaking gear as it was the first time I'd seen it: tripods and apple boxes, metal stands that looked huge, stacks of boxes, and coils of thick extension cords. There was a worktable on the side loaded with electronic parts, tools and soldering irons, and plastic boxes full of nuts, screws, and bolts.

It looked like junk and clutter everywhere, but Bo Masterson seemed completely at home in it.

There was a desk with a desktop computer and monitor against the wall next to the worktable. Bo sat down and pressed a button to boot the computer.

"What are you doing?" I asked.

"I can tap into the CCTV system here. We'll do a quick scan of the building, see what we come up with."

"We can see the whole building from this monitor? Why are we searching then? Just locate her on the monitor."

He turned to me. "Doesn't work that way, Harry. Only the main hallways are on camera. The administrative wing, for instance, doesn't have cameras beyond the entrance foyer."

"At least that's what you thought until you broke into one of the offices and got caught," I said.

Bo turned around and faced Lonnie and Sheba. "Is he always such a smartass?"

"Yes," they both said simultaneously.

He turned back to the monitor as we all stared over his shoulder. There were a series of tiles on the screen, which he blew up one at a time. Each hallway was dimly illuminated by a series of fire escape lights mounted on the walls right at the ceiling. Not everything was clear in this dim light, but a person moving through the hallway would have been easy to spot.

"Nobody there," Bo said. He clicked again. "Nothing there."

He went through every tile. Then he brought up the main menu and clicked another button. Suddenly the exterior grounds of the campus were visible.

"Here's the front view." Bo pointed at the screen, where two cars were parked next to each other in the very front. "There, that silver Audi. It's Ursula's. Nothing but the best for her. And that Ford next to her; I think that's Jack's."

He pointed to another car several slots down. "That little Chevy down there? I think that's Raisa Petrov's. God, they're stupid. If we'd called the cops, they would have had them. They'd be screwed for sure."

"They were counting on us not ratting them out."

"So that means they're here, right?" Lonnie asked over my left shoulder.

Bo nodded. "Yeah, the question is where."

He backed his chair up, scooting us out of the way, and crossed the equipment room to a cork bulletin board. He unpinned a sheet of paper, brought it over to the desk and flattened it out.

"This is a map of the building." He pointed to a place in the back. "This is where we came in. Next to that door is the equipment room."

He slid his finger over the paper. "Across the freight area here is the large soundstage. There's an audio control booth that has a lockable door, but it only locks from the inside. I don't think they're in there or they would have heard us when we came in."

"I didn't realize we were taking such a chance," I said.

Bo continued running his finger over the map. "We come out of here, and that first hallway off to the left is the IT department. There's nothing there but locked offices and one room that's the server room. I don't think they're in there because the security is so tight there's motion control devices. Plus automatic halon extinguishers and all that shit. Whirring fans and HVAC units, dehumidifiers. Definitely not a hospitable place…"

He slid his finger past that hallway. "There's a long hallway here that goes down to the editing labs, color correction suites, and the maintenance crew area. Also the Pro Tools lab."

"Pro Tools?"

"Yeah, the audio booth, recording studio, Foley pits, and a voice-over booth. They could be in there."

Bo stood up. "Now this is where it gets dicey." He turned and faced away from us. "When we get past that intersection, there's a main hallway that goes down to the gallery, then splits off in a Y. To the left leads to the main entrance and the reception desk."

"That's where I came in that day."

He nodded. "Yeah, and the administrative hallway is past that on the other side of the reception desk."

Then he motioned to his right. "The other leg, off to the right, leads down the hallway where all the classrooms are. There's also a screening room off that hallway as well. Past that is the small soundstage."

"There's a second soundstage?" Lonnie asked.

"Yeah. It's smaller than this one across the hall. It's used more for the production classes than for actual shoots."

"So what do we do?" I asked. "Split up? Each take a hallway? Or stay together?"

There was silence for a few beats before Lonnie spoke up. "If we split up, we've got to have some way to communicate. How 'bout this? Two teams, me and Sheba and you and Bo. Everybody sets their phone to vibrate. If we find her, she's likely to have somebody guarding her. We think there are three of them here besides Alex. They'd probably take shifts, so there might only be one person at a time. If we spot 'em, take cover. Text the other team and don't do anything until we're all back together."

I looked at the three of them. "Sounds like a plan to me."

"I do think we should check the soundstage across the freight dock first," Bo said. "Just in case."

I nodded. "Okay."

Bo stepped over to the equipment room door.

"Sheba and I'll take the right leg. We'll go down the hallway and check the labs and the recording studio."

"I've gotta kill the lights before I open the door."

I turned to Bo. "Do it."

He hit the switch and we dived back into that dark so dark you couldn't see the end of your nose.

"You and Bo take the leg to the left," Lonnie continued. "Go around the reception desk, circle around the gallery, and then head down the classroom hallway. When Sheba and I finish scouting out the labs, we'll double back and catch up with you."

I nodded, although it was so dark no one could see it. "Works for me."

We heard a screeching sound from across the way that made

me jump. "Jesus, make some noise," I hissed.

"Probably can't be helped," Sheba whispered.

Then we saw a dim, soft light cutting through the dark. I stepped through the door, leaving the equipment room just as Bo exited the soundstage holding his small flashlight at his side.

"It's clean," he said in a normal voice.

"C'mon, you and I are gonna take the leg around the reception desk and the gallery, then down the classroom hallway. Lonnie and Sheba will catch up with us after they clear the lab hallway.

Bo walked over to the massive double doors leading into the freight area as the three of us followed behind.

"Remember, these hallways are lit," he said, "so we won't need the flashlights as long as we're in the main part. Just stay close to the wall, as far into the shadows as you can."

"Stay quiet and keep alert," Lonnie added.

He pulled the doors open, which thankfully were a little better lubricated than the other doors. They slid open silently and we walked out into a broad hallway that continued on in front of us for a long way. Ten feet or so down, an even wider hallway branched off to the left. As we hit the intersection, the four of us made one last eye contact/group nod and then split up.

Bo led the way, skating as close to the wall as possible, under the beam of the fire escape lights. Everything was silent. I tried not to use the term *dead silent* in my head.

We padded slowly down the hallway, him in the lead and me a couple of steps behind. We stayed as close to the wall as possible, skulking past framed posters, huge photos, a few art pieces that hung on the walls. We passed a closed door and Bo motioned to stop. He put an ear against the door for a second, then turned to me.

"Storage room," he whispered.

I nodded.

We continued on until we got to the place where the hallway split into a Y. As planned, Bo and I ducked down to the left, then continued on in silence. There was nothing, not even the hum of air conditioners as we got to the lobby and the front doors. The reception desk was shrouded in shadow with a couple of blinking lights from a computer and the desk telephone.

Nothing here.

We continued past the counter and over to the locked double doors that led into the administrative wing. Bo fished around in his pockets and came up with a keyring. He held it close to his face and went through the keys in the dim light, holding out one, turning to me and nodding.

He slipped the key into the lock and turned the cylinder. He opened the door and leaned in to listen.

Nothing.

He opened the door further. We slipped in and entered a long hallway. He turned to me. "I don't think we should check every door. If we don't see any light from under the doors and we don't hear anything, it's probably clear."

"Okay."

He led the way and we went down the hallway all the way to the end, where a double oak door was labelled in gold letters: URSULA GILBERT—PRESIDENT. Bo leaned in, put his ear to the door for a few seconds, then backed away and leaned down to examine the crack under the door.

Darkness and silence.

We headed back down the hallway at a faster pace, then exited the administrative wing though the glass double doors. He motioned to the left and we began padding down the hallway, past the gallery, completing the circle that began at the Y split.

Suddenly, Bo stopped, held up a hand. I stopped behind him, holding my breath, alert for any movement, sound, change in air pressure, anything.

And then, in the distance, from somewhere on the other side of the gallery and down the hallway where we'd just been, we heard a sound so distinctive there was no way to mistake it.

A toilet flushed.

Chapter Forty

I instinctively jumped and started toward the sound. Bo put his hand on my shoulder, then shook his head and raised his index finger to his lips.

He leaned in close. "We don't know who it is."

I nodded. He was right; now was not the time to have the bugler sound charge.

We stood there, stock-still, as in the far distance footsteps echoed against the tile floor with no attempt to hide the noise. We both stepped further into the shadows, unsure of whether the steps were coming toward us or away.

Bo edged down the wall to the corner opposite the double doors into the gallery. He peeked around the edge as the sound diminished.

"They're going away from us," I whispered.

"Yeah. Let's go."

We came out from behind the wall and padded down toward the Y intersection. The footsteps were definitely going down the hallway toward the classrooms and not back toward the labs. As we approached the intersection, one of the walls cast a long, deep shadow under the fire escape lights. We slid into the darkness. Bo leaned down and I bent around him; we both peeked around the corner at the same time.

Two people were walking away, their backs to us. The one on the left was definitely a woman, but I couldn't tell who.

The slightly shorter one next to her was Alex. I could hear

the woman on the left saying something to Alex, but her voice was so soft and far away I couldn't make out what it was. Alex's hands were behind her, tied with something. In the dim light, I couldn't tell what.

As we stared, the other woman reached around Alex and opened a tall, wide door. They entered and the door closed behind them.

My heart pounded in my chest. We both pulled back behind the wall.

"That's her," I panted. "That's Alex. They've got her."

"C'mon, Harry, we knew that. Take a breath, calm down."

"Where did they take her?"

"That's the door into the small soundstage. That must be where they've been keeping her. Makes sense, the walls are flyaway and can be made into anything. One common set is a bedroom. There's even a bed and a dresser in the prop room."

"Is there another way to get in there?" I asked.

"Nope. We've got to go in that door they just used."

I pulled out my mobile. My hands were shaking so badly I could barely type, but I managed to get a text off to Lonnie and Sheba. Then I turned to Bo.

"I can't just sit here and wait. We're going to go down there and politely and calmly walk the fuck in. And I'm not leaving without my daughter."

He looked down at me from the six or eight inches he had on me in height.

"Okay. Right behind you…"

I stepped around the corner and started down the hall, in the lead this time. Twenty seconds or so later, I stood at the door to the soundstage, which had to be a least fifteen feet high. Room to get props in, I guess.

I reached out, touched the doorknob, twisted it slowly.

Unlocked.

The door opened inward. I pushed it just a crack. It was completely dark inside. I thought about pulling out the flashlight, but realized that would make too good a target. I pushed the door open further and stepped inside. Behind me, Bo Masterson slipped in as well.

Suddenly, there was an explosion of light from above and beside, from all directions, that blinded me. I squinted, ducked down, raised my hand to cover my eyes. I heard something beside me and realized it was Bo shifting off to my right. I squinted even harder, then forced my eyes open into slits, trying to see anything. The immense room was ablaze with light. I couldn't see anything, but then I heard a muffled voice from the rear of the stage, behind the walls.

"You never learn, do you, Harry?"

My eyes were adjusting rapidly. I kept my hand to my forehead, like saluting, to keep the lights above me away. There was a stage set in front of me, and like Bo said, it was a room made of fake walls, a bed and dresser, some posters on the wall and a faux window with venetian blinds that looked out onto nothing.

From behind one of the flyaway walls, Jack McEwen stepped out. He forced Alex in front of him—his right arm crooked around her neck, a revolver in his left hand—using her as a human shield.

"Daddy," she squeaked.

"Alex, honey, are you okay?" I tried to hide the desperation in my voice.

She nodded. "Your precious little princess is fine," Jack

snarled. "Only I'm not so sure about you. What the fuck do you think you're doing?"

"I came for my daughter. You'll get your money, just like we agreed. All I'm doing is one minor revision to the arrangement. You'll get your money when you let Alex go."

On the other side of the set, a long floor-to-ceiling curtain rustled. Ursula Gilbert and Raisa Petrov stepped out from behind and walked over, stopping about ten feet to Jack's right.

"You're crazy," Ursula said. "Who said you could change the terms on your own?"

Behind her, Raisa Petrov looked terror-stricken, almost shaking. I realized she was the one who'd walked Alex back from the restroom and was talking so soothingly to her.

I pulled out my cell and held it up. "There are two people in my office right now who have their fingers on a keyboard. As soon as I text them Alex is okay and with me, they'll push the button and your money will be in Belize in half-a-second. I can show you."

Then I stopped, turned to Ursula and stared at her.

"Wha—" I said, confused. "What happened to the French accent?"

"You idiot," she snapped. Jack McEwen started laughing.

"You really are gullible, Harry," he said. "Just like everybody else for the past twenty years. Ursula's from Bayonne, a born and bred Jersey girl."

"Well," I said, slipping into a Southern drawl, "butter my butt and call me a biscuit."

"Okay, Harry," McEwen growled again. "You send that text and get that transfer going."

I shook my head. "Not until you let her go."

"It's not happening, Harry."

"I'm not leaving without her, Jack."

He grinned, a mean, even cruel grin. Then he cocked the revolver at this side.

"Then I guess you're not leaving…"

I looked at Alex and we made eye contact. There was fear in her eyes, but determination as well.

"*Hija.*"

Her eyes widened. "*Sí, Papá.*"

Jack McEwen glared at me. "Say, what the—"

"¿Confías en mí?"

She nodded, almost imperceptibly. "*Sí, Papá.*"

"*Cuando le diga, ¡consique abajo!*"

"Shut the hell up, Harry! I'm warning you!' McEwen yelled.

Behind me, I felt air pushing against my back as the door opened. Sheba and Lonnie…

"¿Lista?"

Alex's eyes got even bigger and she gave a slight shake of the head.

McEwen's arm around Alex's neck relaxed just enough for her to bend slightly and start to push away from him. He screamed something unintelligible, raised the revolver and pointed it in my direction. I sensed movement, chaos all around me.

"¡Ahora!" I yelled at the top of my lungs.

We both dropped at the same moment. I went all the way to the floor and Alex got almost all the way there before McEwen tried to grab her. At the same time, he fired the revolver with a loud pop that echoed through the cavernous soundstage. I heard another explosion next to my right ear, a couple of feet away, that made a snapping sound against my eardrum, followed by a continual roar.

Everything went into slow motion, just like in the movies…

Alex screamed as the bullet caught McEwen just above the breastbone and right below his Adam's apple. When he let go of her, she flopped to the floor.

He fell backwards, behind Alex, sprawling face-up, a few feet away. Ursula Gilbert had her hands to her face, wailing like a banshee. Lonnie jumped over me as I lay prone on the floor. He dove past Alex and onto Jack McEwen, kicking the pistol out of the way where it had fallen to the concrete floor.

Sheba, her Sig drawn, jumped over me next, crossing over and drawing down on the two women. Raisa Petrov raised her hands, almost in shock, as Ursula screamed on.

I sprang to my feet and raced the ten feet or so over to Alex. She was on her side on the floor, her hands still tied behind her with cable ties. I plopped down and lifted her into my arms.

"You okay?" I gasped.

She was panting, trying not to sob. "Daddy."

Alex nodded her head. I held her close to me. There was spray of Jack McEwen's blood on the back of her head and blouse.

I looked up at Lonnie and motioned down to her arms. "Knife," I said. "Cut these damn things off her."

Lonnie dropped to a knee and pulled out his Swiss army knife. He sawed away at the cable ties for a few seconds, then her arms were free and around my neck.

Then the real sobbing started, tears pouring down her face, snot running out her nose. She shook uncontrollably for a few seconds, then seemed to settle into my arms. "I knew…" She gasped between words. "I knew you'd come for me."

"It's okay," I said. "You're okay. It's over."

Then she raised her head. "I didn't know you spoke Spanish."

I smiled down at her, tears in my eyes now. "Had two semesters of it in boarding school forty years ago."

She gave me a confused look.

"Thank God for Google translate." Then we both started laughing hysterically.

I scooted a bit so she could get into a sitting position. In doing so, I turned and caught a glimpse out of the corner of my eye.

"Oh, no," I said. "God, no!"

"What?" Alex asked.

Bo Masterson was lying on his back, a few feet behind where we'd been standing. He wasn't moving.

"Honey, I've got to go check on him."

We disentangled and I jumped up, ran over to him.

"Ohmigod," I moaned.

I went down on one knee and leaned down next to him. His huge hulking body was sprawled on the floor, his arms outstretched, the pistol still cradled in his right hand. I looked all over him but couldn't see anything. No blood, no gore… What the hell was going on?

Suddenly, he stirred, then let out a loud moan.

I grabbed his head, one hand on each side, and shook him. "Bo!"

He opened his eyes. "Aw, man, they always told me that would hurt."

"Of course it hurts!" I yelled. "Damn it, man, you just got shot!"

I pulled my hands away from his face and started searching his torso. I shifted; the lighting grid above us was casting my shadow over him. Once I got out of the way, I saw it.

A ragged hole a little larger in diameter than a pencil was

drilled into his safari jacket on the left side of his chest just below the nipple. A tiny, flattened slug filled the hole.

I reached down and tapped his jacket. What should have been soft flesh giving way under my poking finger was hard as a rock. I made a fist and tapped it with my knuckles. It was like rapping on a dinner plate. I tapped all over the jacket, from his belt up to the collar.

I sat back on my haunches, suddenly more exhausted than I'd ever been in my entire life.

"You son of a bitch," I said. "Body armor?"

He laughed and tried to sit up, then groaned and settled back down. "Hey, never leave home without it."

"And all this time I thought you'd put on more weight."

He shook his head. "I told you, Harry. I'm trying to lose a few."

Epilogue

Three Months Later

The Nashville Academy of Cinema Arts was padlocked less than 24 hours after what the media would later call The Gunfight at the Soundstage Corral. A couple of hundred students were left out in the cold, their degree programs twisting slowly, slowly in the wind, but with their student loan repayments completely on track.

Jack McEwen was dead before he hit the floor. Bo Masterson was as good a shot as I expected he'd be.

Ursula Gilbert, Raisa Petrov, and Katy Lederberg were all arrested They bonded out despite the D.A.'s contention that Ursula was a flight risk. They face a laundry list of charges set out by a Grand Jury that will keep everyone tied up in court for years. Publicly, all three of them maintain that it was all Jack McEwen's fault, that they were just helpless pawns taken in by a charismatic and evil man. They all swore that McEwen murdered Leo Walsh on the very soundstage where McEwen himself later died.

Apparently, one late night there was an ugly, final confrontation. And—if what they're telling is anywhere near close to the truth—Leo tried to walk away from the argument when McEwen picked up something called a "C Stand" and bashed him over the head with it. Enraged, McEwen continued to pound him until he was dead, then threw his body in the back of a grip truck and dumped it in the back of the Pancake Palooza parking lot.

Brent Haggerty, the IT guy who ratted out Bo Masterson, wound up skating. He lost his job, though, and I suspect may encounter some difficulty in obtaining another position.

At some point, I expect I'll be called as one of the lead witnesses, along with Bo and almost certainly Alex, and maybe even Lonnie and Sheba. I'm not looking forward to that but will deal with it when the time comes.

When the case broke, it sparked a nationwide media feeding frenzy. Alex, especially, became a minor celebrity for a while. She dealt with it amazingly well. In fact, she dealt with all of this much better than I expected. She was seeing a therapist for counseling once a week for a couple of months but has now backed off to every couple of weeks.

Only the young can truly be that resilient.

Alex double-surprised me by not only deciding to stay in Nashville and go on to Bealesworth, but to live in the dorm as well. I struggled a bit with that one, but after she promised to call and text frequently and to come home at least every other weekend, I let go of it. After the story broke, she became a kind of hero to the other girls and, with the help of Bitsy and Cricket, quickly became one of the inner circle. The folks at Bealesworth were also exceedingly grateful that we didn't hold them responsible for Alex's kidnapping.

It helped that Alex and I made a sizeable, six-figure donation to install video cameras throughout the campus.

Alex later told me, after the dust settled, that she'd gotten a text message that Saturday night that claimed to be from the police. The text message said that I'd been in a serious car wreck and that the police were sending a representative to the school to pick her up and take her to the emergency room. I have no idea how they found her phone number, but who can hide anything in this day and age?

I resisted the urge to fuss at her for not calling my cell to verify all that. She was, after all, only fifteen at the time.

But not for long. Alex turned sixteen two weeks after school began. I would have thought she'd want a big blow-out, but instead she decided to throw a cook-out at the house for a few of her closest Bealesworth friends. Lonnie and Sheba came as well and Lonnie and I manned the grills. The day before, I'd surprised Alex by flying Estella in from Reno, who took the guest room next to Alex's upstairs. I don't think they got much sleep that night. They chattered away in Spanish, with me picking up the occasional word.

Bo Masterson was, of course, cleared of any liability in the death of Jack McEwen. It was a slam-dunk, hands-down case of self-defense. At first, there was a little airborne effluent from the police, especially Lieutenant Akers, over it. So we just told him we'd go on ABC's *20/20* and CBS's *60 Minutes*—both of whom had reached out to us—and explain how this all came about. Curiously, after that discussion we didn't hear anything else from him.

Bo decided he wanted to pursue developing his feature film and his notoriety seemed to open some doors in that regard. Ashley Meadows started working with him on a real business plan and I agreed to kick in a little seed money to get his crowdfunding campaign going.

Speaking of Ashley, she and Hugh moved in together a few weeks later. That was a twinge moment for me, as I'd finally come to grips with the fact that I had a crush on her the size of a Buick. I also knew nothing could ever come of it and the lesson I needed to take away was that I should deal with my own loneliness, that maybe it was time to move on from Marsha and consider letting somebody into my life.

The holidays are upon us now, a time that I normally dread. The holidays were always drudgery to me and something to just get through. With Alex living here now, though, I'm almost looking forward to them. Estella's flying out from Reno again for Thanksgiving. Lonnie got us box seats at the Titans game that weekend. I forgot who they're playing, which no self-respecting football fan would ever do.

Everybody's thrilled.

Leo Walsh's widow, Aileen, put his will into probate, collected the life insurance quite literally a day or two before the grace period expired, and then went to court to have herself declared the sole beneficiary and executor of Leo Walsh's literary estate. She went to L.A. and had a series of meetings and now Leo Walsh's script, *Young Again*, has been optioned and is soon-to-be-a-major-motion-picture. The agent in New York also got her a fat deal for Leo's novel, *In Too Deep*. Maybe Leo's literary reputation can be resurrected after all.

The wheels are in motion to get started on the new business. Our super-lawyer Fallon drew up corporation papers and agreements, did all the due diligence, registered everything properly, and set up all the bank accounts. Then we rented 20,000 square feet of office space in a new technology park out on Centennial Boulevard near the airport where Lonnie keeps his jet. Hugh Caulfield sent word out over his network and soon we had a couple of young hotshot IT guys to take over the German account and he and Donnie Hazzard resigned from Denton & Associates. They're now the CEO and COO of a company called *Prostatévo Technologies*. It's kind of weird around here without them, but Ashley agreed to stay behind and show the new guys the ropes as we wind everything down. When the company closes, she'll move over with Hugh and Donnie.

The new kids can go, too, if they pass Ashley's muster.

So everybody's hard at work and moving on.

Except me.

For a long time after that horrible Saturday evening when I could have lost my daughter, I wandered around in a daze. I went through the motions, made sure Alex was okay and on track, but I don't think I did a very good job of processing this all and taking some kind of care of myself. About six weeks after all this stuff went down, it hit me. The last few months had simply been overwhelming and more than the human psyche could handle. The fuses were blown…

So I packed up and moved out of my office for a while. I got up every morning for months and headed toward the west side of town, a couple of miles from where Alex was living during the week, down Highway 100 to the two Warner Parks. Nashville has two magnificent urban parks, named after a pair of rich, long-dead brothers, that are right next to each other—Percy Warner Park and Edwin Warner Park. For the next two months, I hiked from five to ten miles a day, up and down trails, through the woods, even around and around the Iroquois Steeplechase. I was surrounded by chipmunks and squirrels, wild turkeys and whitetail deer, and the occasional timber rattlesnake. I'd sometimes walk for hours at a time without seeing another person.

I tried to clear my head of the clutter and purge a bunch of bad noise out of my skull. Eventually, everything quieted down. And I decided that while I was never going to hang a shingle up and become a full-time private detective again, the time I spent investigating the homicide of Leo Walsh was the most alive I'd been in years.

I listened to that. I started to disengage from Denton & Associates and took a back seat in the operation of the new company. I'd invest in the company and take a seat on the Board, but that was the extent of it. Corporate life was over for me.

So now I'm just taking care of my daughter, my business affairs, and starting to live life in a different way. I'm looking for new opportunities and waiting to see what the universe throws my way.

This is a new chapter. As the Roman stoic philosopher Seneca wrote a couple thousand years ago, whose words would eventually be immortalized by a garage band from Minnesota, "*Every new beginning comes from some other beginning's end…*"

THE END

Acknowledgements

While writing itself is a solitary and often lonely pursuit, the actual production and publication of a book is a both a collaboration and a team effort. I'm fortunate to have a group of talented and insightful people who were willing to work with me and I am more grateful to them than I can say.

Six very talented writers gave me the gift of their time and feedback as they read early drafts of this book. Randy O'Brien, Jaden Terrell, Wayne McDaniel, Rob Simbeck, Dr. Brian Carlson and Charly Fallon all provided invaluable and selfless feedback. Their sacrifice of time and effort is especially appreciated given that they are all working writers themselves and took time away from their own work to help mine become better. There is no way I can ever repay them except by paying it forward.

Several wise and experienced friends in the movie and publishing business also gave me their thoughts and insights into this book, all of which proved invaluable. Marsha Posner Williams shared her thoughts and insights and made this book much stronger than it would have been otherwise. David Hinton's analysis and critique of an early draft gave me the opportunity to fix several inconsistencies and plot holes, which helped tremendously. Sam Dalton's critique and support was invaluable as well.

Finally, I turned to a few trusted readers who I knew had read the first cycle of Harry James Denton novels when they were published over twenty years ago. I asked them to read the book and give me their thoughts on whether the new book held up to the first six and, in general, what they thought of it. Jim and Justine Veatch (who copyedited several of the earlier books) were incredibly helpful. Susan Reeves, Chris Fenske, Debby Hicks, and Kristen and Kevin Woodward all gave me more support and encouragement than I could have ever hoped for and, in doing so, gave me the courage to move forward with this project.

I also appreciate the hard work Peter Senftleben did in doing the last proofreading and copyediting of this book. His eagle-eyed diligence put the final polish on this manuscript.

I'm also grateful to Cal Sharp, the Creative Director at Caligraphics for his beautiful book design. I'm even more grateful for the patience he demonstrated in working with me.

I'm also incredibly grateful to all the folks at BooksBeNimble, who have become my marketing and promotion partners and given me the hope that somehow this might be an economically viable pursuit. Julie Smith's wisdom and experience and Mittie Staininger's technical expertise and guidance are especially appreciated.

I also want to express my heartfelt appreciation and gratitude to my wife, Shalynn, whose help and support over all these years has been invaluable. I know it's not always easy living with a writer.

About Steven Womack...

Steven Womack is the Edgar and Shamus Award-winning author of **Dead Folks' Blues**, as well as twelve other novels. A former newspaper reporter and writer for United Press International, his debut novel—**Murphy's Fault**—was the only first mystery named to the 1990 *New York Times* Notable Book List.

A screenwriter as well, Womack co-wrote the screenplay for **Proudheart**, an original made-for-cable movie which was nominated for the CableAce Award. He also co-wrote the ABC-TV film **Volcano: Fire On The Mountain**, which was one of the highest-rated TV movies of the year.

In 1995, Womack was the first faculty member hired at the new Watkins Film School in Nashville, which was a program within the Watkins College of Art and the first film school in the state of Tennessee. For the next 25 years, he anchored the screenwriting curriculum, while also serving five years as Chair of the Film School. When the Watkins College of Art closed its doors in May, 2020, he was the longest serving faculty member. Now retired from teaching, he has returned to full-time writing.

Visit Steven's website at:

www.StevenWomack.com